LOVELESS
the pieces of a girl

Laura Ross

Staten House

Staten House

Printed in the United States of America

First Printing, 2023

Staten House Publishing

ISBN 979-8-89778-348-9

Cover photography. Studio M

Contents

Going once
Going twice
Love's for sale
Name your price
Keep hands up
Wave promise to the sky
Persistence is key
Only truth will suffice
It's up for grabs
Anyone can bid
There on display,
it waits
For that someone
who's worth it.
Love's for sale

Prologue

·♥·♥·♥·♥·♥·

"Lay hands on her, Jesus! Rid her of those demons that led her to the drugs and prostitution and tore her away from her motherly duties. Guide her home! For what is man without love?"

"Yes, Lord!" Amora Albert hollered in praise at the TV pastor whose voice ruptured the previous calm quiet that usually existed in our house.

I shook my head as I examined Mama on the living room couch. The quilt passed down from three generations of warrior women in the Albert line covered her minced body entirely. Her pink satin bonnet that usually teemed under the pressure from barely contained afro curls now deflated to one side from emptiness. From baldness. My heart ached to watch her perform her Sunday worship from the cheap sofa in our nearly vacant living room instead of the warm and welcoming congregation of Mt. Goliath's Chapel, our family's home church of god-knows-how-many years. I could have stayed there, stuck like glue in the door frame as I watched her proudly broadcast her love for the Lord in the empty room, but caught notice of her thin body quaking from the exertion of her hymns.

"Mama?" I asked, kneeling in front of her to assess the source of her distress.

She fanned a dismissive hand at me, her eyes trained on the TV. "Cleo, you're blocking the sermon, now. Please move out of the way!"

My hands were all over her: running their way down Mama's back, arms, and legs as if searching for the golden needle in a haystack responsible for her obvious discomfort.

"Cleo!" She protested, pushing me away from her with frail force that felt more like a nudge.

"You're so cold." I mutter, mostly to myself, but she rolls her eyes as if I threw the most ludicrous offense her way.

"I am fine. Just a little chilly, that's it. You need to turn that air conditioning down a few notches, that's all."

I gulped and forced my eyes shut, unwilling to greet the consternation in front of me. In front of both of us. While notorious for our cold winters, it was a sweltering hot day in D.C. I'm sweating like crazy from the heat beaming through the narrow windows.

The air conditioner was broken.

The weather man predicted temperatures in the near nineties all this week, and this day was no exception, but I didn't dare say anything. Couldn't breathe a word of my fear to my fearless mother. It was taking her from me, and I knew it, but I had to be strong.

I don't realize I'm crying until her bony finger wipes a fat tear from my eye.

"Mama's gonna be just fine, Cleo." Her tone was soft and her face tender as she regarded my statue of a body, frozen before her.

I shook my head. "I...I know. But the doctor said—"

"There is no fear in love, my child." She recited the bible verse flawlessly as she gathered me into her rail thin embrace. She's so cold. So, so cold..."Come on, baby." She coaxes as I sob into her chest. "Say it with me. Speak to God..."

"I'm scared, Ma." The blubbered words slip past the caged confines in my heart, and I hug her tight.

"Shhh," She croons while rocking me. "No fear, remember? Tell it to Him..."

I breathe in deep and despite the ice in her touch I'm suddenly warm as I chant the words to 1 John 4:18.

"Perfect love drives out fear; the one who fears is not made perfect in love..."

As we're completing the verse, the TV pastor's question drifts into my mind, and I'm compelled to answer it with the welled-up feelings of futility that's festered in my heart since Mama got her diagnosis. For what is man without love? Loveless.

Part One

"Love was always one of those elusive virtues that had never been all mine..."

1

that girl

· ❤ · ❤ · ❤ · ❤ · ❤ ·

I didn't like to question morals for fear of inherently, or intentionally, doing wrong. However, those lines got blurred real fast whenever Norina Skye entered the building.

I clench the iPhone like a vice in my chubby brown hand, pressing it closer to my face to emit a throaty groan. I knew this would do it, would bring him close to the climax that he needed and I profited from.

Edgar's wheezes blare through the phone, making me nearly gag at the image of his wrinkled pink body writhing in his perfectly pressed suit, his neat slacks bunched around his ankles as he begged the phone to "don't stop."

"Norina, baby please don't stop! You're killing me here." He pleaded, almost as if on cue, to my halting sex noises.

I chuckled darkly, "What did I say about giving me commands? Who's in charge here?"

"You!" He whimpers, out of breath. "It's always you, sweet Norina."

"That right?"

He sputters, "Y-Yes, ma'am!"

"You better keep touching that big piece of meat then. Don't release until I tell you to, either. You understand?" I order before moaning again.

A pause, before he drawls in that country cornbread accent of his, "I-I can't hold on with you moaning in my ear like that sweetness–"

"Shut your filthy little slut mouth, Edgar. Do as I say or this call ends right now."

"Wait, wait!" He pants. "I meant to say, yes ma'am. I won't cum until you tell me to."

I smirk. "Good boy. Now, tell Mama Skye how that hard dick feels. Want me to taste it? Lick up every drop of cum until you're begging for more like my little bitch?"

"Ah!" He garbled in a lust driven agony. "Come suck this big white cock, Norina. I want that so bad. Come back to my condo and do me right…"

"How bad do you want it, little bitch?" I purred my satisfaction, careful to circumvent that request as I always did.

"Bad…" He whined, his pants quickening.

"I bet you want to cum, so bad right now, too."

Another silent pause answers my question, and a faux fury overcomes me. I straighten my back and adjust myself in my dining room seat.

"You there, little bitch?"

His whimpers meet me through the phone, and I ground my teeth.

"Edgar, you better not be cumming! Not until I tell you to."

"Sweet...Norina!" Edgar gasps. "Sorry baby, can't...hold on."

"Fine!" I bellow in agitation. "Cum then, you filthy slut. Remember whose dick that is. Who you belong to. What's my name?"

"Nor...ina!" He wails, and there's a muffled shuffling in the background as I imagined the phone drop from the intensity of his climax.

A radiant power fills my chest at the state of him, of how the amount of feminine energy and potency had the effect it usually did on my customers.

"You there, sweetness?" His ragged voice returned just as I resumed eating my corn flakes.

"I'm here. Don't forget to tip me, baby. Our time is up."

"Oh, Norina," he breathes. "You're the only one who can make me ruin my office like that. I wish you would consider meeting me one day. I'll treat your body so good...just like you do me."

I hear movement in the distance, and the reality of things floats back just then. Norina Skye made her appearance at breakfast time, and I needed her to go before my newly sanctimonious mother could wake up and join me for our usual breakfasts before school.

"You know the deal, Edgar." I respond to his typical complaints after a phone sex session.

While I normally loved his obsession with my boss bitch alter ego because they paid the bills, panic surged through my being at the prospect of being discovered sinning in the morning.

The hallway light came on, and I squealed, "Talk tomorrow, okay sweetie?"

"For real, Norina." He protested as I glanced at the hall. "Let me come take care of you. Bring you back to my place in Greenville and–"

"Cleo, is that you in there?" My mother's voice called out groggily.

Shit. Fuck. Shit, shit, fuck! I swore inwardly before clearing my throat, tossing a quick, "Call me tomorrow, baby!" and pressing the big fat red button on the screen to end the call.

Almost as if sensing the hastily ended call, my phone vibrates with a text message from Him. My...other lover.

HIM: Good morning, boo. I love you.

Groaning from the injustice of Mama's proximity and a keen knowledge that he'd only send fifteen to twenty follow up texts if I didn't respond, I type a hasty reply with shaky fingers.

> **ME**: Morning, boo. Ditto.

Frantic at this point, I shove the smartphone in my denim pocket of my skinny jeans before straightening and diving into my cereal.

That was too close a call, I lamented as I watched Amora Albert trudge into the kitchen with her usual sky blue terry cloth bathrobe and bunny slippers.

"Good morning, Mama." I greeted around a mouthful of corn cereal.

Mama eyed me suspiciously before opening the fridge. "The Lord is willing."

"Amen," I grumbled, heat coloring my cheeks while I scarfed down the rest of the cereal.

I tried to ignore the loud beat of my heart at the intensity of what happened. Of what almost happened.

The real is that I'd almost been caught "working," not for the first time, by my newly devout Christian mother.

"Trice still dropping by to take you to school?" Mom queried between sips of her orange juice.

I hadn't paid attention to her taking the seat across from me at some point, occupying the worn dining room chair and staring at me with even more suspicion. Like her question was pass or fail and I'd been the target of a word trap. This was typical Amora though, I think wearily before casting my shameful gaze to the floor. Since returning to live with her after being solely raised by my Uncle Ferrum and Auntie Laurel, whom I lovingly referred to as Mom and Pop, things had been pretty fine for a while. In exchange for full-time living with the birth mother I suspected Pops never fully trusted, were the weekly dinners I'd been forced to attend. And I tried to finagle myself out of the weekly commitment by up and "forgetting" to show up to one of Mom and Pop's elegantly catered weekly dinners, only to have it blow up in my face.

"We'll host at Amora's next week," Mom told me demurely over the phone after I rattled off the lame excuse. "Since you're so busy with school and all."

That had been enough to get me to never skip another dinner. Mama never said it out loud, but I knew she hated them. And there was no way I'd subject the mother I'd just gotten back to snide comments masked in overt sarcasm from her older brother and his wife.

Mama worked most nights housekeeping at the local motel down the road and her nightly absence afforded me an abundance of alone time. Don't get me wrong, outside of hanging with my girlfriend Trice, spending our Saturday mornings together was an event I'd looked forward to with my overworked mother. But a girl needed her alone time, especially in the line of work I'd found myself in. More real? Mama's meager checks kept the lights on, but that was it. As much as I hated the gig most days, it was moaning perverts like Edgar who allowed me to pay the big girl bills like rent and groceries.

"Um, yeah." I coughed nervously while standing. "Guess I better get ready to go."

"Hold on, ma'am." She says. "I ain't hear a honk yet."

"I know, but…" I trail off, swearing inwardly at my hastiness.

My best friend Patrice Newbern, or Trice, would usually honk her horn two to three times as was signature when it came to picking me up in the mornings for school.

Mama shot me an expectant stare. "But?"

"But…" I started again, wondering how to phrase the fact that I'd been running to avoid lying to her.

And I hated lying to the woman who'd been more like my best friend than any parent to me over the course of my lifetime. We'd always been so tight, like sisters, since we were so close in age at seventeen and thirty-two. She'd always been so carefree, placing importance on the fun of life. Whenever visiting me during court-mandated visits growing up, we'd always have a blast playing cards or dolls. In fact, once she got clean and her visits transformed into me staying nights at whatever house she'd been currently renting, she'd introduced me to the very first love of my life.
I couldn't have been older than maybe ten when she brought me along for one of her "outings" she called it. Really, the trip existed more along the lines of dragging me

to a beauty supply store, flirting with the on-patrol security guard, and sneaking me inside. We had to have nabbed over a hundred bucks in foundation, eye and lip liners, and all sorts of beatification products. What began as the worst day of my life since getting chewed out by my other parents for not washing the dishes, ended in the best way. Mama and I painted each other's faces and modeled the clothes I didn't even notice she threw in the theft bag. A sort of bond formed that day between me and my irresponsibly quirky birth mother, one so strong it fueled everything I did between school and "work." Makeup was my greatest obsession.

Guilty and slightly defeated, I deflate back into my seat.

"Nothing." I mutter.

"I don't mean to be so aggro with you, Cleo. It's these new meds Dr. Alison got me on. Feels like my brain is splitting in half the pain so bad."

"You try the pain meds?"

"The pain meds make me nauseous, and the anti-nausals make me cranky. It's like every pill creates another problem worse than what it's prescribed for."

"Just try to take it easy, today. Okay? Maybe don't go into work if you're hurting." I say.

She grimaces. "Cleo'Nora June. Albert women are fighters. I ain't letting this Sickle Cell run me to the grave when I been fighting it all my life."

"But, Mama!" I start, irritated now by this stubborn woman I loved so much. "Just yesterday you were complaining about your joint pain. And now this? Either go to the doctor or take the day off."

"Baby, it's not that serious. Chill out."

"Chill out?" I mock her, aghast. "Glad to see you taking your health so seriously, Mama. Real mature."

"The Lord says the willing and able shall help others. How I help others is through the work I do."

"Right." I scoffed. "You washing the linens compares to curing the sick and healing the blind."

"Cleo, that's just vicious." She retorts. "Lord knows you weren't raised that way."

You didn't raise me at all! Is what I nearly scream at her, but tamp those words down and hone in on her former statement.

"Sorry, Mama." I whisper, shifting in my seat to face her. "But Cornball can survive the day without you there, you know? Can't he find another maid to fill in for you today?"

I don't mince words where her sleazy shift supervisor is concerned. Cornball Corbin treated all the housekeepers as if they were more than just on his payroll, but possibly on a different payment system the law wouldn't smile so kindly at. His gold grill and crooked smile that twisted his face every time he saw my mother made me want to throttle him by his skinny neck. I often caught him ogling my mother whenever

I'd walk her to Best Stay Motel, and how she responded to the lewd man had me staving off barf. My usually feisty mother who now feared the Lord more than she partied during her occasional appearances in my life, never even looked Cornball in the eyes. Never even stood up for herself whenever he'd refer to her as Amira instead of her actual name, Amora. I made a vow to heal our situation one day. To make more money than the both of us ever fathomed so that we could live cozy in a high rise somewhere. I saved up as much as I could with my Slut Angels earnings, but the rising bills as a direct result of inflation (thanks to gentrification) ate away at my comfy savings. My funds were lower than ever, making me secretly more desperate to find another cash source to pay the rent I'd lied to Mama about paying. To her knowledge, Pops paid our steadily increasing rent. And I knew Mama would shit golden bricks if ever she discovered it wasn't her ever-disapproving big brother paying our rent, but her sinning daughter who made her coins in the same way she did conceiving me. Off the pleasure of nameless nobodies who all but died to me after our thirty or sixty minute phone sex sessions.

Mama's shoulders wiggle with her laughter at my usual pun. "You're right, baby. He sure can."

"Good." I popped up and rounded the table. Kissing her forehead as relief filled me. "Now, go to bed."

"Yes, ma'am." She chuckled.

A loud horn sounds from outside, alerting me of my bestie's arrival to take me to school. I make haste to throw my backpack over my shoulder and run to the front door.

"That's an order!" I tell her while unlocking the door.

"After my doctor's appointment, I promise I'll sleep the rest of the day away." She reassured me with the gentlest tone before I turned back to stare at her. "Your Uncle Ferr is coming to pick me up in an hour for that."

"Keep me posted, Mama." I insist, hating the fear in my heart at yet another doctor's appointment over a failed drug.

I open my mouth to reassure her that everything's going to be okay. To tell her that I loved her despite all the lies I kept inside, but the third horn honk cuts me off.

"Go ahead, sweetie." She says. "And don't forget you've got dinner with your aunt and uncle tonight."

"Okay..." I groaned with an automatic roll of the eyes. "Thanks for the reminder."

"It'll be all right." She crosses the room in no time to meet me at the door and deliver a light kiss upon my forehead. "And remember, I'll be here when you get back, baby girl. Make good choices. Promise?"

I can't resist the warm feeling that lifts my lips in a smile. "Double promise."

The fifth honk just pisses me off as I slam the door and meet my bestie at her car.

"Jesus, I'm here!" I growl while sliding into the passenger seat. "No need for theatrics."

Instead of the playful banter I prayed for each day since her departure, a cold tone greets me as I stare into the depthless eyes of Him. My oppressor, gang lord, and secret boyfriend who I not-so-secretly feared.

"Kept me waiting." Luther snarls in that gravelly voice that tears me to shreds inside. "Again."

"I-I'm sorry."

"You ain't." He says before revving the engine. "But you will be later on. After your punishment."

My doe-eyed gaze shifts to meet the window, where the world is passing us by during the twenty minute drive to Easton Rogue High. I allow my brain to wander towards the past, which is a much safer mental destination instead of my penniless present or frightening future.

Where only loneliness and Luther's punishment awaited me...

2

mortal?

PAST

"Let's be best friends." I say to the Caribbean girl on the ground with long plaits and tears pouring down her face.

I notice by the abrupt hitch in her breathing and dubious crook of her neck while staring at me staring down at her that she's totally distrusting of me. I try to keep an easy smile pasted on my lips in efforts to hide the raw concern. She looks terrible, I think, further examining her dark chocolate skin and the new sand burns those assholes recently put there shortly after recess began.

"State your business," Caribbean Girl demands.

"Cleo," I say while extending a hand to her and pulling her to her feet.

I felt her tiny hand tremble as it touched mine, but didn't mention it as I studied her face some more. Large brown eyes stared right back at me, and I saw the emotion there. Saw something hiding in the background I lowkey resonated with that compelled me to reach out and touch her.

"Oh! S-sorry, I mean my name is Cleo. Not my business."

"Why are you staring?" She snaps, flinching when I come in contact with her cheek but otherwise unmoving.

It was almost as if she expected me to hit her just as Jerome Cooper and his tough-boy gang did earlier.

"Your lip's bleeding." I whisper, allowing my hand to roam her scarred cheek, then to the leaking bottom lip that needed medical attention. "Why did you let them do that to you?"

While unmoving before, my question seemed to be the thing that did it. It was like she'd been snapping out of a trance when she flinched again and leapt out of range of my hands.

"Better yuh mine ol' clothes dan people business, Mooma say." She muttered.

"Mooma?" My face contorted with confusion, sure she'd sprout three heads at some point. "Say what?"

She rolled her eyes. "It be nothing!"

"Okay, then..." I said, pursing my lips. "Sorry."

"What you sorry for?" She frowned this time. "Wasn't you who rubbed my face in the dirt."

Though only eight years old, I felt bad for her. She'd caught nothing but slack since transferring here last week, and often ate her packed lunches by herself in the cafeteria.

It was easy for me to change my appearance or personality to fit in with whatever crowd reigned supreme in those days, but this Caribbean girl kept quiet to herself. I wanted to tell her she'd only make herself a target by being such a stand out loner. That was me not so long ago sitting by myself and desperate for someone – anyone– to just say hi. She had a lot to learn around here if she was going to survive Silver Spring Elementary school.

"And no thanks," She said firmly.

It took me a couple blinks before I realized she'd answered my initial offer of best friendship.

"You don't want to hang out with me?"

She shrugged. "Guess not."

"Oh." I said, doing little to hide my astonishment. "May I ask why?"

Arms crossed, she shot me a hard stare not befitting a young girl.   In fact, she looks years old with the level of weariness and distrust behind her glare. Its intensity makes me shudder slightly.

"What's your deal anyway?" She bites out. "I didn't ask you to ask me to be your friend. Nothing but rotten people at this school."

"I didn't mean to–"

"Do I look afraid?" She spat, stalking me into the jungle gym. "Or foolish? Which one is it? Because I'm getting tired of you rotten American kids treating me like garbage. So, what's your angle?"

"Angle?"

She scoffed. "Here to dump my lunch in the trash can? Pull my hair? If so, then you're too late. Those rotten American boys did enough of that."

My heart beat loudly in my ears while I listened to the torture she'd been exposed to since moving to this country. I remember her introduction speech at the beginning of class last week and winced. Jerome and his cronies, Nicky and Desean, targeted the shy girl with long hair and the funny accent. I turned a blind eye the first week of her torture, looking away whenever catching Jerome steal from her backpack or crumple up her classwork.

"I'm not here for that." I reassured her, or at least tried to.

Her little body was downright shaking from reliving the memories of what had been done to her. And I couldn't explain the need to help her. There were tons of new students, but she'd been the only one my conscience couldn't let me keep turning a blind eye on.

"Then...what?" She breathed, sinking to the ground. "Recess is almost over. You better get out of here before you get caught with Chicken Girl."

I grimaced at the brutal nickname Jerome instituted after dumping one of her homemade lunches that had foreign looking pieces of meat in it. Thus earning her the nickname Chicken Girl.

I sank to her level, stealing a glance around us to make sure we weren't seen. Kids were playing to themselves or respective friend groups, which gave me the courage to look her in the eye.

"That's just Jerome being Jerome. He's funny, right? Try not to take him too seriously. He did the same to me when I first moved here, too. Trust me, ignore him and it'll be over soon."

She nodded. "In other words, let him keep doing this to me until he gets tired or finds another punching bag?"

That's exactly what it was, and my head comprehends the shame of that advice today, but back then?

I grabbed her hand and squeezed it tight. "I think we should be friends. Best friends."

"No." She answered before snatching her hand from mine and turning to stand. "Looks like you have enough friends, Cleo." She seemed to spit my name out like a swear word.

My brain scrambled, totally unsure how to crack this new girl's tough exterior built from fear and distrust. And she wasn't wrong; Lola Fields, Champagne Knox, and Adalyn Carter were the core of my friend group I wiggled my way into for protection shortly after moving here. They looked out for me when Jerome did his worst and stole my backpack one day, then agreed to let me hang with them. But only in school, never for play dates or anything like that. Which I inwardly questioned but outwardly understood. More like, accepted.

My friends sat concealed near one of the nearing jungle gyms, eying our interaction like talent show judges and listening to every word I said.

"Wait!" I exclaimed before grabbing her wrist again and pulling her towards me.

"What the–" She squealed when our bodies collided into a heap onto the playground.

I grunted as the weight of her knocked into me before blinking to orient myself. However, the opportunity I came over here for presented itself crystal clear in that following moment. Chicken Girl's eyes got real wide as they stared into mine, her body lying on top of mine.

Our heavy breaths matched from the exertion and shock of falling, no other sound penetrating the earth as we laid there and just...stared.

Her eyes are softer than I'd ever seen, tugging at my heart strings and amping up the guilt factor.

Holding my breath and closing my eyes, I reached up and stole a quick kiss before shoving her off me.

Chicken Girl crashed into the ground right when I stood up, turned to my girlfriends, and hollered, "I did it!"

"Go, Cleo!" Lola's voice rang out the loudest amongst the small group of cheering third graders. "I knew you would get Chicken Girl to kiss you!"

"You're so gross!" Adalyn wheezed between laughter.

"It was easy," I said with a frail voice.

I did my best not to look at her. Did my best to ignore the wild beat of my heart and tears that demanded to push through my eyes at doing this to her.

"Did she taste like chicken?' Champagne pitched in.

"Um..." I sputtered, fidgeting with my curls and staring at the ground.

But Champagne, like her usual Alpha-self, persisted.

"Come on, Cleo!" She yelled, gaining the attention of more kids from the playground. "Your job was to tell us if she tasted like chicken or not! So, come on, did she?"

"If I tasted like..." Chicken Girl, Caribbean girl, whispered in a broken voice from the ground. I refused to look at her. "You didn't really want to be my friend?"

"Of course not!" Lola preened haughtily with a shake of her ponytails. "Cleo already has friends. Tell her."

Only more silence passed by as the final minutes of recess ticked away. My eyes were shut, and I relished in the darkness it provided me if only to hide a couple of seconds.

I couldn't stand to look at them. Knew I would break if I looked at the damage I caused.

"Fucking tell her!" Champagne snapped, and I heard her footsteps drawing closer to us. "Tell Chicken Girl that she's disgusting and that she should get back on the boat she came from."

Taking a breath, I do it. I open my eyes to peer at the kid I'd called Caribbean Girl, not Chicken Girl, and whose real name I knew but was afraid to use in public.

"You're gr-gross..." I start, but don't get the chance to finish since Chicken Girl stands and bolts towards the classroom.

The entire class breaks out in laughter, as did I. Blending in like I usually did for safety. But whatever that was...what just happened...would be a memory that'd haunt me forever. Especially as I peer closer at Chicken Girl's retreating form and studying the huge chunk of butchered off plaits at the back of her head. It didn't take a rocket scientist to gather that Jerome Cooper, our resident class bully, was the cause of her recent haircut.

Poor Chicken Girl, I almost say, but really it's poor me. I'm the one who was left emotionally and spiritually bankrupt as I think about my fate at Easton Rogue High. In other words, there was nothing wrong with Chicken Girl, but everything in the world was wrong with Nora: the loveless girl I became to protect myself in the years to come.

3

I did nothing

·♥·♥·♥·♥·♥·

The sudden jerk of the car forces me awake. I'm shocked, and not from the realization that I'd fallen asleep, but from the unfamiliar back-alley building we sat parked outside of. I had to blink several times to gauge a clear cut understanding of my surroundings and when recognition refused to come, I shot the driving culprit a confused look.

"This isn't Easton," I said to Luther, whose glacial stare bore into mine at my words.

"So?" He spat. "Never said I was taking you to school anyway."

My eyes slid around to study the area again, still just as befuddled as when I awakened from that odd dream. Not quite a dream, but a memory at just how awful I'd been to Chicken Girl. In the past now, I inwardly chide myself while shaking my swirling head at Luther Noonan's audacity.

"Trice always picked me up every day at seven. Promptly. I guess I assumed you'd do the same."

"Assumptions, huh?" He said, scanning the area while lifting his phone. "Makes an ass outta whoever's doing the assuming."

"Wow." I breathed.

"Wow, what?" He asked absently. "Your homegirl flew the coop last month. She ain't want nothing to do with your scheming ass anymore."

"Luther—"

"You ain't nothing but a liability. You think if I could get rid of your ass, I wouldn't? If you wasn't making me so much money then you'd be just as done as your little boyfriend, too. The fact you still breathing is a privilege. Especially after how you did me."

I open my mouth to respond, but all that comes up is sputtering. I can't think of anything to say to the guy, considering he voiced all my deepest insecurities in the ten minutes I was in his handed-down car. I can't afford to think of... him. My first love. Of Trice, neither. Of everything I lost over the course of one year.

"Sorry, Luther." I whisper while averting my eyes. He had a complex about direct eye contact, and I painfully learned that the hard way when we met last year. "But we agreed to not let my mom know that Trice isn't picking me up in the mornings anymore to avoid unwanted suspicion or questions. You showed up a couple minutes late, and so I thought I'd bring it up. To keep us covered."

A sudden vibration let me know he received a text. His face set in a deep scowl as he fixed his eyes on the screen.

"Yo, this prick need to come on. Got me out here waiting on him like a ugly bitch at prom. Damn."

He grumbled the words, either unaware or willfully ignoring my comment.

"Luther?" I hedged.

"Hmm." He responded while tapping furiously on his phone.

"Did you catch what I said? That we need to be more careful?"

"Fuck!" He roared. And I screamed at the sharp interjection and watched him slam the thin phone out the window. "He got ten minutes before I ride out to Jersey and paid his little shop a visit."

My heart quickened and the familiar dampness formed on my palms when I witnessed Luther spaz out. Fuck, I thought, not another rage. Since Jack Burn, the former leader of the 590's and Trice's ex, got locked up a few months back, Luther had been tasked with running the operations on the outside until further notice. He'd been awful before, sure, but now? He'd break into these fits of rage at random, even at the slightest inconvenience like when the weather man guaranteed a sunny day, then it rained instead. He never said it, but it was clear the stress of running an organized street gang solo took its toll on his mental. There were only one of two things that seemed to calm or distract him enough to get him to chill during the rages, however.

Coking or cumming.

I hurriedly roamed my eyes over the messy car interior in search of his usual drug stash. And nearly cried after finding the usually filled bag of white deflated and empty in the glove compartment. I stole a glance over at my boyfriend, who'd been spiraling even more out of control as his fist connected with the steering wheel. His dark brown knuckles splash with blood before he begins to reign punches into his body: in rapid blows, he strikes his upper chest, shoulders, and head while rocking back and forth. He's muttering something...and I'm as still as a deer in the headlights while I listen to what sounded like death threats murmured under his breath.

"Hey," I start, but he's still rocking and muttering instead of listening to me.

God, I was so scared, but knew something had to be done to stop this. It was clear as day that he'd snorted all the coke that should've lasted him a month, so without options I did what I had to do.

Gulping, I did what I did best. More like, it was Norina responsible for reaching for his bloody hand and forcefully slipping it past the hem in my denim skirt and beyond the seat of my panties. Once at my crotch, I shifted in the seat and manipulated one long digit into my sex. Using his abnormally long fingers to stroke my slit. Call it survivor mode, but the wetness that released on demand before his fingers made contact was just the thing that brought him back.

"Cleo…" He breathed, stilling and taking control of the action beneath my panties. His fingers gained a tempo that had me writhing in the passenger seat. "You're wet as fuck for me."

"Yes, baby." I whimpered as a tide of heat coursed through my body.

It was a lie. A complete fib to give this psychotic jerk credit behind my moisture, but I shut my eyes and pictured something to take my mind off the anger, fear, and disgust exploding inside. "Let me help you feel better?"

"Fuck yeah…" He husked, and I made a conscious effort to ignore the fresh bruises on his face. "Back seat."

I force a smile I don't feel while obeying his command. Coking or cumming is what it took to get him back semi-normal. This time, cumming it was.

"You know just what to…say to get me right, girl. Shit…" He groans before rutting two powerful strokes inside of me.

He seemed to come back to life after the thick streams of his release dribbled down my perched ass. Several minutes pass as we lay in a tangled heap in the backseat, recovering in the aftermath of our sex.

"Gimme your phone," He says in the darkened car.

No loving affirmations or sweet jostling words ever followed our transactional fucking, nothing similar to the way my first love held me moments after we climaxed. But this request throws me off. And makes me wince.

"Um…" I mutter, sitting upright. "My phone? Why?"

"Did you not just see my phone fly through that window a couple minutes ago? Give it here."

I gulp, fear filling me at the prospect of him digging through my contacts. Web presence. Text messages…
What if he saw that text thread?

Luther knew about my Slut Angels job, in fact, it was him who encouraged me to respond to the sleazy under the table and under the guise of an eighteen year old named Norina Skye. My Slut Angles checks scored me a decent wage, but it was the illegal side business I ran on the side that brought the most cash. More like, it brought Luther the most cash since he took the lion share of what I earned and risked my job for.

I provided cam shows to the clients I secretly funneled through Slut Angels, and I almost feel remorse for conning the executives and corporate stakeholders out of their cash for a flash of Norina Skye, but…

I not-so-secretly relished in the control and power from it all. The sounds, the pleasure, and overall excitement that charged the room when I performed for them. In a way, it felt a lot like the love I needed to feel something. Anything.

But I don't know what I'd do if Luther saw that text thread. The same thread I kept muted and that greeted me with a merry "Morning Boo," each day. He'd become so much to me in the months since My First Love left me for good. He, like my bestie, was gone for good. All because I couldn't love them right and fucked everything up.

"Hello?" He said with a wave of his hand, as if trying to signal me back to the current plane.

"My phone, you said?"

"You heard me."

"Right." I stammered, pulling out my cell with a shaky hand and extending it to him.

I had to get ready, I panic inwardly, and do another visual scan in the messy car for potential weapons in case shit went left. Not even a minute passes before he releases a stream of cuss words while staring at my phone screen.

"Yo, what the fuck is this?" He scowls.

His voice is like the blunt end of a weapon. It's so piercing, and I all but cringe from it. What would Trice do in this situation? Or even Chicken Girl? I'm not all that sure why those two questions blare on the loudspeaker in my mind before I open my eyes and stare at him. I needed to think of an answer. And quick. Especially if he was witnessing the forbidden text thread that's gotten me into a familiar trouble with him when I was messing with My First Love.

"Cleo." He growls again, but this time his soulless brown eyes are honing in on me. "There better be an explanation for this shit. You got five seconds."

4

strength in pairs

·♥·♥·♥·♥·♥·

PAST

"Long story short, he fucked the neighbor. Now, I'm out a thousand dollars." Joyce lamented with a single shake of her head before me.

"Girl, you need to leave that husband of yours." Juanita, my cousin and employer, chided between signature pops of her bubblegum while she sectioned off a portion of her client's 3-B curls to be cornrowed.

Joyce, the forty-year old Jewish woman twisted her lips in a way that had her looking her actual age.

"Hold still!" I warned after applying the blush a little too intensely in an undesired area on her cheeks. "Unless you want this to look like a cheap beat?"

"Sorry, Nor." Joyce winces. "And I couldn't leave him, Nita. He's the love of my life." My cousin made a show of rolling her eyes on full display since Joyce had full view of her actions. "I know what it sounds like. I know what I sound like."

"A dumb ass."

"Nita!" I hissed at my unfiltered cousin after applying the client's lip liner. I turned gentler eyes to one of Nita's longest time clients, cupping her face. "Ignore her."

"What I say wrong?" Nita demanded. "She do sound like a dumb ass. Staying with a dude who fucking around on his family ain't forgivable. Or even worth all these tears for!"

I nearly ask about the tears, but that's before I witness the sobs wracking the tiny chest of the tough older lady.

I sink to my knees in panic as I watched my carefully crafted makeup beat bleed from her tears.

"Joyce, girl don't cry!" I begged. "You ruining your make-up..."

"Nita's right." She sobbed.

Nita rolled her eyes again, but this time tight concern on her face existed there as she sank down beside me to meet her eyes. The normally bustling shop was empty today, consisting solely of the three of us. I wasn't here every day, but appreciated Nita for giving me the chance to do the makeup for her client's. The gig didn't pay much at all, and makeup was done only by the request of the select few of her clientele, but any opportunity I got to dabble around in different colored palettes was a win.

"Look," Nita started. "All I'm saying, is you need to get your shit together. How can a man who claims to love you just go around sticking it into whatever hole crosses his path?"

"Graphic," I mumbled.

"No." Joyce cut in. "I get it. I hear what you're saying and I want Larry to do right by me. But if he left us...I don't know what I'd do. He's been like our savior since Ayomide left. I should be lucky he's stuck around, you know? Not many men will cherish another man's leftovers."

My eyes widened as I watched her heart on full display. It was bleeding, I thought, considering the haunted way she used her words and the stricken look on her face. But mine bled right with her. I knew that feeling all too well. Knew what it was like to just shut up and be grateful for the surrogate family created as a result of my mother's bad choices. Mom and Pop, though really my aunt and uncle, were the best parents a girl could ask for. They had the perfect house, perfect salaried careers with 401k, and perfect friends. Mom worked as an Immigration Lawyer and Pops, a retired musician, served as our resident pastor at Mt. Goliath's.

They were the ideal power couple in every way. The only imperfect smidge in their lives was the longing for a child, and after my penniless Mama got pregnant with me from one of her "nameless encounters," my Uncle Ferr stepped in. Uncle Ferr legally adopted me at birth after Mama left me at her big brother's doorstep like a movie network cliche. Mama and Pop's relationship had been strained ever since, but I always sensed there'd been a deeper reason why. And instead of the perfect daughter Mom and Pop longed for, they got me. The girl who'd been super obsessed with dying her hair during her mood changes and practicing makeup in secret whenever she got the chance, since her adopted mother thought face paint was "unsaintly." I should be grateful for them, I found myself chanting the reminder whenever the gloom settled over me. Whenever the longing for Mama, my birth mother I'd been condemned to see monthly, got real bad.

"Cleo!" Someone yelled my nickname, and my head snapped up in its direction.

An hour had passed and my mind must have wandered while I swept the tendrils from the shop floor. I nearly dropped the broom when I met the stone face of Juanita Albert Rojas.

"What?" I barked back at her.

"Don't you 'what' me. I know you heard me talking to you."

I blushed and averted guilty eyes at the knowledge I'd been daydreaming too hard to listen. "I caught most of it."

"Really?" She frowned. "Then what I say?"

A beat, then I caved. "Fuck it. I wasn't paying attention. All right? Now, tell me what you said."

"Girl." She sighed while counting the cash at the front register. "I asked if you'd be okay to lockup today?"

Now it was my turn to frown. "Right now? In the middle of the day?"

"Yeah," She blew out. "Seems like business is drier than usual. And on a Friday, too."

I chewed my lip before answering her. I noticed it, too, but didn't dare voice my concern to her. Nita's Beauty Shop was a D.C. staple; a gathering place of hood bitches and housewives alike to get together and get beautiful. Her shop was an instant success in its seven year lifespan, but it was only recently where the unthinkable happened.

Empty chairs on a Friday afternoon. A true rarity for the beauty gathering place that existed as my third home. Mama's house was second only to Mom and Pop's. And it killed me to watch my cousin's business dwindle.

"It's all those new hair joints opening up since that second mall got built. There's already, like, three style shops not even a couple blocks from here. And with this braid shop is opening across the street..."

Broom forgotten, I crossed the room in an instant to be at her side. "Nita, girl, have some faith. Your loyals are still coming in. You're just going through a season."

She chuckled piteously. "Leave all that faith mumbo jumbo to Uncle Ferr. I live in reality. And for real, Nita's ain't doing too good."

"There's always tomorrow, right?"

"Ta!" She chuffed. "Just another day to babysit empty chairs. Dad would be so upset if he saw this. This salon meant the world to him..."

I watch her face fall at the admission, and I'm immediately hurting for her. Claylin Albert, her father and my uncle, opened this beauty salon over thirty years ago with his devoted husband Julius Rojas. Since Uncle Clay tragically lost his battle to complications from Sickle Cell two years ago, Nita's other father retreated back to his home village in Honduras and transferred legal ownership of the salon to their adopted daughter, Juanita.

"He is so proud of you, cuz." I whisper, heartbroken from the stricken look on her face. It's as if she's reliving something awful.

"Yeah, sure." She said, then wiped her face with a decision made when she added, "I wanted you to hear this from me, okay?"

I leaned against the front reception to steel myself from the impending doom. The finishing blow of information that'd crush me. I had no friends. Nowhere else to go after school other than home or Mt. Goliath's. This place was my sanctuary where I got to do what I loved.

"What is it?" I asked with a shaky breath.

She expelled a huge breath before saying it. "I'll be closing down the shop for the rest of the week. Don't worry, you'll still get paid since your wages barely make a dent in the budget. But I'll let you know next week about plans to reopen. Okay?"

I nodded my head. Truly numb inside. "Yeah."

"I'm fighting this. Don't you worry! This town ain't getting rid of the best braider in the city."

"Damn, right!" I cheered, the hope meter in me nudging upward a little but barely. "And this will blow over. I know it will. It has to. And I'll lock up the shop, so you can get a head start home to be with your babies."

A genuine grin crested her face at the mention of her sons, Frankie J and Julian. "Thanks, Cleo."

"Of course." I pulled her round body to me tight. "Now, scoot! Get out of here and let me worry about the rest. You use that brain for more important matters, like saving this shop!"

She laughed while donning her coat at the front door. "Sure you'll be all right locking up by yourself?"

"What you think?" I shot her a look that conveyed all my annoyance with her statement, coupled with the stress of the shitty news she just gave.

"Okay, okay!" She lamented. "Call me if you need anything."

"I won't!" I called while watching her disappearing body walk away through the glass door.

I didn't rush to lock the front door, instead, I finished sweeping the floor I abandoned earlier. Once done, I moved on to organize the shampoos, the combs, and took extra care to wipe down the tiny corner of my makeup station. It wasn't much, but this tiny nook was where my heart was. And even the thought of Nita closing down and taking this from me for good...

I shuddered from the thought and future I wanted no part of if makeup didn't exist in it.

My mind drifts to a familiar song I caught Pops humming a time or two whenever working on his garage projects. The rap classic, rightfully entitled "Da Madness!" was about a man who'd been so obsessed with a woman's beauty from across the bar, that it had taken everything, his entire soul even, to resist the urge to approach her. Though she'd come to the bar with another male companion she'd looked obviously promised to, the slow blink of her eyes, way her tongue grazed her bottom lip, and sway of her hips brought him to the edge. Fresh, the singer, had been so excited that he gave up resisting. The chorus comes in with–

"Surrender to the Fresh! Surrender to the Madness!" A voice sang from behind.

Off-guard from the invasion, I scream and bolt to the back room.

The only beat that existed now was the rapid beating of my heart that wouldn't bring me ease at the thought of the intruder. How did he get in? I fumed, then smacked myself at the stupid recollection. In my idle cleaning, singing, and dancing, locking the front door was the furthest from my mind. In fact, I'd been so preoccupied with my thoughts that I hadn't even noticed the sky darkened. Mom and Pop would be furious if I didn't get home soon.

"Shit!" I swore while pacing the small storage room filled with buckets of perms and hair tools.

I entertain the idea of calling the cops, but hiss a couple more swear words at the memory of my phone slipping from my pocket during the jog back here. More like, the escape. I'm so damn stupid! Stupid, stupid, stupid–

"Yo, girl." The male's voice calls from outside the door. "What you know about True N' Fresh?"

"Go away!" I scream, willfully ignoring the man's question about the disbanded rap group.

"Uh, my bad." He apologizes, and I note the confusion in his voice. "I ain't mean to sneak up on you like that. Swear to God."

Rage replaces the fear as I point an accusing finger at the locked door.

"Dude are you crazy? Looking for drugs? Which is it? It's got to be either of those if you think walking into a dark building with a 'closed' sign on it to be a good idea. Get the fuck out of here!"

"I said 'my bad.' Chill out for a second. Is Nita here?"

I froze. "Who wants to know?"

"The one doing the asking; I need to see her."

"She's not here."

He chuckles before adding. "Don't even lie. Nita always lockup the shop herself. So, where she at?"

"You're not getting any answers until I do. Now, who the fuck are you?"

He drags out an aggrieved breath, and I can just about hear him grab the back of his neck in frustration.

"What you gonna do if I don't answer? Huh? Call the cops?"

I clear my throat, feigning the brevity required for this fucked up intruder situation.

"Damn right I am. Either talk or leave. Those are your only options. Unless you prefer handcuffs."

"Yo!" He guffawed. "You saying you tryna cuff me?"

"Fuck you!" I screeched and felt my face heat.

This guy was a total asshole and it showed, since panic was the farthest emotion from me. All I wanted now was to punch him. Run home, and punch him.

"What's your name, shorty?" He asked calmly once recovered from the laugh attack.

"Screw you." I retorted. "Now, leave!"

"All right, all right." He conceded after a moment. "Wish granted. I'm outta here."

There was something vaguely familiar about the way he spoke. Don't get me wrong, the dude was all D.C . through-and-through, but there was a latent layer of something I recognized. Like knowing the beat of a song but the lyrics are totally a mystery. Made me frustrated to be honest, and I allowed a couple of minutes to tick by before gauging it safe enough to open the door.

No sight of him. Praise God, Mom would say, and I allowed the panic to whoosh out of my worn body. Today was hell on my joints, hands, and back. As an aspiring cosmetic artist, my hands would often tighten if I pushed it too hard. There was one time a client came to Nita's in desperate need of a foundational redo, considering the previous artist botched it with foundation three times lighter than her skin tone. It took me hours to reverse the damage to her beat, but the results were more than worth the searing pain in my fingers. She looked phenomenal and her referral flooded the shop with new clients.

I vowed to take it easy and maybe see a doctor about this new pain that had my hands cramped and seizing after too much exertion.

But first, I needed to lock the door. No more vagrant weirdos dropping in to see Nita. At least not tonight. After the door was secured, I gave the place a final glance to admire my handiwork. Spic and span I had to say as the gush of pride surged through me. I couldn't let Nita's shop shut down, the thought played through my mind like a playlist on repeat. It meant too much to me to lose it, to lose seeing my favorite cousin who'd accepted my uniqueness and honored my talents. Working here twice a week was the highlight of my life, and I vowed to find a solution to this problem.

The sudden ring of my cell phone rouses me from my day-dreams. I frowned, forgetting my whereabouts for a second before running in search of the sound.

"Mama, wassup?" A man, the same intruder from before, answers shortly after the ringing ends.

I freeze at the realization that makes my heart fall to my toes: the intruder never left. Not only that, but he has my phone. He answered my phone.

"No!" I shout, uncaring if the psycho was armed or not at this point.

I find him in Nita's office, which is sort of the perfect place to hide away from the public eye since it's at the dead back of the building.

"You dick!" I shriek.

He's sitting calmly at the desk with my phone to his ear. There's a large goofy grin on his face I desperately needed to punch off at this point. He stands up.

"Is Cleo here?" He asked into the phone.

"Stop it!" I shout while jumping to snatch the phone from him.

He's so damn tall, or maybe I'm just so damn short. We're settling into a dance of keep away while I leap to grab the phone and he dodges.

"Her boyfriend?" He asks with lifted brows while meeting my eyes. I can see the wheels turning as he seeks to formulate a response. "Yeah. I'm her man."

I pause. Freeze. Hell, I'm completely immobile as the shock of his fake confession seizes me. Panting, I examined the guy I thought to be an intruder. Under the harsh light that filled the tiny office, I can now see his hard face and tan skin. In fact, it strikes a match to someone I knew. Or, at least, someone who attended the same school as me. The same guy I noticed in the crowds and who often flirted mercilessly with all the pretty girls in my grade.

"My name?" He asks the phone again, and I'm powerless to just watch him spurt lies to my mother on the opposite line. "Tyrone. But feel free to call me Ty, miss…?"
A beat of silence as his suggested question hangs in the air. "Ms. Amora."

So it was my birth mother, my Mama, who called instead of my more serious Mom. I wait for the yell or beratement to come blare through the phone at the artfully concocted lie, but it doesn't come.
Instead, he throws a quick,

"Pleasure speaking with you as well, Amora. I'll make sure she's taken care of. And tell her to call you later."

"Mama, wait–" I begin, but the plea dies when he presses the fat red button on the screen.

"So your name is Cleo? I could have sworn it was something else."

Is all he said before plopping the phone in my waiting hand and exiting the office. I'm mindlessly following him before I could even comprehend what just happened.

"What was all of that?" I demand, ignoring that comment about my name. "And why are you still here?!"

He shrugged, and I catch him sinking into one of the stylist chairs.

"You seem so serious all the time. Was just having a little fun. I thought it would make you laugh."

"Ain't shit funny about sneaking into the shop. Or sticking around after I asked you to leave the premises. And there's absolutely no humor in lying to my mother. How fucking dare you?"

"How dare I?" He mirrored.

"Yeah, you asshole!"

Before I get a chance to run, he's out of the chair and in front of me. My chest heaves heavily up and down as my eyes work to take him in. He's scrawny, but long. He had to be at least six foot two. But I'm speechless at the sight of him...so close. More like, the abrupt proximity spellbinds me to only stare into his eyes that stare back into mine. Something...sizzles between us. I wondered if he felt it like I did in that moment, and soon my cheeks heat for a different reason. The same reason that had me crossing my thighs when that smile returned to his face.

"You wrote me off as a violent thug the second you saw me walk in. Right?"

I gulped, because that's exactly what I assumed.

He chuckled. "Thought so. That's not nice, Cleo."

"Stop calling me that." I warn, averting my eyes. "Only my family calls me by that name."

He takes another step in my direction that swallows the remaining distance between us. Oh, fuck.

"And I thought I was your boyfriend, Cleo."

"Quit it!" I step back. "And you're just a clown, Ty. Don't think I didn't recognize you."

His eyebrows wiggle and it looks as if he's fighting off a smile when he says, "So you do know me, then. I thought so. You go by Nora, right? At school?"

I don't respond, just keep my gaze pinned to the floor as I pray for a giant hole to open and swallow me into it. I'm not even sure what made me so embarrassed, but I needed air.
As if sensing my need, he turns away.

"Ain't mean to scare you, for real. But what's a cute girl like you know about rap classics like True N' Fresh? You was spittin mad bars, too."

It takes me a minute to understand him. First, he thought I was...cute? But when I realized he'd referenced the song I'd been rapping to while I cleaned and that he interrupted with his unwanted presence, I sighed. This was not the time nor place I wanted to get into how, or why, that song was ingrained in me since birth.

"Thanks." I respond to the odd compliment. "But it's just a song I heard from around. You know, at cookouts and stuff."

It's not a total lie, but the track was taboo to play at our conservative family reunions and cookouts. Pops preferred to stick to the gospel classics like Marvin Sapp or BeBe and CeCe Winans. But I often caught the pastor rapping the hook to True N' Fresh's "Da Madness" a time or two when he thought nobody was around. But that's a story for another time. One I'll never delve into with this guy.

"I peep that." He said, nodding.

"Wh-why are you here?" I stuttered, forcing myself to get back to the main point of the conversation.

"My bad." He mumbled. "I'll be out of your hair in a minute."

"Good." I said while observing him saunter to the reception desk.

His eyes scan the shop before settling on something at the front desk. "I came to get this."

I frowned when he lifted the rectangular item in his hand. A wallet. I found it a couple hours earlier and figured it was Nita's, so for safekeeping, I stored it at the front desk.

"That's not yours." I said while going over to meet him. "Put it back."

He rolled his eyes before parting the thin fabric, pulling out a card, and presenting it to me.

"Sure as hell ain't mine– what I look like? It's my mom's. She left it here earlier and asked me to pick it up before the shop closed."

I do a quick comparison between the government identification card and him. The white lady who'd been here crying earlier as Nita braided her hair stared back at me. And my mouth fell straight to the floor when I read her name.

"Joyce?" I whispered incredulously. "Joyce Zelman?"

"We look nothing alike, I know." Ty said with a smirk. "Guess I took more from my Nigerian pops side of the gene pool. Ma say if it wasn't for the light skin tone, you wouldn't be able to tell who was who."

I couldn't resist playing the comparison game, hunting like the Crocodile Dundee to find the similarities between the handsome stoner and his Jewish mother.

"Ah!" I squealed. "You have her eyes. See there?"

Ty scowled before studying the ID closer. "You really think so?"

"Without a doubt. You're definitely her son." I say, perturbed by the giddy pride in me for sussing out the similarity.

"Nobody's ever said that before." He said, a look I can't describe on his face.

Fuck, I was blushing again. I felt it just as soon as our eyes reconnected. I was trapped under the spell of his eyes that did magic on me. Ty was one of those untouchable beauties I'd always secretly wondered about, but never got too close to. But right now...as the glimmers of moonlight shone into the darkened shop, I couldn't resist the urge to touch him.

"Do you have a girlfriend?" I asked, unintentionally out loud before covering my mouth and wishing for death. "Shit, forget I asked."

He steps close to me again. "Forgot that quick, huh?"

"Forgot what?"

Our bodies rub against each other and I'm still panting like a rabid animal as I watch him lift my hand to his lips. Then he kisses it, and I die again under a thousand moons as the contact sizzles my sensitive skin.

"You are my girlfriend."

I yank it free as I fight for clarity. "No, I'm not."

"All right then." He says. "Then let me at least walk you home since I promised your moms."

"I..." I nearly protest, but the heat radiating from behind lets me know he's close. Again.

Fuck, when he got this close my brain scrambled and heart flatlined. In other words, the raw need to touch him killed me. What was this feeling?

His hand settles on my shoulder.

"Let me walk you. As a friend, all right? No funny business."

"I guess...I guess that's cool." I whispered.

And that was the night I realized during the long walk home, that I'd met Him. My very first love.

5

release it, my love

·♥·♥·♥·♥·♥·

Days later, my eyes bug at the offensively bold font written in all caps. It's an email. From the head offices of Slut Angels, Inc nonetheless. Surely, I misread the fine print that existed more as a threat under the guise of corporate formalities.

Due to an anonymous complaint, this email serves as an official notice of termination. Your actions have violated the terms outlined in your contract regarding external solicitation of Slut Angels, Inc's established clientele. Please forward your company issued cell phone and other paraphernalia to...

"Fired?!" I breathed the question with a shaky voice and hands to match.

How could this have happened? My mind wanders and skitters frantically as I try to piece together a reason for this. My illegal side hustle involved siphoning clients from Slut Angels and providing them private shows and video exclusives. Risky, I realized this, but so much of my household finances relied on the steady stream of cash afforded to me after a session with Edgar Oakhouse, the Greenville native and CEO of the largest pork production plant in South Carolina. He tipped generously to prevent his secrets from getting out, as did Eugene. Eugene Praxel was a notorious DC business man who'd many wouldn't assume had a kinky foot fetish I indulged via cam shows. The business was all sweet for the past few months, but now it was all over. And for a reason unknown to me, the usual cold fear didn't assault me this time at the thought of word getting back to Luther about how I lost this gig. Fear was an emotion I couldn't afford if it meant getting out of this blemish-free. Even though I owed him everything, rage shoots through my being as I recall the conversation from that morning before school. Rage at Luther's audacity putting me in a situation like that, and heated intrigue when I remembered the man in shadow.

***

"There better be an explanation for this shit. You got five seconds." Luther's hot breath felt more like fire, scorching the air with its heated intensity and menace.

I gulped, unsure how to move, afraid to move under the hard scrutiny of his crescent eyes that denote his half Asian lineage. He's gorgeous, I realize as I watch him alternate his glare between me and my cell phone. If it wasn't for the hatred and obvious drug use, then he'd be the most beautiful thing that's given me attention.

"Cleo," he bit out.

I lifted defensive hands to cover my face in case he lost it and I needed to prepare. But he didn't. Instead, his eyes are still trained on me heavily breathing beside him in the passenger seat.

"Okay, okay." I said in a rush. "I'd been meaning to tell you. It's not what you think."

"I warned you," He sneered. "What did I tell you would happen if you hid from me. Again."

Now that confuses me. I didn't try to hide the mental rollercoaster my brain nearly fell off while I attempted to decipher what he meant.

"What?"

"Here," He threw the phone at me that almost fumbled between my sweaty fingers. "Fuckin unlock it. And don't you think about changing your password without me knowing."

I blinked. Once, twice, totally forcing my heart to come back online and rejoin the chat. A faint memory of changing the four digit passcode last week rises to the surface as I reboot. After being notified by my phone company of the failed hacking attempt, I'd been prompted to change my four digit passcode. But this was definitely a stupid move on my part since I neglected to tell my boyfriend.

"Zero, four, eight, three." I mumbled to him while simultaneously keying the passcode into the phone.

After another warning about never hiding pertinent information like that again, he was growling into my unlocked phone at somebody.

"Be there in ten. Peace."

"Who was that?" I asked once we hit the highway. Several minutes had gone by and only served to heighten my curiosity.

"Your name is Norina. Understand?" He said before pulling into another sketchy parking lot on the opposite side of town.

There were several abandoned homes and businesses on this street I'd been warned against traveling down alone by Pops.

"Come on." Luther demanded, climbing out of the Ford Flex once we made it to our destination.

That destination looked to be, yet another, abandoned deleterious street lined with ramshackle rowhouses. The usual hustle and bustle of downtown didn't exist today, or at least at this time of day. There was an ominous vibe emanating from the area, and I gulped an inward prayer above that Luther hadn't been walking us into some bullshit. Again. I didn't trust the handsome cokehead even under the best circumstances, especially with what happened to My First Love. I couldn't voice my secret suspicions around him having something to do with what happened to him. But even after all of that, I still owed him. Still was indebted to him for life after what I'd done to ruin his.

I'm wallowing in the sins of my past actions when I feel the steel wall of Luther's back. He'd stopped walking just outside, and it took me a minute to notice where we were.

"Jin-Tama?" I breathed curiously, though not really in question. But Luther smirked before answering me anyway.

"Yep." He said while holding the door open. "You goin in, or what?"

My eyes alternated skeptically between the six-foot jack-hole and the chivalrous gesture not befitting the guy I'd been forced to feed drugs to prevent a violent emotional outburst.

He flashed a wide grin at whoever awaited him inside before biting out with gritted teeth, "You better not lose me this deal. Move your ass."

His vague answer to my unspoken questions did nothing to quell the fifty additional ones that sprang up. I opened my mouth to toss one at him, but don't get the chance to.

"Luther!" I whimpered, pain searing my wrist at his deathlock grip that appeared ostensibly intimate.

He's all but dragging me into the vacant Sushi Bar and Asian Bistro I recalled was Trice's favorite places to eat.

The large room is darkened partly by the lack of inside light and barely-risen morning sun hanging in the sky. All that's visible is the clean black tables, where a person dressed in all black is sitting.

"You're late." The man says with a tone so dry it's nearing boredom.

My heart seized at the man's flagrant disregard for respect.
Everyone who was anyone knew better than to cross words
with the new head of the 590's. Unlike Jack Burn who'd
ran the street gang with effortless charm and street wisdom
before getting locked up, Luther had a finite reservoir of
patience. Once that reservoir ran empty, there was no hasta
manana for his victims. But bloody scenes that ended up
with him coking or cumming in me to get the edge off
afterwards.

Luther squeezed my wrist and I fought to conceal the new
wave of agony that almost lost me balance.

"Thanks to that faulty address you gave, we ended up at a
crack house across town." Luther said in a grave tone, but not
with as much cynicism as usual.

This was only getting stranger by the minute as I sought to
identify the man sitting cross-legged at the table. I have to
squint to find his face, and when that's unsuccessful I settle
for examining the nuances of exposed chest and clothing.

His upper half concealed by the shadows of sun, I gaze at
the designer black suit he's wearing. There's not a wrinkle or
crinkle as far as the eye could see, and even his scent was
expensive. Like an imported aroma in the upper thousands
that hadn't likely hit the shelves yet, if at all.

My body...perhaps it's the thing that reacts the most pe-
culiarly under the circumstances. In spite of Luther's death
grip on me, the pain fades into the background as another
sensation sizzles across my skin. It's like the air is running
low on oxygen, since I can't account for the reason behind
the mild pants wracking my chest at the sight of him. Rather,
the half sight of him. Get it together, Cleo! I scream at
myself, using the pain in my wrist as a reminder to float back

to this very unknown situation that might turn bloody in seconds.

"Please, sit." The man instructs.

And I nearly wail in relief at the feel of Luther's release. We sit across from the shadowed man whose smell is still heating my skin in a way I still don't understand.

"Kobayashi-sama will grant you a fifteen minute audience. Your time starts now." He said in a cool even tone that denotes his northern origins.

Perhaps it was Jersey? I wonder. And I'm still baffled at why this man would refer to himself in the third person when Luther clears his throat and straightens.

"Fifteen is peachy." He says with a hint of amusement to this Kobayashi-sama guy. "I'm prepared to make you an offer."

A bit of silence, then Kobayashi-sama ejects into the cold atmosphere,

"Kobayashi-sama would not have traveled to D.C. for any less. Go on."

Kobayashi-sama radiated raw power despite his half shadowed persona. The intensity, and curiosity, of it all had me straightening, too, to listen.

"All right, all right." Luther began. "I'm thinking we can continue with the previous deal. The one you offered last year."

The sun gleamed off the vibrant gold ring on Kobayashi-sama's index finger momentarily blinding me. But I hear his light chuckle.

"Kobayashi-sama's 80/20 offer is no longer valid. Surely, you understand this."

Luther's entire caramel colored face heats with rage, but he keeps his tone otherwise tame.

"Yo, what happened to needing to spread out into the southern markets and shit? D.C. is right between the north and south, where we're running shit."

"You're correct." He counters. "Seems you know your geography, but that's the extent of your knowledge. The Kobayashi's are no longer in need of arrangements on your behalf to operate. We've...sought other means of establishing business in that way."

"Other means like how?" Luther demands, his leg shaking as if in dire need to release the building fury. "You ain't violating our turf."

"Luther, of course not. And if we were trading on your ends, you'd know about it. Word would reach back to you and all-out war would commence. The Kobayashi's arc traders, not warriors. Hailing from a long line of merchants.

We'd never wish to sully the name of the lieutenant turned 590 boss."

Luther's smile turns smug as the man lists out the extent of the 590's influence, and my stomach twists while watching it. To think this bastard took pride in ruining lives all from the high perch of his new boss title. Jack was ruthless, sure, but Luther was brutal. Mental. Dangerous. Ruled the streets with an iron fist that sent him into rages whenever his fragile ego felt his new title be threatened.

"That's right," Luther said while crossing his arms.

"But that's not why we're here." Kobayashi-sama says. "You summoned us. Now briefly explain in five minutes or less why Kobayashi-Sama should further entertain this audience. Clock is ticking."

"Listen," Luther began again. "I think we can make magic together. These streets been booming with all the new people moving into town. More people means higher demand. More people getting high, means more supply. But we ain't selling what y'all got, and I'm thinking we need to diversify our supply. Nah mean?"

No answer, but perhaps Luther sensed his dwindling window of time for his sales pitch.

"The 590's are prepared to negotiate now. We'll move some of your product on our turf, keeping seventy-five percent, and sharing twenty-five as y'alls cut. What you think?"

My jaw fell open at his words. I knew in my heart that this wasn't Luther's grand scheme to diversify. Knew it well, since I saw him smoke and snort most of the product in his charge to redistribute. I took notice that he'd been way more insistent and reliant on my meager earnings from Slut Angels. We split my wages fifty-fifty in the beginning, but now I'd be lucky to see even twenty percent of my checks. I survived now off what little I earned from Nita's shop and illegal side hustle. The once revered street gang Jack turned into a lucrative underground hustle was now in shambles.

He never told me, but he didn't have to. I noticed everything. So this was his plan, I thought as I studied him beside me. Join forces with another gang to stay afloat and save the 590's reputation. An OK plan if I judged it myself, but the chances of Luther starting all-out chaos was too great.

I waited in anxious anticipation for the shadowed man's response.

"That offer would have been tempting a year ago. But things are different now. Very much so. But you know what? Fuck it. Kobayashi-sama's feeling generous today since you brought your woman with you."

So that's why he dragged me to this strange meeting, I gathered, but remained silent. My body heated again at the mention, and I had to resist the moan from escaping my lips at the intense premonition that his eyes were on me. I couldn't see him at all, but even the prospect of this expensive-smelling man giving me attention had my body responding even if my mouth didn't.

"The Kobayashi Clan is prepared to accept those terms, but under a few revisions."

"Shoot," Luther encouraged.

"First, we'll agree to be your supplier, but the profits will be divided at a sixty-five, thirty-five split. Sixty-five going to The Clan and the rest to the 590's."

"What?" Luther yelled, shooting to his feet. "What kind of deal is that?"

"Second." Kobayashi-sama continued as if Luther had not spoken at all. "You'll be honor-bound by contract for a one year term of business. At the six-month mark, we will evaluate liability, profit margin, and potential risks incurred as a result of our deal thus far. You are to liaise with us at the designated rendezvous location once that time arises. You'll be notified via personal messenger. A Clan rep will coordinate those details with you at that time."

"This is fucked up, man!" Luther growled, his entire body trembling with restrained fury as he listened. "No deal."

"Third and final term." Kobayashi-sama announced with a deepening voice and thicker accent. "Never violate the first two terms. If at any point you are caught dishonoring your pact with us, then you will pay dearly."

"Pay, how?"

Another chortle, then he says. "Kobayashi-sama never forgets a face. And his will be the last you'll see should those terms ever be violated."

"Fuck all that noise, man!" Luther swore before turning away. "Y'all talking crazy. Y'all really expect me to accept thirty-five percent of profits made on our turf?"

"You are free to accept or decline them. But the offer is final, and your time is up. Kobayashi-sama's time is precious."

"Fine by me." Luther snarls before yanking me to my feet. "Chop chop, Norina."

A feeling blossomed in my chest as he tugged me towards the door. The need to apologize and beg for reconsideration rode me hard, especially when I thought of the shitty state of our finances. The 590's, while respected, were losing their edge and influence due to late product drops and a coke head de facto boss. What would this deal refusal mean for us? For me? I turned back to steal another glance at the shadowed man and made the decision in a split second.

Freeing myself from Luther's grip, I ran desperately back to the man and for some reason bowed low.

"Please, sir!" I cried while staring at the floor. "Please forgive him. He will reconsider your terms."

"Norina." A voice spoke my fake name, but upon closer inspection and more sun hanging in the air, I could see there were actually two men in the room.

So Jersey Guy wasn't referencing himself in third person, but merely speaking for the other more lethal looking dude in the chair below him. Also, Jersey Guy didn't repeat my name like a prayer, but it was the regal Asian man perched casually in the chair. The man in the chair sat like a king surveying his land, unbothered by Luther's apparent outburst but staring directly at me as he dragged me away.

That heat crept up past my neck at the feeling of being watched again. I could literally feel his intense stare into my downward casted head. This guy could kill me, I realized. Fuck! What was I even doing bowing down before him like the king he appeared to be?

"I beg you!" I whimpered, and the cool air conditioning in the place made me notice the tears that formed amidst my begging. "Please. He'll think about it. He's had a rough time with his partner getting locked up and he doesn't know what he's saying right now."

"Nora!" Luther roared, and it wasn't long before his footsteps sounded behind me. Getting closer.

The yank I expected of Luther's hand never came, and I almost look up to investigate before the same cool voice instructed,

"Maintain your bow." I eeped, and did as he commanded and waited in the silence that followed my pleas. "So which is it?" The king asked.

"Which is what...sir?" I asked probingly.

"Your partner there just referred to you as Nora. So which is it? Norina or Nora?"

I gulped, not entirely certain if I should answer. I'd typically looked to Luther to respond to a question like this. He'd been extremely clear that I was to keep as silent as possible whenever he requested my presence at a deal. In fact, this was the most talking I'd ever done at one of these, and the knowledge of Luther fuming behind me made my body go cold.

"You don't want to say the wrong thing. I understand." His voice lowered, but he wasn't whispering.

It felt as if he gentled it in an effort to reassure me. Like a hunter attempting to calm frightened animals in the woods before exacting a finishing blow. Dreading that fatal hit, I squeezed my eyes shut and shook my head.

"It's all right." He soothes, and I eep again at the feel of his touch. His hand combs through my red curls in one swift, but tender, motion before he adds, "I'll never harm you. It goes against my family's code of ethics to hurt women and children. Show me you understand."

I nod, never meeting his eyes or catching a glimpse at his face but knowing full well the seriousness on it. It was strange, but in this king's presence a surge of security surged through I'd never felt with my mental boyfriend.

"Luther." He clipped out and retracted his hand in the same moment. I mourned the loss of his touch immediately. "Your woman has persuaded me. You have forty-eight hours to accept or decline these terms. If I've not heard from you, then I'll assume your refusal of these conditions."

"I already told y'all hell nah." He bellows.

"And another thing," The king adds. "Take care of your woman. Her honorable actions for your sake benefited you well today. It's clear you do not deserve her."

My pussy throbbed immediately, traitorously, as I listened to the king. He thought of me as honorable? The girl who did all sorts of devilish things in the dark to make ends meet?

"Whatever." Luther grunted, and it wasn't long before I stood and saw the Jersey Guy squaring off with him, preventing him from getting close and disrupting my and the king's conversation.

We left the Bistro and Luther remained silent as we darted towards the parked car. And I sought to ignore the rapid-fire throb and wetness below when I recalled the chill of his words that melted me inside.

6

prime real estate

Laughter erupted from my chest as I clung to Ty for dear life; despite my several pounds over skinny, he'd held and swung our bodies around the empty hair salon while we danced. Even in the new age of iPhone and Spotify, I found it delightful that Tyrone Zelman preferred to use a classic cassette radio as his method for playing the music he liked. More like, obsessed over.

Typically, I'm either bored or disgusted by any True N' Fresh song since it'd been drilled into my ears throughout my childhood, but there was something endearing about Ty's obsession with the disbanded Baltimore-based rap duo that set their decade on fire with the amount of fans they garnered. The group's music included songs about unrequited love, yearning, but also a hint of uplift for the black people in their communities.

Like the one we were jamming to in the empty hair salon of Nita's Beauty Shop. After only a month, I'd taken on locking up the shop solo in the evenings, but not from a sense of duty to my cousin. But more so to linger around on standby in the event Tyrone Zelman came by to "see Nita," or "run an errand for his mom real quick." It was always intriguing to anticipate what his next excuse was to stop by the shop, and I wondered if he was just as curious as me at his nightly appearances.

This night, though, maybe he'd ran out of errands or excuses, since his only explanation for stopping by after Nita unexpectedly took a half day, was that he'd had a surprise for me.

"A surprise?" I asked after allowing him inside. "You don't even know me like that."

"Yeah, so what?" He smirked. "Call it generosity."

Though skeptic, a slow smile I couldn't resist appeared on my face. "Okay, Mr. Generous. Pardon me if I'm a little shocked by that."

He took a large step in my direction that brought our chests to touch. I licked my lips and looked away to fight this gnawing feeling from climbing up my spine whenever I saw him. I hated it. Ty wasn't known as one to smile or goof around at school, it's what spurred his rep as a homicidal maniac and kept people at bay. I'd only ever caught him hanging with a select number of dudes, all popular, that made him an incongruous anomaly beside them. For instance, his proximity to Devin Cooper, star quarterback of our high school junior varsity team, made no sense at all. But despite their evident differences, they'd always looked like they had a good time in each other's company.

Ty reached a hand down to cup my cheek in his.

I stepped away. "What is it that you want from me, anyways?"

His brows knit together in confusion, and perhaps another emotion at our abrupt separation.

"I don't want nothing from you, Nora."

I flailed irritated hands in the air to punctuate my point. And annoyance.

"Sure that's true? Because you've been dropping by here every night now, after the shop closes and when I happen to be alone. I don't believe in coincidences."

"Me neither."

"So, what then?" I demanded with a heavy heart. "Are you here to fuck with me? We never talk or hang out at school, but all of a sudden you're here every day?"

"Not every day." He confesses lowly. "Only Fridays through Mondays after school."

"So what—" I started, then stopped.

Fridays through Mondays after school were specifically when I was shifted to work here. My heart sped up at the notion, at the highly improbable thought that he'd gone out of his way to see me. Me.

I stumbled a bit as I took shaky steps back, eying him like he'd been a mythical creature and sprouted two heads instead of confessing to something that made my body ache.

He matched my stride as I continued backing away until there was only a wall behind me. Now, I was pinned under the intensity of his heated stare and prism within his long arms.

"This ain't no trick. Or game, Nora." He leaned down to whisper in my ear. "I'm feeling you."

"M-Me?" I couldn't help but to feed voice to my doubts.

Nobody ever wanted me, at least not in an honest way that didn't involve profit or sacrifice. Love was always one of those elusive virtues that had never been all mine, but coupled with pretense or selfish gain. I had a sense that my parents loved me, but after Mama's abandonment of me and the accident that hurt Mom, I'd been sure that toleration existed in place of that elusive virtue. That virtue, I hadn't realized until this moment was what I craved desperately.

Ty's gaze penetrated the concrete wall my soul lived behind. And I trembled when he stroked my recently blue-dyed hair.

"Yes. You, Nora. Nobody else." Was all he said before I reached up and kissed him.

I kissed him with everything in me as my body sought the security his words promised. He wanted me. He was kissing me. I couldn't fathom how I'd been so lucky to be the recipient of what I felt was love back then in his arms.

And that's how we ended up jamming to the old True N' Fresh track, "Place Like Home." After several rounds of hard rap classics blasting through his boombox speakers that we laughed and danced to, one of the rap duo's suave R&B tracks filled the room.

Ty cradled me in his arms while we danced slow to the smooth track, and my heart seized when he sang the lyrics in my ear.

"Ain't no better place. Don't let the tears fall down your face, because there ain't no better...place like home. Place like home. I been through time and space but nowhere else could take your place...place like home."

"Ty..." was all I could choke out past the lump of emotions in my throat.

For some reason, the song felt more like a promise. True had been the tenor of the group and I relished in how the retired rap star's words delivered on Ty's lips could make me ache, like live wire, all over with a need to be close to him. It was too much, I decided, but when I went to tug arms apart, Ty tightened around me.

"Ty..."

"Been through too many girls, but none were my world. You bring me to life, Nora...just be by my side, Nora."

Ty, the rugged homicidal bad boy just dubbed my name in a romantic R&B song. The shock of that coupled with the prison of his strong arms around me left me with only one place to go.

Down.

My legs gave out in the midst of his improv'd song with my name involved, and then there was a hollow part of myself that couldn't believe his promise. Or any of it. But...

Instead of anchoring me upright, Ty sank to the ground with me. We soon lay there on the hard linoleum floor of my cousin's shop, listening to the rest of the True N' Fresh album. Once the final song finished, Ty pulled my numb body on top of his so that all I was exposed to was the cushion of him besides the hard floor. He was shielding me, I realized. Thunder sounded from the skies, promising rain and a potential storm to come at any minute. The trickles of rain were the only sounds surrounding us as well as a pregnant silence. We just laid there. Staring at each other for what felt like eons before he said something.

"Storm's coming." He rasped.

I nodded. "I know. We should get home. My parents are gonna birth a baby cow if I don't start walking."

"Nora." Again those strong arms tightened around me. "Don't leave yet. I don't really know how to say this shit, but..."

"But what?" I asked, breathless for some reason.

His jaw flexed before answering. "I like you."

"No, Ty." I shook my head, not quite denying but more so to clear it. "You don't know what you're saying. We don't even hang out in public or school or anything. You'd get clowned by being seen with me."

"Fuck that." He growled. "You think people are crazy enough to approach me with some bullshit like that? You must not be paying attention."

"To what?"

"To me, obviously." He snarled. "Because I see you when you think there ain't nobody looking. See how you try to stay outta the way and keep your head down. You walk around like you got something to be ashamed of, when you should be smiling. That look on your face when we danced? You laughing and smiling and shit? That's how you should be. You so fucking fine, I was sure you wouldn't give an ugly street head like me a shot. But then you did. You opened that door to the shop and let me in. You let me in. That means something to me. You feel me?"

His hands are clasped tightly around mine, forcing the ferocity of his truth into them. I reached up and let my mouth do the answering since I was only tongue tied. I was afraid that if he kept talking that I'd keep falling. I didn't want to do that. I couldn't afford to trust that and not get hurt.

But, in the end, I did. I'd given him my virginity that night in exchange for his loving me in the daylight. One of my conditions for our budding relationship was him claiming me in public, loud and proud instead of in the shadows like now. But nothing could have prepared me for what happened the next day at school.

I sat alone in the cafeteria, per usual, and played idly with the rice and peas mixture served up by the old cafeteria staff. My head had been in cloud nine, or maybe cloud ninety-nine, as I recollected the night before with Ty. The dancing, the laughing, and whispering promises to be there for each other at night and in the light of day where others could see.

I'd been mulling over if what I felt was love for him when the feel of arms wrapping around me tugged me back to the present.

Somebody was...touching me in school. Hugging me. Who would have dared touch me in this way at the risk of their social status? That question was answered with the familiar deep voice crooning in my ear.

"My Nora." Ty breathed, igniting the flames of desire in me as I remembered his mouth exploring places on my body no one had ever ventured before. "You miss me?"

"Yes..." I breathed before leaning into his rich smell of pine and cigars. "Ty, you sure about–"

"You let me worry about that." He interrupted my protests as a wanton moan escaped me.

God, just the feel of his hands exploring my body again made me melt. I didn't even care about the crowd forming behind us or the whispers of judgements and questions. All that mattered was this. Us, in this infinite circle of love that began well before last night. My heart yearned for him the minute he broke into Nita's shop that night. And I was on fire.

"Tyrone!" A cold voice that's distinctly female shouts over the whispering crowd.

Both Ty and I snap out of it to see a statuesque black girl approaching. Her boobs are huge despite her tiny waist and what looked to be a globular ass. Her hair is flat ironed straight past her shoulders, and she's wearing a glare so glacial it makes me shudder.

"Sasha?" Ty barks in confusion, but he doesn't step away from me. "The fuck you doing here, girl?"

'Sasha' taps her foot and her arms cross while she alternates her eyes between me and Ty. There's something about her, maybe it was her stance or frown or mild lilt in her voice that denotes an accent. The accent is faint, but definitely there.

"You're loving up on this bitch? What about us?"

Ty waves a dismissive hand at her. "Bitch, you tweakin. Fuck outta here with all that."

"You're my man!"

"What?" Ty scoffs. "One night together don't make me your man. And that was weeks ago. You're old news and you're interrupting."

Sasha focuses cold brown eyes that ring even more familiar as she steps closer.

"You tryna tell me it's this fat bitch you want? This?"

"She's," Ty emphasized with guttural warning. "All mine. You got some shit to say about that?"

Sasha's eyes round with evident astonishment, then shock, before a cat-like grin spreads on her face.

"Fine by me," she purrs. "Guess you win."

"Win?" I parroted, confused and a tad off balance. "It's not about winning."

"You can have my leftovers, gyal!" She screamed, her accent thickening again. "But I have something of his that you don't!"

The crowd whipped out their phones to record this interaction, and my face heated from the attention. I hated this. The betrayal that began to form in my gut as she kept talking was killing me, but so was the curiosity.

"The fuck you got that Nora don't?" Ty spat at her, his tone bored.

Sasha's evil smile curled into a scowl that detracted from her evident beauty as she said, "Your child, Tyrone."

"My what?" He exclaimed, bewildered.

"Ya heard me." She boasted while staring only at me. "I'm pregnant. And it's yours."

Everything, and I mean it, my entire world blackened after her admission and jeers of the crowd. The future I saw weaving together between Ty and I crumbled in a matter of seconds.

Before I have a chance to blackout or run out of there, Sasha grabs onto my arm and pulls me into her chest. The crowd is going so wild nobody notices this interaction, or her leaning down to whisper in my ear.

"Payback is a bitch."

Her accent on full display and with her face so close to mine, I realize why she rang so familiar to me upon first seeing her. She'd been in my grade and roaming these halls for weeks, and all the while that feeling of being on the brink of recognition rode me when I looked at her.

But I know now. Knew that accent and murderous glare all too well as the little girl I first betrayed in elementary school.

Sasha Kersey, Ty's apparent new baby mama, was Chicken Girl.

7

material girl

·❤·❤·❤·❤·❤·

"What did I tell you about staying out all night, Cleo?" Mom's reprimand awaited me when I crept carefully inside the colonial style house.

There was really no need to tip toe inside since it wasn't detection I was avoiding. It was how I always carried myself in the fifteen years I'd grown up here: careful. My precarious position in the family had been tolerated at best, and so the burning need to not talk back too much or slam the doors too hard whenever upset was likely bred from that. You're not their real daughter, the nagging voice often reminded me in times of great triumph and woe alike. Instead of barking back the saucy retort to Mom's accusatory greeting, I swallow the anger and force the smile to my lips.

"Hiya, Mom." I told her after hanging my coat in the hall closet and entering the open plan kitchen. "And sorry about being late. I walked here from school."

Laurel Albert's gorgeous face contorted into a distasteful grin at my words. "Easton is about a thirty minute walk from this neighborhood. You're over an hour behind."

I gulped, unsure how to translate the truth of today into a digestible lie. How could I tell her the truth? That, although I started the day with the best intentions of actually participating in class, I never even made it to Easton Rogue High. After that intense meeting with the king and his Jersey accented proxy, Luther took me back his mother's house in the hood where he'd traded a few favors with his stepdad for a large bag of white.

"Got some kind of nerve talking to those motherfuckers today." He spat at me where we both sat perched on the filthy living room couch. "That's gonna cost you extra."

"Be reasonable." I whimpered, hot panic boiling my insides at the prospect of him taking any more of my money. "You need that deal. Just think on it, okay?"

"Wait here for a minute..." He said.

An intense look crossed his face before his eyes rolled back and a deep sleep took over. I knew what this meant. Especially as the hour ticks by. Then another. Then two more. Luther was the very definition of paranoid, and it was often I caught him with permanent dark circles lining his eyes. He stated all the time how little he trusted his family of a coked out mom, her drug dealing boyfriend, and his two adult daughters. Malia Parham, the youngest of the two, was who always eyed me with what I suspected as malicious intent. The amount of hatred in her stare only heightened my constant consternation upon entering the large filthy house. His other sister, a six foot masculine-presenting woman was the direct opposite. She made her evident desire for me very clear whenever Luther brought me here.

She went by Squeeze, and while a serial flirt, I sensed she had a kind heart. But she often looked the other way whenever she caught her stepbrother yelling at me. After the fifth hour on sleep patrol, I finally begged his flirtatious stud of a stepsister to take me home. And after a playful back and forth that involved giving her the wrong cell phone number when she asked, I found myself at my aunt and uncle's house just in time for weekly dinner. At least I thought I'd been on time. I wince as I met the eyes of my protective but dreadfully judgmental adoptive mom.

Mom was sharp and discerning like a hawk, never missing a thing. This trait served her well in the courtroom or whenever advocating the rights for undocumented or displaced immigrants. Born to Sudanese immigrants who'd worked tirelessly at menial jobs to support her dreams of attending an Ivy League college, Mom wore her numerous academic achievements with pride. She'd always said that graduating from Harvard in her late parent's honor and marrying the man of her dreams were two of her greatest accomplishments. And even despite the permanent discomfort that reared itself in their presence, I couldn't deny my aunt and uncle's love for each other.

They'd met at one of Pop's concerts in Baltimore, where he and his close friend performed professionally for a little under a decade. Mom watched eagerly from the crowd, and according to Pop, it was like the swarming room of fans melted away when their eyes met. And the rest went down in history, or so he'd always jokingly finished.

"Wait a sec," Mom's brows lift with understanding before her face resets with mild disapproval. "That coach kept you late again, didn't she?"

"Yes!" I answered a little too quickly, I realized, but the lie about my extracurricular activity I'd told to cover for my after school shifts at Nita's fills me with relief. "Um, I mean, yes Mom. Coach Swan ran us extra hard at practice since we'd lost the last game. You know how it goes."

"Sure do." She nodded, her eyes overlooking me as she relives her past position as a high school softball elite. "It's extra strenuous, I know But completely worth it in the end. You'll see."

"Totally."

She rears back with an affronted look on her face while eyeing me down. I squirm.

"Ma'am?" I query.

"You haven't bid your mother a proper hello. Where's my hug, huh?"

"My bad." I chuckle, unable to help myself at her fake annoyance before bending down to embrace her.

I'm all but down on my knees to meet her seated position from her wheelchair.

"That's more like it." She said, her midnight colored cheeks tugging upward in a dazzling smile. "Now, come on! Everyone's waiting in the dining room for you to arrive. They've practically filled up on appetizers, though."

I wince at her use of "everyone," considering the small get-together consisting only of me, Mom and Pop. Other than the wait staff, there'd only ever been the three of us in attendance to the mandatory weekly dinners.

Before I get the chance to question her about it, Uncle Ferr stands up once he sees us walking and wheeling side-by-side into the opulent dining room.

"Our Cleo is home!" He exclaims with outstretched arms, the universal symbol of "get over here and hug me." I do as the gesture demands and force the repeated discomfort down my throat when he pulls back to study me. "My, have you grown! Must have sprouted a solid inch since our last dinner."

I wince again. "No, Pop. I'm still the same shrimp as always."

His large grin reveals spotless, alabaster teeth as he bellows, "That's my daughter! You got that sense of humor from me, you know?"

Even for my ever-jovial pastor uncle, his attitude is ersatz and off-putting. The usual discomfort and inferiority complex that rears its ugly head whenever in their company is heightened ten-fold. Why was he being so theatrically cheery? Sure, Pop was a former performer, but with music, not acting.

"Sit, baby girl." Pop instructs.

And for the first time I realize the reason for his awkward greeting and forced cheer. I didn't doubt his excitement in seeing me, but see the five foot reason he's overcompensating. Her sunken eyes stare at me accompanied by a sorrowful smile. And my heart drops since she's never liked mingling with Uncle Ferr if it could be avoided. Hell, she hadn't ever even been invited to these forced weekly meals my adopted auntie-mom called "soirees."

In fact, his fake joviality makes me mumble the question out loud as I stare at Mama, who looks so uncomfortable she's at the point of squirming in her seat.

"Mama?" I whisper incredulously after sinking into the plush chair. "W-What are you doing here?"

She fidgets, then says, "How was your day at sch—"

"Cleo'Nora!" Mom snarls from the opposite end of the rectangular table. "Don't be rude to our guest."

Her use of the word "guest" almost comes off as a profanity, heating my blood for a second. But, I stifle yet another eye-roll before readjusting.

"Mama," I restarted evenly. "I'm glad you could join us for dinner tonight."

"Me, too." She whispers, her eyes sliding around the room.

My adoptive parents break off into side chatter, something about if the main course of beef wellington would be cooked well done or medium well, but I clear my throat. Loudly.

"Everyone." I start, pulling their attention away from the idle chit chat starting in the room. "Can someone please tell me what's going on?"

"Cleo." Mama begins again, only to be cut off by Pop.

"We'll get to that, Amora." He tells her, like she's a child and not the bearer of the kid he'd raised for fifteen years. He turns to me. "First thing's first. How are your studies going, sweetheart?"

I take a huge breath to calm the rage tide whipping and whirling in me before biting out a response.

"Fine." I say.

"That so?" He answers thoughtfully. "It's not what I heard from your Trigonometry teacher. She said something about you failing the last two exams. And that your progress on the benchmark was below average at best."

Stay calm, Cleo. I coached my inner wolf that begged to spaz out on him. I knew he was just concerned, but his fake cheer coupled with both my parent's lack of acknowledgement of Mama had me seething.

"I've been trying my best, Pop." I said. "It's a difficult subject."

"We understand that." Mom cut in from the other end of the table. She's cradling a half empty wine glass while she talks. "That's why we needed to have this talk."

"Okay...?" I answered.

Pop straightens before turning serious eyes on me.

"We think it'll be best for you to quit the softball team. Before you get mad–" He quips just as I opened my mouth to interject, "you can't afford to flunk this class, Cleo. This is your final semester before graduation. You don't need any more distractions from your studies. College awaits next year and we just know you'll be great, God willing. But without the extracurricular activities."

Fuck! I swore inwardly. No more "softball" meant no more working at Nita's salon. That place had been my lifeline since I began working there at the beginning of high school. This couldn't be happening. This could not be happening!

Recentering, I cleared my throat and directed my measured words towards my adoptive father.

"Pop, please." I said. "I promise I'll work extra hard to ace the class. I'll even go to tutoring."

"Wait a minute." Mama, my real mother, jumped in wearing a stark frown. "What happened to Trice helping you with lessons after school?"

Another lie I'd been caught in that I had to scramble to get out of. Truthfully I hadn't heard from Trice the past month, and while her total absence scares the shit out of me, I can't relay that to the glaring parent trio looming before me. That was tomorrow's mission; I planned to go to her parent's house tomorrow evening after school to check in. I would've loved to admit her behavior was uncharacteristic, but she ghosted me like this in the past. However, we got back on track shortly before she gave birth to her daughter Katrice, but then the love of her life and baby daddy flew the coop all of a sudden without telling her. She hadn't been right since, and I hated Kale McAllen for making her grieve him all over again. And so the three of us it was; Trice, Katy, and me tackling the challenges of teen parenthood and friendship. She'd been the closest thing to a sister, and with every unread text I sent her phone served to make the hairs stand to attention on my neck.

But again, this was tomorrow's mission. One I lied to everyone about, considering the front I sold to my parent trio about Trice currently helping me with my science and math studies.

"Um…"

"What's this I hear about tutoring?" Mom demanded, still holding her wine glass. "You're doing tutoring and softball?"

"Cleo isn't on any softball team," Mama added, her tone going stern and curt. "Cleo'Nora June. Explain."

A loud bang sounded at the head of the table nearing the kitchen. It's Pop. His face is blank as stone and though balled, his trembling hands send vibrations through the table.

"Family!" His voice rang out. Gentle, but authoritative. "Now isn't the time for this. Let us bow our heads in prayer."

Confused, I babbled, "But I—"

"Dear God," Pop began, his graying eyebrows knitting together as his lids drift closed.

His hands ball into conjoined fists and I sulk into my seat. There's no way I'd get in a word edgewise when he began in prayer—when he turned from Uncle Ferr to Pastor Albert.

Stealing a quick glance, I notice both Mama and Mom's heads tilted downward in similar fashion while they muttered their own prayers. Weekly dinner felt more like Pop's weekly bible study, I gathered, but kept my lips sealed as he continued his interruptive words of worship.

"Father," Pop said. "Please bless us this night, and every night to come. Illuminate the darkest corners of our hearts so that we may learn to love and live righteously. Live the best in Your image."

"Amen." Mom mumbled, wine forgotten.

"We know that you are a forgiving God. A loving God. An accepting god. Even a wrathful God when deserving. But please hear our call tonight. Our cries for mercy."

"Yes!" Mom sang.

"And healing." He spoke the last words with an evident note of sorrow. Like he'd been holding onto something that released in that statement and with tightly clasped hands.

Healing? I wondered, but still kept my eyes shut and hands clasped as well.

I don't have to wonder long about what he meant by invoking the healing powers of God. I also don't need to guess any longer at Mama's surprise arrival at the weekly dinners she'd always said made her feel looked down on and less than, considering Auntie Laurel's sharp sarcasm and disapproval of her.

"God," Pop whimpered in a faltering voice. "We bring forth as many prayer warriors as we can in our dire hour of need. Same as with our late brother Clay, we ask that you rid Amora Mae of this sickness the doctor's claim she won't make it through. We rebuke that terminal diagnosis in the name of Jesus!"

I'm certain if Mom had the ability, she'd have stood to her feet and praise danced her affirmation at Pop's prayer. But not me.

I only stare blankly at Mama, whose eyes are now openly staring right back at me. Slow tears trickle down her face, and I go numb at what he just said.

"I'm sorry," She mouths behind a strained smile.

8

take the box

.♥.♥.♥.♥.♥.

I pace the length of my tiny bedroom while fuming into the phone at my best friend. The disastrous dinner "soiree" ended about an hour ago, and I straight up stewed in the backseat of Pop's truck during the short drive home. I noticed Mama's frequent worried glances at me in the rearview mirror as she talked about the importance of prayer where it came to her terminal diagnosis she kept from me. She'd been nodding at him like she understood, but I knew her concern for me trumped whatever haphazard sermon from Pastor Albert.

In pajamas, I sink into the twin sized bed we'd kept in the family for many years and continued my telephone tirade.

"Trice, you wouldn't believe it if you were here." I bite out. "I knew I should have went with her to that doctor's appointment yesterday instead of Uncle Ferr. Why break such news to me in that way? I mean, fucking liver cancer?!"

Though I yelled, my heart split into pieces at the veracity of all this, of what this meant for Mama. What would this mean for her future and how would I fit in it? It wasn't fair. We lived together for a total of two and a half years, at the start of high school when she rented this house and vowed to keep the bills paid in order to get me back. Shocking everyone, Mama got clean and got a job to afford the place. Those were always two of Pop's conditions if she wanted to obtain temporary custody of me. It was no shock to me though, since I believed in Mama's ability to hustle and make things happen. Though our relationship mimicked more of what Trice and I had as the best "beaches," I never told her how much I respected her. How much my love for her had been the only thing that kept me from crying myself to sleep at nights during my childhood with auntie and uncle. I loved my de facto parents, but they never understood me. But Mama did. Still does. And perhaps that's the reason she doesn't follow me when I stomp into my bedroom and slam the door behind me.

"Beach." I whimper helplessly into the phone. "Liver cancer. I'm...I'm..."

Gonna lose my mama, I think, unable to choke the words my heart can't believe.

Soon, I'm greeted by a cool voice letting me know the mailbox is full and can no longer receive messages. Grumpily, I slam the phone into the bed and scream into the pillows. Of course the mailbox was full. I'd called Trice several times over the course of the month to no avail. Raw desperation and loneliness drove me to call her anyway. To text her every day and check on her. And when those didn't quell the urgent need to talk to her, I'd resorted to the voicemails. But now, the mailbox was full, a literal and additional barrier keeping me from contacting my bestie like I'd soon be permanently robbed of the opportunity to speak with my dying mother.

My body quakes with unchecked rage before I'm scream-ing into the pillows again. This wasn't fair, this wasn't fair this wasn't—-

The buzz from my phone restarts my heart for a second, and I answer it without even checking the ID.

"Beach?"

There's a shuffling before I'm met with a gruff response.

"Norina?" He probes, and I flinch, not quite able to believe this man called my phone.

My personal cell phone.

"Edgar?" I panted.

"That's right! It's me, baby. I told you you were my every-thing. And I'm here for you."

"Edgar!" I hissed his name like an obscenity, trying to keep a leash on the anger that demanded I scream at him. Mama couldn't hear this. Not my recently saintly mother who'd make me eat soap now for all the shit this man was about to eat for contacting me in this highly unprofessional way.

"What are you doing calling my personal number? Tell me right now how the fuck you think I should treat this situation?"

"Norina, baby, please don't be sore about this. It doesn't matter how I got your number. I need you with me tonight. Say yes."

"Fuck, no!" I snarled. "And yes it matters how you got access to my personal information. Edgar, level with me here. How would you feel if you were in my shoes?"

He pauses before answering in that southern accent, "Loved. I'd feel incredibly loved and would appreciate your efforts to make my dreams come true."

I pinched the bridge of my nose, wary from this conversation, yet not emotionally prepared to deal with how he got all this access to me. Since my Slut Angels, Inc contract ended yesterday, my accounts should have been deactivated. Even so, I never provided Slut Angels with authentic details. Far as they knew, Norina Skye was a twenty-one year old administrative assistant in Baltimore, struggling to make ends-meet.

"Edgar," I say in a tone much more gentler than my rage demanded. "Don't call this number again. Okay, hun?"

"Not okay, darling." He stated firmly. "You are my woman. And I haven't heard from you since you got the news. We can be fully together now, man and wife just as God intended without all that Slut Angels nonsense. Give me your address and I'll come scoop you up by morning."

The audacity. The bravery. The absolute insanity of it all was what I couldn't fathom. Again, I couldn't afford fear right now with all that was going on with Mama. Swift action was all that would truly aid this situation. Even though I was pissed at her, it was my duty to keep her safe. Especially from the weirdos that I allowed in.

But a cold realization settles over me before I bite back another warning.

"You knew I got fired?" I inquired numbly. "Wait, wait. You didn't just know– you were behind it. Weren't you?"

"I wouldn't word it that way, buttercup." He crooned. "I did what needed to be done. So now you can be my woman. All mine. Let me take care of you. I already have an Amex card with your name on it whenever you're ready. I'll take you shopping, on vacations, you name it, it's yours! Just say yes."

I choke on my own tongue from the horror. Edgar filed that complaint against me? He lost me my job? And now he wanted me to be...his woman?

As if he could see me, I shook my head. "Edgar. You know I can't do that."

"I'm an old man!" He exclaimed, his voice deepening then turning deadpan. "At the end of my life. I want to live out these last few years in happiness. With the woman I love beside me."

"And I hope you find her." I cut in. "But that isn't me. I'm not who you think I am. Don't call here again."

I almost hit the big red button on the screen, but freeze at his next words.

"You hang up this phone and I'll make your life a living hell. Cancer ain't the worst thing that'll happen to your dear mama if you deny me again. Understand?"

My jaw drops in mute shock, but I don't respond. And this apparently fuels more of his fire.

"Norina!" He roars. "Tell me you understand what I'm saying."

"I do," I warble on unsteady breath. "I understand."

"Good, girl." He sings. "I'll give you a couple of days to get ready for me. Then I'm coming to get you."

"Hang on!" I exclaim, frantically searching for every weapon in my social charm arsenal. Think Cleo! Think, think, think! I stopped my pacing and breathed slow before relaying the perfectly concocted lie to my crazy client. "Baby," I purr. "A girl needs more time than that to prepare for such an adventure."

"All right." He said. "How long you need?"

I took another breath. "At least a week. Give me one week to get my affairs in order, and I'm all yours. Okay?"

"I don't know, buttercup." He hedged. "A week is a mighty long time to—"

"All." I interrupted, moaning the words. "Yours. In every...single...way. To fuck. To taste. Whatever you want, however you want it."

"Hot damn," he breathed. "You got it, baby. Give me a little something to tide me over till then."

Another hour of outlining in vivid detail the things I'd do to his body and how hot he'd gotten me about this new life he promised, before we hung up. Tears spring from my eyes at what had just happened. This psycho knew me. Not my name, but where I lived. My mother's health information. He got me fired from my seedy under the table gig, too. And maybe it wasn't the most respectable position, but it was mine. An area in my life where I got to be someone else. But now here I was; stalked and with a ticking time bomb over my head that existed in the form of a mere week to get my plan together. To get myself, and Mama, out of harm's way.

Another few minutes of sulking passes and the familiar aroma of fried meat assails my senses. All that fury, fear, and disappointment temporarily suspends when I unconsciously rise to investigate the smell.

Of course, it's my mother.

She's back in her blue bathrobe and bonnet, and I crook my head to study the mundane scene. Her back faces me when I enter the small dining area that opens to the tiny kitchen – totally opposite of the grandeur of Mom and Pop's several feet long cooking quarters– but she's shimmying to some unheard song while at the stove.

"Hey, my love." She sings, rooted to the spot.

"You're...frying chicken?" I asked, not quite believing it.

She shrugs. "Yeah. I figured I would since I couldn't sleep, and that catered beef wellington mess looked too pink for me to finish. Not sure where Ferr developed the taste for uncooked meat considering he grew up in our Mama's house who didn't play that, but go figure. Regardless, I'm hungry and cooking for you relaxes me."

I gulped, taking in her words as I sat down at the table. "Never said I was hungry."

"No need." She states, then turns with a plate full of fried heaven in her hands before setting it on the wooden table. Fuck me and my traitorous stomach. As if in full agreement with Mama, it growls loudly at the sight.

"Mama knows." She says, winking at me with a large grin.

We soon break off into a cozy laughter as we eat the pile of fried dark meat. Dark meat was my favorite part of the chicken, considering it had been the parts I wasn't allowed to eat growing up with Mom and Pop.

"The dark meat is too fatty," Mom scolded me during one of her grand Thanksgiving parties after I reached for the turkey thigh. "Eat the breast like we talked about. Okay?"

Not okay, I answered now. But remembered nodding as that familiar wave of displacement settled in.

My hands clung to the plate of chicken thighs I'd demolished alone, realizing Mama had eaten only a piece before stopping and watching me stuff my face.

"Aren't you hungry?" I asked her.

"Not as hungry as I am concerned for you. I am sorry for putting you through that back there. Think you could ever forgive me?"

I chewed more quickly. "It's fine."

"My love," she mewed, reaching for my hand. "You don't believe that. Just like I know that was such a fucked up way to go about explaining the diagnosis to you. I'm sorry."

"It's fine. Really." I told her, despite my hand that squeezes her like a vice. Like she'll disappear if I don't hold on. My breath quavers as I add, "It's fine."

"May I hug you, my love?" She asked, and I shook my head with more insistence on how "fine" I was. Mama opens her arms. "Please?"

I hesitate, but panic when she releases her hand from mine. The sudden act scares me, and it feels like I lost her as I feared. One minute I'm glaring at her, but the next? I can't stop myself from shuddering when our bodies meet for the hug I needed.

"I'm sorry." She cries, but her voice is calm while she strokes my hair.

"Mama..." I keened as I held her for dear life. "Why?"

I ask, and maybe she gets my unspoken question since she holds me tighter and whispers.

"I'm not leaving you. That cancer can kiss my ass! I'm here, Cleo."

"But it's cancer!"

"But I'm your mama!" She wails. "And I ain't letting this Sickle Cell stop me from living like it did Clay. I understand this may be God's wrath designed to punish me for my old days of sinning, but this cancer ain't meet somebody like me. I'll kick its ass before it takes me from you."

Sobs and snot coated my face and transferred to her chest as I listened. But I'm not convinced. The storm in my heart not calmed by her positivity on all this. All it felt was the only words I let slip past the barrier of my lips.

"I just got you back." My voice warbles. "Now you're leaving me again. All by myself."

"Listen to me, Cleo." She demands with way more conviction than before as she pulls us apart. "Listen up good. I'm here. And I know there's nothing I could say to make you believe I ain't leaving, but trust in God, okay? And believe me in action instead of promises. So...I wasn't sure if this was the right time to show you this, but...follow me."

"What...?" I quietly probe but follow her scuttling form into her bedroom.

"Wait here." She instructs when I follow her inside. I occupy the queen sized bed instead while I wait for her to come back. And she does, but carrying a shoebox with a brand name I'd never seen before.

"What is this?" I question her when she sits beside me on the bed.

"Take it."

"What is this?" I repeat.

"Proof, my love." She says softly, just as I'm removing the top from the shoe box.

My eye saucer at the expensive jewelry, old photographs, and a small blue Kodak camera that looks to belong from another decade. I take a moment to study the single photo of the young girl. She's wearing a huge grin with a baby in her arms. And even though the baby is in the middle of a crying fit, the young woman's smile radiates nothing but pure joy. Her large curls are full and lush, and her chocolate complexion glows despite the poor camera quality. She is absolutely gorgeous, I gather before looking up at her.

"Mama?"

A sad smile crests her face when she responds. "That was me right after I had you. You couldn't have been no more than a week old."

"We look so much alike." I whisper, still observing the woman's beauty.

Mama nods. "See those items in that box there?"

"Yeah."

"I moved around a lot before, and after, giving birth to you. And there are so many things I regret. When the doctor told me you'd be a girl, I panicked because I thought I wasn't capable of raising a respectable young lady. I feared that my mistakes would hurt you or turn you into me, since that hard life was all I knew. I even took you away from your father, and..." Mama blew out hard. "And he didn't deserve that. He offered to quit his entire career to help me raise you, but I refused. How could I be responsible for taking that away from him? His music meant everything, and I'd be damned if I turned out to be one of those girls set to pop out his baby and ruin his life in court. So, I lied. I lied and said you weren't his before running away."

She paused, rocking herself and shutting her eyes. She looked tortured, reliving those memories.

"Why did you give me up?" I couldn't stop the question that ate into my conscience since I'd been old enough to comprehend memory. "Because of my dad?"

"No, love!" She reassured me. "That's not it. But I think it's time you learned the truth of what happened. After I gave birth to you, I was so happy to become a mother. To think, this young, stupid girl from the hood who'd never had any real parents of her own was now a mother. Though painful, birthing you was the best day of my life."

"Really?" I whispered.

"Of course, Cleo." She insisted while clasping my hand. "But, of course, with sunshine can often come rain. Not even twenty-four hours passed before my big brother came to the hospital. He brought that bitch wife of his and a representative from Child Protective Services, who explained that I had twenty-four hours to surrender my newborn baby to Ferrum Albert. Of course, I was only fifteen years old at the time, homeless and with a major drug problem. Your uncle took custody of you that day, and pain only followed in the days after that."

"Wait, what?" I beseeched, rearing back at her words. "Pop told me you left me at his doorstep with a note begging him to take me in since you didn't want me. To raise me since you were too young and unfit."

Mama shook her head, as if resigned to the tale but not totally in disbelief that her big brother would go so far.

"No, baby. He's right about only two parts of that equation. Sure I was young and potentially unfit because of the drug situation, but I always loved you. I always wanted you. That never happened. He came to that hospital and took you from me. That photo you're staring at is the first time your uncle let me see you since birth. I got tossed into foster care and ran away after the man in that home tried to touch me. But...no, baby. You were always wanted and loved by me."

I shook all over, appalled and on fire from this news I never knew about. It had all been a lie? My loving parents were total liars.

"I got clean when I turned eighteen. After that, I got a job and a nice apartment. Since your uncle had full custody, I had to get his approval before you were granted to spend time with me. I tried so hard to keep it together, did everything that he, and the judge, required of me to get you back. But it got so hard. Ferrum made my life impossible when I tried to take you for the weekends or even spend time. He's a loving man, that's for certain, but he's threatened by me. He could never give his wife a child, and I did, so he appreciated that. But there was always something missing when it came to you. Every job I got, something would go wrong and end me up fired. Every apartment wasn't quite up to livable standards that I found for us. He blocked me every chance he got with his money and influence. I fought tooth and nail to even get the supervised visits. But I never gave up. Ever. You know why?"

"Because you wanted revenge? On Uncle Ferr?"

She pulled me into her arms then, a surprised look on her face and wonder in her voice. "You still don't get it? That I'd do anything for you. I'd kill for you, my baby girl. You are my entire world, Cleo'Nora June Albert. All those items in that box are a collection of my most precious values I picked up over the years. Starting when my parents died when I was a little girl, so much had been taken from me. Everything I loved most, you included. The drugs numbed the ache of wanting, but can't you see? I don't need those no more. I love you so much cancer doesn't even get a say. I finally have you home...with me...so, please..."

She chokes on a sob as her body shakes with emotion. The shoebox is long forgotten at this point.

"Don't count me out. Have faith in me, okay?" She begs behind a mask of tears.

I nod, my chest feeling as heavy as my heart that's pounding with such force I'm sure it'll fall out. There's a lot of doubt and fear in my mind from the events of the day, the threats from Edgar, horror of Luther, and disappointment from the liars pretending to be my parents. But in this moment with her, my mother by heart and blood, there's no doubt or fear when I speak into her shoulder. "Double promise."

"That's my girl." She says. "Give me a smile."

"Mama..." I groan.

"If you don't give me one willingly I'll force it out of you..."

I widened my eyes in horror, knowing full well her next actions. "Mama, don't!"

"Too late!" She warns, and soon I'm pinned to the bed while her fingers tickle my sides, causing the forced laughter to rise to the surface.

I hated getting tickled, she knew that, but real laughter mixes in with the forced one as we lay across her bed, emotionally spent while recovering from the intensity of the previous conversation.

"Take this, too." Mama declared after digging into her jean pockets.

She produced a small piece of notebook paper, and there's an address on it.

"Whose address is this?" I hedged.

"That's not important right now." She said. "But always know this place will be a safe space if you're ever in need of one. Even after I'm gone."

I grimace. "After you're gone...?"

"Yes." She asserts, and I don't wonder too long about what she means. She isn't running out to the store, or going on a trip. But it was death, her death, that was implied.

"No." I shook my head. "Don't talk like that!"

"Cleo." Mama states firmly, wiping the stray tear from her eye. "Go there and ask for Janice. She'll know what to do. Okay?"

A tense minute ticks by as we stare at each other. Then I falter. Mama's not backing down, and I won't acknowledge her upcoming demise with a verbal response. So I just nod, unable to say anything else.

"Okay, love. Thank you."

She leaves the room after a few minutes, claiming her bladder was on fire after having to fill up on drinks at Mom and Pop's house, since the food was alive.
My mind turns back to sulking, at least it almost does, before the buzz from my phone returns. I'd forgotten the device in my back pocket, desperately wanting to put as much distance between it and me from that Edgar situation.
Everything freezes, however, when I read the screen. It's a text message. From my long awaited best friend and Beach, Trice. Tears form as I read the message for the third time.

TRICE: Hello Nora. Sorry I've been so distant. Want to drop by tomorrow and hang out? I'm dying to catch you up on all that's been going on.

9

night to remember

I remember the day he came to live with us. It was a cold January afternoon and an intense ice-rain just completed its course into blanketing the town in more Winter and less sunshine. As a huge Barbie fanatic, I could always be found in my usual spot within my parent's Silver Springs ginormous house: the playroom. Or, rather, my playroom, which technically functioned within a small nook in the attic where no sound could be heard beyond its ultra-reinforced walls.

I performed lots of dye experiments back then on my dolls, however, ones I knew would end in a tongue lashing from my parents should they ever see the state of the high end collector's models. Mom went ballistic the year before about my collectors '99 edition Holiday Treasures doll. I got the doll on Christmas day and by the next, her hair was amateurly dyed from blonde, to highlight green. It was one of the rare moments in my time in the Silver Springs mansion that pride filled me. And upon showing my Mom, instead of the warm smile and "good job, baby!" like I expected from my birth Mama at my efforts, she'd all but shook with rage. Rage that I'd been so careless during my administrations by mutilating the four hundred dollar doll. She actually used the word 'mutilate.' The woman I respected as my mother actually looked upon my interests with disgust, like it was a phase from which time would force me to outgrow instead of the passion that made me feel alive.

I'd done a similar thing to my Cafe Day doll Mama got me one day during her "outings." Though the dollar store doll was so cheap it had a brand name foreign to me, Mama spent several hours with me in her then apartment living room, where we sat on the floor amidst laughing and snacking while creating the perfect shade of candy apple red. We dyed the doll, whom I named Norina after me and Mama named Skye due to her deep blue eyes, and danced the night away. She didn't have much furniture and I'd also understand later how her spending that night with me cost her the waitress gig Uncle Ferr pulled strings for her to get without a high school diploma. We passed out from dancing and dying the night away at the expense of her job, because Mama valued me over all else. Unlike Mom.

"Crap!" I swore under my breath after getting sprayed with the permanent pink hair dye Mama secretly thefted for me.

After another several minutes of frantically scrubbing the stain on my hand as quietly as I could in the upstairs bathroom, I sighed. I kept my cosmetic experiments upstairs for good reason since Mom's disapproval, so I crept downstairs and scanned the dark kitchen to make sure the coast was clear. To avoid detection meant everything, I thought, and screeched when the lights came on as I determinedly scrubbed at the sink.

"Cleo!" Mom sang when she saw me.

Her eyes flitted to the pink stains all over my clothes, and I flinched in preparation for the cross examination. But it never came. Instead, she jogged over and lifted me in the air. An act only Mama and I engaged in while we swayed to old school hip hop tracks in one of her many apartments.

But the shock on my face was written there by Mom's athletic arms twirling us both around in the mansion kitchen.

"Mommy!" I giggled, despite myself. "I'm getting dizzy!"

After another minute of twirling and giggling, then she replanted me on the floor before kneeling to meet my gaze.

"Cleo'Nora," She whispered with light in her eyes. "Is that hair dye on your clothes again?"

I froze. There it was– that mind numbing displacement that kicked in whenever she was near. For a moment everything was mysteriously fun. Abnormal for the legal eagle spirit of my adoptive mother, but otherwise warm in the place of the cold criticism when she usually saw me "acting out."

I fidgeted, unsure whether to confirm or deny.

Maybe she was sick or something. Yeah, that had to be the cause for the upward tug of her lips. A smile?

"I bet you get pretty lonely in this big ole house, huh?"

Though only five years old, I ran her words through an imaginary AI processor in consideration before nodding my head.

"I thought so." She said, a tinge of sadness in her voice.
"I'm sorry, Mommy."

She frowned. "Sorry for what?"

"For..." I hesitated. "For mutilating my Holiday Treasure
Barbie."

Her frown remained as though she sought to find the
memory of my words. Then she smiled again. "That's in the
past, sweetheart."

A tear ran down my cheek. "I'm sorry! It's all my fault you
get so angry! Because I don't follow the rules. And because
I'm a bad girl."

"Cleo, listen." Mom held me with firm hands, and it was
then when I noticed my body trembling. "It's all right. You
play with dolls, you're a kid! That's okay. You'll grow out of
these silly little behaviors when you're my age. But right now,
I have some awesome news!"

"Awesome news?"

"Yes, honey!" She sang. "Follow me into the living room.
Remember that conversation your father and I had with you
last year?"

I didn't, but it didn't take long for familiarity to spark once
we left the kitchen. We walked hand in hand into the large
quarters where Pop and a little kid sat on the sofa. Their conversation was an animated one, punctuated by exaggerated

flapping gestures and animal noises from them both. All talk ceased when they got a look at Mom and me entering.

"My Cleo!" Pop greeted with just as much cheer as Mom a few seconds prior. He stood up. "What's all that paint doing on your clothes again?"

"Never mind that!" Mom chirped before I could fidget. She all but dragged me to the center of the room where the little boy with light brown skin and slanted eyes stared at me. "Cleo, say hello to Ashawn."

"Who are you?" I made my confusion clear and sized him up. "And why are you so skinny?"

"Cleo!" Mom chided, rushing to the foreign boy's side and pulling him into her arms. "Sorry, Ashawn. Our daughter has a sense of humor. What about you? You like games?"

Why was Mommy talking to this strange kid like he'd combust at any moment? Like he was fragile as glass or volatile as a bomb. Either way, both Mom and Pop treaded carefully when regarding him.

"I like cards," this "Ashawn" boy answered neutrally.

"Cleo likes cards, too, right?" Mom asked in a tone several octaves higher than usual.

That familiar urge to fidget came to me again, and I held my tongue for fear of saying the wrong thing again.

"Right?" Mom repeated.

I drew my lips tight, sealing them and refusing to say anything else. I didn't like their eyes. All of them. They gazed at me in a way that had me unsure if it was Ashawn or me that existed as the stranger.

Fire flashed behind Mom's eyes that let me know she was about to detonate. And perhaps I should have said something, anything, lied even to appease her questions. But I...just didn't like their eyes.

Pop rested a hand to Mom's elbow. "Calm now, Laurel. This is all new to our daughter. Give her some time to adjust to it. All in good time, Lord willing."

"Amen." Mom said almost automatically after Pop spoke of the Lord. "Your father is right. Cleo, why don't you show Ashawn your playroom? I'm sure that'll make him feel more at home."

I nodded.

Suddenly, Ashawn's face twisted in what looked to be confusion and wonder as he stared at me. "So, is she my sister now?"

His question shocked me so bad I caught myself yelling, "No!"

"Not exactly, honey." Mom answered his question as if I hadn't just screamed at him. "We'll explain this all to you later. But for now, Cleo is being unreasonable. Could you both just go upstairs and explore while Ferrum and I have a chat?"

Though it stormed on this day, Ashawn's thousand-watt smile was ultra-violet when he nodded. "Yes, ma'am."

Mom melted at his respectful agreement and she raised a hand to her chest. "You're quite the gentleman."

"Not really, ma'am." He said. "I really like you, though. I like you all. Everybody has been super nice."

"You're not my brother!" I screamed bloody murder mere inches from his face.

Ashawn didn't miss a best though. His smile grew wider as he regarded me. "I like you, too Cleo."

My face warmed from his words, but at the time I didn't know why. But subsequent embarrassment filled me when I crossed my arms and pouted. There were those stares again, but this time it was only coming from Mom and Pop. It was them who regarded me like the adopted alien I was, instead of a troubled little girl. An unknown emotion greeted me when I met the little boy's eyes though.

"I'll take care of her." Ashawn, the boy I'd met a mere five minutes prior, grabbed my smaller hand and guided me up the stairs in my own home. "Come on!"

"Dinner will be ready at five, kids!" Mom called, but I didn't care.

I allowed the world to blur beyond our footsteps into the attic-turned-playroom and shook my head when he let me go. He walked around the room, studying every corner and doll that lined the wall shelves with a keen focus.

"You didn't have to drag me in here!" I fumed.

"Sorry." He kept his eyes on one of the dolls with vibrant red coils and party dress. "I like this one."

I froze. Not quite believing that someone, more so a boy, could walk in here and like my most coveted toys. Feeling much too seen, I ran over and ripped the doll from view. Clutching it to my middle as if I'd been making a pass towards the intersection of a football game.

"Stop looking at my stuff!" I whined.

He laughed good naturedly, causing the laugh lines in his mouth to extend. A question floated to my mind then. "How old are you anyway?"

"Eight years old."

"Well, why do you act so grown up?" I demanded, more curious than pissed off.

"No, I don't." He huffed, but I noted his reddening cheeks as I watched him sink to the floor near my dollhouse.
"Want to play dolls?"

"What?"

"You like dolls, right?" He asked while toying with the dollhouse. "Instead of cards?"

I think it was the shock. We'll blame that emotion for the hours' worth of doll playing that followed his questions. I'd had so much fun, and we laughed for hours on end about games, friends, and what our favorite shows were.

"Your favorite show is My Little Pony?" He asked, bewildered.

I frowned. "What's the matter with that? I love all the colors!"

He laughed at me. "That makes sense."

"Shut up!" I whined then smacked his arm. "What's your favorite show- Big Stupid hairy Head?"

"Ouch!" He chuckled, then sobered as he said, "And no. First 48."

"What kinda stupid show is that?" I giggled. But he didn't join me in the merriment while he stared at the tuxedoed Ken doll.

He averted his eyes. "I like it. It's a crime show about cops stopping bad guys. I want to be like that when I grow up. Stopping bad guys before they can hurt good people."

"Oh..." I whispered, trailing off in thought.

It was much too real for my then five year old brain to comprehend at the time. I just quieted, sensing the pensiveness in his body language.

"Mr. Ferrum and Ms. Laurel are good people." he spoke plaintively, though with still some hushed emotion I couldn't understand.

"I guess." I shrugged.

"No, really. Y'all are nice. Good. And I hope I get to stay with you forever and be the best big brother!"

10

missed opportunities

❤ · ❤ · ❤ · ❤ · ❤

I never liked the winter, nor any weather that demanded wearing anything heavier than a cardigan. I'm all but cursing the Lord's name in vain through chattering teeth as I look both ways down the suburban streets. The sight of the large blue colonial house, nestled between trees and an identically grand one on its left, sent chills up my spine. And, no, the chills weren't to be attributed to the wintry winds whipping through my orange hoodie and leggings, but the gut-punch of apprehension assailing my conscience.

What would Trice say when I saw her again? Sure, she'd fallen off the face of the planet in the past after ending things with Jack, but we patched up since then. Our friendship, while initially fake, blossomed into a sisterhood I didn't know I needed. I tried to be there for her even after she became a single parent, but then her texts became fewer and far between. Again. In fact, an eerie suspicion rises in my mind before I tamp it down and knock on her front door.

The door swung open to reveal a smiling Mr. Newbern, the man I recognized as Trice's father. I wasn't too versed on what he did for a living, but I remembered it having something to do working in the state attorney general's offices. We connected on a deeper level having both been the product of lawyer parents, citing the immense pressures placed on us to become second versions of themselves.

"I love my dad," Trice told me one day during our car ride from school. "But he's quite absent. And when he is there, he's harsh– though not in an obvious way. He keeps this poker face that doesn't convey his true opinion of you. When he gets that look...?"

She trailed off, and I fought the second wave of chills at the memory and at the sight of the six foot man who appeared as an older, male copy of my Beach.

"Hi, Mr. Newbern!" I said nervously between shivers.

"Ms. Albert?" He probed with an even tone, right before a lash of wind whipped between our bodies. "Get in here before you freeze to death!"

I yelped at the feel of his arms wrapping around me and tugging me until we crashed into the opulent foyer. I noted his hand lingering an extra minute before he took a full step back.

"Sorry to cause you trouble." I mumbled, heat scalding my cheeks from the clumsy move.

"No trouble at all, Ms. Albert."

"Nora," I corrected. "Nora is fine. Let's do away with the formalities since Trice and I are best friends."

He cracked a wide smile. "That's right. I apologize for the misnomer. Please come in and have a seat, Nora."

I hesitated, my eyes shooting a searching look towards the suggested sitting room and the stairs.

His eyes were almost golden under the amber lighting in the foyer, sparkling a mischievous glint and heightening my nervousness.

"I see," He said with a nod. "You're visiting that daughter of mine."

I winced. "Um, yeah. Not to be rude or anything, but I'm really excited to see my best friend. It's been almost a month now and she promised to fill me in on the details of all of this."

"Nora, Nora." Mr. Newbern chided before folding my hand in his. He spoke while simultaneously massaging my knuckles. The action was soothing, but also shiver-inducing. "Explanation not needed. Don't worry. I know you and Patrice are long overdue for some girl talk– am I right?"

I chuckled. His mismatched colloquialism spoken with firm articulation broke up some of the tension in the room.

A quiet befell the room as we just stood there. Stood there staring at each other with silent questions hanging like living vines in the air. But when he opened his mouth to speak, I jumped first.

"So, is Trice asleep?" I asked, deciding to get right to business in spite of the unease that filled me all of a sudden when I snatched my hand back.

He made a face that was a cross between distressed and exasperated before composing. He blinked two full times as he said, "Patrice went to the store. But don't worry, she sent me a message saying she'll arrive shortly."

"Okay..." My mouth worked the word out with a measured nod. "That's cool. What about Katy?"

"Apologies," he supplied. "She took Katy with her. Ran out of formula. I insisted Patrice visit the grocer for the items, but she refused. There's apparently some niche children's store in Silver Spring she was excited to go to."

"Hang on." I reared back at that. "Silver Spring, as in, Silver Spring, Maryland?"

"Correct."

I fought the rising panic threatening to take over to properly assess this situation. Currently, I was standing in an empty house with Patrice's father. The same one who made it a point, in Trice's eyes, to avoid being home. The same man who traveled so often for work that his own granddaughter barely recognized him. My heart raced at a thought I didn't want to give voice or power as I took in huge gulps of air to calm. Figure this shit out, Cleo. I warned myself, even when the urge to run hit its peak the second he took a step towards me.

"I hear you're a collector?" I probed, praying my efforts to mask the terror were successful. "Of spirits?"

And perhaps they were, since he answered in a composed voice, "Oh, yes. I carry a global collection of only the best spirits. Spirits I wouldn't credit young ladies like yourself to take interest in."

"Oh, yeah!" I gushed out the lie. "My dad drinks all sorts of expensive wines, mostly French imports. I know a tannin or two about it."

Mr. Newbern's grin didn't reveal his amusement, but another emotion I couldn't figure out. Nonetheless, I continued with the lie to see where this conversation went. He crossed his arms. "You're a lovely surprise, Nora. Where has Patrice been hiding you all this time?"

"Nowhere, Mr. Newbern." I replied sweetly. "It's just, you aren't usually around whenever I come over."

"Call me Patrick." He maintained that smile as he said, "Missed opportunities, huh?"

"Sure." I shrugged and scanned the empty, haunted-feeling room where almost no light could be seen aside from an upstairs one. "Anyways, if Trice is going to be there for a while, then I can meet her. Which store did you say she went?"

"I believe it's called Paisley's."

"Thanks." I said while adjusting my thin hoodie. "I'll see if I can meet her there."

"Wait!" He urged, a bit frantic as he watched my hand rest on the doorknob. "Do you drive?"

I froze, feeling guilty all of a sudden for the next lie delivered to the kind older man. I shook my head, needing to clear it of the harboring suspicion of Mr. Newbern I suspected festered from Trice's tales. She spoke about him as if he'd been the worst dad ever instead of the nice guy who welcomed me into his home, apparently without any knowledge of my arrival.

Deflating, I turned back to face him. "I don't."

"How about this?" He started and I studied his face crack with another interesting smile. I looked for this poker face Trice talked about, but in fact it's sincere concern shining in those bright brown eyes there instead. He extends a hand to me. "Come with me to my study. You look exhausted and I can see you trembling from here from the cold. Let's you get inside, warm up, and we chitchat a little until that daughter of mine comes home. Sound good?"

Be kind, Cleo. My Mama's motto drifts back to the forefront during my ruminations on his offer: Be kind, and make good choices. Those were Mama's words, not mine, but I'm fighting the tension building in my chest as I seek to claim the words as my own. A kind girl wouldn't refute the nice guy's offer. I couldn't disrespect Trice like that, my thoughts skittering back to the memory of how I used and even wrestled with the shy girl in this very home in middle school. Another minute of tortured thinking, and fast-forward ten minutes later, I'm sitting with the nice father of my Beach in the small corner office in his house.

"You a fan of stories, Nora?" Patrick asked between sips of his expensive bourbon.

We were situated now inside the office: he behind his desk and me on the plush couch he assured me doubled as a bed when he worked late nights.

I tried not to make it a habit of checking my phone every thirty seconds, praying that Trice would come home, burst inside the room, say "hi Dad. Bye, Dad!" and take me back to the sanctuary of her bedroom. Where we'd powwow about the updates happening in her life, effectively pressing the resume button on our stalled friendship that existed as my lifeline.

"Um," I cleared my throat. "Not really. I mean, sure sometimes, but I'm not a huge reader or anything."

His brows lifted. "That right?"

"Yeah," I shrugged. "Between the two of us, Trice is the academic. More her style, less mine. You know?"

"That's very intriguing. Patrice does value her studies more than most, a fact her mother and I adore about her. An intelligent girl."

"The best." I cheered, genuinely pleased to hear him speak her praises.

"At least most of the time." He added in a voice so low it took a few minutes for me to register the cold insertion.

"What are you talking about?"
He shifted in his plush computer chair, an uncomfortable look on his perfect face. A face so chiseled only a few peppered gray strands in his shaved hair denoted his age. "Everything all right?" I asked after noting the hitch in his breathing.

"Allow me to tell you a story." He whispered so low I asked him to repeat it, "Please." He added desperately.

"Uh, okay..."

He went on to relate the tale of a man named Aniko. He'd been a poor street kid who fell in love with a girl well above his strata. After several failed attempts at winning the girl's affections, Aniko gave up. He was soon doomed to watch the girl date rich suitors from afar, and then it dawned on him: money. He'd needed more of it if he had any hopes of winning the girl of his dreams over. After the mysterious and sudden demise of his father, he'd come to inherit his policy cash at seventeen. He'd used that same cash to put himself through college, then law school, and once he'd landed his dream position in a high profile law firm out of law school, Aniko reached out to the same girl from years ago only to discover she'd been dead for over a year. She'd died during a childbirth complication.

I hadn't noticed the tears falling down my face until Patrick said, "No tears, Nora. Trust me, there is a silver lining to this tale."

"Go on." I sniffled, eager to now hear the rest of this story.

"Right." Patrick answered, downed another swallow of bourbon, then continued. "Well, turns out that girl's death story was only a cover up. It was later discovered that her husband at the time, a world renowned surgeon, poisoned her after she'd given birth and relegated her death as a neonatal complication. Her husband found the girl's diary where there were several old letters addressed to her. From Aniko. In the diary…she states how unhappy she is in her marriage to the surgeon and how she wishes her life turned out differently. She also notes that she'd been watching Aniko through the years, same as he did her, and she wished she would have given their love a chance. It was believed those notes sparked the motive for the surgeon to end the girl's life. A life cut entirely too short…"

"Poor Aniko." I sobbed, wiping the tears with the backs of my palms. "What ever happened to him?"

Patrick flashes a sad smile, his eyes staring into what looked to be the past. "He met another successful woman, working to become a licensed marriage and family counselor. Even though he grew to adore the loyal woman who'd been compatible to him in every way, he'd always ached for a chance to go back. To make things different, just as the girl of his dreams wrote. However, his new girlfriend refused to marry him until he changed his name to something more palatable. A name much more befitting a future politician.

So, he did. Aniko and this new woman soon married and even welcomed two beautiful children. A boy, who mirrored his mother in looks and grit, and a little girl Aniko swore to protect from a similar fate."

An eerie sense of suspicion reared its head full force on the inside of my mind. This was no cautionary tale, I figured, considering the obvious similarities to reality.

"Hang on." I shifted slightly in my seat to stare at him more directly. "Are you...Aniko?"

Patrick stood up then and was soon standing before me. There was another, unreadable emotion on his face, and I wondered if this was the poker face Trice warned me about. The expression made the hairs stand up on my arms and had me fumbling in my pocket for my phone.

"It's been quite a while since anyone's referred to me by my original name. I like it."

I didn't reveal it, but held firm the phone in my pocket. "Then why don't you change it back?"

"Perhaps, I should clarify." He took a step towards me. "I like the sound of my name on your lips, I meant."

I wriggled back, my breathing frenzied as I sought to create some space between us. But he drew nearer, and before I get the chance to bolt out of there, he sinks low to entrap me between his arms.

"Mr. Newbern!" I panted. "Where is Trice?"

"That daughter of mine." He said dryly. "I told her she'd be cut off if she didn't stop seeing that little Irish bastard. That family was trash well before those murders occurred. Can't you see, Nora? She's heading down the same path as Aniko–settling with the hardships life dealt her. That boy and that baby are her hardships. Her innocence was tainted by that family. And now...now..."

The reddening of his cheeks and fury in his eyes puts me in mind of Luther during one of his rages. Taking a deep breath, I do what seems to always work when calming my dangerous boyfriend. Since I wasn't sure if coking or cumming were vices of his I could manipulate, I default to the next best thing.

I fought to steady my trembling hand when I reached up to cup his cheek. His eyes flickered shut for a moment and he leaned into it.

"You tried your best with your family. I'm sorry you were forced to change so completely that you lost yourself in a life you didn't want."

"Thank you..." He strangled out.

"Of course." I supplied soothingly despite my terror. "But you need to understand that you were not responsible for what happened to the girl. Or her husband's actions. Just like you need to learn to accept the people in your life for who they are. Trice thinks you hate her."

He recoiled as if I'd slapped him. "She what?"

"She does. You're never home. And when you are, you avoid everyone in this tiny office of secrets. Get to know your family. The real them. Trust me, it's no fun living in the loveless zone, thinking that your existence in your family is tolerated, or worse, unwanted."

His eyes avert to the floor, as if he's processing this information. "I love my daughter."

"She's not just 'your daughter.' Her name is Trice. You speak about her as if she's this complication you've been saddled with instead of a concerned father. She's human, like you, and she loves you."

He's silent and his arms are still encased around me, limiting my movements. However, I realize the veracity of my words to the fallen guy before me. Realized how I needed to take my own advice in dealing with the amount of unprocessed trauma associated with my upbringing. I spoke ad nauseam about this loveless zone because it's where I lived in my uncle's household. Just because I'd never been sure, didn't mean they certainly didn't love me. Just like now, this could be resolved with a simple conversation. And I vowed that, if I ever made it out of here, that I'd do that. Have that difficult conversation with my parents about what really happened regarding my entry into this world.

"What's her name?" I asked.

He doesn't even hesitate or ask for clarification. "Her name was Nora."

My hand stilled on his cheek. "The girl...from the story...her name was Nora?"

"Yes." He nodded.

"Super weird." I mumbled, and when he turned unreadable eyes on me, I recentered. "I mean, what are the odds that the former love of your life's name matched mine?"

"You're a woman wiser than your years, Nora. And the first time I laid eyes on you sucked all the air out of my body. Not only did Patrice's best friend have a name, same as my soulmate's, but she was identical. In looks, stature, and even charm. But I kept my distance. I know, especially in my line of work, how dangerous getting involved with a minor was. But you'll be eighteen in a few months, right?"

That mind numbing fear resurges despite my efforts to tamp it down with pseudo calm. This was just plain creepy, and I couldn't take it anymore. Fury accompanied the fear involved in propelling me forward. I shoved him with all my might, which was insufficient against the man with way more muscle than I pegged him for at first. He collapsed on top of me, and now our bodies squished together in a tight embrace I fought against.

"Let me go!" I sneered, getting in as many punches as possible on his back. But he didn't move.

"Nora, my love." He simpered while stroking my dyed hair. "You've come back to me. We can be together now. You have no idea how long I've waited for you – for this moment!"

"Stop it!" I screamed then coughed when his hand clamped over my mouth. His red rimmed eyes flared with insanity as he hissed at me.

"Nobody's gonna hear you! Stop fighting this love, Nora! Is it money you want? I'm rich now baby, take it all!"

Some shuffling noises sounded before a literal money shower rained over me.

We fought for another few seconds before I became utterly winded. Maybe all that crazy deflated from him, too, since he collapsed on top of me again. His hand fell to my side as his head laid against my breasts heaving in rapid up and down motions from the exertion.

"Let me go." I whimpered, still afraid for my life but my mind seeking to hatch another escape.

Coking or cumming. Coking or cumming. Coking or...

Taking a deep breath and totally unsure if this next move would be my last, I reached down between us until I felt the hard piece of flesh contained behind jeans. I nearly barfed at the contact that had him moaning in surprise, then ecstasy.

"Nora..." He groaned. His face was fully buried into my chest. "Not yet. Not...old enough...."

I gulped. "I know. But I'm ready now. I need you."

He shuddered. "Oh, Nora...you're killing me here..."

Same as a phone sex session, I channeled Norina Skye to enact the finishing blow. I gripped his hard flesh once more, and couldn't hold back my smile.

"Let me go freshen up for you. I want to be ready for you. I've wanted you for so many years, even back then when I said I didn't. I should have chosen you." My voice was coy, kitten-like, and just the right amount of tantalizing to draw another shudder from him.

"I knew it, baby! My Nora. My Nora…mines all along." His words were rushed and unintelligible.

I reached a free hand up to stroke his hair. "Yours."

"Yes, yes, yes…"

"I need to go to the lady's room, okay? Where can I freshen up for you. I want to give you my best."

He tightened around me, as if that was answer enough. No way in hell he'd release me unless I played this right.

"Pretty please…" I squeezed his arousal again. "Aniko?"

A warm, or hot, sensation met my touch after I purred his true name. His entire body shivered with the intensity of his climax, and I kept the confident grin the terror in me didn't truly feel. After another minute of swearing and shuddering, he finally released me.

"Hurry back, beautiful." He insisted in a dreamy tone before collapsing back onto the sofa.

"Of course." I hummed agreeably before power-walking into the hallway.

Once I was sure he wouldn't chase or follow, I ran down the steps and towards the room where I felt the safest.

Trice, I begged inwardly from the fear and need to see my smiling best friend. What's going on? Why text me only to leave me alone with the monster upstairs? Was this some sort of grand setup? I quickly disbanded that thought, confident in my best friend's love for me. She would never do that. Never, ever put me in a situation like this even if my cooperation with the 590's led to so many of her troubles.

"Trice!" I cried before pushing her bedroom door open.

Then I froze. No, more like, melted into a heap on the empty floor of her once furnished bedroom. Where a queen sized bed with a gold fixtures frame was nestled was now gone. The corner where she kept Katy's crib was also gone. In fact, the entire room looked as if it had been scrubbed entirely, emptied of any personal items that would let the onlooker know a teenage girl resided here.

I clamped a hand over my mouth when a cold realization settled over me. That text message Trice sent me earlier wasn't sent by her. But it originated from the monster upstairs. It made sense now why so many alarm bells rang when I first entered the house. Trice would have never gone out of town alone. It just wasn't like her. As a nervous driver, she'd dragged me almost everywhere when she was first gifted the car. Also, Paisley's was a children's clothing outlet, and it was so upscale that I remembered Trice's comment about them being too bougie to carry baby formula when we visited a few months ago.

All of it was a lie. A lure. A trap set by Patrick Newbern to get me here alone. But if he had Trice's phone, then where was she?

Bitter disappointment and cold terror fueled my numb movements towards the bathroom. Once inside, I locked the door and whipped out my phone. Without looking, I dialed one of the numbers at the top of the call log and did something I rarely did since Luther's unofficial induction as the new 590 Head.

Pulled rank.

"Nora?" She asked after picking up. "Is everything okay?"

"Come get me." I said, my voice a hollow version of itself as I told her the address. "Right now."

"But–"

"That's an order." I barked before hanging up and hanging my head in my hands.

11

Colorado

"You're so easy to be with, you know?" Ty whispered while withdrawing himself from my heat and enfolding me in his arms.

With my back drawn to him, I frowned and adjusted myself in a more comfortable position on the cold hard slab of linoleum floor. Cleaning supplies and the strong smell of bleach permeated the air around our half naked bodies, a welcome cover-up to disguise the smell of our sex in this frequently used janitor's closet.

"What's that supposed to mean?"

I felt him shrug. "You know."

"Um, I actually don't. Hence, my question."

A silence stretched between us, alerting me of the sudden arrival of one of his many mood changes. Judging from his heavily drawn breaths and tightened hold around my middle, I'd say anger this time. Or maybe annoyance?
"Everything okay?" I can't help but ask.

"What would you say if I told you I broke it off with Sasha?"

My cheeks heat from the unexpected question and emotional turn in the conversation. But I play it cool as I respond, "That's, uh, I mean...that sucks. Is what I'd say."

He laughs. "Just how I thought you'd respond. You're so silly, girl. Real innocent and shit. I fucks with that."

"Thanks," I say wryly. "But where is all this coming from, Ty?"

He shrugged. "You know."

"I seriously don't."

"I better not be the only one in love here." His words were punctuated at the end with an aggrieved exhale.

The witty retort kept readily prepared whenever he was in my presence never made it past my lips. Suddenly, in that moment, it was just he and I. Not anyone else. Not Sasha. Or my parents. Or even the students shuffling to get to their classes outside the janitor closet door.
I sat up, willing my inflamed body to ignore the feelings his hand on my thigh incited.

"You're in love?" I choked out.

He sat up, too, drawing my body closer to his. "Not just with any ole body."

"Stop playing, Ty."

"I ain't."

"But you are!" I exclaimed. "You stay fucking with my feelings."

"Yo, baby. Chill." He soothed. "It was just a question. And you right. I was just fucking with you."

I shirked off his arms. "See!"

"Wait a minute!" He urged while I knelt to stand. "It ain't our time yet. Let me get my shit straight with the BM."

'BM' meaning baby mom, or Sasha. I knew that by now from our coded text message exchanges on a daily. Since publicly gaming and claiming Ty as hers, Sasha had made his life miserable. I wanted nothing to do with him after that display, but somehow we found our way back to each other. He'd pop up after my work shifts after a month of zero contact. Though I screamed I wanted nothing to do with him, my heart pleaded differently. It went from actively ignoring or yelling at him to stop coming by Nita's after school, to conceding a month later after his mother came in and all but begged me to remain friends with him.

"You're his only friend, Nora." She pleaded stormily while I secured her first lash. "I worry about the company my son keeps when I'm not looking, but when the two of you hung out he started coming with me to Temple again. If only you see how he worries me and his Bubbe."

Nothing prophetic, but hearing how my presence made any sort of an impact on anyone's life for the better...on his life for the better, my first true love...call me crazy. But I unblocked him and we re-launched our journey as if we hadn't fallen off. Ty was one of my closest friends, he saw me inside and out like nobody in my family ever did. I believed it when he said he cared about me. Believed his promises to leave Sasha after the babies were born.

I deflated from his words. Fell back into the cold floor ever-so-grateful the darkness enshrouded any facial expressions from view.

"I believe you, babe." Was all I said.

"Do you, though?" He competed. "Every time I even mention the L word you fight me. Why it gotta be like that?"

"Because that's how it is! Look around."

I can't see him, but know he followed my instruction from the shift in his seated position.

"What of it?"

"What of it?" I parroted. "We just finished fucking in the janitor's closet. This is where we are. This is all we'll be until you break things off with her. I'm your second choice."

"Never that."

"I've been that. But listen. I'm not angry, babe. I understand the situation you're in. We'll have our time in the sun one day."

I'm in his arms suddenly and without knowing it.

"You're my girl whether you know it or wanna deny it or not. I don't deserve you, Nor. But let me do something for you."

"Do what?"

"Take you out to dinner. At a real restaurant with the fancy wine and flowers and shit. You feel me?"

I reared back. "Um, okay. You think that's a good idea?"

He shrugged. "I offered, didn't I?"

"Well, yeah." My voice was measured. "But again, you're not exactly the most single man right now."

"Yeah, cuz I got you." He growled teasingly.

"No!" I shoved him. "You got Sasha. Remember her? Your girlfriend, and mother of your kids? What will happen when she finds out you're even talking to me? She hates my fucking guts, and it's got nothing to do with you. We got history and…I don't exactly blame her."

"Listen to me real good, cuz I'm only gonna say this once."

I'm not exactly sure how much time passed as we stared at each other in the darkened room, but I coached myself on calming down. The air thickened and my heart constricted at whatever he was about to say next. What if it was "get out bitch, you'll never be my real girl"? I couldn't stomach the idea of him not visiting the shop to see me every other day. Or hearing from Joyce how happy I made her only son when she came by Nita's. He wasn't perfect, neither was I, but we were so good together.

The mere thought of rejection from him right now made me...

"After my Pops cleaned out our savings and left us for dead, I felt this...this emptiness. Like all I been doing since he left was going through the motions that came with the day-to-day. Yeah, I kick it here and there with the occasional party or two, but not all the parties in the damn planet opened me up the way you do. I ain't no pussy or nothing, so I'mma say this one time: You are earth. You ain't my universe, but you're an important part of it. You give me life. How can I not love somebody who taught me how to feel life again?"

I chewed on my lip, but when I tried to look away he grabbed my chin to force our eyes to meet.

"I ain't been the best boyfriend, so I won't even call myself that. I know I need to earn that. But can you just stay my Earth? Give me some more life like you always do, and I'll do the rest."

"Ty..." I whispered, teary and unsure, but otherwise touched beyond belief. I wrapped my arms around him. "I'm sorry for doubting you."

"Don't be sorry, Nor." His arms tightened. "Just don't stop believing in me. I can't take that."

I refused to cry all over his exposed shoulder. He didn't need that, but I felt so raw. So seen in a way like never before. Logic constantly made me question my reasons to keep seeing a taken man. A man with twin infants, at that. But it's him. My feelings for Ty ran deeper than normal love.

"You're the sun, then," I said in his ear. "If I'm your earth, then you're the sun since you make me so damn warm."

He laughed. "Nah baby. Then that would mean you revolve around me. You got that backwards."

It was my turn to laugh at that, though his words did just that: they warmed me.

We adjust so that I sat fully on his lap with my legs wrapped around his waist. School would end soon, and Trice would be looking for me if I didn't hurry up and leave. But my mind flits to his previous offer.

"So you have another surprise for me then?" I purred.

"Yeah." He sang. "Sorta. I'm taking you on the best fucking date of your life."

I recalled his underemployed status and raised a brow, wondering how he'd summon enough capital to foot the bill to an extravagant night out.

"Is that..." I began to ask, but felt the awkwardness set in. "I mean, are you able to afford...that?"

He laughs again, but it's drier this time. "Don't you worry about me. I got the hookup."

Funny how he denied his sun-status considering the rays of light his promises filled me with. He was vibrant, and an effervescent presence I didn't know I craved until he was taken from me. Forever.

12

cause and effect

·♥·♥·♥·♥·♥·

"You all right?" Sasha's tremulous voice carried with it a slight trace of her buried accent.

"Just drive." I commanded, and released an unconscious breath when the SUV accelerated at a suspicious rate, mismatching the pace of the tranquil suburban neighborhood.

A heavy silence accompanied us during the rest of the drive down Toronto Boulevard, then by the familiar shops a few blocks from Mama's house. I didn't need to tell her where to, since this had been the extent of our relationship since Jack went away and Luther assumed complete control over the 590's. Whenever I called–which was rare– it was routine: pick me up and take me home.

"Nora." She stated seconds after parking in front of the small blue house.

"Yeah?" I sighed, not looking at her.

She rested a hand on my shoulder. "Look at me."

Squeezing my eyes shut, I shrugged her off. "Leave me alone. I'm home. Your duty is fulfilled."

"I know, but..." She trailed off, and her hesitation worked to worsen my nerves that were already shooting off the charts after that strange interaction with Patrick Newbern.

Even though staring more than one second at the girl who represented all the dark parts about who I truly was, the true ugliness of Cleo'Nora Albert, I found her round eyes misting at the sight of me. Her long hair, historically flat ironed to death, is in a messy pile of curls at the top of her head. Though chocolate skinned, the red ring around her eyes is visible. Same for the bags under them. Her nails are chipped, I noticed, and more than a little concern clouded the usual evasive annoyance that colored my emotions when it came to her.

"But I can't keep doing this. I...I..."

"You...what?" I asked.

She gulped. "Mooma. She gone."

"Sasha..." I didn't know what to say to the former subject of my bullying.

I spent so much time in my own head, wrapped up in cleaning Luther's blunders or getting money the best ways I knew how to support the life I wanted. It took my brain a moment to register Sasha Kersey, the Trinidadian girl who made Tyrone's life miserable towards the end. I tried so hard to atone for the hell I put her through in elementary, even went as far as becoming Latisha Millard's dog, but Sasha's animosity became a living thing. She vowed to take all the thing's most precious to me away. To make my life the same kind of hell I created for her in elementary. After Ty and Jack disappeared, rank changed in my favor, making me the de facto co-head of the 590's as Luther's girl. I didn't want the damn title, so I kept to the shadows in school and the streets. And even though Sasha moved to Maryland with her grandparents, she was still indebted to me. That meant that even though she escaped this town where all her dreams fell apart after Ty, I could command her as I wanted. I didn't like to pull rank, but times like this called for using every resource possible to escape unscathed.

"I don't know what to do. First my uncle last year. Then Tyrone. Now Mooma. My Mooma!" She hung her head in her hands and shook with tears.

I just sat there, watching her in a daze for a second before sighing. But I vaguely recalled elementary school, her use of that term I later researched to mean "mother." Considering my own Mama's condition, my heart immediately split when my brain finished processing.

"Your mom...she passed?" The words squeaked from me.

"Two days ago. It was a terrible accident and I found her at the staircase landing..." She responded, a hint of that hidden accent poking to the surface with her dreadful admission. "But what am I saying? You hate my guts. Especially after taking your man, Queen 590."

"I wouldn't have asked if I hated you. And don't call me Queen." I decided not to comment on the 'taking your man' part.

She scoffed and theatrically raised her hands in mock surrender. "All hail the Queen. Apologies for insinuating you had a heart. It takes a heart to hate. You straight up don't give a fuck about my life. So, pardon me."

"Where is all this coming from, huh?" I growled, my fuse blowing each time she opened her mouth. "I didn't ask you about your life. You went all teary-eyed with me."

She wiped her eyes again. "I'm just sick and tired of this punishment. I left town. I don't want any part of the sinking ship from that tired ass gang. Luther is moving real messy and it's affecting us all."

"I know." I said, sinking into the chair a bit as I looked on at my Mama's small blue house. "I just...I know. Let me take care of him."
"Take care?!" She exclaimed. "You call rushing into my grandparent's house and taking all my money 'taking care?'"

"He did what?" I asked.

She exhaled harshly before saying, "He came into my home last night. Where my children lay. Demanding I pay him back for betraying The Family. He's still punishing me for Tyrone. I swear it. I mean haven't we paid enough with that video?"

That video. Her voice rings out on the last two words and I close my eyes. My mind and gut lurches at the memory of that video...what he made me do...the morning after...all the shame...

I blinked the tears at bay, hardening my voice to speak to her from a fake place of calm. She was full blown sobbing.

"Sasha, I'm sorry about your mom." I said, meaning it.

She studied my eyes for a hard minute, then deflated.

"I'm sorry for being so coarse with you. She'll be so happy to be sent home on the words of Pastor Albert. Her memorial is tomorrow, and now I don't have any money to gather the flowers or buy her a decent outfit to rest in. He needs to be stopped."

At the mention of my adopted father, I harden. I had some words for his traitor ass soon, but those have to wait for later. Her family were devout members of St. Goliath's, my family's church, so it made sense Uncle Ferr would preside over the funeral. I don't let my disappointment for him show on my face though. Instead, I nod my head, a tight feeling in my chest from the promise I can't keep. But I reassure her anyway.

"All right." She says, satisfied. "Call me if you need anything else."

"I mean it when I say I'll take care of Luther. He's awful, I know. But we can't go against him if we want to stay alive. The Family is punishing both of us for being with Ty."

A wry chuckle escaped her lips. "I'm so fucking sick of this 590 Family bullshit."

I almost agree, but don't. I didn't want to let her in on my plans to find Trice. To find the truth about what happened to her and get the fuck out of here once and for all. There was nothing left for me in DC. And now I had a ticking time clock on my head until Edgar made his move. Three days to be exact.

"Everything will be all right." I assured her again. "Put the video behind you. He won't use it against you. You just let me know if he goes to your house again."

"Oh…" She breathes with a startled look of surprise on her face. "You're…helping me?"

I shrugged, considering our relationship since Tyrone died. "Helping you, helps me."

"Right."

"Text me the address of the funeral." I say before climbing out and shutting the door to her confused "why?"

Moments after she revs the engine and leaves, I make my way inside the house, only to slink to the floor as the events of the day rush over me. My hands shake violently and I have to bite my tongue to keep the scream away.

Where. Was. Trice?!

Why was her room empty? Why was her father lying about it?

Why did he come on to me?

And, perhaps the most terrifying question of all: what was I going to do about Edgar?

And now Luther was robbing Sasha the day before her mother's funeral? I want to ask how one man can stoop so low, but reconsider. It's Luther Noonan, of all people. The guy who has to get sky high to avoid dealing with his real life. Like this severe cash flow issue it looks like I'll have to solve myself.

I try to remember Ty: his smile, his laugh, and presence that demanded respect and exuded power. What would he do?

"You are earth," He breathed so many times in my ear when our bodies joined as one. "Give me life. Love you, Nora."

"Love me..." The words escaped me before I could stop them.

I stood up, taking in several gulps of air to recompose and assess. Earth is strong. She is strength and she gives life. Memories of the hurricane in '08 that took the lives of some of my relatives in New Orleans came to mind. Earth is strong. She is strength, and she gives life.

But she can also take it away.

I had to lean into the power Ty saw in me, even if I don't see it myself. A plan formed in my mind during the short walk to the motel Mama worked at.

"She's didn't come in today." One of the maids with limited English skills answered when I asked the whereabouts of my mother.

I checked the time on my phone again, sure this was around the time she'd be on shift.

"Are you sure?" I asked the short Hispanic lady.

She looked troubled when she answered, "She's not here. Corbin is out as well."

She added that last part when she saw me head towards the building where his office was. This was super strange, considering Mama worked a full shift on the weekends. It was Saturday, and she'd be expecting me at this time to swing by and walk her home.

My brain is still wracking itself on the trek back home. Maybe she went to the grocery store, I surmised as I stared in to the empty fridge. I recalled her mentioning how she wanted to fry some catfish tonight. My mouth watered at the thought of something homemade, warm, and overall soul fulfilling. Her cooking was nothing like Mom's, who pretty much catered every meal since I'd lived under their roof. The one time she cooked me something was when she burned my grilled cheese so bad the fire marshals had to be called. She learned the hard way that day to never leave cheese sandwiches on an open grill. For an hour. Unattended.

My uncle worries so much about Mom all the time, even more so since her spinal cord injury, but since then he forbade her from cooking anything.

I'm still laughing from the memory as I walk through the house. If I didn't hear from Mama in an hour then I resolved to calling the police. I didn't want to entertain the idea of her hurt or in trouble, but I couldn't be too sure. I was full blown in a gang, and indebted to some seriously bad people who literally wanted to kidnap me at all costs. So precaution never hurt.

Though normally off-limits, I decided to check her room. I'm now in my pajamas and have already scarfed down a PB&J, but I needed to cover all my bases to find her even if she was only out shopping for food.

Her room was across from mine, so I figured I'd just pop in to check it.

But I didn't make it past the threshold. A man, half naked and zipping up his corny leather pants walks out with his head turned. He's laughing at something I can't hear.

"Amora, woman." He says, winded. "You sure do know how to put a smile on a man's face. Meeting up at your house is a decent change of pace from that dank ass motel."

Then I heard her. The woman who gave herself to God mere months ago when she let me live with her. The woman who stayed on me about being safe and protecting my heart where it pertained to guys. And she was doing this?

"You make my job easy." She says demurely and in a tone I'd never heard before.

"Keep that cookie reserved for me, and I'll make sure them bills stay paid. You hear me?"

"Loud and clear." She sang from inside her room. "See you tomorrow?"

"Long as I'm alive to see it, damn sure will." He proclaimed while turning around.

"Mama!" I hollered when he met my eyes.

"Oh, shit." He barked, partly from shock and partly from fear. "Mora I thought you said your daughter was spending the day at her friend's house or something?"

Mama ran to her bedroom door, barely looking at me as she began to shove the man I hated towards the front door.

"Shit, baby, no need to be so aggressive, I'm leavin'." He barked.

"Out!" She sneered before her final shove pushed him out the house. His clothes followed.

"Please tell me that wasn't who I thought it was?" I whispered in horror as I inched into the living room. Her back was to me.

"Cleo," she says in a voice so small I barely heard it, "I can explain."

I don't say anything, because...well. What could I say?
She wraps arms around her thin body, and her cheap satin robe looks so large on her at that moment. She's shaking, I note from where I'm standing, but I try to listen as explains herself.

"It-It started as a one-time thing," she started again. "The bills were getting to be too much, and those itty bitty checks weren't nearly enough to show Ferrum I could take care of you. H-He keeps trying to take you away from me. I just got you back, and I'm tryin so hard to stay the straight and narrow but–"

I don't let her finish. Instead, I'm bolting towards Mama to wrap my arms around her. I feel it. All of her shame and anger and utter humiliation at what just happened. I can't judge her because she is me, I realize, and do my best to anchor her to me as she trembles in my arms.

"Thank you, Cleo." She breathes. "Thank you for understanding your Mama. And not being disappointed in me."

"I can't be." I tell her once she's turned to face me. "Mama, I don't fully understand why you're doing this with Cornball Corbin, but I want to. Let's...talk. Okay?"

She frowns. "Talk?"

"Yeah." I respond quickly. "There's a few things we need to work out, and it looks like you could use some girl talk. Am I right?"

13

seventh hour

•❤•❤•❤•❤•❤•

"Y'all got roaches?" Pop blurted shortly after opening the door to his mega mansion and allowing us inside. Though 'allowing' isn't exactly the word I'd use to describe banging on his front door and stomping past him.

Pop's usually composed face twists into a confused sneer after I fire off the hasty explanation for Mama and I's sudden appearance at the Albert house. In truth, the house isn't really a mansion, more like a huge two-story craftsman with way more bedrooms than they needed since I moved out.

"Yep," I answered, trying to ignore the rapid beating of my heart when I sat on the living room couch. Both Mama and Pop join me soon after. "Huge ones. All over the place. Which is why we can't live there."

"At least for right now." Mama interjected, her flushed cheeks denoting the same nervousness that made my heart race. She sat beside me. "This will only be a temporary solution to this very fixable problem. Right Cleo?"

Her question was aimed at me, though it's something else she's asking. Meeting her gaze, I nod. "Yes."

Before I allow my mind time to wander back to the hastily concocted plan and conversation from earlier tonight, I
blink in surprise from Pop snapping his fingers in my face.

"Earth to Cleo!" He harrumphs in a hard voice not befitting
his silk robe and bunny slipper attire. "Y'all telling me the
reason you're standing at my front door in the middle of the
night is because of a roach infestation?"

I suppressed the instinct to shrink into myself like usual
when he berated me. Recalling what Mama told me earlier,
and the secrets I shared with her, and my mind was made. I
couldn't shrink back and wither away like I wanted if it meant
our plan would fail. After all, it took a lot of pride on Mama's
part to even set foot on her big brother's land like this again.
He was the reason for so much of our pain and misfortune.
He was the one who robbed a young girl of her only child
and forced her out of her life at infancy.

***

"I don't want you hating your uncle." Mama said to me after
kicking Cornball Corbin out the house. We sat on the living
room sofa and she'd just finished crying when she broached
the subject of Uncle Ferr, or Pop. "He's a man of God, and
is doing his best for our family. I know I told you about our
history, but that's all it is. Ours. Not yours. So, please don't
hate him for what he did in the past."

I shook my head at that. At all of that. "Don't you hear yourself? Covering up for a Jesus-fanatic narcissist who throws
the Good Book at you to justify his shitty behavior? Y'all's

history is my history, too. Period. Ain't I a part of your story he keeps trying to rewrite?"

"I..." She sighed, conflicted. "I am trying so hard to forgive. You need to, too."

I sucked my teeth at that, the conversation sort of aggravating the hell out of me. "All due respect Mama, but I'm almost eighteen years old. I decide what I need."

"Ouch, Cleo." She grimaced, and then the guilt came after her next words. "I get it. I wasn't there the way you needed me to be growing up."

Damn it Cleo, I inwardly scold before turning to fully face my saddened mother. "Mama–"

"Wait." She cut me off with a raise of her hand. "I want to make this plain and clear. You don't need to forgive anyone, and neither do I. You're right. I could choose to sit here, bitter as hell towards my big brother for the things he did to me. But that ain't what's in my heart. Not anymore. I don't hate him now that I understand it for what it is. The long and short of things is he took you in when I had nobody else in the world to rely on. Do I like the way he did it? No. But I sure do respect a man who took in a child his wife didn't give birth to to make sure she grew up nothing like me."

"Mama," I said in a small voice, hating the anguish in hers. "I do want to be like you. I am you."

She smiles. "No, baby. You're not me. I grew up hungry. And I thank God you never had to experience what going to sleep without a meal is like. Ferrum kept you safe, so for that..."

"I get it," I said, pulling her into my arms. "And I'm sorry for talking about him like I did. Makes me sound like a spoiled little girl."

"I'd rather you that, than living the way I had to." Suddenly, a haunted look passes her face as she pulls back. "That wasn't living. That was survival."

I wanted her to know that, though I did grow up with so much more opportunities ever afforded to her, I still respected her. Though I walked in on her doing the very thing Pop's threatened to rescind her custodial rights over, I still loved her. I realized at that moment that I didn't hate my uncle. But I despised everything that threatened to cut my time with my mother short: Uncle Ferr, cancer, Edgar— all of it was enough to get my blood boiling and adrenaline pumping for the right reasons: fuel. I'd use this new resolve to keep my mother with me for as long as possible and all costs. Which made me have to ask.

"Are you and Corbin...together?" I asked.

She stared at me for so long in silence that I feared she wouldn't answer. "No."

"Okay," I answered. "So, was that just a friendly visit or..."

"I don't work at the motel!" She blurted out. "There it is. God's honest truth. And I don't wanna talk about any of it beyond this."

"Hold up." I stood up, outraged by the news. "He fired you?!"

"Not...exactly. No. But I don't want to talk about it."

"How can he even do that? Is it legal? Was it because of your diagnosis?"

"Cleo!" She yelled, a piteous look on her face. "That's enough."

I sat back down. "Aren't we girl chatting?"

"This isn't just girl chatting, Cleo. This is my life."

"And I wanna hear about it. Please, Mama. I promise I won't judge."

"No."

"Mama." My voice broke with the word. "Please. There's something I need to talk to you about, and it's big. But I want to be there for you. I want to open up to you about this, but...I just need to know you'll understand. And won't hate me."

She cupped my cheek then, concern growing on her beautiful brown face. "Never."

A few minutes of silence stretched between us, willing me to get my breathing together. The plan was– is–simple: honesty. I couldn't rely on Norina Skye to get me through this interaction, or the strength from Ty's encouraging words.

Because in reality is where I lived, and where my first love was taken from.

"All right." I said, punctuating the words with a stiffening of my back as I turned to face her again. "We need to leave."

It took a moment for the shock to register on Mama's face, but when it did, she reared her neck back as if I'd slapped her. "Say what, now?"

I sighed. "I...um...I'm in the service industry."

"Of course you are. Working at Nita's isn't exactly labor intensive, but it sure is a service"

I pinched the bridge of my nose in irritation. How was I going to get through this? Far as Aunt Laurel knew, the extracurricular activity taking place every other day was softball, umpired by an overambitious coach who kept me late nights for practice. I couldn't tell them the truth. That Juanita's salon was the only true place, besides being with Mama, where I was truly myself. My parents despised the "culture" of hair salons, but I knew that shit was code for "we don't want Nita's blackness to rub off on you, just in case you catch a case of going down the wrong path."

Nita was hood. Nita was real. And I always appreciated her for pushing me like nobody else did. So it was time to be real with Mama, so I could allow her inside.

"Not that kind of service." I started. "It's in the men-servicing industry. The pleasure one."

Her jaw fell slack, and there was the horror I expected to well into her eyes. Silent tears are coursing down her face before she cups her hands over her mouth. To my surprise though, she releases a scream so agonizing it makes me tear up too. So I just sit there staring at her, not sure what to do to make the fraction of my truth more digestible for her.

"I'm sorry." I whispered as she began to pace the room. "I told you I understood you–"

"No!" She hollered, jabbing a furious finger at me. "You don't get to relate to this. You don't get to use this as some sort of teachable moment. You. Are. Not. Me!"

I open my mouth to explain, but she's pacing so fast and mumbling stuff I can't understand that it doesn't allow me to get a word in.

"This isn't great news, I know." I said.

She laughs mirthlessly. "Cleo, what do you want me to say to that, huh? I missed out on so much of your life, that maybe I'm doing this whole 'raising you' all wrong. But tell me how I should respond to my teenage daughter who just admitted to me that she's sleeping with men for money. Hmm?!"

"Let me explain!"

"You've done enough of that, child!" She yelled in my face as I stood up. "We need to pray now."

"No!" I fume. "Let me finish! I don't sleep with men for money. It's just phone sex, I swear! And occasionally I do cam shows, but that's all. I swear to–"

"Don't!" She hollered, tears streaming down her face. I'm shaken as she takes my shoulders in her hands and squeezes with a manic ferocity. That look in her eyes...it isn't her. "Don't take the Lord's name in vain. Don't you dare do it. We'll work this out."

"There's nothing to work out, Mama." I whimpered. "I'm sorry for lying. But please believe me when I say I understand you."

Without warning, she sinks to the floor in a pitiful puddle of robe and legs. I fall down with her, fear making my heart race when her eyes roll in her head and color drains from her face.

"Mama?" I shook her, and for a minute her eyes were completely closed as the sobs wracked her body. "Mama!"

"I'm okay." She breathed. "I'm fine. And I'm sorry. I get dizzy sometimes since the doctor doubled my dose."

I hugged the shit out of her, terrified from the other truths that threatened the time I got with Mama.

"It's okay. I'm here." I said.

She nods. "This disease took so much out of me I couldn't go to work anymore. That motel was too much strain on me to entertain making any money there. And I know you think

Corbin is mean, but he isn't. I promise. He had to let me go when Glenda found me passed out in one of the rooms I was cleaning. She reported it to Corbin, and voila. Job gone."

"Passed out, as in, you fell asleep while cleaning?" I asked, afraid of the actual truth she was hinting.

She smiled limpidly. "Sort of."

"You fainted, didn't you?" I asked, and the guilty way she averted her eyes was proof enough I'd been right. I re-arranged her in my arms. "Mama, when did this happen?"

She shrugged. "Maybe six or seven months ago. That's the first time the doc upped my dose. And yeah, I get a little dizzy sometimes. But it reduces the hospital runs. So, I deal with it. However..."

"Yeah?"

"It lost me my job. And since Ferr would use that as lever-age to take you away from me, then..."

I nodded, more truth dawning on me from what she didn't give voice. And my gut wrenched at how long she admitted to literally suffering in silence just to keep me.

"All of that pain..." I said. "All of that suffering...why do it? I thought your health was on the up-and-up. Why do this?"

She cupped a hand to my cheek again, and the warmth spread from her touch into me. If my mother's love was a living thing, capable of sprouting arms and legs, then I'd attribute it for lifting me up weightlessly through the air. She didn't need to say it for me to get it. Because I felt it for her, too.

"I asked Corbin if we could set up this...arrangement. He's been lonely since his wife died and I think this offers comfort, in a way. He has every opportunity to rat me out to your uncle, being he's one of his old homeboys from before. But he doesn't, and I'm grateful. It's just...you weren't supposed to be home so early."

Now she squeezes me, but I feel the truth rush out of me like a bitter sneeze. "Mama, we need to get out of here. Tonight."

"Why is that?"

"One of my...clients. He's out to get me, and I don't know how he got my information, but he did. And he's coming to take me away if we don't get somewhere safe for a little bit."

"Calm down, sweetie." She said, holding me again. "Now who is this man and what do you need me to do?"

***

And that's how we ended up on my adoptive parents' doorstep three hours later. We came up with a story that seemed reasonable enough to get Pop to believe us. Or at least that's what I hoped, banking on his serious fear of most things that crawl.

"Yes," I said, answering his question about if we really had roaches or not. "Lots of them. And they've become a problem."

"All right, then..." He said, his wrinkled face wrinkling some more as he stood there with his hands on his hips. "We'll figure this out. Mora, did you call the landlord last week like I told you to after the rat situation?"

"Wait, what?" I asked them both.

Mama cleared her throat before speaking. "Not exactly, no. And that was an isolated incident I thought we agreed to keep private ."

"Yeah, well." He said. "That's all fucked now, ain't it? Why didn't you call him like I told you to? Even though that vermin was on the sidewalk, it still could get in the house. Now you're telling me you been letting roaches roam free where my child lays her head?"

"Ferrum, wait—"

"Didn't I warn you in the beginning that if even a single ounce of harm comes to my daughter because of you, that you'd be sued six ways to Sunday?"

Mama, who'd always been so strong and proud, was now crumbling at her big brother's feet. Pleading to him like he's been her God, instead of the monstrous older sibling who weaponized The Word against her.

"Ferr, listen to me–"

He kicked his legs free from her arms as I stared at the scene with horror. What the...

"I had a real long ass day with the Kersey's planning funeral arrangements. This is not the day to fuck with me. You had one chance to get this right. One!" He roared 'one' in Mama's face, making me flinch. Pop's eyes were dark red as he continued his tirade. "I'm heading over to the house right now. And if that house is in any sort of squalor, then Cleo will be moving back home. With her real parents. Tonight and for good. You hear me?"

Mama's sobbing uncontrollably now, and my body is literally frozen at the spot as I tried to reconcile the horrible plan for what it was. This backfired. I mean, really really backfired in both our faces, and now my uncle was practically promising to rescind custody.

"I'm sorry!" Mama cries before slapping her hands together. "Don't take her from me again...I couldn't take it. I don't know what I'll do if you take my baby away again!"

He knelt low to whisper, "Then you talk to God. Pray to Him for forgiveness."

"I have!"

"Right now!" He screamed. "Tell him how fucking selfish you are to come crawling back over here. Begging me to take you in because you couldn't provide for your daughter. This is the same story as seventeen years ago, on replay."

"F-Father God, hear my cry. Forgive me for my sins, Lord…" Mama's mumbling a rushed, watery version of her usual prayer at his feet as I observe the scene in mute terror.

I'd never seen my uncle this way. Ever the easygoing sit-com dad, he hadn't even so much as cursed in front of me. I found myself holding back giggles whenever I eavesdropped on him idly rapping to a lewd True N' Fresh song, prudishly muting over the swear words and obscene descriptors for an attractive woman. But this…that look in his eyes…was no laughing matter. He looked straight up feral. Like a rabid animal set to sink its teeth into its prey. And that prey was my mother, on the floor and pleading with Lord Ferrum to not take me away.

"I'm meeting with Howard tomorrow. We'll see what he has to say about this." He said, cold and clipped while Mama mumbled more prayers.

Oh no. There was only one Howard I could ever recall meeting. One who embodied every negative lawyer stereo-type I fought against since I was little, considering the good person I thought my attorney Mom to be.

"What the fuck is going on down here?" A voice demanded from the stairwell. Looking up and unfreezing, I see who it is.

It's my auntie Laurel, or Mom, rolling into the room in her wheelchair and a satin bonnet on her head.

She looks on at the scene in a similar way that I did. In total shock. "Amora? Cleo? What are y'all doing here so late?"

Pop ran an aggrieved hand over his wrinkled face. "Mora saying our girl's living in less than favorable conditions." He said.

Mom's eyes widened at the news before she looked at Mama. "Explain this."

There was that look again, I noted inwardly. Mama's usually straightened shoulders are now slumped over as her eyes hit the floor. Her shame and fear a tangible thing biting into the atmosphere.

"It's not what you think." She whispered.

"Well all we know right now is that our daughter, who we entrusted in your care, is living in filth. How do you suggest we think? Or act?" Mom fired off at her after Pop explained our hastily concocted lie for being here.

I hated that Mama was taking the heat for this.
As if unfreezing, I jumped to my feet and ran towards her, grabbing onto her shoulder when I finally stopped in front of her chair.

"Auntie," I started breathlessly, "it's the neighbors. They're the reason why all those rats end up in our yard."

"You expect me to believe she hasn't coached you on what to say to us?" Auntie asks coldly with a pointed look at my mother.

Though she's sitting in a wheelchair, she always held this air about her that made her seem to look down on those she addressed from some high perch.

"I don't know what you expect." Mama said, clearing her throat as she found her voice. "But that's not important right now. The important thing is that we need a place to live for right now. Let us crash here, we'll be out of your hair in a week."

"Plead your fucking case then, Amora!" Auntie bit out. "In court, a defendant doesn't just ask nicely for the outcome they want. No. There's a narrative. Some evidential proof behind why the judge should even consider passing judgment on those claims. So plead your case."

"I just did." Mama said, her voice wavering but otherwise firming up.

I scrub my face, totally exhausted from these unexpected versions of events today. All my aching body demanded at this moment was a hot shower and a resolution to this nonsense. I hated Mama taking the heat for the last minute plan we agreed on for our escape until I sorted this Edgar mess out. Lay low in Auntie and Uncle's for about a week under the false report of roach sightings in our pristine home. Mama always took pride in our clean home, which Pop should know since he made it a point to visit as often as he could to inspect it. But this encounter proved so much, essentially how little my uncle needed as just cause to file for custody again. Even an obvious lie.

So much about my origin story was beginning to unfurl and rewrite itself from the fantasy sold to me years ago.

The air changed in a way, considering the long silence falling into the room. We're all still for a few more seconds when Mama visibly straightens to face her wedded oppressors.

She looks at Pop first.

"How dare you sit up there and speak to me like I'm some sorry chick you just met? Really, Ferr, do you hear how she's talking to me? See how she looks at me like I laid with the devil himself when you aren't around? God damnit I am a person! A real, live, living person who makes mistakes and even fails more times than she can win. And for all the wrong I've done in my life, just know I'm paying for it. But nobody deserves to get treated like you do me. Your little sister?!"

Pop opens his mouth to sputter when Mama points dangerously at him.

"Don't feed me anymore of your religious bigotry candy coated in Holy lies! You're dead wrong. And you know it. Attorney Howard Stapleton. Tuh! Shame on you for even breathing that awful man's name into the air."

I hold my breath as my mind draws the image of the grubby lawyer Mama mentioned. The same one who spearheaded my removal from her care even years ago.

Pop hung his head low while Mama turned her frigid glare at Auntie Laurel.

"And you." Mama started, walking slowly towards the wheelchair-bound older woman. "Always taking so much pride in your athletic, honor-rolled daughter. Do you even talk to her?"

"Of course!" Auntie spat. "We talk all the time. I did raise her, after all."

"That you did." Mama said with a dry chuckle. "And after sixteen years of raising that child under your own roof you know nothing about who she really is. I mean, come on, softball? Does that even sound like something Cleo would be remotely interested in?"

"Our daughter is a little confused right now is all—"

"Did you even know about Tyrone?" Mama demanded, making my heart drop by her mentioning his name.

"Mama!" I called, panicked. "Wait!"

"Cleo's boyfriend was the sweetest soul to ever grace our lives. Always came by with a smile. Always willing to spend time with her and not afraid to put in some chores when my joint pain got real bad. He was the best thing for her, and he loved her."

"Mama..." I pleaded. "Please don't say it."

My heart was shattering again. Making me relive all those painful memories of Ty. Of our first real date, where he told me he'd gotten a job at a pizza shop. He showed up at my front door with a car that obviously didn't belong to him and proceeded to take me to one of the fanciest restaurants I'd ever been to. Maggio's, the romantic Italian eatery, was called, and he confessed that night that he loved me and wanted to be with me for real, instead of Sasha. I was his first choice. ME! But then the next day came. And from the combination of events told by the news and by Devin Cooper, who'd been there to rush him to the hospital, he'd went to collect the car he'd borrowed from Devin the evening he got shot.

"That poor boy was gunned down like a dog." Mama said my true horrors out loud. "He was killed! And where were you both when this happened? When her pain got so bad that she couldn't eat or go to school? I stayed up all those nights with her when she...when she begged to die right with him. I was there. Not any of you when she really needed it."

"Cleo, is that true?" Pop asked numbly.

All I could do was hang my head, so ashamed now that it was all out in the open. Afraid of the inevitable: them kicking us out when we needed it most and disowning me for good like I always feared. Too scared to say anything, I braced myself for the worst.

"Evidential proof you want?" Mama hollered, white knuckling the arms of Auntie's chair so tight I was scared she push her over.

But before I get the chance to intervene, Mama stands back, and with one sharp tug, rips the loose t-shirt off her thin chest. Her naked breasts and stomach are exposed, drawing loud gasps from us all.

"Amora, what the hell?!" Auntie shrieks while shielding her eyes.

"This is your evidence!" Mama yells while pointing to the deep stretch marks whelped all over her belly. There's also a long scar I'd never seen before lining her underbelly from the left to the right side of her pelvis. "Twelve hours I labored in agony trying to push my baby girl out of me. But she wouldn't come. An emergency C-section was what it took to get her here safely. I was in that room all alone! No parents. Not even her father was by my side when they told me the cord was wrapped around her neck and choking the life out of her. So look at these scars, Laurel! Look at them!"

Mama forced Auntie's hands to lay at her sides.
"These scars are my proof. They are my truth. I am her mother. Her only mother, and you will respect me. I'm not that same strung out little girl anymore and I understand– and appreciate– your concerns for Cleo. I been clean for eight years. Eight! Doesn't that account for something? We're not back in that hospital room and God's been putting on my heart to forgive."

"I know my daughter." Auntie Laurel mumbles in a shaky breath. "She'd never hide anything from us."

I take a steadying breath before rising from the couch I'd not recalled sitting in mid Mama's speech. It was time to be honest, I told myself. No more lies and hurt. It had to stop with us. And now.

"Mama's right." I start. "You don't really know me."

"Nonsense!" Pop blurted out.

"No, seriously. I've never went to Softball practice a day in my life, nor am I on any team for it. I have a friend on the team who clues me in after all the games so that I know exactly what to tell you both."

"That's not right..." If I had to describe the raw emotion on Auntie Laurel's face, then it had to be hurt.

Pure pain from the lies I just confirmed.
I took a step in her direction as I spoke.
"It is right. Trice doesn't tutor me anymore since I don't know where she is. She left town and even her own parents are being shady about the details. In fact, her being gone has stressed me out so bad I haven't even had time to work."

"You have a job." Auntie Laurel tacked on. Her voice not even asking, but a dry statement she'd provided in expectation of the worst.

"Of course she does!" Mama answered for me. "You see what I'm saying? Y'all looked after my child, but don't even know her. Look at that beautiful face. She's wearing a full face of makeup, and you know who did it? She did! She's got real talent that me and her cousin see could take her somewhere. I thank Juanita for giving our girl a chance to be herself and develop her skills."

I smiled at Mama, so thankful she got me. I never even opened up to her about how beautician work made me truly feel, but of course she knew. Mama knew me and that's what made us tight. I never needed to hide things from her, at least not until recently.

"Thank you, Mama." I said with a totally warm heart.

"No thanks required." She beamed. "Because I pay attention. I know my baby inside and out. Do y'all?"

Both Auntie and Pop shared guilty glances that served as an answer enough to that question.

Mama sighed. And before I knew it, came to stand beside me at the center of the room.

"I'd prefer it if we had this conversation in private, but I guess now's a better time than any. Speaking of Nita..."

"Yeah?" I asked, gulping hard from fear.

Mama took another breath. "She called to tell me she's closing down shop. At least in D.C."

It took several seconds for her words to register, but when they did, a shocked "what?!" escaped my lips before the tears fell.

"I know you're upset! But the new building owner made her an offer she couldn't refuse. While she's closing operations in this town, she plans to reopen a new shop down south. She called to ask my permission to take you with her. To live and work as an official apprentice after you graduate. I told her it was your decision since you'll be eighteen soon, but...I think it's a good opportunity. Baby this is the break you need! Especially after all of this."

My head spun from the bumrush of information. I sort
of figured she'd fire me soon since I hadn't shown up to the
shop in a while since Trice left. My troubled brain put two
and two together real quick:

Nita was closing down shop and reopening down south.
And she wanted me to come with her. To live and learn in
a new town where there was no drama. No Luther. And no
more lying to my pseudo parents for their acceptance.

I looked at all the hope shining in my mother's eyes.

"Is this for real?"

She nodded before hugging me tight to her chest. "It's real.
But only if you want it to be."

"Only if I want I want it to be..." I breathed in disbelief. "I..."

"No!" Auntie roared from her side of the room. "You aren't
going to live with that hood rat ass cousin of yours anywhere!
She's got civil fines, child support cases, and a record! We
won't let you go anywhere with her!"

"Stop it, Mom!" I screamed at her. "Can't you see living
here was killing me? That every second I'm around you both
it makes me feel so unworthy and uncomfortable. You want a
mathlete honor student for a daughter, and that's never been
me. And I'm sorry I'll never live up to those expectations. But
I'm me! What's wrong with me?"

Tears rolled down Auntie's eyes at my words, but I kept
going.

"What's wrong with me?" I repeated/blubbered to her.

"Nothing, baby!"

"Then why can't you accept me the way I am?"
Out of nowhere, Pop fell to the floor. But not because he collapsed. My eyes gape in shock as I study the six foot surly pastor on his hands and knees the same way Mama was, breathing laboriously and crawling over to me. He stopped at my feet and balled his hands tight.

"Pop?" I probed carefully.

"Cleo'Nora June." He mumbled, flashing shining, blood-shot eyes at me. "Forgive us."

"What?" Everyone in the room asked in sync.

"You...you believe we don't...love you? That you're unworthy? I...my God, we did you so wrong. That's not it at all."

"Oh, Ferr." Mama breathed sadly as she watched him below.

"We did you wrong, too." He added as their eyes met. "I shouldn't have taken Cleo from you that way. Or make your life hell when you did your best with the limited resources you had to get her back. I'm your big brother, and what would Mama say to me if she survived that car accident? What would our father call the man I turned into? Better yet, what would God say?"

"You're the Pastor, Ferrum." Mama whispered. "Don't you talk to God?"

He shrugged piteously. "Sure. But just because he talk
don't mean I'm always in a place to receive His word. Like
right now. This ain't the way. Us, screaming at each other
ain't the way."

"Baby– " Auntie cut in, but Pop raised a hand to silence her.

"No more, Laurel." He said. "We can't keep covering this
up. Our girl is hurting…and we did that. So, it's only fair we
make right some of our wrongs tonight. We got some news
a few hours ago that we originally thought to keep from you.
But no…this is what's right."

"Are you sure this is the time?" Auntie asked her husband
softly while wheeling further into the room.

She sat beside him now as he remained hunched on the
floor, stroking his back in wayward concern.

"The time is now." He confirmed. "Ladies, please have a
seat. There's something you should know."

It's not the disownment I expected or the firm throw out
I thought was imminent that comes. Instead, Pop wipes his
eyes before looking at us with a pensive, guilty expression
that wasn't there before. He looks wrung out, but from something that's happened long before us showing up to their
front doors. And I was right.
"We got a call this morning from Monroe." He said.

Mama frowned. "Monroe? As in, Money Row your old
manager?"

"Yes." Auntie finished deferentially. "He called to inform us of a terrible crime that happened last week."

"What terrible crime?" Mama asked suspiciously while holding on to me. We've already sat on the couch but I fought the urge to spring up and shake the information out of them.

"Mora." Pop says while staring my mother dead in the eyes. "Stan is dead."

A long silence stretches between them, charging the air and making Mama's gasps that much more distinct.

"D-Dead?" She squeaks, fanning herself. "Stan? You're lying."

"I'm not." He mutters, another agonized wave of tears coursing down his otherwise grim face. "Monroe wouldn't have lied about that. He knows to only contact me where only serious legal matters arise regarding the old business. This is one of those matters."

I frowned, trying to piece together how any of this random information was relevant or even the slightest bit related to me. That name rings a vague familiarity, but other than that, I was the only bewildered party in the room.

Or maybe I wasn't. Considering Mama's shocked chuckling.

"You've got it all wrong." She laughed. "Stan isn't dead. Maybe Money lied to you."

"He didn't!" Pop snapped. "He wouldn't. And that explains why he hadn't accepted any of my calls or responded to the letters I sent...."

"Letters?" I ask, but then it dawns on me as they continue talking about 'the old business,' and 'Money-Row.' "Are you talking about True N' Fresh stuff?"

"Yes." He answered, voice hollow. "And I knew you'd want proof, so here." He tells my mother, handing her his phone. There's a webpage from a local news site pulled up, where the confirmation of my questions were answered in big bold letterhead across the top page:

FORMER RAP STAR FOUND DEAD BEHIND NY NIGHTCLUB.

I briefly skim the first paragraph where the reporter writes about the random act of gun violence that claimed the life of Stanley True, the other half of the Baltimore rap duo formed with Ferrum Albert. The article continued to describe the grisly scene and how funeral arrangements were ongoing for the former True N' Fresh rap star.

"The funeral will be privately held at his family's estate in Baltimore." Pop said slowly. "And I thought you should hear it from me, Mora. I am so sorry."

Mama's cradling the phone to her chest now and rocking back and forth. She releases an anguished cry so wrought with pain that it makes me stumble back. Stanley True was one of Pop's best friends as they grew up in the same Baltimore projects together. They gained small town fame before signing to KrewTown records and blowing up back in the day and officially becoming True N' Fresh.

"I'm sorry you lost your friend, Pop." I said, meaning it.

"He was more like a brother to me, and I let him down. I don't deserve any of the blessings that came my way since what I did to him...."

"What happened?" I asked, trying my best to console my wailing mother.

"STANLEY!!!!" Mama cried before wrapping her arms around me. "Cleo, I'm sorry. So so so sorry!"

"Mama...?"

"I thought there'd be more time!" She groaned in my ear. "Thought I'd go first...not him. He loved you so much."

"What? Who?" I asked. "None of this makes sense! I'm sorry for your loss, but why is it such a big deal?"

More sobs and wailing before Pop clears his throat and says, "Stanley True is your biological father, Cleo."

14

unsung hero

·❤·❤·❤·❤·❤·

Turns out I attend a funeral after all, but it isn't the one I promised Chicken Girl. Three days have passed and Mama and I are sitting inside Pop's black SUV alone and nestled together in the back seat. We're both trembling as we hold onto each other and pretend to ignore the ongoing funeral procession of my biological father, Stanley True.

"I don't think I can do this," Mama whispers brokenly with a hand muffling her mouth.

I take a deep breath because, really, that's all I can do to gain some composure in this situation. Though the countdown ended, Edgar never showed nor were there any looming dangers to watch for around the corners. In fact, I even manage to get some work done, including reconnecting with my cousin Nita to have the much needed discussion about my employment at the salon. It was an emotional conversation, and my eyes misted as I recalled the raw emotion in her voice when she described how it felt to lock the doors for the final time since selling the building.

"Hate that you're not coming with me girl." She sniffled after I declined the beauty apprenticeship she'd offered through Mama. "But know you always have a place to come back to if anything ever happens. I'll keep a chair open for you should you ever decide to move to South Carolina. Got some good beauty schools down there too."

"Thanks girl," I said teary-eyed while drawing her in for a hug. "And I'll remember that. But I need to take care of Mama while she fights this disease. You understand."

"Course I do." She replied. "You know I do. This sickle cell runs heavy in our family. Daddy suffered so much towards the end with the joint pain. Auntie Mora will stay in my prayers."

"Thank you."

"And so will you." She insisted while holding me tight. "Taking care of your mom while finishing high school will be a lot. So try to look out for your mental, okay?"

I nodded. "I will. I promise."

But my promise had been a lie. How could I look out for my mental when Mama's was so fragile? Especially as we sat hidden inside the car and pretending the entire funeral party didn't even exist.

"We don't have to get out the car if you're not ready." I tell her, forcing the calm in my voice though I'm really stressed enough to scream.

"It wasn't supposed to be like this!" She hissed while collapsing into more sobs. Her black bodycon dress and feathered hat concealing her in the dark corner. I stroked her arm.

"We can leave if you want." I say in a small voice, silently pleading with her to take the bait.

Stanley True, of True N' Fresh, was my biological father. Even thinking the words made my head spin. The fact that everyone lied to me during my childhood should have been enough to make me incensed, but all I feel when I look towards the funeral party with Auntie and Uncle mixed in is abject exhaustion. I'm one thousand percent tired by all of this. I one million percent wished to be back in the shop as if these last three weeks haven't happened.

But much to my chagrin, my mother shakes her head.

"He is your father." She said, her voice more resolute than ten minutes ago. "And it was always my purpose to have the two of you meet. Especially since I got the diagnosis. It gave me so much peace to know that you'd have him after I left this earth. But now..."

"Stop talking like that!" I bark, pissed now that she kept speaking on her own demise like it was a guaranteed thing instead of a prognosis. "You aren't going anywhere."

"I might." She whispers, her head in her hands. "And even the prospect of leaving you here alone makes me regret so much. Makes me regret choosing the party life over securing a better life for you. Over making choices that led you away from God and ending up more like me than ever. Oh God, what have I done?"

I was full blown shaking her now.

"You did nothing wrong, Ma!" I exclaimed with hot tears in my eyes. "I am fine. We are fine!"

"You say that, but..."

"But what?" I asked.

"What about your dreams?"

I frown at her. So completely confounded by the pivot in the conversation. What did her dying have anything to do with my dreams? What did they matter anyway when she was in this condition and there was a possibility that my stupidity may have put her in harm's way?

"My dream is to be a good daughter. Make sure you're healthy and happy." I say forthright.

That seemed to aggravate her more.

"No!" She hollers. "I am your mother, damn it! I should be saying that to you. I should be supporting you so that you can become the best god damn beautician this world has ever seen. Instead you're deciding to give it all up for me. I let your daddy down by keeping him away from you all these years. And now he's gone. I refuse to hold you back like I did with the first love of my life."

"You aren't."

"Go to South Carolina." She demanded with a watery voice.

"I'm staying."

"Get out of here!" She screamed so loud in my face that my ears rang.

Without warning, she reached out to push me. It took me all of a few seconds to realize she's been trying to push me out of the car. I slapped her hand away before she could push the handle and roll me out of there. We're full blown fighting at this point. Fists flying, wig snatching, and grunting ensued to rock the cramped SUV as we went at it. Glancing out the window, I notice we've caught the attention from a few of the funeral attendees, but the pastor continues to speak as if there isn't a battle happening a few feet away in the parking lot.

"I won't let you die!" I growl while on top of her. Her arms are straining with the exertion of her dwindling strength as she pushes against my shoulders. "Why do you keep letting me down?!"

Suddenly she freezes. As if my words immediately disarm her. We're both panting and I send a cautious gaze her way as I study her limp body beneath me. Her eyes take on a faraway look as the tears swell.

"Letting you down..." She repeats. "Forgive me, Cleo. I shouldn't have hit you. I shouldn't have pushed you away...should have told you sooner...fuck! I did it again."

Sobs wracked her body again and instead of calming her this time, I can't resist the words that slip past my lips.

"Tell me why you lied," I say. Hollow inside. "Tell me the real reason you weren't there and why I'm just now learning that my father wasn't some rando like I'd been told my entire life!"

She doesn't answer, but she doesn't have to. Her wounded cries mimic a dying animal more than a soul wrought human. It's like my words slice into her, but I needed the truth more than her comfort this once.

"That story about Uncle Ferr taking me away from you during the first twenty-four hours of my life is a lie...isn't it? He didn't really take me away after all did he? Tell me the truth."

"Cleo..." She sobs, attempting to cover her face with her hands but unsuccessful since they're bearing the weight of my hold on her wrists. "Let me go."

"Why am I just now finding out about Stanley True, huh?" I continue the onslaught. "Whenever you came around when I was young Uncle Ferr would get so angry. And now I see. It wasn't anger at all. He was...he was terrified of you. But why?"

She shook and fought some. "No!"

"Stop lying to me for fucking once Amora!" I seethed, not even feeling the tears from years of pent up resentment and futility and anger and ungodly lovelessness rattling my chest. My heart, breaking in two as I squeezed her wrists like a vice. "Why weren't you there?!"

"Because you ruined my fucking life, Cleo!" She yelled.

And it takes me a few seconds to put together her bitter words as I fight to restabilize above her.

"W-What?"

"It's true, all right?" She groaned. "Stan and I were doomed the moment we met. Even though Ferr warned him to stay away from me – that I was no good– that idiot still wouldn't leave me alone. I admit I used him for every dime he had to feed my addiction. When True N' Fresh were at the height of their careers and set to sign those million dollar contracts with that label...I messed it all up."

"How?"

"They were set to perform for that label. All they had to do was show up, perform for that talent scout, and seal the deal. Stan was with me that night instead of on stage. I don't really remember everything...I just remember being so high out of my mind and Stan trying to stop me from ruining my life. He ran out of money that night since he'd given it all to me the morning prior. Course I smoked that up. I told him to leave me alone. But he wouldn't give up on me. Wouldn't even leave me to destroy my own life when I tried to rob that convenience store. He let the cops arrest him, too, instead of admitting to them that I robbed him. That's the kind of love he had for me. And I fucked it all up.

"They missed the show. Lost out on the record deal and ended up taking a savage deal with a lesser known label that landed them in financial trouble. KrewTown still owns the rights to several of their songs. I ran away when I discovered I was pregnant with you. I knew you were Stan's, since he'd been the first and only man I ever been with. Stan spent so much time looking for me, but I knew just how to stay unfound. When I showed up almost a year later and heavily pregnant, I was going through withdrawal so bad..."

She pauses as more tears squeeze from her eyes.

"I gave birth to you two days later. But Ferr never stole you from me. I...I..."

"What did you do?" I demanded, on the edge losing my mind if she lied to me again. "Be real with me...for once."

She sighed morosely before saying, "Ferr and Laurel came to the hospital to visit me. But that was all. There was never any lawyers or social workers. Just me begging them both for cash after all the nurses left. The cravings were so bad since I forced myself to stay clean throughout that pregnancy. I was willing to do anything to get high one more time. So...your uncle made me a deal. He agreed to take you–to raise you–as his own since Laurel couldn't get pregnant. In exchange for me staying out of your life for good. He also agreed to keep your existence a secret from Stan even though the group disbanded after that deal gone bad. I happily took the money he offered, bought a bus pass, and lived couch to couch for the years that followed."

I blinked several times as my heart crumbled in my chest.

"You...sold me?"

"I..." she started, then nodded. "I did."

"You just gave me away? Just like that?"

"Cleo, it wasn't that easy. My body ached in your absence, baby girl. Trust me. I felt every excruciating minute we were apart."

"But you didn't stay." I mumbled, falling back into my seat even as the funeral carried on outside.

My father was dead and my mother was slowly dying to me. The woman she sold herself as was slowly withering away as did my devotion to her.

All the pieces came together at that moment. Why Pop fought so hard to keep her out of our lives. Why Mom never wanted me to acknowledge the deeply damaged woman as my mama. She wasn't jealous or threatened by our budding relationship, but merely concerned for her only daughter in the hands of the one woman who had the power to hurt her again. Mama leaving me left a hole so deep in my soul that I projected that incompleteness onto my parents who'd loved me after all. Amora Albert was the cause of my lack of my faith in people and certainly at the heart of why I clung to such toxic constants in my life.

Sure, Trice was my best friend. My Beach even. But the real, is that she totally jumped ship when I needed her the most. Left me in this small town filled with gang members who wanted my head on a good day.

And Ty, though the love of my life when he was alive, was just as unavailable. He'd never leave Sasha for me. I was always his second choice. Same as I was Mama's, since it was really drugs she chose first and foremost.

Fuck that. Fuck this. Fuck everybody.

"I need space right now." I say while scrambling off of her and unlocking the door opposite of the funeral party.

I climb out ignoring her protests for me to come back and storm off into a secluded section of the graveyard. I can almost feel Mom and Pop's worried gazes on my back as I stomp into the seclusion of a distant brush down the hill.

Without anything else to do, I hang my head in my hands and cry. I cry so hard that it feels like there's no more water left in my body. I cry until there's no more tears to cry or enough air in my body. Soon the sobs mutate into dry-heaving, and as if on cue with the vibe of my life right now the rain starts to pour in buckets. I don't have the energy to run for cover. Instead, I sit there and let the mud cover my Converses and rain soak my red quick weave. My mascara that I painstakingly applied this morning runs down my face. Making me feel truly as ugly as I felt. Mirroring what I felt inside. My entire life was a lie. My mother was the true villain even though she'd been the unsung hero I tried to protect all these years against my adoptive parents' judgment. I protected her when she never cared about me, at least not the way she should have. Mama was my hero. The one who understood me so much. Yet all I'd ever been was the thing that ruined her life.

The vibrations in my black skinny jeans let me know I've got a call coming in. I'm sort of grateful for the welcome distraction then confused as I study the familiar number on the screen.

"Nora, listen to me. You've got to get out of there!" It's Sasha, and she's screaming frantically into the phone.

I stand up. "Sasha, slow down." I say. "What are you talking about? Get out of where?"

"You're at a funeral in Baltimore, right?"

My blood chills with her frank admission. "How did you know–"

"There be no time for that!" She shouted. "Pastor Albert told the church he'd be at that funeral today and I managed to get the address from him. No time for details, but you need to be prepared for what's to come."

"For what to come? Sasha you're not making any sense right now."

"It's Luther." She hisses. "He came back for more money again and said he'd kill me if I didn't tell him where you were. Have you been ducking him?"

"Um, well. Yes." I admit, too exhausted to lie. "I have nothing to say to him right now. What does he want?"

"He wasn't right." She said. "He looked all shaken up and went crazy when I told him I didn't know where you were. He came to my mother's funeral with some white man with him."

"A white man?" I say, my mind reeling with whoever that could be. "Are you sure?"

"I'm certain!" She squeals in that accent. "I know we don't have the best relationship since Latisha and our shared history with Tyrone, but I'm scared for you. And I don't want you hurt. Not if I can avoid it. You need to get out of there. Right now."

"Sasha, I can't just leave." I lament, pacing now and looking over my shoulder. "I'm at my father's funeral."

"What?!" She screeched, and I get her up to speed on this being my biological father's funeral and not the one she'd thought. "Thank heavens" she breathed. "Me can't take no more death this day."

"Neither can I." I say, sorrow etched in my heart at the amount of dying that took place in thirty six hours. "I'm sure it's fine. He's probably just mad because I haven't checked in with him in a few days."

Nothing coking or cumming can't fix, I commiserate bitterly, feeling so sorry for my life just then.

"Nora, you're not getting it." She says deadpan. "That man he was with..."

She doesn't need to finish that sentence. Not at all, since the man in question is walking directly towards me as I watch him exit the car from the parking lot. He's parked far enough away that the funeral party wouldn't have witnessed him stalk towards me across the field and down the embankment where I was. Alone.

But there's no man with him like Sasha warns. He's totally alone and I'm completely frozen in place by his unexpected arrival.

I hang up the phone without another word and tuck it into my pocket.

"Luther." I greet him, voice shaky but my chin held high in spite of it. "What do you want?"

A slow, dark grin twists his face as he lets out a laugh.

"My girlfriend disappears on me when I send for her and I'm not allowed to be a little upset about it? I should ask you the same thing."

I scowled. "What are you talking about?"

He took a step closer to me. I took a step back.

"I'm asking you the same thing, girl. What do you want?"

"I don't understand what you're asking."

Again, he takes a large step towards me to close the gap between us, while I take a giant step backwards.

"What did I tell you about lying to me, bitch? Hiding passwords from me. Getting secret boyfriends on the side like I'm stupid enough to believe you been faithful to only me. Outside of that half Jewish motherfucker who else you been fuckin with?"

My brain fogged. Not quite comprehending what was unraveling. He came all the way to a funeral to accuse me of cheating on him? I couldn't convey the terror, so I just stood my ground and listened without confirming or denying anything. It didn't take much to provoke him. I learned that the hard way. And I fight to hold the facade as he brings up my relationship with Tyrone Zelman.

He steps forward.

"It wasn't enough that you took away the only shot at a real family I ever had, Cleo. Wasn't enough that I took you back even after creepin around with the half Jew. Now I see you been talking to some dude way up in Wisconsin through some dating app? When will the lies and destruction end with you? You burn everything you touch. I'm sorry about your mom, but you're the real cancer around here."

The scared girl, timid Cleo, melts away as I observe him through strained squinted eyes. All there is in front of me is red. Fuck this. Fuck that. Fuck everybody! I chant again. My mind slowly losing the war from holding back so much after all these years.

My fists move as agents of my will and act as a direct result of my limited capacity for bullshit. I hit him. I punched him so hard several times over. Pound after pound of flesh made my knuckles ache but brought me sweet release as I unloaded years of trauma, heartbreak, and emotions across his strong face and jaw.

After five more minutes of hitting, I realize he's not hitting me back like Mama did earlier. Not fighting me or laying me flat on my ass like I know is within his capacity to do so.

Instead he's smiling. Blood coating his white teeth but otherwise an emotionless manic glint shines in his eyes as he spits the blood from his mouth. Then looks down at me.

"Done?" He asks, his tone bordering bored.

"Fuck you." I spat, hating the limited impact of my fury on him despite the effect of his presence near me.

How he had that ability to shatter any sense of peace or safety in a matter of seconds just by existing beside me. And he wondered why I strayed?

Sure I was dating another guy online. And I looked forward to his daily texts in the mornings and nightly check-ins with me. He told me every day that he loved me, and even though I'd never gotten his real name, RichBoy02 showered me with more love than anyone in my real life. But I still wonder how Luther found out about this.

"I took that deal from that Kobayashi family." Luther says casually amidst my inner turmoil. "Took it and had some real fun. That supply he left the 590's to distribute tasted real good and disappeared real quick. It's good shit. But now it's gone and he's expecting me to pay up. And soon."

"Luther." I bite out. "You accepted that deal with the Kobayashi's...and smoked the entire supply? Do you have any idea how dead you're gonna be when that man doesn't get his money?"

A knowing look illuminated his face as he nods.

"Just like I thought." He stated. "So you're fucking him, too. Eh? That's what all this was about? That why you obeyed him like his little bitch when he told you to bow back in that restaurant?"

My mind skitters back to memories of the lethal Asian king and the heat he made me feel. Though enraged, the mere thought of the man I couldn't see heats me in ways other than anger. However, now isn't the time for that.

"Luther, you are absolutely insane." I say, holding my chin high despite the rain pouring and his proximity.

"You can't even spare me the decency to lie. Wow. And to think, when Eddie told me he wanted you I turned him down at first."

Ice trickles over my skin at what he was saying.

"You...you what?"

"Come get her." He says into the phone I didn't see him fish from his suit pocket before hanging up. "This could have been so simple had you been loyal. To me for once."

"Luther wait!"

In the distance, a white man in an expensively tailored suit descends the hill Luther did previously in getting to me. There's no spark of recognition. No indication that this rando person had any knowledge of who we are until he stops short a few feet from us. A wide grin on his face and a twinkle in his green eyes.

"Sweet Norina." He says over the loud whipping rain. "Ready to go home?"

I don't know his face, yet that voice can't be confused with anyone else. Nor that nickname uttered with an accent as southern as cornbread.

"E-Edgar?!" I gasp.

He extends his arms. "That's right baby! Come to daddy. Come give your future husband a kiss for old time's sake."

"I don't fucking know you!" I screech, backing away from both of them.

Luther speaks up. "Eddie and me worked out a little...arrangement. Since I needed cash to pay back Kobayashi and he wanted you, the deal was a no-brainer. And he so graciously provided me with full access to your cell phone records and online search history."

The frequent requests from my cell phone company to change my password due to "unforeseen hacking attempts." I couldn't believe it. It was like my life was on a vicious repeat, a broken record of the worst kind of chance. Making me realize for the second time today...

"You sold me?"

The easy grin on his face disappears into an angry snarl as he leaps in front of me. I'm frozen to the spot like the usual deer in the headlights as he grabs my neck and squeezes. Gasping for air, I fight his hold to no avail.

"Sold you?" He growls in my face. "Don't forget you gave yourself to me. You are mine. To fuck. To sell. To let live or die..."

"Mom and Pop..." I choked out. "Will see you..."

"Fuck them!" He barks. "I don't give a fuck about them no more. I don't even give a fuck about myself. But I do give a fuck about you owing me and getting what you deserve for fucking once. I ain't spare no bullets on your little half Jew boyfriend, so don't expect me to spare any on you. Fucking cunt."

The world fuzzies, and I don't have the mental capacity to sort out what he just admitted. The thing I feared. The thing I knew in my heart of hearts to be true.

"You killed..." I squeezed out. "Ty...rone."

Another slow smile before answers. "He touched what was mine. I don't like to share. Truth is I barely remember it."

"Ease up on her now Luther." Edgar cautioned behind us. "If she's damaged that's coming out of your pay."

That's what makes him release me after I nearly lose consciousness. I fall to the ground gasping for air.

"You...monster!" I rasped as I wheezed on all fours. I try to catch my breath and lose, falling on to the ground.

"Norina!" Edgar calls worriedly. I hear him standing over me as the battle for lucidity becomes harder and harder.

"You'll go with him." Luther starts. "Or Tyrone won't be the only one pushing up daisies today."

I barely have the time to think. Barely can fuse the brain power together to put rational sentences together to answer him. But a will to live like never before and protect the parents who'd I misjudged all these years rears up.

Staring into his cold eyes, I choke out a weak, "I'll go."

And the feeling of being carried hurriedly into a car and driven long down the road are my final memories as I succumb to a deep sleep.

Part Two

"You. Are. Not. Me!"

15

Sorry

•♥•♥•♥•♥•♥•

I swayed to the melodic chorus playing through my newly installed wall speakers as the music took over me. A true easterner at heart, the smooth R&B singing from the hook in Wu-Tang's *"Can It Be All So Simple,"* flowed easily past my lips while I danced with a cup in my hand. In all actuality, the cup is a wine glass filled to the brim with expensive spirits my father would appreciate had he still been a part of my life.

My heart plummeted as I danced and submerged myself in the memories. The past. I didn't like to let my mind linger there too long in fear of what those feelings might make me do. Something stupid, that's for sure, like call Pop and beg him to rescue me from this strange plantation-style mansion. Or call Mom to tell her how sorry I was for, yet again, being the burden-child in her life by up and disappearing ten months ago. Maybe even worse, hitching a ride back to our tiny blue house in DC and getting the hug I desperately needed from Mama.

No, Cleo! I admonish internally before stumbling over a sock on my bedroom floor. She isn't Mama anymore, but a lying, deceitful, manipulative bitch who literally admitted your birth ruined her life.

I wait for the hate, the white-hot fury to pulse through my veins like it did at Stanley's funeral, but...

The tears are the only things that force their way through the barrier around my heart. Falling to my knees, I chuck the expensive Cabernet Sauvignon and don't bother flinching when it shatters upon striking the wall. Red wine oozed down the solid white paint and I sort of resonated with it, being that I oozed onto the floor with an unattractive plop.

The chill lyrics reverberated like a siren's call in my ears: why couldn't everything just be simple?

I'm cradling my knees when Raekwon sings about dedicating the song to both winners and losers when a familiar voice interrupts my weekly pity party.

"Ms. Oakhouse?" The high-pitched voice of Luanne, the Oakhouse housekeeper, beckoned from the cracked door.

I didn't bother to look at her, knowing full well her apprehensive speech before she even launched into it.

"Ms. Oakhouse!"

"That's not my name!" I roared before chucking the closest object beside me at her. A sock was my weapon of choice this day, but at least she got my point. "It's Nora, or nothing at all."

"Ms. Oakhouse." She simpered while entering the room. "You made quite the mess this time. Mr. Oakhouse isn't gonna like that you've been drinking unsupervised. Again."

The added "again" resonated with much more sass than the other words preceding it. I shrugged, not needing to cast a glance at her to know she'd been busy scrubbing the wine stains with gumption.

"Maybe your precious Mr. Oakhouse shouldn't hold an underaged woman against her will into living in this ridiculous fucking house. How old is this antebellum prison anyways?" I slurred a bit, but caught the dribble running down my mouth.

"The Oakhouse Estate turned hundred years old this past year," She stated with dignity. "And under the eyes of the law, you are of legal age of consent. How can you even be an underaged woman? Them two words just don't go right."

"Whatever." I murmured, still holding myself at the knees and praying she'd just go away. "Don't you have better things to do than bother me?"

She stood in front of me now. "Not really. 'Less you want to help me steam the linens on the fourth floor?"

"Pssst." I smirked. "Screw that."

"Then getting dressed it is. Today is an important day. Remember?" She sang this while effortlessly standing me upright.

Of course, I fought it, but the six foot woman was firmly built and lifted couches as though it were part of some military training.

Luanne frequently spoke lovingly of being raised by simple parents with strict family values. The Brigitte Nielsen lookalike took every chance she could to preach about the difference between good and bad women. Or the wife's role to service and obey her man as he pleased being the basis for a strong relationship.

"I'm not going today," I groaned while slamming against the lush queen mattress.

Ghostface's verse on mad lives being up for grabs abruptly cuts off and I jerk upwards to glare at the old witch standing at the speaker controls at the wall.

"Hey!" I barked, incensed by her audacity.

"Young wives-to-be shouldn't be listening to such God-awful nonsense. Be better for you to read instead in your pastime."

I wobbled over to her to growl in her face. "Don't touch my music. Don't call me a wife-to-be."

A sympathetic frown dawns her face momentarily before she rests a hand down on my shoulder. Our height difference is hilarious, her six-foot to my five-foot, but 'ha-ha' is the furthest from my vocab right now.

"Having another bad day I see." She assesses when I smack her hands off me. "Best get yourself together before we see Madam Chelsea for lessons."

"I'm. Not. GOING!" I all but roar at her.

"You're already behind, sugar." She said casually while scooting me towards the door.

Immediately, my heart raced at the prospect of not only seeing the condescending etiquette teacher I called Wife Coach, but at leaving this room. This room, though really a guest room situated beside the service quarters downstairs, was the only place I had to myself.

Since Edgar forced me to live here ten months ago, he'd been oddly kind and attentive when I refused to come out of the bedroom for the first week here. After having lied to my parents about suddenly deciding to take Juanita's offer for apprenticeship in Greenville South Carolina, I'd been an erratic mess once Edgar's bodyguards dragged me inside this prison. And was surprised that he granted me this room he had custom built for me.

"I want you to consider this house your own, sweet Norina." He said outside the locked bedroom door one night. "You're the woman of this house, so I want you to be comfortable. You'll get there one day. But until that day comes I might have a solution to get you warmed up."

Another month of holding myself inside the bedroom initially meant for both Edgar and I, and I woke to the shock of a lifetime. Literally.

I awakened inside this small bedroom modeled after my DC room in Mama's house. How he pulled this off in such a short turnaround time was beyond me, and beyond creepy considering the place a dead ringer for my at-home bedroom. But I spent every night here in the past ten months of my captivity without even a complaint from Edgar Oakhouse. Other than our daily breakfasts and nightly "suppers," our paths never crossed. He worked all the time at the pork plant, Oak N' Sons, and kept me busy too with etiquette training, tennis lessons, French lessons, dive instruction, personal training and charity planning. While I despised the others, I grew to love charity planning, which consisted of researching small business, nonprofits, and organizations that Oak N' Sons could donate to. I was tasked to plan the yearly charity event for the family business since I was being groomed as the future Mrs. Norina Oakhouse. Bleh.

My days passed on an endless, numb loop of training and event planning so routine that I frowned when Luanne dragged me into the large, pristine bathroom near the service quarters.

"Where are we–" I began and screamed as the cold water poured down my entire body. The shower. I was in the shower where this bitch rained ice-cold water all over my fully-clothed body. I turned an even icier glare at her through my natural curls Edgar insisted I dyed back to their original color. Boring black. "You twat!"

"Yeah, yeah, yeah." Luanne chided. "Thank me later. But we are so behind schedule that there's no time to get you properly sobered. Stop all this drinking!"

"Let me leave the property for more than an hour by myself." I shot back.

But she was quick with it.

"You know you aren't allowed to leave the premises unattended, Ms. Oakhouse."

I lunged for her, but she was quick again to disarm me with a mere one arm holding me back against the shower wall.

"Let me go!" I holler while kicking and screaming.

"You better behave before I send for Colin!" She shrieked, knowing that threat would definitely compose me.

"Not Colin!" I whispered, not drunk, but still not sober enough to put on a facade to hide my true fear of the can- tankerous guard. He was more enforcer in the crude way he addressed everyone. He'd been the same guard to shove me into the car that day and haul me here.

"She giving you problems today, Ms. Luanne?"

As if on call the entire time, a menacing voice bellows from behind Luanne at the bathroom door. Luanne stared pointedly at me. I shook my head to confirm how non-prob- lematic I swore to be from then on.

"We're good." She answered while eying me suspiciously. "Just a little hiccup is all."

"You let me know if I need to step in at all. All right?" His dark, deep voice resembled gunpowder.

"All right." She said after turning off the faucet and yanking me out. "Boss is gonna flip if you're late to Charm Class."

"Why?" I asked, totally confused why Edgar would sud- denly care about my routine since he's typically long gone before I wake.

She doesn't answer, and she never does in the fifteen extra minutes it takes for me to dress in the appropriate yellow sundress and white cardigan. We're walking silently, yet tense, to the grand dining room with expensive China stacked in the center of the table.

The long rectangular table that could seat up to twenty is totally bare except for the China in the center of it as well as the man seated at the far end. The sun blinds him from my view and I'm all of a sudden reminded of being in that dark Japanese restaurant, where the mysterious Asian King sat shrouded in darkness.

"Go on," Luanne grumbles when I pause and stare at the odd scene where my etiquette lessons usually take place every Tuesday.

"Right..." I mutter, then take tentative steps towards the man in a white suit.

Upon closer inspection, two plates of fried food are placed before him. There's one plate in front of him and another at the seat nearest.

"Norina, is it?" He asks.

"Um, sure," I say awkwardly. "Hi."

"Where are my manners? Here." He stands and pulls the seat out beside him

"Thank you." I say, a bit shaken as I occupy the offered seat. "Will my Charm lesson still be taking place?"

Though I have no clue who this man is with sandy blond hair and crystal blue eyes, I decide to hold my tongue and let it ride. Afraid of the guards standing closely behind him.

"Yes, of course." He answered politely after sitting down. "You hungry?"

I picked the fork up and stabbed into a piece of fried okra without a complaint and nearly moaned when the thin crust touched my tongue.

The man chuckled before eating a piece, too. "Seems so."

We finished our food in a weird silence, and though I wasn't even hungry I still ate. I ate because I feared not eating would land me in trouble that involved Colin.

"Ms. Pauly sure knows her way 'round a skillet and hot grease!" The man exclaimed while patting his stomach.

It took me a minute to understand that he'd been referencing the old cook, a Latina woman who worked and lived here for the past twenty years. I don't dare voice the obvious racist stereotype keeping the overworked chef here for the long hours she did on call night and day. Instead, I smile deferentially.

"Sure does," I say.

The man pins me with an odd stare, like he's trying to listen to my thoughts before speaking.

"Name's Trace Oakhouse, ma'am." He extends a hand. "Old Edgar's son."

"Oh." I say, because I'm not sure how else to react to Edgar's son, of Oak N' Sons, sitting here where Madam Chelsea should be. I shake his hand. "Norina."

Instead of shaking my offered hand, he folds it gently in his own, turning it palm side down before bringing it to his lips.

"I know that." A lazy smile forms on his face that reveals his brilliant white teeth.

Our eyes held each other for a short period before I snatched my hand away like it scorched. I ignored the way my heart pounded out of control when I asked, "What the hell do you want?"

Not drunk Nora would come to eventually regret the tersely worded question later, but the current Nora was on her first bottle of wine for the day and craving another to numb up the pain of existing here.

That treacherous smile flashed again before he answered, but not the answer I expected. "What's your sign?"

I faltered. "Um, my what?"

"Your sign. Come on now, you know. Your zodiac? Are you a fish?"

"No, I'm a human being." This conversation was making my head hurt. "How is this relevant?"

A full belly laugh, then: "You can tell a lot about a person by their star sign. Right now you're giving off major fish or water energy. Pa's a Sagittarius, which speaks for itself."

Mind rippling with confusion and the need to return to my room, I indulge in his little game. "March third is my birthday."

"A fish, indeed." His eyes rolled a few times in consideration before he said, "My instinct never fails."

I shifted in my seat uncomfortably, but also to calm the dizzying effects from the Cab Sav from earlier. My skin crawled for some odd reason I couldn't understand just then and a bad feeling overtook me from this line of questioning. It felt like there was something he wasn't saying–information he'd been withholding– and judging from the grievous expressions worn by the house staff, it was something awful.

I gripped my fork tight before asking, "Are you...in town for work or a visit?"

His smile was wide, revealing white teeth and the same mild gap as Edgar. "Why, I'm glad you asked. Suppose we'll call these matters business related."

"I apologize for cursing at you earlier." I say, trying to pull Nora from the ocean of wine-brain.

His eyes lasered into me at that, and I wrestled with the urge to crawl away. Then he spoke, his next words shocking me in place. I had to ask him to repeat them.

"Touch me."

I drew back. "Why, sir?"

"You may call me Trace and nothing less." His voice took on a hard edge, as did his blue eyes where a quiet storm of emotions raged. I watched in astonishment as he took my hands in his. "I feel your cooling, watering energy too. As a Taurus, our chi complement each other."

A minute of silence passes as I observe his eyes float closed. He looks as though he's meditating or praying or maybe both. My heart is the loudest thing in my ears as another two minutes of more silent hand-holding ensues.

Then his eyes open to reveal...tranquility? Maybe he did pray, I consider since he appears refreshed and polite again.

"You're here for those etiquette lessons, right?"

"Yes."

"See them there plates in the middle of the table?"

"Yes." I repeated stiffly.

"Go ahead and fix them up just right."

"Excuse me, sir but–"

"Trace." He corrects with that renewed politeness. "We're acquainted now, remember, Norina?"

"Pardon me," I stutter. "Trace. Where is my Charm Instructor? Madam Chelsea?"

Trace doesn't answer, but nods towards the plates instead. "Set the table. Show me what you've learned from those etiquette lessons."

Cleo would protest in this situation. Demand this weirdo explain his presence here and why he wanted me to perform this strange task. But Cleo is dead, I remind myself not for the first time. If the forcible prison stint in this antebellum palace didn't kill her, then the daily booze did.

I take a deep, steadying breath before I stand and deliver on the directive from the handsomely strange son of Edgar's. My mind wandered as I set the table. Where was Edgar? Why send in his son to oversee this weird task when I had a Charm tutor to do it? I was so off-schedule at this point that there was no way I was getting to French lessons on time.

Twenty silent minutes of place setting for twenty nonexistent attendants passed. After placing the final dessert fork I stood back to study my work.

Trace, clapping, comes beside me where I note our obvious height difference.

"Excellent job," He congratulated me with another one of those dishonest grins and penetrating stares. "Looks like Pa was right about you. You are something special. We'll hang on to those Charm lessons."

"Excuse me?"

I took a step back to look up at him. This was all so confusing. None of his words made any sense. Why would he be the one deciding the fate of my classes and routine instead of Edgar Oakhouse himself?

"Where is Edgar?" I ask, crossing my arms and doing the utmost to keep my voice level.

The answer to my evident turmoil comes when a grim expression settles onto Trace's face. He casts sullen eyes towards the floor before meeting mine.

"Pa was found in his office this morning." His voice hitches on the final word.

I frown. "Found? What do you mean by that? Was he lost?"

"Naw," he rasps, jaw flexing before carefully adding, "he's dead."

16

ruined humans

· ♥ · ♥ · ♥ · ♥ · ♥ ·

"That's it, Nora! Give me three more reps and we'll be done for the day." Pascual exclaimed beside my sweaty body.

My body screamed at the exertion from the grueling bicep curls. We'd leveled up since last week from ten to thirteen pounders and I felt every second of that mistake. Sweat poured down my natural curls, blinding me so bad I was forced to rapid-blink them away. I nearly lost my balance at the twelfth rep from the pulling on sore joints.

"Don't you give up now girl!" My usually flamboyant personal trainer cheered when I bent at the waist for relief. He got real close. "Remember what we talked about? Who are you doing this for? Me?"

"No." I breathed after several swift inhalations.

"Your parents? Teachers? Friends?"

More breaths, then "no..."

I couldn't tell him how neither of those groups had any real contact or fulfilling relationships with me any longer. Mostly from the fact that it was shame I felt whenever thoughts of Mama, Mom and Pop, or even Trice emerged. The nearly fatal hyperventilating also posed a barrier in relaying any polysyllabic words from me.

The sun shone bright and threateningly in the sky this afternoon, and I was already mentally drained from French lessons two hours prior. Add the physical strain from an intense sesh with my joyous, yet equally intense, personal trainer in the hot outdoor gym and that was it for me. My knees buckled from the enervation before I sank to the concrete.

"No, no, no!" Pascual, the hulking, handsome Brazilian fitness nut I grew close to since my imprisonment in the Oakhouse estate said before hunkering down beside me. "Don't you give up girl!"

"But my body's gonna break in half." I huffed, breathing heavy.

"Look how far you've come though, girl! Remember where we started five months ago? And that sore back you didn't even realize was a problem worsening by your weight?"

"I remember." I breathe, visions of how winded running a lap would get me.

Or even lifting a five pound dumbbell. Though mentally miserable in Edgar's prison, I hated to admit all the activities I nicknamed "Wife Grooming" improved the physical. Since leaving home, I was halfway fluent in schoolroom French, dropped sixty pounds thanks to Pascual, and even knew how to set a table. Edgar warned that I'd be a proper wife to him once we made it to the aisle, and a proper wife was well-educated and maintained a busy life of activities. I hated Edgar, but grew to love event planning. I'd been HBIC organizing this year's Christmas Thanks Ball, an event that honored the Oak N' sons sponsors and investors. The businesses and charities that Oak N' Sons invested in or donated to were also welcomed. And I managed the list. I managed most of it, and....

I didn't hate it.

While merely July, the event took lots of time and preparation. And I'm glad most of it was done with caterers booked, location secured, and guest list double confirmed. Though the glaring difference remained: Edgar was dead. So what would be the fate of the Ball this year?

"What's on that mind of yours, Nora?" Pascual asked with a nudge of his elbow.

"Nothing!" I squeaked.

We sat pretzel-style on the cool ground facing each other. Me now averting my gaze from the probing hunk of a trainer of mine.

"Oh don't you 'nothing' me young lady!" He snapped after glancing at his watch. "If you got tea to spill, you better spill it! We got thirty minutes left to this session so that leaves us plenty time to talk dirty."

"Not dirty." I couldn't help but laugh. "I was just thinking about the Ball. Now Edgar's gone, I don't really know what to do with...anything."

He sighed. "Oh girl. I thought you couldn't stand that wrinkly-ass old man?"

"Sure," I shrugged. "But he was a part of my normal here. Now it looks like Trace isn't going anywhere, so..."

"He did practically move back in since the old man kicked the bucket last week."

"Yeah." I blew out.

Trace Oakhouse did, in fact, move back into the estate which once was his childhood home. Even stranger, he moved immediately into Edgar's old room what felt like seconds after that weird lunch we had. We barely spoke to each other outside of the occasional greeting when we'd pass each other in the halls or if he walked in on one of my lessons.

"Esquisito. I don't got a good feeling about him, girl. Can't you just leave? Aren't you free now the old man's morto?"

Dead, I translated inwardly. Edgar was dead, but I didn't quite know what to do. I couldn't return home since Luther threatened to hurt my parents if I ever showed my face in DC.

My shoulders slumped. "Pas, it's not that simple. I have nowhere to go."

"Nonsense!" He exclaimed with a dramatic clap of his hands. "You can stay on my couch anytime babe."

Tempting, I think, just before another harsh reality sets in. "I'm followed everywhere. Plus, there's no way Edgar would have ever hired you on without having a full surveillance of your apartment at all times."

"Si." He exhaled. "I had to sign a waiver and an NDA just to get this job three years back. If I hadn't needed the money so badly I would have thrown that contract in his face!"

I smile at him, my heart warm for the first time in days since learning of Edgar's passing. Not from sorrow, but from the unknown. Trace reinforced that life would continue as normal even with his father dead. But it felt like I'd been waiting on a bed of nails until he made his move. Would he kick me out? Pimp me out? Force me into his bed like Edgar groomed me to do?

I covered his hand with mine.

"Thanks for looking out for me, Pas."

He slapped my hand away and pulled me into his chest.

"Forget that girl, come here! You are my girl, no matter what. And when we make it out of here we'll get drinks. On the beach. Where we'll both have our pick of the litter of hot guys to choose from. Si?"

"Si." I hugged him back and blinked the tears away at his wholeheartedness. "Speaking of hot guys, what's the tea on your new beau?"

His joyous face crumbled at the mention of the guy he admitted to being in love with after their third date two days ago.

"Girl." He huffed. "Fuck him."

"Wait, what?" I asked. "But I thought he was one of the good ones?"

"Shin is so far in the closet he's practically walking around with his dirty laundry! I mean it. You should see the way he hides me."

His voice fell and my anger rose because, oh hell no. Pas was such a great friend to me in the five month stint here that I practically considered him a brother. No way could I see anyone hiding the Brazilian god who mirrored a buffer, more effervescent David Castañeda.

I twisted to turn a nasty sneer on him. "Are you fucking kidding me?!"

"No." He answered, tone flat. "I wish, but no. Even after I told him my ex-boyfriend horror story with Jake. That conservative farmer took me for a ride but not worse than how Shin is doing me. He was all right the first few dates– the hand-holding, PDA, and compliments were so refreshing. But two nights ago things just...fell apart. I haven't heard from him since."

I paused, gathering the info in my head before probing gently, "Oh no, Pas. Two nights ago. That's when you made love."

Not a question, more of an inference, but he nodded all the same with that depleted look on his gorgeous face. The sky began to darken, letting me know that our time was running out before he had to leave and my next Wife Grooming activity began.

"I made love." He spat angrily, rocking himself. "He fucked me. Even today, I miss his emotionally-avoidant ass and that's still fucking me."

Tears coursed down his tan cheeks and I sprang into action; wrapping myself around him just like he did me when I needed a cry. I stroked his back as I spoke.

"Try to calm down, babe. Calm down and forget about him. Besides, you'll have another great adventure someday with the right guy. Crying over him will only make it harder for Mr. Right to find you."

He shook his head. "I'm ruined."

"You aren't 'ruined'."

"I am ruined." He sniffled into my shoulder. "Because even though he ghosted me after the best sex ever, I'm still the fool for falling in love with him. Like, glutton for punishment or what?"

"Maybe something happened, you know?"

"Like what?"

"Like…like…a family emergency?" My attempt at an excuse was lame, but I didn't want to see him so down if he was truly in love.

He waved a hand away at that as we separated. His wet curls hung freely down his face making him look that much more crestfallen as he continued talking.

"It's been a whole twenty-four hours! We went from texting every ten minutes to this?! I don't care if his uncle was the pope or if he got gout– nothing constitutes this. He held me in his arms when I told that story about Jake. Nobody has ever treated me with such tenderness after that. Though I admit it isn't a story I openly share."

"Give him time, babe." I whispered. "That's all I say. I can't relate to everything you've been through, but I know a broken heart. I live with that every day. So trust me when I say give it time and you may be surprised."

"Time." He breathed. "An evil bitch, ain't she?"

"That, she is." I say. "But she's constant, too. Don't give up on love yet."

"I can't say it was love I felt for Shin– still feel. The tenderness he made me feel wasn't everything. And I'm not looking for everything. It just can't mean nothing. And I'm scared our time together was just another hit-and-run bump in the dark."

My first thought was getting him some concealer since his face grew puffy from crying. I willfully made no comment on his statements about love, since it was always something never afforded to me. I preferred to keep my affection-trauma to myself these days so as not to rub my loveless charm on others.

"Everything's gonna be okay." I offered with a hopeful grin.

A tight smile formed on his face like he'd been about to say something, then he blinked, and it was gone. Had I hurt him in some way? Before I had the chance to ask, he says something that makes me frown.

"You better call your cousin." He said out of nowhere between wiping the snot from his nose. "She's been leaving you text messages that don't sound like she's very happy with you."

I sighed in exasperation. I knew exactly what cousin Pas referred to since he kept my secret phone for me. It was the best way to sneak phone calls to Nita, who agreed to lie to my parents for me about my whereabouts: they straight up believed I lived and worked with Nita's new shop downtown full time, and I appreciated her for fielding the calls and lying for me. Though there was some small seed of guilt in me for persuading my cousin to exact this lie— especially since Mom already disapproved of her.

But at a time like this, when my only true friend was hurting, talking to Nita fell on the unnecessary side.

"What? Did she say why?" I asked.

"No." He said before producing the small iPhone and extending it to me. "You know I don't like to read your text messages."

"But you totally can." I laughed, unlocking the phone. "You're the only one who knows the passcode in case of emergencies."

"Just because I can, doesn't mean I should. It's an abuse of power. That's not what decent people do." His words were emphatic though his tone never hitched over deadpan.

That's not what decent people do. His words rang loud and true in my ears. Resonating somewhere buried within my heart. I wasn't being a decent person. Not in the slightest. Suddenly that ache for my family and guilt reared up, making me hang my head in shame for a second.

"Sorry, Pas." I whispered. "You are such an awesome friend."

He smiled at that and squeezed my hand. "You, too. Now, go call your cousin to make sure she's all right. Your session is almost up and I don't want to make that uncouth but ungodly handsome Pitbull suspicious."

I laughed at his description of Colin, Edgar's perpetually angry bodyguard and babysitter of me. He was right. After another minute of jesting, I walked to the corner of the yard and hid behind the house to make the call.

"Why haven't you been answering your fucking phone, Cleo?!" Nita screamed the second the line connected.

"Sorry, cuz." I said regretfully. "I told you my schedule has been nuts."

"That psychotic fiancé of yours still keeps you locked up, doesn't he?"

I didn't respond, because what the hell should I say? She's not wrong, but I can't let her know she's right either.

"Rich." A mirthless laugh accompanied her dry statement. "Just rich. An actual emergency happens and your head is so far shoved up this nameless fiancé's ass that you can't come out for a second to consider how it might affect your family. Real funny, Cleo!"

"Wait, what do you mean emergency? What's wrong?"

"Why bother? Not like you give a damn anyways."

"Juanita!" I hissed. "Don't do this!"

"Cleo'Nora!" She hollered even louder, making me have to yank the phone from my ear. "I'm not doing anything. It's you doing the doing."

"Please just talk to me. Are Mom and Dad all right? What about Mama?"

"You know where my shop is. You want answers, you meet me here."

"Nita, wait–"

The line, of course, goes dead. Since she hangs up on me, leaving me to panic and worry and question:

What was happening back home?

17

white-winged dove

· ❤ · ❤ · ❤ · ❤ · ❤ ·

I stride into the Oakhouse Estate/prison with fervor and hellbent on talking to Trace Oakhouse about my situation. I try not to let Pascual's warnings about the thirty-year old Oakhouse heir fester into doubt, too.

"Be careful talking to Trace Oakhouse, babe. Rumor on the street is that he killed his wife last year to cash out on her family's fortune. A little funny now he's back and someone else is suddenly dead without cause. Watch your back..."

I will Pas, I say a mental note to him and myself in attempts to reassure both parties that what I was about to do was logical and safe. Logical and safe. Just chant it till you believe it, Cleo.

I nearly make it to the door of Edgar's study (or Trace's new study, I supposed) when his voice stops me.

"What's so suspicious about a cremation?" Trace snarls into what I believe is a phone, considering the pause before he spoke again. "You trying to tell me how to run my family? Our business? An empire in the Pork Production industry has fallen and all's y'all care about is how I'm smearing the face of the brand? To hell with your input, Amanda!"

Amanda? I ask inwardly, my mind racing to identify a face to that familiar name. If I wasn't mistaken, Amanda Lake headed Oak N' Sons public relations unit. She was nice enough to me in my brief interactions with her, but very uptight where it pertained to the company's liability and image. Fitting for her role, I supposed. But what was she saying to Trace that got him so upset?

A sharp bang made me jump before he started talking again. Or yelling, would be the appropriate term.

"My apologies, Ms. Lake, if I miscommunicated. See, you're employed by me, and I don't ask anybody on my payroll for a goddamn thing. You hear?"

No one deserved to be spoken to like that. I shook my head as I listened to the pause, during which I assumed she apologized since his tone lightened.

"No need to be sorry. Sorry don't make me money. Be better. All right now."

I rapped gently on the thick oak double doors at the assumed conclusion of that call. But I entered anyway, noting him standing instead of sitting at Edgar's desk.

"Norina!" He exclaimed with a wide boyish grin when I stopped at the front of the desk. "Come, sit, get comfortable."

"Thanks." I mumbled when he came around the desk to offer one of the two chairs facing the desk to me.

I awkwardly plopped into it and averted my eyes from his penetrating blue ones.

To my awe, he sat right beside me in the adjacent chair instead of at the main desk. Odd, I noted.

"Lessons been going all right?" He asked.

"Oh, yes. Yes, thanks for asking."

Another huge grin spread across his face, making me notice how absolutely gorgeous he was. Gorgeous, but super sus. And with apparent anger issues like a certain someone who threatened to hurt my family if I returned to DC.
Similar to that certain someone, I avoided looking him directly in the eyes.

"Something I can help you with, beautiful?" His voice was...dare I steal Pas's word...tender.

Like he'd been addressing someone he cared about or known for a while. I didn't fit into either of those buckets, so this only heightened my paranoia.

I cleared my suddenly parched throat and squirmed when I responded, "No. Uh, yeah. Sorry, I mean yes sir."

"Naw," He said lazily while leaning back in the chair. "Trace is fine."

"O-Okay." I stuttered.

"Is it?"

"Mm-hmm."

"Good," He answered, looking so pleased as if I'd given him a gift. "Let me hear you say it, Ms. Norina. Call me by my name."

I gulped, hating this seat all of a sudden since it was so close to him.

"I...um..."

"Go on." He prodded.

"Trace." I whispered, my cheeks hot.

"See there? That wasn't so bad. Was it?" His voice dropped a level. One that sent chills though me, but not in a good way. I needed out.

"Trace, I need your permission to go out. Today. I'll send lots of proof when I'm gone and promise not to run off. I swear. Just please let me go on my own. It's sort of an emergency."

"Sort of?" He asked. "Or is?"

"It is. A family emergency." I rushed out.

He nodded, taking my words in with an actual note of consideration. "Okay."

"Okay?"

"Yeah. Okay. Go ahead."

"But I–" I started, then fell short. Did he just say what I think he did? "I...can go?"

He shrugged. "I don't see why not. Didn't you say it was an emergency?"

"Yes," I answered on guard, preparing to counter should this be a trick. Or a trap. "It's late on a Wednesday evening, and I can just...leave? Without a guard or escort or whatever?"

"Did you want one?" His question was almost sarcastic, but I didn't have the capacity to acknowledge it.

"I don't, it's just..."

"My father wouldn't have let you out of his sight without some guard breathing up your dress. Am I right?"

I blinked, considering then answered truthfully. "Yeah."

"Good news for you." He rasped upon standing and walking over to the bar of expensive spirits. "I ain't my daddy. And you ain't no little girl that need chaperoning. Just be back before dinner."

I stared, mystified, at his white pants suit attempting to let his words sink in. He was letting me go? Just like that?

"Thank you, Trace." I murmured, still confused as I stood up.

Each step towards the door felt like a risk. Like a lie, and I treated each one as if there were land mines of whatever trap he set for me to detonate. Pure, raw, relief hits my body just as I twist the doorknob before he speaks. God, why did he have to speak?!

"Assume you heard about my wife by now, eh?"

I freeze. Pas's warning sent immediate alarms through my already foggy brain. On the outside, I merely take a second before twisting to face him at the bar.

"No, I don't believe I did." I lied.

He only stared at me from across the room. None of us saying anything amidst the tension so thick I could hear my breaths. This entire situation brought memories of Trice's dad to my mind. Me, desperate and waiting for any scrap of information regarding my best friend's whereabouts. All for it to be a trick, like this one. One set up artfully based on my desires. Which, in this, case, was to get to Nita's salon.

My heart lodged in my chest when he began to trudge over to me. Unlike last time, I stood my ground. Prepared to kick his tiny nuts in should he try anything funny. I was sick of getting treated like trash for...well, for nothing! After all, I was the prisoner here.

"I believe you did," He said silkily, pinning me into the door and bringing his lips so close to mine.

"I didn't," I said, voice firm.

His eyes bore into mine for another minute, as if trying to sus out the truth there. Brandy hard on his breath, he leaned in close to my ear to breathe a chilling message.

"I oughta tell you bout her sometime. You remind me of her. She had so much water in her...same as you."

That I didn't expect. It takes me a turn to realize he's referencing that zodiac sign mumbo jumbo again. I turned in his arms slightly to respond.

"Is she black, too?"

Trace's laughter disarmed him enough to straighten and take a step backwards. Though his eyes still promised something dark and menacing I didn't like.

"Have a wonderful evening Norina Skye. I'll be here when you get back."

18

back in

• ♥ • ♥ • ♥ • ♥ • ♥ •

"You get two hours. Max." Colin spat after I exited the black Range.

The moon shone high and bright in the night sky and I grunted a terse, "okay," before jetting to the front doors of Nita's Beauty & Nail Bar. The building was a quaint, older one that looked as a permanent fixture on Church Street. It was older in age but not rundown, I noted, since the painting looked fresh and floor-to-ceiling glass windows gave it a chic appeal. Had I not been in so much of a rush to get to the bottom of this emergency, I'd have been more inquisitive and thrilled about my cousin extending nail services to her shop, too.

Right now was definitely not one of those times.

"Nita!" I called.

Banging on the door like no tomorrow and praying she'd be there. The older building looked like a two-story, if I wasn't mistaken, so maybe she lived in the apartment on the top floor? Did an apartment even exist on the top floor?

I swore under my breath after the fifth call-and-knock combo produced no results of my cousin. Shit. Maybe I underestimated it. Or assumed she'd just, I don't know, be at the location she dropped me via text?

After memorizing the address, I gave the secret phone back to Pascual. So now I just stood there. Phoneless. Penniless. And without a fucking clue where to even begin to get answers.

I'm wrestling with the notion of throwing my expensive Sketchers at the front window when the sound of chains and locks rattling behind the salon happen.

"Cleo?" Nita breathes, horrified, as though she's witnessing a ghost at her door. Hand on her heart, she asks, "That really you?"

"Yeah," I squeak, and even though I'm furious at her for so many reasons, I can't help it.

We're rushing towards each other like the couple from the Notebook, without all the kissing. No, instead we're squealing and crying and twirling in each other's arms in the otherwise quiet street.

"I didn't think you'd actually show up," She said after we'd made it inside and all the crying subsided.

"Of course. You said this was an emergency!" I reared back. "Which reminds me. What's wrong?"

Nita's rocking a silk wrap and purple robe that barely shields her voluptuous curves. She's gorgeous as usual, but there's something off about her. Her movements were a bit staggered and her tone overly elated. Nita was sort of known to give it to you straight, no chaser, and often abrasively. There were only two occasions I caught her merry in any way: Getting her hair done and drunk as hell.

I frowned at my cousin. Whose cheeks are flushed a deep pink and are flushing darker by the second under the light fixture in the hall.

"You've been drinking," I said aridly.

"I had a sip of some wine after work." She said indignantly before turning away.

She's all but running to the staircase in the back of the room filled with style seats, and I have to thank Pascual for the heavy cardio since it's big easy to keep up with her almost-run.

I tugged on her silk robe sleeve once my legs caught up to her scurrying towards a door beyond the top step landing.

"Ouch! Quit it!" She whined, but not before pausing completely and collapsing against the door. "Don't kill my high."

"Why are you acting so evasive?" I asked, arms akimbo while regarding her.

"My shop..." She whined, her face crumpled into her hands.

I looked around the dark second floor, certain this was the entrance to a top floor apartment like I originally figured. There wasn't much to the naked eye since it was dark.

"What about it?"

"One of my loans fell through, so that means I can't buy new wash stations or fund the nail bar services. Top that off, my only employee quit today. I couldn't blame her though, because she didn't get paid. I'd have left, too."

"Oh, cuz..." I breathed, saddened to see my strong cousin crumbling before me within the first ten minutes of seeing her.

I took a step towards her then and wrapped my arms around her thin top half. Nita was built differently from me; where I was evenly thick all over, she possessed a tiny upper body and rounded lower one may not expect upon looking at her sitting down.

"It's okay," I soothed her, stroking the taller woman's head lying on my shoulder. "Like I told you back in DC, we'll fix this by any means. Even if I have to sell my right kidney."

She pulled back to cast the most awed expression at me, as if I dug into my stomach and ripped the kidney out in front of her instead of promising it for sale later.

"What are you doing in Greenville, Cleo?"

I bit down hard on my lip. I totally wasn't expecting the conversation to go down that road just yet and it took me a minute to rebalance before saying, "You already know why."

She folded her arms, as though her tears were a mere afterthought or figment of my imagination. "Yeah. I remember the bologna answer you gave ten months ago when you begged me to lie to your parents, Auntie Mora included, about working here at my shop. When in actuality you've never even set foot inside."

"I've been meaning to visit," I say lamely, but Nita mows right over my incoming lie with her words.

"Cut the crap, cuz. I ain't your parents so there's no need to keep up with the lies."

"We'll talk more about it later. I promise."

"Fuck later!" She hissed, jumping into my face as I slowly tracked backwards down the stairs. "I thought we were better than this. What is going on with you? Uncle Ferr and Auntie Mora get more worried every time they call and hear another excuse about why you too busy to come to the phone. But it ain't just them—I'm worried too. I'm scared you're in danger and won't open up to us for some reason."

I shook my head, fear wrestling with the truth right beneath my tongue. I want to yell at her to stop. I want to ball up and cry or, even better, run back to the Oakhouse prison and drink my problems away. But I can't. I'm trapped in this interaction that felt a lot more like an ambush instead of an emergency.

I took another step back, but Nita latched onto my shoulders holding me in place. "You gotta understand where I'm coming from, girl. You run away from home in the middle of the night and end up here. In the same town as your only relative in this place and have yet to see me. I'm glad you've stayed in touch through short calls and texts. I'm also glad you offered to help support my shop, but you need to level with me. How are you in any position to support me? Are you a secret millionaire or something?"

A dry chuckle escapes past my lips before I say, "I wish. Then I wouldn't be in this mess in the first place."

"You say that," she starts curiously, "but that just makes me more confused."

"I can't go into details, Nita. Please try to understand that."

A long, hard stare before she grabs my hand and ushers me down the stairs.

"Hey, where are we—" I begin to whine, then cut short when I realize where she's dragged me.

We're downstairs now, in the beauty shop area I only caught a brief glimpse of when I chased her upstairs. Though now I get the full view of the place after she flicks a light on and...damn.

My heart stuttered at the intricate designs on the walls, several styling sections and color-coded hair products lining the huge mirrors in front of the style seats. Royal colors of deep purple and gold mark every corner of the room from the gold door knobs at the front to the purple writing on the front window that read: Nita's Beauty & Nail Bar.

This place was her dream come true, I realized in admiration and warm awe. That familiar feeling of security rose in me as I gazed at the one place that's felt most like home in the twenty minutes I've been here than that twisted mansion.

"Nita, you've outdone yourself." I breathe, my eyes still bouncing from every detail in the room like they'd been plastered on a major motion flick. "It's perfect."

I didn't see her, but heard her smile as she responded. "I know. Put every single cent of my savings into this place, and then some. This is supposed to be my fresh start…"

"It still can be,"

"Before we get into that, turn around girl." Her soft voice instructs me, and I notice again that we've stopped in front of one of the style seats. Right where a huge floor-to-ceiling mirror is fixed beyond.

"Why should I turn—" I gasped when I glimpsed at what stood before me.

Two women, one in a purple silk robe and bonnet on her head. Her sable skin is glowing, for lack of a better word, under the mirror lights and besides her frown, she looks drop dead gorgeous. But it isn't her beauty that makes me gasp in shock. It's the woman beside her.

She's wearing black leggings and black tank top. A light blue jacket covers her unusually thin frame and there are heavy bags under her eyes. As though she hasn't slept in days or wiped away her mascara. Her hair is a tangled fro of curls that are clean, but wild and unruly. Though darker skinned, there's a yellowish paleness to her complexion that's just downright unhealthy.

A single tear slips down my face as I watch the bonneted woman wrap her arm around the battered one.

"Do you see yourself?" Nita asked gently.

"Is that...is that what I look like?" I asked, raw agony in my voice from what I was witnessing.

Nita nodded. "Where's my cousin under all that? Your hair is in its natural color. You look years older than me judging from the state of your skin, and you've lost so much weight..." She quieted for a beat then added brokenly, "Cleo, where are you?"

"I'm here." I whimpered, her every word striking something deep in my gut. In my chest.

It's like the mirror is cracking from the image I created, but in reality, it's me that's been cracking. A skincare regimen and or thorough deep conditioning was never a part of my life now that I lived here. Every day was spent sulking in my own woe. So sad and guilty about the problems I cause my entire family and terrified about the prospect of returning home to dead parents.

My entire body shudders from the thoughts and her words combined, and I soon crumble to the floor.

Nita catches me before I hit the floor and I melt in her arms as she croons in my ear. "Everything's gonna be all right. I'm right here when you feel like talking about it. Okay?"

"Okay," I nod, sniffling and sobbing into her chest like her eighteen month old son, Julian. Which reminded me... "Where are the boys?"

"Girl, don't you worry! My friend Yuri is looking after them for the night while I get my shit together with this salon. As you saw, I was busy with the self-pity parade over here. Didn't want the boys to see me that way."

Her tone darkens as another wave of silence befalls the large room.

"I get not wanting to be seen at your worst. Trust me, I do. And, uh, Nita?"

She sits up to stare into my eyes. "Yeah?"

"Thank you."

***

Heavy knocks come at the salon doors a couple hours later that make us both freeze. Time flew by in an endless stream of laughing and crying and apologizing that I hadn't even thought to keep an eye on the time.

We remained on the salon floor regaling tales from the past and catching each other up on recent developments in our lives. I'd learned that Nita was taking self-defense classes regularly since she'd moved to town last year. This was also the place where she met her friend Yuri, a Japanese expat who'd moved from New Jersey. She and Nita bonded over their interests in beauty and widowed statuses. Yuri moved to Greenville to get a fresh start after her husband died, and this closely mirrored Nita's situation since her late boyfriend died from a brutal car crash nearly two years ago. Leaving her with two young sons to raise all on her own and a crap ton of debt accrued to keep her shop running. Top that with a serving of legal issues her late boyfriend's family tried to pursue after she left town with their only grandsons.

"Legal issues?" I'd probed before shoveling a spoonful of pistachio ice cream down my throat during our salon-floor chit chat. "As in, custody stuff?"

She nodded, a distant emotion in her eyes. "Yes. After Farookh died they tried to argue me as an unfit parent. Saying it would be in kids' best interest to be raised in a well-established home. Pure hogshit is what that sounded like to me. The judge thought so, too and ruled in my favor."

"Gosh," I breathed, barely able to fathom that my cousin was going through so much hardship behind the scenes with this. Then came the guilt. "Sorry I've not been around much to support you through this. This must be hard to undertake alone, in a new city, and a relaunched business."

"It is hard." She shrugged. "But it's worth it. Not all things in life worth fighting for are going to be easy. I wish it was, but that isn't reality. Plus, I got a good community. Since daddy died, it's practically been all on me to keep it together for my kids. My friends and favorite cousin make life much more bearable though, I do admit."

I took her hand in mine. "I'm here now. I promise not to disappear again. I want to be your favorite cousin again. I want us to be tight again."

She squeezed my hand. "Then let's be that again. Come live with me. I don't have much, but I can make room for you if it gets you out of this situation you're in."

"Thanks, but I can't. Not yet."

"What are you waiting for?" She demanded. "This guy really has you under his finger, huh? What's he got on you that's making you so resistant towards leaving?"

"Nothing, he..." I struggled to lace some truth in. "We're just keeping a low profile these days. I'm not in danger, Nita. I'm fine."

"'Fine' is all well and good. But are you happy?"

Happy...I thought. That word had been one of those imagery emotions that existed in my past. When I lived with Mama and worked at Nita's part time. Back when I used to secretly spend time with My First Love and he swung me around while we danced to R&B classics under the moonlight.

I cleared my throat. "I'm fine."

Nita's face fell while she scrutinized mine, probably detecting me trying to hold it together despite the obvious lie.

"If you won't leave, then just remember my door is always open. Same as Uncle Ferr's and Auntie Mora's: you have support in us, Cleo. I promise you that."

"I know that now. Thanks." I said, meaning it while trying to stave off tears.

"I have a phenomenal group of friends from my self-defense class, too. So can you promise me you'll show up for some sessions?"

"Self-defense class?"

"Yes!" She effused. "No joke, they're so helpful. They've helped me feel strong and empowered since Farookh passed. I want you to join me for a couple of sessions. Okay?"

I sighed, already feeling myself caving at her request since it had been so refreshing hanging out with my cousin again. I wanted more of this. More time spent with the people who mattered most.

"I'll come." I agreed and chewed my lips while my mind turned with another idea. "Let me help you, too. Okay?"

Another skeptic frown twisted her face as she watched me dig into my jacket pocket to produce a silver Amex card. "For the salon." I said.

"Wait a minute." She splayed her hands in front of me as if blocking off rays from the sun. "What's this?"

I laughed and took her hand in mine. "This is for you. A thank you for being there for me when I need it, even after all this time."

"Cleo..."

"Take it." I said with finality before closing her hand around the card. "I don't use this thing anyway. And I know this creates more questions than answers right now, but I promise this isn't a burden. Whatever debts you need to pay or outstanding bills prevent you from operating at full capacity for the salon, I want you to take care of them. On me."

"Cleo, I..." She stammered, breathless. "I can't. Girl, I can't with all good conscience spend your hard-earned money on—"

"I don't mind, cuz." I told her, vehement and earnest as I possibly could be to emphasize my point. To show how much I wanted to support her any way I could like she did for me all these years. "Take it."

"I can't pay you back. Not for a while."

"Well, that's great. Since I don't expect a dime back, then that makes us square."

A look crossed her face that asked so many questions. I want to reveal to her the true reason I can't leave the Oakhouse Estate. I can't let her know about my last failed attempt at running and the awful consequences that ensued. I couldn't put myself through that again. So, in place of sharing this with her, I inwardly willed her to take this card as an equivalent exchange.

"I love you," She whispered. Then she threw her arms around me and we both giggled as we tumbled to the floor. "Let me know if there's anything I can do for you. Anything. I got you."

We're laying with our backs to the floor now, breathing hard as the truth settles between us. Some version of the truth, I suppose. I turned to her.

"Actually, there is."

"Anything." She says. "I got you."

"Let me come back."

"Back?"

"Yeah." I said, "To the shop. As your makeup artist."

Nita opens her mouth to respond when the knock comes at the door. Hard. Loud. Angry.

We freeze, and turn in the direction of the entryway hall where the late night knocker is continuously pounding on the glass door as if something's on fire.

Nita stands up. "Yo, who the fuck is that knocking on my door like that?"

"Late night caller?" I tease, trying to keep the panic out of my voice at the knocker's heavy, persistent pounding.

"Girl, I ain't dating nobody," She remarked while tiptoeing towards the door. "But whoever the fuck this is is about to get the beatdown of their life if they don't stop banging!"

Nita's yelling the words, projecting them loudly so there's no mistake who she's talking about. I'm sure the knocker hears what she says because he pauses to holler, "Norina!" before more banging ensues.

"Norina?" Nita asks, bewildered as she turns to me. "This guy got the wrong address."

"Oh fuck," I breathe, my heart dropping to my toes at the realization that my two hour window came and went over thirty minutes ago. I definitely knew the identity of the night knocker.

It was Colin. The Oakhouse's most ruthless body guard and head of security on the estate. I'd never seen the guy smile once in the ten months I'd seen him. And he surely wouldn't be smiling once he saw me tonight.

I shot to my feet. "I have to go!"

"What? Hell no I'm not letting you go with that psycho pounding on the door like that!"

"Nita, I don't have time to explain!"

"No need!" She exclaimed before pulling her phone out. "Leave the explanation for the police."

Shit! I think, not exactly sure what to say to prevent her from calling the cops. I couldn't exactly tell her that my late forced fiancé's guard was insane about me being on time. Or that he came to collect me by any forcible means possible on boss orders.

Turns out I didn't need to explain and Nita never makes the call. We both screamed as a loud crash of shattering glass sounded after the final series of brutal knocks.

"What the fuck?!" Nita screamed as we clutched each other in fright.

A dark, hulking figure appears in the ill-lit entryway. He's standing to his foreboding six foot-plus height and glaring at us. Or, should I say, me.
In a swift second, Nita breaks away from me to grab a blow-dryer.

"Nita, no!" I shout, but it's too late. With a banshee screech, she charges at Colin with the heavy hair accessory raised.

"You bastard!" She cries and only manages to get one hit in before Colin dodges and tackles her to the floor. Nita squirms under him, her arms pinned by his hands but her legs flailing wildly. "You broke my door, you asshole! Cleo, get my phone! Call the cops to take this trash away."

My head is swirling from the turn of events. So much so that it takes me a minute to register that my cousin is being restrained by a very powerful, very dangerous, man. A man so lethal the entire house staff quieted whenever he entered the room. He stalked the halls of the mansion like he owned it. Or like he dared anyone to tell him otherwise. Which I never did.

"Colin, let her go. She's innocent." I tell him with hopes my pleas would reach him.

His eyes never leave Nita's face, but he says, "You're over time. Boss is gonna be pissed you missed dinner."

"I know," I said, my gut wrenching at the memory of Trace's only rule. To show up for daily dinners, same as I did with Edgar. "I'll talk to Trace later. We'll work it out."

Colin's face contorted for a second. "I don't fucking care. My mission was to return you to that house by six o' clock. You're over time."

"You know this asshole?" Nita questioned breathlessly from the floor due to the weight of Colin on her chest. "Can you get the fuck up off me?"

"I'll explain later," I told Nita. "Colin, let's go."

Colin stood up with military speed and watched Nita struggle to stand. "Sorry about your door. Should've moved quicker to answer."

"Like I'm answering the door at this late hour with some psycho banging at it? This look like a horror flick to you? Because, newsflash, only the black girls get sacrificed in those plots. I ain't one of them." Nita's answer came with a full neck roll.

"Yeah, well, this should cover it." Colin said before chucking a wad of bills to the heavily glassed floor.

"Dickhead." She mumbled. Then she winced as she tried to bend over and pick up the cash wad.

"S'wrong with you?" Colin beat me to the question, eying her with suspicion and a foreign look of concern. Wait, was that concern written on his face? The emotion was so human I thought I'd imagined it on the beast darkening the entryway.

Nita glared at him. "I just got laid flat over several shards of glass. Now they're embedded in my back. Guess who's responsible for that?"

"Please take us to the hospital." I ask Colin while rushing over to my cousin. "She's hurt."

Nita waved me away. "I'll be fine, Cleo. Seriously."

"No, you won't!" I asserted, pissed now. "We're taking you to the hospital!"

"Only place you're going is back home." Colin cut in, addressing me. "I got orders, and you're already over time."

"Let me see," I mumbled while rolling her robe down. I studied the bright red blood pouring down her purple sleeves and vibrated from fury. "We're taking you to a hospital."

"Cleo, I'm fine." Nita whispered, her voice small for some reason as she redressed.

"St. Francis is a couple minutes away, we'll take you." I insisted, "This isn't up for discussion."

"You're right!" She exclaimed, fully facing me. "I'm not hurt that bad. I'm more pissed than in pain."

"I am not leaving without you."

"Too. Damn. Bad!" She growled.

"Nita!"

"Cleo!"

We're shouting over each other, all but physically sparring for dominance in this conversation. I'm fully resolved to drag her stubborn ass out of there by the time Colin clears his throat. We quiet and redirect our attention to the highly irritated man in the room.

"Norina," he growls with zero patience in his rough tone, yet with a new exhaustion winning over. "To the car. Now."

I didn't usually stand my ground with Colin considering he frightened the shit out of me and wore an ever-fixed frown. But I straightened my back, readying for battle against this very non-negotiable topic. No way would I leave my cousin to bleed alone in pain.

"No!" I hissed. "I'm not leaving her here to–"

"Think twice before interrupting me again." He warned. "Get in the car. The woman said she'll be fine, so believe in that and follow orders."

"Oh, hell no!" Nita thundered at Colin, who turned his predatory glower at her. But unlike me, my cousin didn't back down. "Don't you talk to my cousin like that!"

"Hmm," He hummed. His eyes studied her as if she'd been on display at a museum. Interested and wonder in his words when he says, "don't nobody raise their voice at me. Haven't done so in a long time."

She crossed her arms and took a step towards him. "Don't expect more than that from me, buddy."

"Buddy?" He countered, rearing his head back. "All right. We'll do this. Norina," he addressed me, but his eyes never left Nita, "you're still over time. I'll drop you at home and take care of this woman afterwards."

"Really?" I asked, renewed hope in my heart at the prospect of getting medical treatment for her. "You'll really do that for her?"

Perhaps I was the only grateful one, considering this out of character offer from the frigid beast of a man who typically eliminated anyone who disagreed with his command. Because Nita rolled her eyes at his offer.

"Don't do me any favors," she said to him.

An amused, threatening promise of a smile curled his lips. "According to your cousin here, I'm a lot of things. But I ain't a liar. You got my word I'll get her to safety."

"Thank you." I said once all the wind whooshed out of me.

A strange energy charged the room, as if there was something crackling between the two as the silence descended. I raised a curious brow at it, but made sure to keep my comments private when we made the drive back to the Oakhouse Estate.

19

haunted mansions

KIMMY

"Can you stop ignoring me?"

I pretended not to hear the unknown ghost's question as I went about pouring milk in my Raisin Bran. I could practically hear Vonnie's, my wife's, gag as the cool skim submerged my cinnamon raisin goodness I consistently tell her is good for her. A groan escapes my lips after taking the first spoonful. So darn good. Excited, I munch happily away at the bowl while simultaneously scrolling through social media. I'm hyper adept at ignoring ghosts (spirits, I called them) at this point. So adept that I merely tuck into the blanket as I adjust into the cozy position onto the living room couch.

"Yo, Miss?" The spirit called again.

What was the name of that song again? I thought while scrolling down the Insta page of the new rock band Vonnie became super into the past month. Their new hit song featured a nameless, faceless, vocalist whose voice charmed my hard-to-please wife out of a crappy mood after a feud with her twin brother.

As if hearing my thoughts, 84 Vipers' new track plays during the fifth scroll down their band page.

"Like a sickness in my blood, your pure love, it leaves me hurting. Love just leaves me burning..."

I'm humming along to the soulful chorus and lowkey giving Vonnie all the props for finding this hidden gem of a band. The Vipers were sort of new to the rock scene and made a couple EP's here and there that were semi-successful. But their fanbase, and fame, skyrocketed from the clout of featuring a mysterious vocalist. Her voice was like a siren's song, a drug, resigning me to agree with the chorus's message: her voice was like a burning poison, but in the best way.

"Like a sickness in my—"

"Hey, bitch!" The spirit interjects my love song with an accompanying crash.

I yelped when I caught our expensive abstract flower vase hit the floor. Water and fresh picked lilies scattered to our small cabin front door space. To my chagrin and fury, our eyes connect for the first time since he manifested yesterday afternoon during my and Vonnie's evening walks.

"That's it!" I grunt.

Cozy blanket and Raisin Bran abandoned, I stomp over to the snarling spirit towering over me by a foot.

He's handsome, and not familiar in the slightest, but something inside me knows he wants something. Likely it's something I can give or help with, and I always hated that about this gift my Granny said made me special. I'm not feeling too special right now, especially since it takes all my strength not to scream at this guy.

"Do you have any idea how much something like that costs?"

"Fuck that shit," He snapped, barely glancing at the damage he's caused. "If breaking glasses is what it take to get some fucking recognition around here, then I'll break another one."

Find your center, Kimmy. I have to warn myself of the words I chanted to my wife during one of her panic attacks. I was pretty close to panicking, but chose to breathe through it. Michael, my wife's twin brother and my unofficial second spouse, often told me to embrace what makes me 'Kimmy.' To trust myself above all else because I've got grit. Sounds silly that my wife's spiritual twin encourages me like this, but I love it. No one had ever told me that I was strong. So many years of running from spirits, and now here I was enjoying a bowl of cereal while in the same room with one. An angry one if I had to guess.

He's donned in a loose white T and bagging jeans that make him look like something from an Omarion video. Except, there isn't quite an icebox where his heart used to be but a thin, translucent version of himself visible only to me.

Nonetheless, neither of these observations would magically rebuild my broken vase. I crossed my arms and glared.

"Congratulations. You've won my attention. Now what do you want?"

"I ain't won nothing," he snorted. "Don't even know where I am."

"Wait a minute," I frowned, vase forgotten momentarily to address this spirit's abject confusion. Usually, spirits walked among us without being seen nor having the ability to inter-act with the corporeal world. Usually. "You don't know where you are?"

"I'm speaking plain fucking English, ain't I?"

"We won't accomplish anything if you keep cursing at me."

He breathed hard while I watched him noticeably consider my words.

"All right, whatever. But I've been running around this Podunk jungle all damn day to get somebody's attention. Everybody acting like I pissed them off or some shit the way they ignoring me."

"Oh, no," I sighed, my heart tearing for the confused spirit.

It wasn't often I crossed paths with a spirit so unaware. So lost. Even now, I could tell he wasn't really an angry douchebag like I pegged him to be upon shattering my vase. The tall, brown skinned guy who looked no older than seventeen was utterly helpless. My nerves ease a little from compassion as I take a step closer.

"I'm so sorry to hear you're lost. And we're on a farm, not in a jungle." I say, treading lightly since his spirit was strong.

Strong enough even to hurt me if I spoke out of turn. "What's your name?"

"Yo, what happened to me?" His voice broke with the words. "My body don't feel right. I don't feel right. I don't know where the fuck I am and…"

"And everything's not what it seems?" I finished for him gently. "I understand."

In a flash only a ghost could achieve, he's in my face. And while the air is cold due to his less than living nature, his breath is as hot as July as he growls in my face.

"This coming from the bitch who ignored me for an entire day to finish her cereal. You don't understand shit!"

His front pushed me back against the couch where I fell clumsily onto the cushions. The air chilled to an intensifying degree, putting me in mind of Heath Shay, my departed brother in law. His spirit had been so strong, fueled by so many of his regrets and failures that he'd had the power to not only interact with the living, but shake entire foundations of houses. Heath had long since crossed over, but that eerie chill this nameless spirit is emitting makes me shiver from the memories and the temp in the room.

"I'm s-sorry to up-s-set you!" I stammer, feeling like little Kimberly from Jersey again.

The same one who cowered away from her fears instead of confronting them with brass knuckles like Vonnie now did. Michael's calm settles over me like a warm blanket all of a sudden, and it feels like he's borrowing me some of his tranquility to breathe through this. Then that calm dissipates. Dissipates until all that's left is a rage so intense I know it's given by my equally intense wife.

"I ain't letting nobody kick me around again. Neither will you. Understand?" She said to me after our wedding, where my mother's rapist was revealed as my uncle for the entire party to see. "Screw everybody. It's you and me."

You and me, I think. Emboldened by those words and comforted by her unintentionally sage outlook on life. Vonnie started like me. Meek, afraid, and voiceless. After that wedding controversy, she turned into a new woman. Someone bolder and older than her twenty years and ready to punch her adversities in the gut.

"Dumb bitch." He spat above me with a self-satisfied smirk.

Without hesitation, I reared up and applied Vonnie's logic to the situation. I punched him square and hard in the gut until he flew back onto the floor. His ass causing a loud thud in the room I'm sure damaged the floor. I'd never felt so bold. So powerful and all bad as I straddled the douchebag and aimed a finger in his face.

"Respect me!" I roared like a mad woman. "Or go the fuck away. You're dead, not me. So fuck off for an eternity alone knowing you pissed off the only help you're gonna get in this lifetime."

"Get off me crazy–" He began to protest and struggle beneath me to no avail. Not because my strength was near enough to keep him pinned, but because he froze. A look so jarring on his face concern reared itself in me without notice. "Did you just say I was dead?"

"Uh..." I chewed on my lip before nodding. "Yes."

"You fucking with me." He said, more so self convincingly while his eyes drifted into the distance. "You gotta be kidding me."

I rolled off of him to stand. But he remained on the floor. Stunned.

"I might be of some assistance to explain, but you need to be nicer."

No answer. At least, not a verbal one, since his horrified stare and wail spoke for itself. Though a departed spirit, I hear his soul wrenching through the painful howls of his sobs. So much raw agony that it's tangible, eating up the entire room and I feel tears prick my eyes. I don't know this guy. I've never even had a conversation with this guy. But a sudden rush of feelings roll through me and leave me raw. Not knowing what else to do, I sink to the floor. Pulling him upright and into my arms.

"Please calm down."

"No!" He groans the same instant the floors begin to rattle. "That ain't right!"

The windows make a noise recognizable from the Heath days. They're about to shatter into millions of pieces, the same as him. And I don't know what else to do but hold him. It wasn't quite me holding him though, and it was hard to explain what propelled my arms to squeeze him tighter. I needed him to know everything was okay.

"Kimmy!" A voice, a familiar voice calls out to me firmly. The emotion in it isn't fury, but I know that voice from anywhere. "Babe. What is this?"

"Baby!" I call back to Vonnie at the door. She's just standing there, staring at me with a hard look that's just as icy as the room. "Sorry if this looks strange. It's a spirit. He needs me right now."

Her jaw works a moment before she says, "Get away from him."

"What?" I asked, flabbergasted by her blatant coldness and perturbed by it.

She takes one step into the house, her top half a bikini and bottoms were basketball shorts. Fitting, since she just returned from swimming earlier now that she was used to it. She'd hated water, always did, but I helped her to swim and now she couldn't stay out of the pool we had built in our yard. I was proud of her, but not right now. Right now, she was scaring me by her callousness and unwillingness to calm the situation.

"Babe!" I called when she wouldn't answer. She gulped hard and held a balled fist to her mouth as though she'd throw up. Then it dawned on me. "Vonnie, can you see him?"

"Vonnie's in the other room right now." She said, and suddenly I realized my mistake.

Vonnie wasn't acting like herself because she wasn't. This was Michael, or Mikey, her twin brother who lived within her in spirit and who I loved just as hard. His usual kind eyes, so bright with passion and optimism, are hard. Dark brown pebbles in his sockets that glare at the two of us. Me, rocking the screaming ghost, and the ghost...well, screaming.

"Right." I say, recomposing myself. "Sorry, Mike. Mind giving me a hand with him?"

He shakes his head. "Kimmy, get the hell out of that house. Right now."

I notice he's standing on the porch, his hand still balled at his nose as if there was a stench in the air. Why was he acting this way? And most importantly...

"Where's Vonnie?"

"She..." He hesitated. "She, uh, slipped away. Think she may have felt this spirit in here before we walked in and disappeared somewhere...inside."

"Mind Manson..." I breathe, not needing him to finish the sentence. "Shit. We gotta get her back. I don't like when she just disappears like that."

"You're not the only one." Mike says, still glaring at the spirit. "I was in the middle of a nap when she made me Take Over."

"Oh, Yvonne." I whisper, needing her here right now. By my side to get me through this situation instead of huddling down in her mental cave. Then a thought struck me. "You have any idea who this guy is?"

Another pause before he nodded. "Yeah, but I came to talk to you. About something important and time sensitive."

"You do know him?!" I squeaked, my ears ringing over the guy's cries. "Sir, please calm down!"

"What's his name?" I ask Mike, who still looks uneasy and unwilling to enter our house.

"We should talk, Kimmy. Outside. Away from that!" Mike spat the words with an irritated twist of his round lips.

The nameless spirit made a jerking motion that nearly flung me to the other side of the room. Thank heavens for my competitive swim days and all the underlying muscle it afforded me, or else I'd have been hurt.

"No time for that!" I hollered over the wailing spirit thrashing below my wrestle-hold on him. "Mike, please help me! I need to calm him down, but I'll need his name."

"But—"

"Please!" I begged, hating the indecision and agony on his face.

Right when he opens his mouth to crack the case, to solve the forty-eight hour mystery who's been haunting me, the guy howls from the floor.

"Nora! I'm sorry!"

20

take a seat

·❤·❤·❤·❤·❤·

"Heading out!" I call excitedly before leaving the Oakhouse prison.

With all the open access freedom Trace granted, the prison felt a lot less like the stronghold Edgar kept it. It was more like, well, a mansion. A super huge mansion I got to leave and return every day, so long as it was before the intriguing suppers alone with Trace Oakhouse.

A solid month flew by without incident, and for a change I felt good. I'd gained, according to my cousin, a much needed five pounds and my hair was done. I now rocked long yarn braids laced with blonde that Nita administered as a welcome aboard gift since I started working at her shop again. Well, it was more like volunteering since I insisted she keep her money. I mean, I lived in a freaking mansion for Christ sake! Not the little blue house of my dreams and with my parents, but in a lavish plantation-style fortress nonetheless. Nita's was still developing, and I even requested a time to speak with Trace about potentially adding the salon to our small business support list. Shit, not our, I meant the Oakhouse Small Business Support fund. I had to reprimand the small voice dying for belonging whenever it reared up.

Instead of drowning that voice out with hard liquor in solitude like I normally did, I chose to invest time with Nita. Same as before, her shop became a home away from hazardous home life with Mom and Pop. My days were filled now between Ball Prep, Wife Grooming, and volunteering at Nita's Hair & Beauty Bar. My days were full, but my heart ran on empty.

Lately, the need to see my family intensified the longer I hung around my cousin. It was like old times, but with new clientele. I'd arrive at eleven in the morning, set up my cosmetic station Nita so kindly set up for me now that the cash flow was in much better state, and continue on with my day beautifying clients. The makeup business was solid in DC, but booming down south. Since my client base practically tripled compared to what it was back home. I loved every minute of girl talk and shampooed secrets that never left the premises and resumed after each client visit.

The salon was thriving, and as a token of Nita's perpetual gratitude for my financial assistance, there awaited a gift basket at my station every morning. I'd chastise her against it, swearing there was no way I'd be able to eat through baskets full of fruits and snacks every day without ending up in the hospital from diabetic shock. After several more heated verbal battles on the subject, she'd resigned to flowers instead. And I smiled each day when I walked into a new flower placed at my station before an appointment.

Today it was magnolias.

Warmth spread throughout my body and I couldn't suppress the smile as I lifted the flower and twirled it between my fingers. She didn't need to keep thanking me, is what I wished I could tell her, but I know Nita. Proud, mature, and gracious to a fault and this shop was her dream. If this made her feel good, then I wouldn't stop her.

"Nora, your eleven thirty called to say she'd be a couple minutes late," Aryanna said from the front desk.

I smiled at the new receptionist and answered, "No prob! Cool of her to give us a notice."

"Yeah, she sounded not from around here. And really excited to get her hair and makeup done."

"I love that!" I said, meaning it, since meeting with new clients meant the world to me, too. Greenville locals were also so kind compared to individuals who'd often show up late or not at all sometimes back home. I'd gotten so accustomed to the whole southern hospitality thing and wondered when the ball would burst. When the veil of perfection would fall from this perfect little haven that had somehow been constructed around my life.

"Better hope she gets here soon since we're closing early today," Nita sang coming down the stairs from her upstairs apartment.

I stilled. "Closing early?"

"Yeah, girl." Aryanna chirped from the front desk while shuffling through some papers. "Because of that festival happening today until five. The streets will be a nightmare to get through."

"True that," Nita confirmed from an empty style seat. "Be lucky if we make it to the parking deck at all in the middle of all that. Don't you remember?"

"Must have slipped my mind," I mumble past a clog in my throat. My heart and hopes sink at the thought of going back to that awful house and being near Trace Oakhouse any longer than necessary.

I school my face quickly to a blank mask, so as to not reveal the dread flaring in me at the bleak prospect of returning home immediately after this eleven thirty appointment. I must do a good job at hiding that dread since Nita and Aryanna share a laugh I'm too zoned out to pay attention to.

"Frankie is all excited about this damn festival, too." Nita laughs with a warm smile on her face. "That boy is so much like his daddy. Passionate about the things he cares about. Since he met Koichi they've been so tight, and it's nice my baby's finally got a friend to relate to down here."

A faint smile lifted my lips at the mention of her six year old son, Frankie J, we called him since he'd been his late father's namesake. Best word to describe him was saint level genius since he'd been obsessed with every aspect of Asian culture. I couldn't deny the level of cuteness the best friend pair presented during times Koichi would visit the shop and geek out with Frankie J in history books, instead of action figures.

"What kind of festival is it?" I asked Nita.

"Something called the Obon Festival. It's all about honoring one's ancestors and is open to the public if y'all wanna come. Frankie is practically salivating to show me his rendition of the Bon dance."

"Thanks, but count me out," Aryanna says. "Gotta hot date tonight, and I'm super thankful for the extra time to prepare."

"Boo, you suck!" Nita mocks jokingly. "You're getting way more action than me on a Friday night. Pray I don't pass out from boredom y'all."

"Try to have fun, though, girl!" Aryanna cheered and I noted her packing her bag for the day. "You going, Nora?"

"I..." I stammered, unsure if this fell within the scope of my newfound semi-freedom. I clutched the phone in my pocket in thought. "I'll have to check with, well, you know who to make sure there's nothing planned for later."

Neither of them joined my wry chuckle, which is why I never brought up my home life in the salon. Nita folded arms across her chest and rolled her eyes while Aryanna made a face before falling silent.

"What?" I asked.

"Oh, nothing." Ary said, polite as always. Unlike Nita.

"I promised last month that I'd keep my mouth shut if I had nothing nice to say. And I never have anything nice to say about that controlling psycho you go home to."

"Nita..." I groaned, really not trying to go there.

"I didn't say anything!" She effused. "Some fiancé you got that won't let you see your little cousin's festival debut."

I rolled my eyes. "It's not like that. He'll let me if I just keep him informed."

Her eyes rolled even harder. "Sure. Keep him informed, my ass. More like ask his permission."

"Gosh, you're a real bitch when you wanna be." I couldn't help the words, and welcomed/expected her gasp. "You got no clue. About anything."

"Well, how about you fill me in on the details, for once. Like I asked you to a month ago!"

"It's not that fucking simple!"

"But it is, though. You just open your mouth, and make words. Like ones that explain why you had to practically beg him for a cell phone. That don't even sound like you to beg a man for anything."

"Leave it alone." I warn. We're walking toward each other now like merging tornadoes, set to destroy anything in each other's paths to get close and wreak havoc. I was tired of having to defend myself to her. There was concern, then there was Nita. Always extra. Always doing the most where the most was not needed. Did she even understand the sacrifices I made to be here?

"Ladies, let's settle down." Ary cautioned, coming between us. "We've got a client."

I almost ignored her. Almost disregard the two women standing at the front door to focus my energy on my meddling cousin who consistently took things too far. To knock her ass down a peg and stop prying. But I don't get the chance to do that, or otherwise, because of the familiar voice that calls out to us. To me.

"How I've missed you ladies!" The white lady sang from the front desk. She's holding an African American toddler and the silk wrap on her head is one I recognized from not too long ago.

Nita hollers her excitement and runs over to her while I just freeze. "Miss Joyce!" She says.

"Oy, hi my girl!" Joyce says. "Told you I'd come for a visit soon. I have no plans on abandoning the best hairdresser in the universe. Sorry I'm late! Traffic is a beast out there."

Seeing her...Joyce Zelman...the mother of My First Love and physical representation of all that I'd lost. Of who I'd lost during the numb months in Greenville...rattled the shit out of me.

"Nor!" Joyce called out. "Same goes for the best MUA in all of DC. I've missed you all."

"I..." I stammered, my eyes glazing over at the scene. "I've missed you, too."

My throat is dry as I watch the reunion, and I wrestle with the urge to run far away. Since it's not just one ghost from my past, but two. And her eyes are scathing as she watches me from across the room with another toddler in her arms.

"Where are my manners?" Joyce said before indicating the woman beside her with a strained smile. "Nita. Nora. Meet Sasha. My grandkids' mother."

A beat of silence clouds the room that would have registered as awkward should I not been frozen with terror. Seeing them both here...at once...just what was this?

"Nice to meet you, Sasha. Welcome to my salon," Nita says to her.

Sasha flashes a small smile, barely acknowledging the greeting. Then she moves. Marching to stand before me to hiss, "We need to talk. Right now."

21

labyrinth

·❤·❤·❤·❤·❤·

"We need to talk. Right now." Sasha says only to me while bouncing the toddler in her arms. The toddler whose brown eyes and fae-like beauty looks just as spellbinding as their father's, making their parentage unmistakable.

A tight smile, just as strained as the one Joyce flashed Sasha upon entering the shop, formed on my face as I looked beyond Chicken Girl to face the confused crowd. Staring at us.

"Hey, cuz, cool if we borrow your apartment to chat in private for a moment?" I asked Nita.

"Y'all know each other?" Joyce answered instead.

"Uh, sort of. Yes. We're old friends from back home." I responded to her, a total lie, but I needed to say just enough to get out of range from their prying eyes.

The loud music lets me know the Obon Festival is beginning, and I oddly feel compelled not to miss it. To call Trace and beg him to let me go, or attend the once a year event anyway and ask for forgiveness later. Either way, the quicker we got this chat over with, the better.

While I missed Joyce, I couldn't really look at her without caving in. Or totally crashing.

Nita flashed me another scathing glare, one that screamed "what else are you hiding?!" But she handed the keys over without another word.

After asking Joyce to watch the kids, I shut and locked the front door of Nita's quaint upstairs unit moments later. Now we're staring at each other in the living room, no sound but our deep breathing around us.

Sasha folded her arms and I noted an emotion accompanying the anger in her eyes as she stared down at me. "You got a lot of nerve to leave town the way you did."

"You got that same nerve coming down to Greenville the way you did." I countered, ready for the double-sided battle that always occurred between us whenever we spoke. "What are you doing here anyway?"

She stepped closer. "Why did you leave?!"

"I'm not answering that." I said calm, plain, and as deadpan as possible. "Thirty seconds or I'm leaving. I do have a client to get to before closing time."

A frustrated tear spills down her cheek, and I school more neutrality over myself. Not engaging with Sasha was always best, because when she got going, she didn't stop. "The way you dismiss me. You act as if nothing ever happened between—"

"Twenty seconds left," I said, totally not going down that path. "Did something happen back home? Anything with Luther?"

"Luther is...God, he's gonna stay the way he is. Awful." She sniffed, then continued, "when you were there he wasn't as bad. Now..."

"Did he hurt you?"

Her eyes scan the premises as if looking for the very man in the room. Then she gulped. "He sold nearly all my things. Nora, there's nothing left and now me and the boys are forced to live with Joyce. She despises me."

I scowled, anger burning bright and hot in my gut as she continued speaking about all the devastation Luther was able to wreak on the gang. He apparently didn't stop at selling every valuable from most of the women, but firearms from the men, too. Sasha had been grudgingly loyal and willing to withstand his worsening behavior, but soon he demanded her paychecks. Yet his latest crime was unforgivable.

"He held your son at gunpoint?" I repeated the words I couldn't believe. Not processing how one man could stoop as low to threaten a two year old.

She wiped the tears from her cheeks and shot me a look so full of agony I fought back a tear myself. "We need you. Please come back. Deal with him."

Though I sympathized, I shook my head. "I can't."

"Can't? Or do you mean that you won't? There's a clear difference between the two. And we can't stand too much more of this."

"Then move away, like I did. Luther is insane, but his reach is pretty limited now he's fucked up most of his relationships with other surrounding gangs."

"You are not understanding!" She hissed. "I got grandparents to take care of. Me can't leave. What happens to them if so?"

"I don't know," I told her with a crumbling heart, "but that's not my life anymore. I can't go back. His influence is limited, but not gone. If I go back he'll take everything I love. I can't risk that. I won't risk that."

She buried her head in her hands, fully sobbing now. I notice her hair is frizzy, unkempt compared to her typical bone straight from the result of too many perms. The color in her skin is off, too. Like all the sun's been sucked out of her, same as me when I first got to Greenville.

Not one detail about her resembles the regal baddie who caught Ty's eye and there are so many things I want to say to her. The first one being, "Sasha, I am sorry."

She doesn't answer but sobs harder. Like a dying animal after a finishing blow. Like she's held on for too long to something and is without hope.

"I'm sorry. Look at me." I command, losing the edge in my voice. "I know it's really late, but I truly mean it. How I treated you back then was just unacceptable. I realized I never apologized for that."

"Don't," she blubbers with her thick Caribbean twang permeating her speech. "Just forget it."

"I'm selfish, I know." I say before grabbing her shoulders and forcing her to look at me. "What do you really want from me?"

Though closed before, her eyes blink open. Pitiful tears continue to waterfall down her face but she's otherwise silent. My head fills with questions but is surprisingly clear when I catch her eyes linger on my eyes then settle on my lips.

"I..." She squeaks, "I want...the graveyard...you and me..."

I don't give her a chance to finish as I pull her forward and capture her lips in a deep, exploratory kiss. She melts in my arms, and though I'm a couple inches shorter, she falls into me like a second skin. Or maybe like a second coat, since every nerve opens wide and sets my skin ablaze. I didn't know what I was doing, to be honest—I just felt. I just couldn't bear the guilt of watching her hurt because of me anymore. Especially after hearing Luther began her on the same path as me before I was practically banished. To think she was going through what I endured for the gang's sake in my absence? Even after the hell I put her through in elementary school?

My mind drifts briefly to the events after Ty's funeral, in the graveyard, and the fire ignites again. Though I'd been frozen cold inside and out, somehow Sasha and I argued, which turned into fist fighting the day after the funeral. After going to visit his grave that day and seeing her there, too, I just couldn't bear to watch from the shadows anymore. Couldn't stand to see the bitch he claimed ruined his life cry over his grave. The details are foggy since I was half drunk at the time, but we ended up back at Mama's house, in my room where we'd woke up after several rounds of angry, drunk sex.

All for it to be unknowingly caught on camera. The tech set up in my room for the illicit cam shows I told no one about, were turned on. Turned on and filmed us mid-act. Luther got his hands on the tapes and threatened to ruin our lives if ever we betrayed him. And everything went downhill from there.

"Nora..." Sasha moans into my mouth. I grunt when she shoves me up against the front door and lifts me into a strad-dling position around her waist. She's surprisingly strong for her slim build, but I'm burning up still. Anxious. Regretful, but anticipating. "I want to...to touch you. Can I touch you again? Same as before...?"

I nod my consent before a firework of stars exploded be-hind my lids at the feel of her intrusion. The crook of her finger latched onto my G spot, and I moaned an immediate, powerful release in her neck.

"Sasha…" I say, a breathless and throaty beg into her ear, "I meant it. I am…s-sorry."

"It don't matter no more," she sang, sultry and low while continuously fucking me into the door with more fingers. I bite down on her revealed shoulder to keep from screaming through the second orgasm. My juices create loud sloshes of sound around her searching fingers. "I just want you. I want us. I'm ready to give you everything if you'll have me."

"This is…" I moaned, "what you really want."

She licked my right lobe, sucking the sensitive appendage between her lips I didn't even realize could be a source of pleasure. "Have me, Nora."

"Tyrone…" I breathed, rocking against her digits in a rutting frenzy. "Not you. Loved him…"

"He loved you." She moaned. And I'm undone at the sight of her slurping my juices from her fingers, sucking the evidence of my extreme arousal as if it was the sweetest nectar. Like it'd been a remedy for something due to the roll of her eyes and whimper she emitted around her submerged fingers. "He loved you just like I loved you. Don't you get it, silly gyal?"

I shook my head, my brain under a complete fog of pleasure. Not able to answer that.

She kissed me again. Slow, sensual, and in a way that made me understand the phrase slow burn before separating and saying, "Silly gyal. We argued about you. All our fights were about having you. You think I didn't know he was fucking you while we were together? Tyrone couldn't resist ya. And neither could I. He...told me he'd try to talk to you about being with both of us. So that we could all have what we want. But Ty got greedy..."

"No!" I moaned, the fog trying to clear from my head but my pussy still clenching and riding her offered fingers scraping over my clit. "Ty...and you...wanted to share me?"

She cupped my face, an adoring look on hers. "Not at first. But I didn't ever think you'd be into me. I liked Ty enough, but you...it was always you. Since you kissed me on the playground, it's always been you." Her face turned sour for a moment. "But you had Patrice. You fawned over her after Ty was killed. I couldn't get near you if I tried."

Ty. My First Love. Trice. Leaving me. The graveyard. Suddenly all those terrible visions of reality float back and sobers me. Sobers me enough to realize what I was doing and who I was doing it with.

"Stop!" I commanded, willing my breathing to normalize after shoving her away from me. "I can't think with you...doing that. Sasha, this is so fucked up."

A helpless look of dread twists her face. "You asked. I answered you with the truth. I'm laying my cards on the table here. And I want to be with you. I'll even move to this Podunk little town if that's what it takes to be together. Luther wants me to...be his. He keeps threatening me with this tape, and...I don't care! If it really comes to light, then that means we can just be together sooner. I'm not ashamed anymore."

Tears course down my face as more reality crashes. I cupped her face, "This isn't right. What happened between us at that grave, then the tape, I regret. Not because we had sex. But because of the reasons why. Sasha, you are beautiful. You are so wonderful and I kick myself every day for not being the real friend both you and I needed back in the day, because...look at what that could've blossomed into."

She closes her eyes. "So do I..."

I smile, sadness beating my heart at my next words. "I can help you get away from Luther. I do consider you a friend, and you don't deserve what he's putting you through, too. But us being together wouldn't be true for me. When I see you, I see Ty. Everything that I lost and can never have. I want Ty. And to be with you would be unfair since you'll never be that."

"Nora, wait—"

"You are wonderful." I whisper, marveling at her eyes I'm now noticing are hazel in color. "So damn gorgeous with a gorgeous soul to match. I can't be with you."

"Can't," she bites out, "Or won't."

Even though my heart didn't belong to Sasha that way I couldn't imagine why we couldn't remain close. For so long we tiptoed around these feelings. So long we talked around each other, at each other, but never to each other. This felt like, for the first time in a long time, the start of something new and could be unique to us. Convoluted now, for sure, but

I had the best feeling that we'd survive this storm. Ty couldn't make it with us to the other side and for him, I decided to trust me.

"You are earth," He breathed so many times in my ear when our bodies joined as one. "Give me life. Love you, Nora."

Love me...

An expression I'd never witnessed formed on her face and I smiled, somehow feeling the light pouring into the gentle forehead nudge she'd given me.

"There's still time." She whispered helplessly. "Still time for us to leave all of this behind. I thank you for understanding me, though. And for listening. But if you won't come back home, then we can just go. Start over, maybe, as friends."

"No. I'm done running." I said, tears gathered in my eyes as I shook my head. "Thank you for bringing me this small ounce of happiness. You helped me figure out what needs to be done. For real and for good."

"What's that?" She asked.

Heavy pounds on the door make us both jump out of our skins. Of course, it's Nita.

"Sorry, cuz!" I shout, mortified by the fact that we'd practically had sex in her living room. I was also horrified that the private moment I requested morphed into a full thirty minutes. Damn it, I swear internally while readjusting my pink sundress. "Sorry we kept you guys waiting—"

Instead of Nita standing at the apartment threshold with a scowl, it's someone I totally don't recognize. She's a tiny thing, I first noted, observing her minced frame covered by a white kimono with red flowers. Her skin was the color of alabaster, whiter than white that lets me know she's painted this way intentionally.

She resembles a tiny Asian doll, so cute and almost as if she's crawled out of her box. The cute girl beams up at both Sasha and I, where I finally notice the deep scar along the right side of her face. It's puckered and healed with age, but there's a deep brown mutation which gives her a sort of frightening countenance.

"You breathing hard, gyal." Sasha penetrated the silence. "Are you in trouble?"

"I need person skilled in face arts." Her voice was like a light twitter, carrying on the breeze with an urgency. I blinked a few times before understanding dawned on me.

"Oh, yeah. That's me. I'm the makeup artist here at Nita's. Do you have an appointment?"

"*Yurushite kudasai*, ma'am!" She bowed to me. "No time! I need your help right this instant! It is matter of—how do you say—life and death!"

22

the first step

KIMMY

The gentle summer breeze whizzes through my strawberry blonde curls and I take a deep breath to take it all in. The familiar sounds of insects chitter in the distance, which doesn't quite measure up to the bright sun shining down on my face as I sit in this empty park. The park feels familiar, like a vague memory from somewhere deep in the past I can't quite grasp. But as I look around the vacant lot void of any children on the playground a sense of peace floods me. It's almost like I should panic, but can't. As if an invisible sheen of calm spray is sprayed into the empty space and I'm the only one capable of breathing it in. Keeping with that simile, I do just that. Taking the deepest breath possible and closing my eyes to find that center again.

"Pretty dress," a little falsetto says.

My eyes fly open from the suddenness of the child's appearance. Where had she come from?

Taking a couple more of those steadying breaths, I gulp. Then respond to the little girl. "Thanks. Yours is pretty, too."

"Really? You think that, miss?"

"Yes," I tell her, quickly studying her pink Sunday school dress and shiny black shoes with white lace socks peeking out. That same ghost of familiarity plagues me just as it did when I found myself in this empty park. It was like she was familiar, but not exactly.

She smiled, revealing bright white teeth with one missing in the front. "Mikey said you were pretty, too. He was right!"

"Wait, what?" I sputtered. "Mikey told you I was pretty. When?"

"When he came to visit me, silly!"

"Right..." I said, contemplating before adding, "when would he have visited you, little girl? And who are you?"

"Hmm," she hummed in thought while poking an index finger into her cheek. "I'll tell you my name and when Mikey visited."

"Great!" I breathed, not realizing the breath I'd been holding until it rushed out of me. After adjusting myself, I turned to her more fully on the park bench. "Let's have it, then."

Her three pigtails shook as she shook her head. Denying me?

"So, you don't really know Mikey?"

"Absolutely, I do! Mikey is so kind. And stubborn. He met my daddy, too. "

"Okay then," I start, "then when was he here?"

"Unh unh." She vocalized. "That's not how this works, Kimmy. Do you like games?"

I thought for a second, remembering how much fun playing video games with Vonnie was, considering I'd deemed all games as meaningless in a past life.

I shrugged. "Sure. But why is that important?"

"I love Tag." She said as a slow sly smile poured over her face. "Catch me if you can, and then we'll trade stories. Okay?"

"No, no, no, wait!" I started, but it was no use.

She bolted towards the jungle gym now swarming with children. Where did all these kids come from? Did they magically gather during our conversation? Impossible, I thought, considering the huge crowds of kids. There was no way that many little people could have gathered without a sight or a peep, or even stranger, without adult oversight. Looking around, I noticed I was the only adult for miles sitting at the park bench.

Don't think about it too much, I coached myself as I stood up. There were so many children running and screaming and playing that it seemed unnatural. Or, rather, unnormal like they were too preoccupied to stop for a breath or notice me approaching. I could do this, I could do this, I could do this, I chanted before plunging into the crowd.

The minute I enter the crowd, the sky darkens. Then the temperature drops from its sunny breeze to a glacial chill. Snow pours down over us, the kids included, but maybe I was the only cold one since they never stopped playing and chasing each other.

"Little girl!" I called out. "Where did you go?"

"Get away from me, camel!" A child's voice shouted.

"W-What?" I demanded and shivered at the same time. But not from the cold. The chill down my spine came from that old nickname. The nickname I hadn't heard in over a decade.

"Kimmy the camel!" A voice screamed.

"Look at her long legs! Long legs like a camel! Kimmy Kimmy camel leg."

"S-Stop it!" I yelled over the voices and screams, walking in circles. "What is this?!"

The kids, who I assumed were NPC's (non-playable characters) at this point, ran faster. Faster than was humanly possible until blurs of speed and light surrounded me. My head hurt from this.

"How could someone even be with a schizo like you?" Another voice, but this time I knew it as Felicia Winters,

my high school crush who'd flat out rejected me in front
of my entire class after her recently deceased grandmother
cornered me during homeroom. "Crazy Kim you should be
called."

"I'm NOT crazy!" I shouted into the speedy winds that
upgraded to gale force strength.

The children's laughter becomes screeches of something animalistic, piercing my eardrums so intensely I'd be
shocked if I didn't make it out of this permanently deaf.

"I'm blaming you for all of it. For taking advantage of me,
my brother, and my body. That's all on you to deal with. Take
it up with your god for punishment, or your therapist. It's
not my deal..."

My heart stills at the previous argument. It's Vonnie, my
wife's bitter words spat at me after she caught me and her
brother having sex. I'd felt so low then. So, so, impossibly low
to get caught making love to the girl's body I'd all but drooled
over when I first moved down south. We'd since moved past
that and our disastrous wedding, but...

"Vonnie?" I shout for her warmth but am met with more
ice-cold wind and snow. My head hurts. Everything is a total
mess and the screams? They've heightened and intensified
to ear bleeding heights.

This had to stop.

Everything's a blur when I reopened my eyes. So blurry
I'm not able to make form or figure out of anything but a

pair of red eyes a couple feet away. Frantic, I do the next best thing whenever I find myself in the middle of a lucid dream to wake up. Bring my hand up to my lips and bite down. Hard.

"Catch me if you can, Kimmy!" A guttural, animal voice taunts from beyond.

It's nothing like the adorable little girl who greeted me earlier. But then I pull my palm away and study it. There's blood. So much blood there after my bite that it oddly brings me back to reality.

In the matter of an instant, I'm warmed by...something. The winds and laughter had stopped long enough for another voice to pierce the air.

"I'll be your number one fan, cheering you from the sidelines and encouraging you to follow that dream if that's really what you want. Okay?"

Tears prick my eyes at the sound of the first non-bitter voice echoing through the blur circle. I also recognize where the warmth comes from, too. It's all the warm fuzzies I felt after Vonnie uttered the words. Telling me she's been my number one fan, without question or recompense from my shitty actions. She's always been that shining light amidst my own storm. Anchoring me back home even when she didn't realize it. Like now.

Certain and clear now, I met the red-eyed gaze beyond the blur circle and barked, "Helen! I see you."

"No!" The guttural creature I can't see roars before the ground shakes. The whole thing feels rather horror-movie chic, but I don't tear my eyes away from the red beams until they've disappeared completely.

Just as soon as it appeared, the summer day returned. Along with the serenity of the chittering insect noises and the heat. The children have disappeared, all but one, since the same little girl is sitting on the ground. She's clapping excitedly.

"Congratulations!" She cheered. "Mikey told us you were smart, but wow! Good job at catching me."

"What just happened?"

She ushers for me to come closer. Suspicious, I do it, and wince when she brings her hands up to cup my face.

"You won! Now I must keep my end of the deal." She effused while wiggling from excitement. "This is the Center. Neither heaven nor hell, but a middle place where spirits come to be reborn. And rest. Always stand here from now on, okay?"

I nodded. "Okay."

A warm knowing smile crests her face. "Good. I can't give you all the details, but I will honor our deal. Mikey visited during Yvonne's coma. He wants to come Home."

I laughed, a loud, foolhardy camel-Kimmy sort of laugh that leaves me wrung out by the time it stops. I break away from her to wipe my eyes. "That's ridiculous. This has got to be a nightmare."

"Oh, Kimmy," she breathed in a sympathetic tone. "You're not dreaming. Mikey doesn't have much time left. He's with you now, but he shouldn't be. He promised to honor both your and Yvonne's dreams before he departs."

"Stop talking nonsense you evil little fairy!" I hissed.

She laughed and clapped. "Good one! No one's called me a fairy before. I like it better than Helen."

That reminded me...

"Helen," I began, "she's Mikey and Vonnie's mother, right?"

"I..." A sad smile tainted the warmth on her face. Then she looks up with unshed tears in her eyes. "She wasn't a good mommy. She hurt them. But Mikey's hurting now too. Can't you see that?"

Funny. Seconds ago I'd been dead set on murdering the mischievous little fairy. Now I knelt down to her height and placed hands on her shoulders to rid that sad look on her face.

"What does he need from me?" I asked. "I don't want Mikey to hurt either, and I see you don't. What can I do to help him, uh...get home?"

Her smile returned, reminding me of Vonnie's face after she'd won a difficult level of her video game. She cupped my face again. "Answer 'yes' to his question when you go back. Okay?"

I frowned. "Answer 'yes'?"

"Mmhm." She nodded. "He wants to honor your dreams, both of you. This will make his efforts easier. And help Yvonne realize hers. Mikey can't stay much longer without breaching our deal."

"Right," I mumbled, knowing better than to violate a deal with a spirit once made. "You mean I help Vonnie realize her dream so he can move on? Find peace?"

She nodded once.

"Why all of this, huh?" I ask, indignant once more. "Why all the theatrics of walking me through my own torturous memories to get here? None of this makes any sense."

"Such a smart girl." She whispers. "I showed you those memories to make sure you were strong enough for the task of helping the twins."

"And if I wasn't?"

She remained silent, but there was no need to speak. I understood the ramifications of failing that weird test, of losing that weird game. A loss meant I wouldn't have come back home, to either of them. Leaving Mikey forever trapped in a Mind Mansion of suffering.

As if sensing my anger, she reaches for my cheek again. Cupping it, and whispering, "You are clever and strong. I had no doubt you'd win."

"Helen—"

"Shh," she whispered, chanting something non-English before adding at the end, "Help him through. Answer him yes. Only you can do this."

"I can't do it."

"You can do it, Kimmy," she said. "It was great meeting you. Love them both to bring her back. Let him honor your dreams."

"Please wait!"

"You can do it!" She repeated, the world blackening and distorting her voice. "You can do it, Kimmy. Come back."

"Wait a minute..." I rasp, my throat is so dry all of a sudden. Warm hands stroke my cheek before I feel the wetness on my forehead. Is it raining?

"Come back to me, Kim." More rain, then, "Don't leave her. Not yet, not yet, not yet! You can do it, baby."

"Vonnie," I rasp once her face comes into view. The world is spinning and my mind is foggy. My body feels heavy with the weight of stiff limbs. "I'm here."

"Not Vonnie," he says darkly and in a way that lets me know it's Mikey, not his sister. There's something soft below me and I marvel at the lush sensations of warmth and plushness. I'm on a bed. "Where'd you go?"

"Where am I?"

A pause before he responded carefully. "It's morning time. You slept all day yesterday and wouldn't wake up. Vonnie tried waking you and panicked when she saw you weren't responding. Are you okay?"

I nodded, my heart steeling at the thought of triggering my wife.

"Thank god!" He breathed before covering me with his body. "I couldn't handle it if I lost you. It would break her."

His hands are rough and strong, nothing like Vonnie's soft ones she took painstaking care of with the best lotions and potions. I realize two things in that moment that had me leaping from the bed:

First, it didn't rain on my forehead. Instead, Mikey's tears spilled into my face tricking me into thinking I was back at that playground and Helen's ghost decided to throw in an extra rain storm to the Tag game.

Second, it was Mikey beside me. This wouldn't normally scare the shit out of me, but it was Mikey beside me. As in, Michael Masters the male! In the blood and flesh. Since he'd rocked a similar afro as his fraternal twin sister used to, it had been easy to mistake this grown man for her. But if his breast-less, taught upper half wasn't proof enough of his manhood, then his naked glory did. All his naked glory that revealed something pulsing to life once my eyes landed on it.

"Who the fuck are you?" I screamed, looking around the room for a weapon, any weapon, to hammer this nude psycho to pieces.

He climbs out of the bed, too. "Kimmy, calm down. It's not what you think. It's still me, Mikey."

"Mikey, my ass!" I hollered before charging at him. We fell in a tangled heap back onto the bed and somehow I finesse my way on top of him. Straddling his hard hips with mine and wrapping my hands around his throat. "Who are you?"

"Still Mikey," he chokes out.

"Stop acting stupid and tell me what you did with my wife! Or I swear I'll kill you right here."

He fought my hold for a second, bringing his legs up in a way that slid me down his body. And, dear freaking heavens, I could have died when I stared in horror at my bare breasts.

I was naked, too!

I'm suddenly regretting my decision to sleep in the nude since being married when I feel his dick, long and thick, throb beneath my opening. We stared into each other's eyes as a wave of heat passed between us, floating into the atmosphere with the knowledge that it'd only take one thrust to—

"Shit!" I swore when Mikey flipped me on my back, taking advantage of the distraction. "Get away from me," I said winded, all the anger draining from my words when he nestled himself between my open legs. My pussy pulsed then clenched at the feel of him so, so close.

"Will you listen to me for a second?" He demanded, low and grumbling its vibrations all the way down my body. "Kimmy, it's still me."

"Then where is Vonnie?"

He gulped. "She slunk away into the Mind Mansion when she couldn't wake you. Next thing I know, I'm waking up beside you, but as me! A man. Vonnie's totally gone. I checked. She's nowhere inside my head or in the house."

"Gone?" I whispered, crestfallen and broken. It's like a thousand shards of glass have taken residence in my hollow heart at the knowledge that Vonnie was gone. And it felt like my fault. "No, no, no!"

"You were babbling stuff in your sleep earlier." He said, his face dark and stone cold. "Did you...see a little girl and an old man?"

"A little..." I began, then the flood of memories of those terrible visions came back. Helen, running and laughing through the playground called The Center. All the bad memories. Her message. Her warning. "No old man, but there was a little girl. Yes, um, her name was Hel—"

"Don't say it," Mikey warns slowly, bringing his hand to my lips. "Not right now. Did she give you a message?"

I nodded after he removed his hand. "Yes, she said...she said..."

"You can do it, beautiful." He encouraged me while stroking my hair. "What did she say? This might be the only way we can get Vonnie back."

I had to trust him, I thought even as the memory of that vision evaded me. Felt like it happened centuries ago instead of minutes ago, and I'm struggling to figure it out. What did she say?

"Find your center," He crooned in my ear. "That's what you always tell my sister, right? You try it, too. Just breathe, relax, and focus. Focus on the message."

"Right," I breathed in thought, staring into his eyes that held so much fear laced with compassion. I did as he said, and focused on Little Helen's words and how he'd made a deal to return to that strange purgatorial arena she called... "The Center! My dreams, uh...something about you not being able to go Home until you've honored our dreams?"

He frowns, contemplating for a second, before he says, "The promise I made."

"She also said you'd made a deal."

"She's right." He stated. "I can't break it, and I sense this is the old man's way of expediting the process."

"Old man?" I asked, totally confused.

He sighed. "My grandpa."

"You mean your late grandpa? I thought he'd passed on," I said, remembering Vonnie telling me how she'd never met either of her biological grandparents since they'd all died before she was born.

"Exactly. It's a long story. But just know I don't belong here. I can't stay much longer, since I promised them I'd help you both accomplish your dreams before it was my time."

Had he been talking to someone without my particular skill set of seeing spirits, then they'd have him committed on the spot. But he's not talking to just anybody. It's me, and I recall how both he and Vonnie believed me when I told them about my abilities. Dubious at first of course, but never buying into the Crazy Kimmy spiel. And I wouldn't disbelieve him either.

"Kimmy, what's the one thing you want the most?" He asked tenderly. "The one thing you want to achieve, establish, or overcome?"

My dreams, I realized. He wants to help me accomplish my dreams. Without a second thought, I told him. "To be a mother and grow our family."

A loud silence befalls the room. It's like the air and atmosphere shifted into a stilted mass, weighing heavily on my lungs despite the extremely tall man covering my naked body. The knowledge that he was naked—that we were bare—completely in this moment makes me squirm awkwardly beneath him.

If Mikey was feeling any of that awkwardness, then he hid it well. Since he brings his lips to mine and kisses me deep, and works himself closer into my heated folds.

"That's the answer," he husked against my lips in wonder. "The old man didn't expedite the process. He made the process possible..."

"Michael..." I groaned, all logical thoughts flying out the open window as my body spasmed and pussy clenched beneath his length. Just one movement, I purred inwardly. Just one thrust forward and he'd be fully seated inside my moist channel, "...please..."

"May I?" He kisses me again, not ever honoring my pleas to whet the monstrous lust blooming on a cloud of desire. He cups my face. "Let me make your dreams come true."

"We shouldn't...?" I groaned when another wave of desire rolled through my body. I sprung up, my body an oven and pussy drenching the sheets. What was this feeling coming over me?

"I need your answer, baby." He crooned while aligning his dick, oozing at this point, at my center. "May I honor your dreams of becoming a mother? Let me do this for you..."

Little Helen's words of warning echo inside my mind from nowhere. "Help him through. Answer him 'yes.' Only you can do this..."

Unable to help myself, I reach up to cup his cheek. Which is more contoured than Vonnie's, I note. "Are you in pain? Living inside Vonnie this way?"

I can tell he doesn't expect the question since he quickly shuts his eyes. "Yeah. A bit more complicated to explain, but yeah. Don't get me wrong I love being there for my sis. But this ain't living. It's..."

"Suffering." I finish for him, Little Helen's words ring truer as my next thoughts.

Only I can do this, I think, to help him get Home. To help him not hurt anymore...

I wanted this. I needed this. And my body? Well, it responded for me in the most primal way possible when I reached up and trilled "yes!" in his ear before delving in for another kiss.

The kiss starts out tender and exploratory. In fact, it's so tender my body is brimming with anticipation and I'm dizzy with pleasure when we part. I loved his smile. A distant part of me marvels at glimpsing this side of him. In male form and taking control. His nature is usually mild when he Takes Over in Vonnie's body. Ever the rational one, the Yin to my wife's Yang and constantly coming up with solutions to our problems.

Not today.

Today, he is the problem. More like, he's responsible for the excitement and Armageddon-level panic blooming in my chest with the need to be filled, so completely, with his seed. To be seeded, bred, and absolutely fucked.

I half-expect the conscientious side of him to take over, to hesitate or overthink sinking his hard shaft inside of my readied wetness. But he doesn't, and I scream out into the morning sun as he embeds himself to the hilt inside of my womb.

I cup a hand to my belly and thrash from side to side from the tornado of sensations: There's pain, and pressure, but oh is it fucking sweet. Maybe Mikey feels it too, because he drops his mouth into my neck to roar as jets of warm seed pump into me after the first stroke.

"K-Kimmy!" He keened. "Waited so long...for this. So sorry."

"It's all right." I crooned into his ear since he hadn't yet brought his head back up from my neck. "You're perfect."

We're eerily still while we hold each other in the twilight of his release. A solid minute goes by and several more streams of his seed are flowing into me, and damn my greediness. My pussy is clenching around his wood in an attempt to milk all of his cum.

Once the ebb of his arousal stops, he pulls out and sits up on his elbows to stare into my eyes. His are dark whirlpools that say so much despite his silence. In them, I see his appreciation for me. I see how much he longed to hold me in his arms instead of through his sister's. I see so many thank yous, thank you for believing in me and thank you for forgiving me for the wrongs done in the past.

"You are my reason to keep fighting." He breathed after kissing my nose. "You've always seen me for me. Always saw the man inside who loves you just as hard as his twin sis."

"Because you are." I agree.

His forehead comes to rest on mine as he says his next words. And they absolutely tear me apart.

"I'm not gonna just miss you after this is over, baby." His voice, so haunted, hitches on the final word. "This is going to break me in fucking half."

"Oh, Mikey." I warble with a splintering heart. "No matter how many times I help spirits get to the other side this part never gets easier. But this feels impossible. You...your love...is everything"

He shakes his head. "You are everything. My all and one and only. I can't thank you enough for risking it all for me and Vonnie. You don't have to and still you do. You're like the sun in that way, so bright I can't stand to look at you sometimes. Thank you for giving me the honor of honoring your dreams. You are my second chance. I'm so fucking honored to fill your belly with life just like you did with me, my forever lifeline. Just...thank you."

"I'll never forget you." I whimper, my face already so wet from our combined tears collecting there. "Never!"

I don't recall when it happened, but his dick reanimates between my folds. Then he pushes into me with a gaining rhythm, my heart is beating out of control and pussy clenching, drawing him in like it never wants him out.

"Say it again." He growls. "Tell me again."

"I'll..." I panted between his wild thrusts as he jackhammered me into the bed. "I'll never forget you, baby."

"Again..." He strains between more hard strokes into my waters.

My brain is reorganizing and recomposing, but I managed out a weak, "Never forget," as he thrusts so hard and so powerful I feel them deep inside my womb as my insides vibrate from the impact.

"Again, beautiful!" He groaned as if his crash and run impact was hurting him more than it set my body alight with fire. "I'll never let you go unless you tell my crazy ass you won't forget me after I'm gone. Make me believe it!"

I wrap my arms around his neck, riding the waves of passion into another dizzying sensation. Something grips my insides, my womb, and a bright flash of light explodes behind my already straining lids. This orgasm obliterates me.

"So good, so good, never stop...!" I've cum, though my clenching channel spasms for more, and he delivers. He doesn't stop, not even after another powerful wave of climax shivers through me. "M-Mike..."

"Ah...Kim...tell me...tell me!" He's not even making sense anymore, but I don't dare dishonor his command.

"I'll never lose you in my heart, Mikey!" I plead, but it's more of a sob as the tears flow freely between our fusing bodies. "You'll never die to me. Never."

"Kimmy!" His face contorts into the most pained grimace and my eyes flutter closed to focus on staving off the fifth orgasm. It'll kill me, just like his facial expression did and his deeper, longer strokes stoked more of the flames inside my hearth. "Don't make me go alone...so tired of...being alone."

"Yes!" I say in understanding of what he meant. He didn't want to cum alone. Neither did I. It felt like the world would explode right when we did as we crested our climax together under the sun. But I hold him tighter and whisper my words of love into his ear. "Let's do this. Let's cum together."

"You're safe with me." He guts out, and just like we promised, my walls spasm around his staff. Right when buckets of his release spill into my womb, coating my inner walls and opening me wider to allow all of him inside.

The room is quiet after our breathing calms, and I twist inside his arms to smile up at him. "I love you."

"I'll never stop loving you." He whispers, his eyes and heart, like mine, so filled with emotion I nearly choked on the intensity of it. I gasp when his hand comes to rest on my belly. "She'll be so beautiful when she's born— the best of both of us. Don't forget to tell her that she's made from love. I will cherish you all. Forever."

23

let love in

·♥·♥·♥·♥·♥·

After dabbing the final patch of snow white foundation over the puckered scar I twist her around in the chair for the grand reveal.

"What do you think?" I asked the timid, yet formally gowned, girl in the mirror. "Crisis averted?"

Her face is blank as she assesses the finish beat job. She'd requested I use my highest quality materials, which is often reserved for client's who are used to specific brands on their skin or who just want the very best. So, in keeping with her urgent request to perfect the doll look, I pulled out all the stops even after the shop had long since closed for the day.

Nita and Frankie J hurried to the festival happening on Main Street, and Ary went off to get ready for her date. After Joyce's hair was perfectly slayed to the gods by Nita, I promised to comp her makeup the following day to accommodate the timid doll's request.

"Seems she needs it more than me," Joyce commented after Sasha and I returned downstairs. "Scars like that take a miracle to cover and heal from. And I'm not just talking about on the outside."

None of us said anything to that, but twenty minutes and a ton of promises to reconvene with our DC guests later, and here we were. Both the nameless timid girl whose expression I can't decipher as she studies her completed beat job.

"I can redo it if you don't like it," I offer, but it's selfish since I had no interest in perfecting her look. It was more of a need to avoid going back to the Oakhouse Estate earlier than necessary. Colin would be by soon to collect me, I knew.

Unexpectedly, she shoots to her feet and pounces on me; her arms are like tightening wire around my plusher frame, but our heights are the same.

"Shitsure shimasu!" She squeals in my ear before stepping back, composing, and bowing. "Allow me to repay your kindness."

"Oh, no need!" I tell her while fanning my hands. "You've already overpaid and over tipped enough. Really, I'm just glad to help out."

Her eyes widened from the shock of my rejection. "No, no! This will not do. Allow me to extend gratitude for, erm, late minute request."

"It's fine," I reassured her. "Besides, don't you have a festival to get to?"

A quick glance at her gown she informed me was called *Yukata*, she yelps. Then bows again. *"Sumimasen*. Please disregard manners...am called Yume Kobayashi. Call me Yume-chan, please."

That name rings vaguely true in some form in my memory. It's so specific, though, and I don't really get a chance to think about it after she straightens and asks for my name.

"I go by Nora," I say, bowing for some reason. "Just Nora. Nice to meet you Yume-chan."

"Hai!" She says then grabs my elbow. "I must pay back for kindness, Nora. Allow me teach you *Bon Odori*. It is dance. Come!" She spoke so fast in her broken English that it was hard to understand her.

"Hold up!" I protested, but in spite of them, she managed to drag me outside, barely giving me enough time to lock the doors before plunging out to the open crowd of people.

There are so many people on the streets, dancing and taking pictures. Food trucks are lined along the streets and a large parade of similarly robed children perform a dance that gets the crowd going. I feel so oddly placed in my highlighter pink sundress and butt length blonde yarn braids. While I'm not the darkest one there, I'm still in the minority since there aren't many black people in attendance.

Yume-chan stops near a gaggle of similarly dressed tiny women, making me take notice of the dance routine that was soon to commence.

"This *Bon Odori*, Japanese dance for honor ancestors. Watch me, please? I show you."

Finding it incredibly impossible to deny her at this point, I nod. "Knock 'em dead!"

My cheeks heat from the embarrassment and the confused look on her face from my stupid expression.

"It means, good luck. Super out of context though, so sorry about that." I stammered and then pushed her gently toward the forming dance group.

"Yes, luck!" She said after a look of understanding dawned on her. "Will knock dead. For you!"

I can't resist the chuckle as I watch Yume-chan begin dancing. The music sounds like flutist work, giving the instrumental an ancient, Geisha quality to it. Out of place as I was, I still enjoyed the show. Or display. Or performance? Whichever it was called, I found the music...different than anything I'd ever heard before. Not the usual 90's rap I blasted in my private room on the estate, but melodic nonetheless.

Suddenly, the dance group retrieve paper hand fans and throw them in the air before catching them with a graceful bow. The entire move was so demure and cute I applauded them. While my claps were the loudest, they weren't solo. Several onlookers put their hands together and even begin mimicking the dancing with huge smiles.

The entire display is nothing short of beautiful. All of it. Dancing was clearly Yume-chan's calling, seeing as that timid girl from before melted away with every move and sway of her fan.

The sudden urge to pee overcomes me quicker than expected, and I'm shimmying as the music simmers down. Perhaps I could run back to Nita's to relieve my bladder and return before Yume-chan notices? The walk from the salon was about five minutes down Church Street, quick enough for me to pee and run back in time for her to finish. Resolved, I swiveled around to begin the trek. Only to slam into the hard, unforgiving chest of a stranger, a man, standing directly behind me.

"Fuck, watch it, dude!" I protest, rubbing my affected forehead that crudely met his lower chest.

Despite the loud flute music the rumble of laughter is audible from his chest. All the hairs rise on my skin and an eerie feeling overcomes me.

"I do believe *you* ran into *me*." He says, no amusement in his voice or emotion. It's like this jerk is trying to goad me with his overt sarcasm.

I fold my arms under my breasts and glare up at him. The sun beams into my eyes and conceals his face from me, but no matter. This jerk would feel my wrath because I was sick of entitled men like him, messing with honest, hard working women.

"Well, if you weren't standing so close you wouldn't have been hit. Dude, you were so close I felt you practically breathing on my neck."

He leans down, close to my ear and whispers, "Like this?"

A faint lift of his right cheek, not a smile, lets me know he's totally amused by this despite him not wanting to be. The smell of his cologne makes my mouth water instantly from the memories. He smelled like morning dew or rain on a paved street mixed with mint. A unique scent I wouldn't forget, yet...

The entire world fades while we stare into each other's eyes. The sun also shifts in a way that allows me to view his entire profile, and I'm all but panting. Despite the summer temperatures in the near hundreds, this man is clad in black jeans and black muscle fit tee. The dark leather jacket completes the look. His hair is pulled up into a high man-bun and shaved on the sides, a very modern style not befitting this occasion. But then again, I didn't fit this occasion so in that sense we matched. His shark eyes narrow on me and I'm rendered frozen to the spot, spellbound and stupefied by him. Again.

"K-Kobayashi-sama," I whisper, my heart hollowed by the sight of him and chill in my veins. "You're...here."

"Hello," he bowed his head slightly, "Now that I have you to myself you can finally answer my question."

I shook my head, so many visions of Luther and that awful Jin-Tama meeting climbing to the surface. The man looks just as regal as he did from before. There's like an air about him that's commanding and much more terrifying than Luther ever was.

"What question?"

A deep scowl mars his perfect face before he asks, "your name. Are you called Nora, or Norina?"

"Oh," I said, breathing hard and backing away a few inches. The crowds and the music and cheering was making my head swirl. "That."

"Yes, that." He took a step closer. "Who are you?"

Did he really have the nerve to ask me that? Wasn't he the one who barged into me, whether on purpose or accidentally I didn't know. But I did know that I needed out of there. Pronto.

"I, um—" I start, but don't get to finish since another famil- iar voice trills as they approach us.

"Nora-san!" Yume-chan sings while coming up from be- hind. "What did you think of the dance?"

"I, um..." I started again, my eyes alternating between her and the Asian king from long ago. "You were great, Yume-chan. Thank you for inviting me to watch it."

She jumped excitedly and clapped her hands together. It was as if the compliment was a lottery offering instead of a few halfhearted words. But she giggles all the same and beams a sweet smile at me...that was before she noticed the Asian king, too.

Her entire demeanor shifted from overjoyed to consternated. She bows instantly towards him.

"Oni-sama," She greets robotically, *"Sumimasen,* I did not see you standing there."

"Nora." The Asian king squinted curious brown eyes at me as if seeing me in a new light and totally ignoring her greeting. "You've become acquainted with my sister. Tell me how that came to pass since she's never visited this city before today."

My words are lost, like all sense of language took a vacation in the guy's midst and I'm sputtering at him. Yume-chan Kobayashi. That was it! She was related to him, the Kobayashi-sama Luther snapped at during the business deal gone awry.

Yume-chan, still bent, answers for me. "There is no trouble, brother. Met Nora for makeup. She covered face scar. See?"

He nodded in appreciation after studying the area where her scar was, carefully concealed under the expensive product she rush-purchased from me.

"Nora," The Asian king said. "This is your handiwork?"

"Hai," Yume-chan said.

"The question was meant for Nora. Do not speak out of turn again."

Ruder beyond rude, I thought, and Yume-chan's acquiescence and withdrawal revives one of those strong emotions from the ashes: Fury. I stare him in the eyes.

"Don't you talk to her like that!" I growl. "She was only answering your question which, in all actuality, really isn't any of your damn business."

"Nora-san, no." Yume-chan begs. "No matter. He no disrespect. I disrespect."

I held a hand up to silence her. "Oh, hell no. He one hundred percent disrespected you. Speak up and tell him to kick rocks."

"You are petulant." The Asian king comments in that same cold tone that was pissing me off.

"Yeah, well you're an asshole."

He opens his mouth to say something else, but I give him the hand and turn to address his sister. "Thank you for inviting me, Yume-chan. I'll be taking my leave now."

Yume-chan gawked at my hand in his face, horrified but otherwise nodding. *"Hai."*

I let my glare linger on his stony face for a few moments. Still afraid on the inside but fed up with those feelings. Turning on my heel, I quickly walked back to the salon and cried out in relief as the pee whooshed out of me on the toilet several minutes later.

Tears fell in waves down my face and sobs wracked my chest. From fear? Yes, but also from what his presence here meant. Luther sold me to pay him back, which meant that even he'd been cautious not to be in his debt since Luther owed several other loan sharks that looked way scarier than The Asian king. That told me he was the real deal. That he also was a part of the past I numbly hid from in South Carolina coming back to haunt me.

What did he want? And better yet, why me? He could have easily noticed me and minded his business. Left me alone to numbly trudge through my sentence at the Oakhouse Estate, or until I figured out how to escape again. I wasn't sure of anything, but the reminder that a full bottle of vodka awaited me in my secret stash in my room back home had me typing a hasty response to Colin once I freed my phone.

> **ME**: Can you pick me up? Nita's closed early.

After several minutes ticked by without response—abnormal for the ever-punctual Colin—I dialed the number attached to his contact. Five rings, no answer. Again, very unusual for my only ride back home to not respond to his unwilling charge.

Without any other options, I dial the number of the girl I hated seeing again under this circumstance. So similar to the last time I'd last seen her picking me up from the Newbern house.

"Wam, Nora?" Sasha spoke all business into the phone. "What's the matter— you crying?"

I sniffled. "I'm all right, Sasha. Really."

"You don't sound all right. We just checked into the hotel, but I can come get you."

"Thanks," I whimper, so grateful she didn't ask me to explain myself. "I'd appreciate it. I could order a Lyft if—"

"Nonsense!" She groused. "Are you still at the salon?"

"Yes."

"Good." She breathed. "Hang tight. See you in ten."

I thank her again before hanging up. So, so thankful she didn't let me request that rideshare since the last thing I wanted was a forced conversation with a stranger during the twenty-minute ride back to the estate.

Breathe Cleo, I tell myself. Just breathe and the rest will work itself out later. I didn't desire to be around Trace Oakhouse, but I needed to go back and recoup my strategy. As much as I hated the hastily concocted plan I had to do it. I didn't know why this man came to Greenville of all places, but I doubted it had to do with coincidence. Coincidences were for the young and stupid to believe, and I still felt both of those while I sat in a bathroom stall and sobbed like a young fool.

Sasha will pick me up, no questions asked, and take me back to the house. There, I'll regroup.

But again, things don't quite happen that way. Mollified for the moment, I flush and open the tiny stall door to wash my hands.

"Hello, Nora." No other than the Asian king greeted me with a sinister smile.

He'd been leaned up against the automatic hand dryer and blocking my path to the sink...and the door. My only option was to stand there and fight or try to wrestle him down to reach the door. Either way, I had to fight.

Nostalgia makes the moment feel full circle, considering I'd met Ty in a similar way as an intruder inside the salon.

"You ought to lock your doors," he said plainly and took steps toward me. "Or else something monstrous may slip in."

24

anything she wants

· ♥ · ♥ · ♥ · ♥ · ♥ ·

"You ought to lock your doors," he said plainly and took steps toward me. "Or else something monstrous may slip in."

Same as moments ago this strange man leaves me flustered. I mean it; I went from boo-hoo crying ugly tears to stunned silence in seconds. Totally freaked out and not truly knowing what else to do I slam the stall door closed. Yet another similarity to my and Tyrone's first meeting— me barricading until he promised to go away.

Except, like I suspect, the Asian king makes zero efforts to leave.

"Are we not acquaintances, Nora?" He asked with the same emotionless automaton tone from the festival. "Don't hide."

"Sir," I said between the heavy pants I was sure would kill me. "I don't know what it is you think you know about me, but I've got nothing to do with...those matters anymore. I've left it behind."

"Interesting." He answered. "Let's you come out and we'll talk further about those...matters."

"Are you insane? Or maybe just stupid? I told you I've got nothing to do with 590 business anymore."

"I won't argue with a stall door, Nora. Come out and we'll have that chat that keeps getting interrupted one way or another."

I took a deep breath, huge waves of consternation and irritation colliding into my resolve to remain hidden. To stay in my safe bubble that's surrounded me nearly a year since living in this town. This guy, whoever he was and whatever he wanted from me, brought it all back. Luther, gang drama, and the constant helplessness.

"If I go out there to talk to you will you promise to leave?" I asked wearily.

A beat, then, "You have my word."

I opened the door slowly, taking a tentative peek beyond the thin door that was a poor shield in reality should the king decide to renege and attack. Or touch me...

I bite my lip to tamp down the flames of lust igniting my insides at the sight of him. Still in black, his hands are raised as though I'm an officer of the law and have threatened to search him. His pale skin looks nearly porcelain, an odd contrast to the pale yellow wallpaper in the common restroom downstairs. His complexion is also telling of his origin. Clearly he didn't reside in the south since most Asian and White natives rocked a distinct tan.

The only difference to this handsome man whose looks were unrivaled by any popular K-pop singer is his black gloves. An eerie feeling settles into my stomach as I inch backwards towards the door with my eyes never leaving him.

"Hey!" I yelped when he dropped his hands at his sides. "Stay. Put."

This time he does smile, but it's wicked as he re-raises his hands over his head. "Yes, of course, Nora."

That eerie feeling unloosed another chain over my fury when I paused to glare at him. "Will you stop that?"

"Stop what?"

"Saying my name like that."

"Apologies. Am I mispronouncing it? Yume's been chattering about how Nora's charitable deeds helped her win the Bon Odori performance contest."

"Me?" I asked deflating a bit as a warmth spread through me. "She said that? I didn't know it was a contest."

He shook his head. "It isn't. At least, in Japan it isn't. Obon is merely a Buddhist celebratory affair all throughout the country during the summer where dance is mere performance. Nothing more. It's quite different in America."

A bitter sneer forms on his face, making me question something. "And this displeases you?"

"My list of displeasures far outnumber anything that's pleased me since arriving in this country."

"Sorry to hear that," I say to that extremely pessimistic statement.

A forlorn pain resounds in my gut at his admission that he'd not been able to enjoy anything since arriving here. Then I mentally slap myself for forgetting that he was the dangerous intruder from my past and that I was escaping.

"Don't be," he grunted, steeling his features and lowering his hands. "My displeasures shouldn't concern you."

"I decide what concerns me." I retort without thinking about it. Then gulp when, in the next instant, he leaps over to block the exit with his massive body and impossibly long legs. He isn't particularly tall, about five foot eight, but that's still several inches beyond my frame. My utterly weaponless frame.

"Nora," he breathes out in a thick accent. "You're worried about me?"

"Uh," I gasped, "I'd worry about anyone who'd practically admit to being chronically unhappy."

He glowers at me, but there's a latent emotion hiding under all that rage. Something akin to the lovelessness I'd felt since young. Though I understand this was his attempt at scaring me I allowed my body to move without thinking about it.

He gasped when my hand came to stroke his cheek. "What are you doing?"

"It's all right," I soothed. "I know that pain, too. It's like a suit of armor people like us wear to keep others away. Even the ones who do care and love us."

"Nora..."

"You keep saying my name like that..." I commented, still piecing together the emotions I identified with that were becoming more plain on his face. "But I don't know yours."

His eyes fluttered closed and he breathed in deep. Like he was trying to keep his cool. Or restrain himself from something, I didn't know. Then he brought his hand up over mine, stilling it.

"Takeo."

"Takeo." I said, running the name over my tongue like a new flavor of ice cream. "Takeo Kobayashi."

"Do not speak my name in that way." He growled and I gasped when his hand squeezed mine. "I have honor."

"Of course, you do." I agreed. "If you didn't, then you would have hurt me by now." My mind skitters back to his initial statement when we met at Jin-Tama. "Hurting women isn't your family's way, right?"

"You are correct." His voice is tight, like speaking was actually bringing him pain.

"Have faith in the people around you," I stated in spite of the pain in my hand from his tight grasp. "You have to. Learn to trust that people love you. And you're valued just as you are."

His eyes flare open. And I yelp when he slams my body into the tiled wall and kisses me. The kiss isn't gentle like Sasha's but it's hard and insistent, our tongues dueling inside each other's mouths.

"You dared to run from me at the festival." He chewed out all while palming my breast. "Now you stare at me with those big brown eyes as though nothing is wrong. As though your very existence in this backwards little town is not reflective of the larger issue at hand."

"There is no issue. I don't want any trouble," I groaned as his mouth went to my neck and bit down. Hard. I squeal from the mountain of pleasure coursing from the afflicted zone down to my pussy.

His eyes bore back into mine in no time, but his hands play a different game at strumming my clit. "You even have the nerve to pity me."

"No, I don't!" I gasp as the orgasm tugs at my insides.

"Do not lie!" He growls into my face, our eyes never leaving each other's. "And do not look at me."

I groan from the rockets of intense sensation shooting through my nervous system, but otherwise hold his gaze.

This infuriates him.

"Do not look at me!" His voice morphed from cool and collected to unhinged, crazy even and as my orgasm crested I reached over to capture his bottom lip into my mouth. Biting down and drawing blood into my mouth as I drag my teeth over the soft flesh. "Fuck!" He bleats behind a rapid succession of words in Japanese.

Something tears, and there's no need to look down and confirm if the thin material of my Torrid sundress is the victim of his frantically exploring hands. I cry as surges of delicious pleasure assail me when he latches his mouth around my nipple.

"You wish to know...why I say your name?" He grunts between sucks of my hardened bud. "Right, Nora?"

"Yes!" I moaned, not as an answer to his question since there's zero room for reasonable thought.

He continues anyway. "Nora is derived from the word 'honor.'"

"Takeo..." I breathed, unable to stomach all the sensations at once.

He drew another long suckle of my breast and I buckled in his arms. "I meant it when I said Noonan-san did not deserve you. He is a worm, spineless, and without a shred of dignity in his body."

Noonan-san, I realized, was Luther. My ex-boyfriend and punisher. The mention of him nearly sobers me. Nearly. The feel of his teeth against my sensitive areola provokes an immediate release of warm waters down below, where I notice his large, veined, dick is on full display through his jeans.

"I have honor," he repeats that phrase again, still massaging my breasts when he stands up to stare at me through hooded crescent eyes. "You will be mine."

My head spins as I work to understand. "What does any of that mean?"

That's when I noticed the knife in his hands, and things happened very fast after that.

"Takeo!" I screamed when he brought the large blade to rest at my throat. "I thought...I thought you didn't harm—"

"This is different." He responded, his tone back to a cold mask of ice. "You, just like your scheming partner, are a worm. Without honor. Without dignity. And it's time you pay for your crimes against my clan."

"I don't understand!" I cried, shaking as the knife pierced my neck ever so slightly. "I told you I'm not a part of that anymore. Me and Luther are done."

"A perfect actress." He grunts. "Now where is he?"

"I don't know!" I sobbed, my hands on his chest. "Please don't do this. I'll pay you whatever he owes."

"It is too late for that!" He roars in my face. "Only his life will do. He must be punished. But now he's suddenly nowhere to be found and his whore is playing fairytale in some antebellum mansion. No, Nora. Money will not suffice this time."

"Takeo," I whimpered. "I don't know what to say."

"I am valued just as I am." He spat my words back at me. "More lies. More bullshit. To think I let myself get carried away like this..."

"I'll give you whatever you want." I groaned as I fought and pushed against his body. Realizing now why he was wearing gloves. So as not to get his hands dirty. "Get away from me! Help!"

"No one will hear you," He chuckled while pinning me back against the wall. "You will be mine. We'll see how Noo-nan-san takes to his merchandise being taken from under him."

Maniacal laughter permeates the bathroom and I'm sobbing and screaming and kicking and then, just like that, it all stops. A gunshot blasts into the small space, knocking the self-proclaimed monster away from me. He flies into the stall clutching his shoulder and hollering in rapid Japanese.

"Cleo!" Somebody hollers at the door. It's Nita, holding a gun alongside a shaken looking Sasha.

25

November nights

•♥•♥•♥•♥•♥•

"Tell me right now just what the hell is going on?" Sasha demanded while gunning the SUV down the backroads to the Oakhouse Estate ten minutes later.

I'm shaking all over from what could have happened—what almost happened, and cringe when his strange smirk reappears in my mind and all of a sudden the knife is at my throat again.

"Nora?!"

Then comes the strange pleasure he allowed me to feel. His hands all over my body, massaging my tits and traveling south to my aching core. Fear dueled with the passion building in me, yet this somehow made both emotions stronger as I grazed over the minor cut in my neck from the knife. It stung to the touch and created a new spray of moisture in my already ruined panties. Ever grateful to Nita for letting me borrow her sweatshirt and red thigh cut shorts, since my fingers would be playing their own tune down below from the pain and pleasure.

"Damn it—Nora!" Sasha's frantic voice finally registers amidst my daydreaming. "Are you with me?"

I blinked once. Twice. Before answering her. "I'm right here."

"Right..." She said, deflating a bit before refocusing on the road. "I don't like this at all. Do you know that man?"

"Not really," I answered neutrally, my gaze fixed on the passing trees speed by.

She makes an irritated noise with her throat. "Then why was he holding a knife to your neck?!"

I shrugged. In a bit of a daze and unbothered by any of it.

"There is more to that story. He's your obvious choice since it was clear you'd gone farther than we had just this morning. Judging from that huge dick of his and that look on your face."

Though her words were bitter, I didn't pay them much mind. Merely stared out the window and counted the clouds in the sky. My mind was replaying the entire day, from waking up in the best mood to ending it with a knife at my throat. I should be scared, and sure I was, but...

The mere thought of the Asian king called Takeo's large body of muscles blanketing me against that wall...the smell of his cologne...him calling me 'honor.' That peculiar energy that charged the room from Jin-Tama intensified in the salon bathroom, if at all possible. I'm panting from the fact that he could have killed me, right there on the spot and without a witness since Nita had stalled for so long on installing security cameras. My thoughts return to Nita, who'd oddly handled shooting a guy fairly well.

"Sasha, please take Cleo upstairs to get her changed." She ordered after locking the bleeding man in the bathroom and dragging me through the salon. My dress was destroyed and what remained intact was sprayed in blood. "Afterwards, take her home until we can sort this out. Shit! I'll need to close shop for the next few days to deal with this."

I'd been staring into space, same as now, as Sasha dragged me upstairs and dressed me in the sweater/booty short ensemble. She took delicate care to wash the blood off my body and speak to me, but her words weren't penetrating the stratus cloud surrounding my brain. Like now.

"Sweetie, I know you're in shock. But you got to perk up and talk to me. Me can't help if you don't tell me how you got in trouble with that Kobayashi fellow."

Several more minutes pass and I count forty-five additional cloud shapes drift by before my face plummets into the dash. The car hits an abrupt stop and that zaps the neurons back online enough for me to twist around and glare at her.

"Slow the fuck down, Sasha!" I screech from the depths of my lungs at her, wiping away the stray blood from the impact of what appeared to have been her slamming on brakes.

"Now she's back!" She exclaims. "Perk it up and talk to me."

"You—"

"I'm a bitch, I know." She sneers but dismisses me with a wave as she cranks the engine back up and resumes the journey down the country roads. "At least you're awake."

Hot fury obliterates any trace of sympathy or camaraderie felt between us in an instant. And it doesn't matter that she'd practically fucked me into a wall this morning. Or that she needs my help to escape the boyfriend who's forced her down a similar path as me. None of that shit matters, at least in this minute, when I reach over and yank the steering wheel.

"Are you crazy?!" She screamed as the car swiveled into the opposite lane. "Get off!"

I glared at her. "No! Since you don't care about road safety, why should I?"

"Nora," she bit out, "remove your hands. Right now!"

"No." I growled and gripped the wheel tighter.

Headlights from a car journeying down the opposite lane shine before us, and I lowkey relish in her terrified groan.

"Nora, please! We'll crash right into them if you don't let go."

Right before the car makes contact, I release it. Sasha veers quickly into the correct lane, swearing and shouting all kinds of threats to me. The gates to the Oakhouse Estate show up from the distance and let me know we're now close. Close to my room and bottle of vodka I desperately needed as a balm to my dread and now headache from the car injury.

"Why are you really in Greenville?" I asked coldly. Carefully, so as not to lose whatever calm is left after that near deadly head on collision and run in with Takeo Kobayashi.

"What are you talking about?" She asked, but I noted her avert her eyes quickly at my question.

We're feet away from the estate and at this point I had no intention of sugarcoating anything from her. Head pounding, I reached into the glove compartment that fell open after she slammed on brakes.

"Do you think I'm stupid?" I barked, waving the charcoal Glock in the air. "This is Luther's gun."

"My God!" She breathes in horror after slamming on the brakes again. Except, this time we're parked just beyond the gates of the estate and I didn't fly into the dash from impact. Instead, she reaches for the gun. "Put that down!"

"Do not touch me!" I demanded as I evaded her grab. "Answer. My. Question."

She chewed on her lip and fidgeted with her shirt sleeve before answering. "You wasn't supposed to see that."

"If you hadn't slammed on brakes like a maniac, then the glove compartment wouldn't have just fallen open to reveal this old thing. I would know, after all, considering this is LUTHER'S CAR! And his gun. So no more lies, Sasha."

Tears stream down her face. "Oh, god, it's all fucked up. I fucked it all up!"

"What did you fuck up?"

She continues to cry and rock in her seat, not responding to me. My heart in my throat, I do the unthinkable towards the girl I vowed to safeguard and never harm again since elementary school. I raise the gun to her.

"Nora, I can explain everything!"

"Do it. Now."

"Okay!" She blubbers before wiping her nose. "I was sent here to...to bring you back to DC."

"That's not all." I cocked the gun. "Keep talking. Or I swear I'll use this thing. Fucking traitor."

"Okay, okay!" She screeched while holding her hands up. "He s-said to bring you back. The money's all gone, Nora! He needs you back and he sent me here to get you. I think he's fucked up, again, royally."

My stomach drops as I realize something. "And he sent you down here, with his favorite gun, to bring me back. With, or against, my will. That about sums it up?"

She reaches out for me, but I dodge her again, keeping the gun trained on her. If I didn't get out of the car, security would surely chase after this nefarious-looking Ford Flex chilling a couple feet from the property. No doubt about it.

Settling for hugging herself, she weeps. Weeps long and hard and in a way that puts me in mind of cruel and unusual torture, like there's a slow knife entering her body from several entrance points.

"I didn't mean for this to happen. Not like this. I promise, Nora."

I glared, so pissed I could spit. "Your promises mean nothing. I can't trust that. I won't trust that."

"Are you...going to kill me then?"

"Ugh, shut up!" I spat, wiping the blood pooling from the forehead gash. "I just don't understand this."

"I told ya I'm so sorry!" She cried. "Luther gave me no other options. He says he'll kill my grandparents if I don't bring you back. Or..."

"Or get rid of me." I finished for her, shaking my head. "I don't get it. Why not finish me off himself? Why send you, with a car full of babies, to kill me when he could easily do it?"

She gulped before answering. "He's made some big enemies. Enemies all over, including the Kobayashi fellow I'd met in passing during one of the drops. Everybody wants him, so he needs you."

I nod, taking her words in. The scorned look on Takeo's face made so much sense now. He thought I was working with Luther.

"I wasn't supposed to take my boys. Or even Joyce. But I planned to take you with me and run away. Back to Trinidad."

"And Joyce cosigned this little plan of yours?"

"Kind of," she chuffed. "She's in a similar situation with her man, and said she'd rather be with her grandkids if she had to choose between them, and him."

My mind flits to Larry, her current husband and the step-dad Ty despised. I recalled all of his stories about how he'd never want to be home if he was home, too. Or how he felt his presence in the house was the only thing keeping the retired policeman from hitting his mother. After Joyce's comment regarding Yume-chan's scar, a sinking, sorrowful realization that Ty's hunch came to fruition guts me.

Sasha finally gets a hold of my wrist and there's a desperate look in her eyes as she says, "I love you. I would never intentionally harm you babygyal. I could never even consider it. My plan the entire time was to stay long enough to convince you to come away with us. With me."

Luther, like I figured, was on the decline and getting worse by the day since I'd been sold. Though I hated the bastard, a small part of me pities what he became. Feeling partly responsible for it as well as the many lives his actions have affected, like Sasha and her family. I should have done something sooner to prevent this. Taking a deep breath, I toss the gun back into the glove compartment.

"Give me your phone."

She scowls. "Wait, why?"

"Just hand it here, okay? Before I change my mind about this."

"What are you doing?" She asked after handing me the iPhone. "Don't you have a phone?"

I don't explain that my phone was likely bugged, and thus not useful for this next task. "Do you know Luther's location?"

"Well, no." She said, considering. "Nora, what's the meaning of all dis?"

The line trills three times before his heavily accented baritone answers into the phone. "Hello?"

"Pascual, it's Nora," I say while adjusting my sweater. "I need a huge, last minute favor. I promise I'll pay you back one hundred times over."

"A hundred times over?" He laughs. "Now, I'm listening. But girl you know I got you. Whatever it is, I'm down."

I smiled briefly at my ride or die friend before rattling off my request.

"Girl are you sure?" He hedged in a troubled tone. "Of course, I don't mind. But are you in some sort of trouble? Did that Trace Oakhouse do something to you?"

I bite my lip, because there's no way I can explain it all within the five or so minutes left until the security came over to the car. Clock was ticking.

"No time to explain, Pas. But I love you and appreciate you for this! You'll hear from me soon."

"Nora—"

"Sorry!" I groan before hanging up. I'm speed dialing the next number with shaky fingers, feeling time slip away with every passing second.

"Who you calling now?" Sasha asked, her face intrigued but still scared.

"Hey, Nita." I say into the phone. "Need you to do me a solid."

"Is everything all right?" She asks. "Are you hurt?"

"Not really," I mumbled.

"Good," she breathes out in relief. "I'm closing the shop for a few days until we figure out this intruder situation. Can't believe that fucker escaped."

Now that makes me pause. "Wait, the guy got away? Dude from the bathroom?"

"Sure did," she groused. "Don't you worry about it. I...have a friend who's helping me solve this without all the yellow tape. Know what I mean?"

"Uh..." I said, trailing off because I had to make sure I was hearing what I thought I was hearing. My cousin had under the table help to capture the Asian king? "Nita, please be safe. Be smart about this. Call the police and don't play detective on my account, okay?"

She sucks in her teeth. "Screw that shit! That psycho broke into my business and ASSAULTED you! He needs to pay for what he did."

"Pay?" I asked, my already pained head hurting more from her vague, questionably legal threats. "I don't have much time for this. Nita, I need to collect on a favor."

"What's up? And why are you calling from this weird ass DC number?"

I glance at Sasha, whose hanging on to my every word. "I'll need you to look after Sasha, Joyce, and the kids for a while. No time for details, but they need a place to stay until I get some things sorted out."

"What?!" Both Sasha and Nita thunder simultaneously.

A pause, then Nita adds, "Cleo, this better not be about that crooked-ass fiancé! Has he done something—"

"Please!" I whimper, the final shred of confidence coming loose by the minute. "Please, do this for me. Sasha will tell you as much as she's able to in a few minutes."

"Okay, fine." She grumbled. "I suppose I owe you after you helped drag my business from the coals. I got you."

"Thanks."

"This time!" She warns. "Next time you do more shady shit I'm telling your parents. Fuck, I should just tell them anyways."

"Please don't do that!" I beg, truly beg because I couldn't handle it if either of my parents got involved in more of my bullshit. "This is my mess to clean. I'll call you soon to let you know I'm okay."

"Nora, what are you doing?" Sasha whispered, her eyes filled with tears and wonder and another emotion I can't decipher. "You don't have to do this."

"I know." I grumble, "but I also know Luther. He manipulated you into this, and I'm stopping him the only way I know how. It's my responsibility to end this. Once and for all."

Sobs rack the thin girl's body, and I can't take any more of it. I reach my hand up to caress her face, taking notice of her soft skin and the dampness from the tears there. She looks at me.

"I'm doing this for you, too." I soothe. "I know you, as well. You wouldn't hurt me, no matter how much I might deserve it. Evil isn't who you are—that's Luther."

"I really am sorry. You're going to all this trouble for me."

"It's for me, too." I assured her, gripping her cheek harder. "I need to end this. I let Luther get this bad after I robbed him of a family when we were kids. It's all my fault he turned out this way."

She opens her mouth to ask me something, but I don't let her. Disconnecting my hand from her face instead, I'm soon scouring through the contacts in her phone.

"Which one's his?"

"His? Who?" She queried, so confused. Then an awareness hits her and she's shaking her head. "Nora, no. I will not let you call him."

Pursing my lips, I fold her hand in mine and squeeze. Willing all my regrets and apologies into that simple gesture. "I have to do this."

"You do not need to sacrifice yourself for anyone!" She yelled. "Silly gyal. I came all the way down here to give you a chance to live."

"I tried," I started feebly. "I tried to live a normal life. Tried to make do with the situation he forced upon me by living in this town filled with strangers. Far away from my only family. But it seems I've been running just as much as he has. It's time to end this. And it ends with me."

"This is ridiculous." She whispered, snatching the phone from me and landing on a screen. Then she hands it back. "His number is there. He'll hang up after two minutes since he believes the number is being traced."

"Thank you." I tell her, raising the phone to my ear after dialing.

"Be. Careful." She bites out, her eyes brimming with concern and absolute fear. "He'll be furious that I've let you live this long."

I nod, sending her small reassuring smile as the line rings. And rings. And rings. And rings.

A cool voice informs me to leave a message at the beep, and I decide to just disconnect. Perplexed the most paranoid guy on the planet wouldn't answer his phone. Right when I'm about to ask if this was the correct number, the phone rings in my hand. Feeling more like an active grenade than a vibrating mobile device.

"You got her?" Luther asks, his voice sounding harder, more grim, than the last time I heard it eleven months ago at my father's funeral.

No words come since that usual fear rears and chokes me up, not for the first time upon hearing him speak. This, of course, infuriates him.

"One minute left bitch," he growls. "Did you get her or not?"

I take a mental breath before speaking into the phone. It was now or never.

"You won't be seeing Sasha again." I say, not sure if I sounded as frightened as I felt.

Deep, resounding laughter permeates the phone. In fact, it's more of a movie villain cackle if anything. "Hold up, hold up, hold up. This ain't who I think it is, is it?"

"Who else would it be, Luther?" I spit. "You fucking idiot."

"Miss Cleo'Nora June." He laughs again. "South Carolina got you too big for your britches or what? Must have forgot who you talking to."

"I didn't." I bite out. "My mind is clear and I know exactly what I'm saying. You can't control me anymore. And Sasha's not playing into your little games either. She's with me, and she's safe."

"Miss Sasha must have also forgot I got her granny and grampy with me."

"You're bluffing."

"Am I, though?" He asked, his voice acidic and sarcastic. "Sound a whole lot like what her mama said before I kicked her fat ass down them steps."

LAURA ROSS

"You what?" She demanded, her eyes crazy. The phone isn't on speaker, but the volume is turned all the way up and Luther was never a whisperer. Much too brazen for that. "Me Mooma...that...that be you who—"

"Pushed her down the steps after she wouldn't cough up that jewelry on her neck? Yeah. That was done by yours truly. Didn't know eight flights could kill a lady, but hey. Tad bit of collateral damage never hurt nobody."

Sasha's dark brown face is bright red, as was her eyes. I felt control slipping from the situation and worked to grab the reins again.

"Sasha, please calm down." I tell her. "He's doing this to goad you—"

"You bastard!" She screams before launching her entire body at the phone, as if he was right in front of her instead of hundreds of miles away. "I will kill you!!"

As I'm wrestling her to stay still, his loud hyena laugh permeates the car. Louder and louder, my head starts to scramble as control flees me. As it always did due to Luther's mind games. He had a way of taking your worst fucking fear and twisting it to the most excruciating point. To the point Sasha was at, considering her screaming and rattling in her seat from the anguish and rage.

"I knew you had a thing for my girl, Sasha." He chuckled. "Think I'm stupid? Knew your bitch ass would switch up since you and Nora cut from the same damn cloth. Forever biting the hand that feeds you greedy bitches. Makes me sick."

"I hate you!" She screams.

"Yeah, I hate me, too." He supplies. "Now what is it that you want, Miss Cleo'Nora June?"

"No!" I whine, hating the loss of power the conversation was taking. Like it always had. "You don't get to call me that. And I'm calling to level with you. To make a deal."

"A deal, huh?"

"Yes." I say. "You've made enemies Luther. Big ones. Enemies that won't take kindly to you snorting through more of their product."

He stays quiet, and despite Sasha's hushed keens of pain, I continue. Knowing I've got him right where I want him.

"Edgar is dead, and I have access to a lot of money. I can help you. I can make you a very rich man if you let me."

"The fuck's the catch?" He demands.

I take a deep breath, squeezing Sasha's hand for strength before saying it. Saying the words I thought I'd never have to say again. "Leave everyone alone. I mean it. Don't involve anyone else in this business that's uniquely ours. You'll leave my parents alone and Sasha's family. Even the rest of the gang. You'll do no more harm to anyone else if I agree to come back. If you can agree to that, then I'm all yours. Along with all the money I can get my hands on from the Oakhouse Estate."

More silence on his end as he considers. And I'm waiting with baited breath as my worst enemy ruminates on the terms of my impending imprisonment. Praying to the stars above that he'll take the deal because I can't handle anyone else hurting because of me anymore.

"This a fucking trap." He grunted. "I'm out of here."

"Wait, no!" I hollered, tears in my eyes at what he might do if he hung up this phone. Would he go for my parents first or Sasha's? I had to get him to agree to this, even if it meant my freedom was on the line. "Please, don't go. Please."

Even more silence, and my mind is whirling from the pulsating headache and fear. I had to do something. Say whatever to get him to agree.

"Ashawn," I pleaded with my former foster brother, using his government name. It feels strange on my tongue due to my lack of using it since he'd been forcibly removed from our home ten years ago after the fire. I pray it does the trick and doesn't send him up the wall from fury. I wait. Wait for the explosion to come but it never does. "It's me, remember? Cleo. It's still me and I'm sorry if I ever hurt you. But you got to hear me. I'm begging you."

He expels a huge breath that leads me to believe he's been waiting on the same bated breath as me. Then he bites into the phone, clear, cold, and succinct. "All right. Meet me in three days at the address I text you."

He disconnects the call and I let out a relieved breath. He took it! He took the deal! Now I could return to my sentence with Ashawn Luther in peace knowing I did the best to protect everyone. Even at the expense of me.

26

game over

·♥·♥·♥·♥·♥·

Two days left until it was all over. I felt the ticking of time chipping steadily away with every passing minute the following morning. Sasha, Joyce, and the kids retreated back to Nita's without incident. But not before I spoke with an apologetic Joyce over the phone.

"Nor, I am so sorry about all this." She said between tears. "Should have told you sooner that we were really moving instead of visiting. Hate to involve you in my late son's baby mama drama."

"Her name's Sasha. And she's doing her best." I asserted. "You don't owe me a thing, girl. But cut her some slack."

"Yeah, yeah." She tuts. "I know she's trying. And she didn't need to bring me with her, but I am grateful—even if it doesn't come off that way. You know I can be a cranky old bitch."

I laughed at that, a true belly laugh that felt good coming out and despite my last minute plans.

"Gosh, I miss that son of mine." She said, recovering from laughter as I did. "I just wished he could have asked you out, before..."

"I know," I whispered, my heart in shreds from the subject much too close to home. "Me, too."

"I've been team Nora from the beginning, you know? The way he'd grill me after my hair appointments was ridiculous! I got so tired of hearing, 'how is the makeup girl?' this and 'is the makeup girl dating anybody?' that. He was a mess. The madness wouldn't have ended if I never left my wallet behind at the salon on purpose that day. Heaven knows I loved my bub, but he needed the push."

Speechless wasn't the word to describe my current state. My jaw fell completely slack while I absorbed her words and the shock.

"Are you saying you...plotted this from the beginning?"

"Plot is a strong term," she chuckled. "Let's use strategize. My Tyrone was such a gentle boy, always so sensitive and passionate about those he cared about. As an only child, he was my best friend but easily misunderstood. Trust me, it was the push he needed."

Funny. Had she been talking to anyone on the subject of her son's sensitivity they'd have laughed. He built a reputation on streets as well as school as being one of those brooding bad boys. So insanely handsome that it compensated for his short fuse and limited social skills. However, it was clear to me that they'd had him pegged so wrong, since the version of Ty revealed to me was the same one his mother spoke of: calm, sensitive, and vulnerable. Yeah, his delivery was rather curt, but I liked it that way. I'd never wondered about his feelings for me, and the usual tears that form whenever anyone speaks his name doesn't come. In fact, there's an eerie sense of peace I'm filled with just thinking about his smile and words that had that warming effect on me.

"He was my favorite person in the entire world. I'm glad you pushed him." I told her, my heart heavy but words strong and true. A brief silence ensues, heavy with the weight of our memories of the guy who'd gone too soon. For a reason that had everything to do with me...and Luther...and that constant mess that kept us toxically tethered. "Hey, we'll talk soon. Okay?"

"Don't be a stranger, Nor." The strong old lady stated. "You're all I have left of him. The real him, you know?"

"I won't." I assured her before ending the call and commencing the first stages of my hasty plan.

After sending Sasha off, I ran inside the house, bypassing Luanne's snide questioning about why I was home so early as I jetted to my bedroom. My head was in a whirlwind of thought, the first being what I'd do once I saw Luther again and how to handle seeing my parents for the first time in eleven months.

Would they even want to see me? After all this time filled with lies and radio silence on my end, perhaps they gave up on me. Like I feared, but secretly understood.

All thoughts of next steps and parent-doubt hit a brick wall after I opened the door to my room to discover...nothing. Everything—my bed, clothes, speakers, makeup—it was all gone. As if this tiny little room of refuge never existed. The Dior backpack, usually empty on the closet floor, I'd planned to fill to the brim with a few clothes and as many valuables as possible. Now it was gone, along with everything imaginable I held sacred in this shitty place.

And that's how I end up waking from a fitful sleep on the bathroom floor, disoriented and in the same sweatshirt from yesterday.

Yesterday. The rush of yesterday's events flood my already foggy brain and I groan. Hating the way things turned out. Hating how all this was happening because of my cowardice and avoidance of the actual problem lurking underway. Luther, nee Ashawn, promised he'd make my life hell if I ever disobeyed him. And after we'd ran into each other at a party almost two years ago, he'd lured me into giving him my heart before he revealed himself to be Ashawn, my former foster brother who left us on the worst terms. Terms that I was truly at fault for instead of him, so when he told me that I was his I did my best to go along with it. Didn't ask any probing questions about the 'why' or his mental state to insist his former foster sister to be his girl, but...

I shouldn't have blindly played into his hand. Like now, I found that I was always falling in line in spite of myself. Forever that loveless little girl in the Albert house who'd been admittedly disposed of after birth, never feeling like she belonged.

Why did I give them the power to decide my worth? The question sank into my being right after the visions of Luther's abuse did. After the scenes of Takeo holding me at knife point as well as Edgar's strict supervision over my life detonate inside my mind like a truth bomb, I straighten.

I would be the spinner of my own fate. The decider and executioner for a change instead of the numb recipient of somebody else's wrath.

Standing up, I yank the door open with fierce resolve to proceed with my plan. To pack my shit and get the fuck out of here to face my oppressor. Instead of the empty second floor hallway, I collide into a formidable brick wall of muscle.

"Nora. Hey." It's Colin, who awkwardly stares down at me in a way I'd never seen before. "Got a minute?"

I grunt once I recovered from the forehead slam into his pecs. An eerie realization settled over me, and maybe it's all the time spent with Nita's forwardness, but I end up asking, "Where the hell have you been?"

A slight chuckle, then he responds, "Fair of you to ask since I'd ghosted you yesterday. As your protector, that's on me. Sorry about that."

"Hang on a sec," I mumble, warring with the notion that I'd hit my head somewhere as I listened to him say the words I'd not been sure he was capable of. "You're...apologizing. To me?"

A lazy shrug, then "Yeah, don't be a dick about it, Nora."

"And that, too," I added. "You're calling me Nora."

"So what?"

"So, everything." I start. "I've been begging everyone in this house to call me that for a year, yet all of a sudden you're talking to me like we're friends."

"Fuck that." He grunts. "I'm your guard. That's it."

"Hmm," I hum, not sold and not understanding where this soft side was coming from. "Okay, then. So where were you yesterday?"

The sheepish expression dies on his face, transforming into something stark and menacing. His chest swells as he says next, "Taking care of business. That's all you need to know for now."

"For now?" I ask.

"Fuck, all y'all Albert women this damn demanding? Just chill out. And listen to me good."

All Albert women? Just what was that supposed to mean? The only other Albert woman I could fathom him mentioning was Juanita, AKA my cousin who couldn't stand his guts. Anytime they were in the same vicinity all hell broke loose. I opened my mouth to question him more about it before he held a finger to his mouth.

"Quiet for now." He orders. "Just listen. Trace sent for you."

I rolled my eyes, visions of what he'd done—what he insisted—pushing into my mind. "There's nothing for me to say to him."

"Hear me out, though."

"No!" I hissed. "He emptied out my entire bedroom—the only place of sanity in this house—and moved all my stuff to his bedroom suite. After I confronted him about it, he'd laughed about how childish I was and told me it was time to 'stop playing pretend.' As if I'm a rebellious child instead of the nineteen year old woman he's forcing to sleep in his bed from now on. Told me I was 'rightly his.' Whatever the fuck that means."

"He did that?" Colin took a step backwards, a strange disoriented look on his face. Then he met my eyes. "Actually said that to you?"

I pause. "Uh, yeah. Why do you think I slept on the bathroom floor? No way am I sleeping in there with him. Is he crazy?"

Another stunned look and more silence punctuated the air between us. His face and tone are equally grim as he says, "Need to make a call. Stay put."

"Colin, wait!" I call after him but he's already disappeared down the hall in seconds.

I had no clue where the bravado to even look him in the eyes came from all of sudden, much less, be so forward with him about my feelings and situation. For so long he'd been the hulking shadow I'd often fear to be in the same room with for longer than sixty seconds, and now he was here. After being mysteriously gone all of yesterday, he was here now. Standing in front of me and calling me by my name. My actual name.

Ten minutes of waiting turned into twenty real quick, and by the twenty-fifth I gave up. Just dismissed this weird kindness as some charade of Trace's, sending Colin in to do his bidding instead of doing it himself. Remembering that I'd be living for myself now, I walked down the hall, descending the long staircase in no time to peek into the kitchen.

Thank goodness, I breathe inwardly. It's empty. There's no Miss Pauly singing at the double oven or any of the wait staff in sight as I tiptoe towards the fridge.

"We gotta stop meeting like this." A voice floats in from behind me at the entrance.

"Oh my god!" I yelp, nearly choking on the hushpuppy crammed in my mouth. After a few fitful swallows of the sweet onion bread, I face the jack-hole with a glare. "What the fuck is your deal? Sneaking up on me like that?"

If my unladylike behavior bothered Trace Oakhouse in the slightest, then he didn't show it. Instead, the lopsided grin on his face and slow stroll further inside the kitchen revealed only his comfort and—dare I frustratingly note—amusement. The blue-eyed jerk is openly laughing at my shock as if yesterday never happened.

"Hard to sneak up on anybody in my own house. How'd you sleep last night?"

Excruciating, was the first honest word that came to mind as an answer to that question, but then I stop. Realizing, once again, that he's goading me. He'd know exactly how I slept in the cramped room, where only two rolls of toilet paper served as my pillows on the harsh tile. Sure, the mansion had at least twelve bedrooms, but none of them had locks on the doors. None except the bathrooms on the second floor, where I slept fitfully.

But I stood tall and answered with grace.

"Fine, thanks."

His smile was like acid, curving slowly up his face while his pungent cologne stunk up the room. He moved closer and extended a hand to me.

"Sweet Norina," he said. "I apologize for working through the day and night and never leaving time for you. You deserve better than that. Let me give it to you."

I eyed his hand wearily. "I don't want anything you have to give."

"Now, don't be difficult."

"I'm not," I countered, crossing my arms. "I'm very busy today with Ball prep."

Not a total lie, since I would be on the phone with caterers or updating the guest list for the Ball a mere four months away. Though it isn't the total truth, since my plan involved packing my bag and getting out of here. Like, today. Luther gave me three days to make the trek to an address in DC where we'd meet, I paid him in full, and he'd disappear. For good. Never to threaten or harm anybody else who crossed paths with me. I'm grateful for the support system that flocked together without my notice over the past year. Including Pascual and his willingness to harbor me for the next few days since he'd apparently moved to a new apartment in Clemson.

Everything was lining up just right under the circumstances. Now it was on me to get the hard part out of the way: escaping Trace Oakhouse unnoticed and with a whole lot of cash.

He leaned up against the fridge, putting me in mind of those Westerns Pop used to love forcing me to watch with him, even if only to laugh at my squeamishness over the shooting scenes.

"Stubborn as a fish." He muttered.

"What are you talking about?"

"Doesn't make sense does it?" He said plaintively. "Because it doesn't. The phrase is 'stubborn as a bull,' which is a Taurus. And that ain't you. Know the traits of a fish, Norina?"

I breathed in deep, in restraint, trying not to deliver the cuss out this guy more than deserved for disrupting my life. For making my skin crawl in a multitude of ways whenever he got near me. Remembering the plan, I put on a sweet Norina smile and play along.

"I'm a Pisces. So, maybe, moodiness?"

"Not quite," he chuffed. "But close. Fish, or Pisces, are known for their creativity. Their capacity for imaginative thinking."

"Cool?"

He smiled considerably. "Cool, indeed. But that ain't so cool for this little circumstance we found ourselves in today. I don't appreciate you lying to me."

A cold chill ran up my spine as I listened to him. My body froze to the spot.

"Seems you used that imaginative thinking of yours to conjure up this fantasy world, in which, I'd overlook the several thousands of dollars wired to some beauty salon downtown."

Fuck. So he knew about that. I'd happily given the Amex Edgar gifted me without a spending limit to my cousin last month. Even wired her a few heavy bands of cash to her bank accounts and wrote them off as charitable donations, so as not to trigger an alert to Accounting. It was all for naught.

I found the strength to turn to him. "Trace, it's not what you think."

"So now you're telling me how to think?"

"No!"

"Then to me, it sounds like a nasty case of money laundering for your friend downtown."

"What? Please, don't do that! There's a simple explanation for this. I was only trying to help my cousin. And it worked! She's doing well and has agreed to pay back every cent."

He glared at me through icy ocean eyes. "Where's the ink?"

After studying my confused expression at what I assumed was another southern phrase, he sighed exasperatedly. "The contract, Norina! Did you put the deal in writing?"

"No." I whispered, chewing my lip guilty. Hating myself for being so stupid and not expecting this outcome. "She will pay it back. She promised me."

"All this imagination talk," he spat while pacing the length of the wide, white kitchen. "Figures Pa would get mixed up with a foolish girl from the sea. How in the hell is a promise gonna pay back that money?"

I gulped. "She-She gave me her word—"

In a flash he's pinning me to the fridge. My body squished between him and the cool glass surface of the smart appliance. He leaned in close to my ear and growled, "Since when have business deals ever been settled over pinky promise? Do you have any idea how liable this makes us? For Oak N' Sons?"

"I'm sorry!" I whimpered, my eyes pressed shut to avoid looking into the crazy. "Why does it matter, though? A few thousand dollars shouldn't hurt a multimillion dollar business. Should it?"

He's quiet for a moment, and in that brief silence all I hear is his harsh breaths, billowing over my forehead like a hot fan of wind. I don't know exactly what else to do or say, or even if what I said was a total no-no. Edgar and I never discussed finances. Hell, we barely discussed anything outside of the same forced supers Trace still forces me to attend between him and I. Sensing I'd fucked up in a major way, I pry open my eyes. Then gasp at what I see.

As a makeup artist, I know a good cover up when I see one. It wasn't uncommon for Nita's regulars to come in with a beat job that made them look, well, beat. Not beat to the gawds, but beat up.

Trace's coverup is an obvious disaster on wheels. Since he's close enough I can spot the much too bright foundation covering the purple ring around his eye. There's also a tooth missing from his bottom row of teeth I'm not quite sure how I missed once he entered the room. He looks like a total wreck.

"Your face..." I trail off, not knowing how to best ask about who put the shiner there.

"I fucked up the job, I know." He said after several jaw flexes. "Don't you bother with it."

"How did that happen?" I couldn't help but ask despite his warnings. That old caretaker heart of mine was bleeding again at the sight of another unhinged man with a beaten face.

"Don't bother with it." He warned again with his tightly closed eyes.

"I'll help you cover it up. I'm good at that, you know?"

His eyes remain closed, a mixture of what I'd call shame and embarrassment roiling together on his face. However, I don't give him the chance to go crazy on me. Don't even think twice about what I'm doing until after I've dragged him to the master bedroom suite and sat him in front of the vanity mirror Edgar bought for me a while ago. It'd never been used because I had no reason to do my makeup or feel pretty. But now, here I was, using this bleeding heart of mine painting over Trace's fresh scars in the very room I'd rebelled against entering since moving in.

"You're good." He breathed, studying my handiwork in the mirror once finished.

I blushed at the compliment that always felt so good in my heart after hearing a client's praise. "Don't mention it."

"Really, Norina." He said again but looking at me this time. "I see what my Pa saw in you. You're as true a person as ever. Don't ever lose that."

Slightly put off by the additional complement, I merely smile and nod. Then something overcomes me, and in this raw space of admittance I can't help but blurt out, "Please stop calling me that. Nora, is my name. It's always been Nora."

He frowns, processes, then says, "Why'd you introduce yourself as Norina first we met?"

I sag a bit in response. "Edgar, erm, Mr. Oakhouse liked to call me that. But Norina...isn't really me. Not at all."

After a minute, he rose and met my eyes. And for a while we stand like this. Saying nothing and seeking everything in each other's stare.

"I don't like misnaming people," He starts. "Nora, it is, from now on. I'll deal with anybody who calls you anything other than that. All right?"

"Uh...sure." I said, his earnestness coming off as major creep vibes still, but not so much as before. Right now, I can sense his gratitude, but also something more ominous underway. I braced myself.

And bracing myself was right. Since the next thing he asks nearly makes me stumble into the floor.

"You...you said what?" I stammered.

"Are you on any form of birth control?" He repeats the question with a hint of amusement. An amusement only he delights in since the question just triggers my fight or flight.

I shake my head, forcing my brain to process his totally out of line questioning. On autopilot, I numbly nod once.

"Yeah?" I breathe, recalling the monthly pill I demanded Edgar provide as a condition of me leaving my refuge room. The refuge room Trace had emptied.

He chuckled darkly at that, at my confusion, and pulled me into his arms. My face buried in his hard chest while he spoke.

"You ain't sound too sure of that." He said. "So is it a yes, or no?"

"Yes." My mouth says. "Yes."

The decent guy from several moments ago disappeared, clearly, and in his place sprouted this Dr. Jekyll person. The same guy who emptied my refuge room. The same guy who cornered me inside the kitchen and demanded money I didn't have back.

His hands explore my hair, digging into the plaits on my scalp. Then roaming lower past my neck and down my back. I'm still wearing Nita's sweater since I had no chance to change and shower since yesterday, but that doesn't stop him. With a quick yank, my sweater is ripped over my head and onto the floor, my breasts on full display since I wasn't wearing a bra.

"Gorgeous..." he whispers, his eyes honed in on me, stalking me as I take furtive steps backwards into the wall.

"Trace..." I breathe, horrified at where his line of questioning entailed and history repeating itself several times over. From Luther. From Mr. Newbern. Takeo Kobayashi, and now this...

Love, that elusive virtue Ty always claimed to harbor for me, was never all mine. Never. This was proof of it.

"You and I are gonna make some beautiful brown babies in no time. Just you watch. You're what I need, Nora."

"Get away from me!" I screamed, so hard and loud my throat burned from the intensity of it. History, repeating itself all over, my brain seems to keep reminding me. I was a prisoner all over again. A slave to someone else's wrath and pinned down because of it. I had to get away. I had to get away. I had to—

Right when he reached for my exposed breasts I remembered. Remembered the thing I swiped from Luther's car yesterday and tucked into my pants pocket. In a split second, I reach for it and direct it with wobbly fingers at his forehead.

"Nora," he whispers, shock resonating in his voice just before the caution did. "Where did you get that gun?"

I will my sweaty hands still and force the nozzle into his exposed flesh. The same frozen girl from Mr. Newbern's office a dead memory as I clung to the weapon I had no knowledge of using before. Resolving to be the predator for once, instead of the prey, sends a calm wave over my body and I glare at him. Hating him more than I'd ever hated anything for his abuse of power.

"Raise your hands and kneel on the floor." I command him.

That same smug smile from before returned as he looked at me. "You won't shoot."

"On the floor. Now. Or else."

He laughs. "Takes two kinds of people to shoot somebody: crazy or gutsy. Judging from your eyes ain't neither one of those inside of you."

"Shut up!" I scream, then chew on my lip, feeling like he figured me out. Feeling a bit too seen and worried he may have called my bluff.

How was I even sure if this thing had bullets in it? How to even fire it? Though part of an affluent crime organization back home, these parts were left to the soldiers, Saint Millard called the men who served under him in the 590's. Luther, Jack, Felix even, were the hired guns of the gang. Not the women. Our jobs were to look good at all times and remain available. Pretty trophies in a sea of crime, but not this time.

Fuck that, I thought and inwardly decided to rage against that shit. I wasn't a 590 girl anymore. Luther wasn't here and neither were my friends or parents. Nobody's coming, I thought. Nobody would come to save me from this unless I did something.

Without a second thought, I pushed every ounce of power I had into smacking him with the gun. Blood spewed from his mouth and spattered onto my face. Instead of giving into the instinct to wipe it away, I approached the guy on the floor carefully.

Trace just laid there, cradling his bleeding mouth and hissing threats at me about what he'd do once he stood up.

"You bitch!" He swore after I kicked him in the shin. His attempt to stand plundered by, yet another, kick to his other leg. "Go easy, all right?"

"How's it feel, Trace? To have your life reduced to a final second? Your power stripped away?" My words were seething as I stood over him, writhing on the floor. I got lower to meet his ice cold stare. "Men. What you all do to women is disgusting. I should kill you."

His eyes search mine while he breathes, "You wouldn't."

"Stop telling me what I'd do! You don't fucking know me!" My voice was hoarse from yelling so much. But he needed to get it. "What do you want from me?"

"I told you." He whispered. "Since Pa passed, you are rightfully mine. Promised to me since I'm the next in line to the Oakhouse fortune."

"Figures," I chuff. "This is all about your precious money. Let's get this straight." I crouch on all fours to meet his stare for stare, gun poised at his temple. "I am mine. Nobody else's."

He shook his head. "No."

"Say you understand." I demand, pressing the gun deeper into the side of his head. "Or I will use this."

"I won't say that." He said, flashing bloodstained teeth behind a sick smile.

"I will kill you!" I growled while raising the gun. "Just like you killed your wife."

He froze. Smile vanished as he stared at me in absolute disbelief. "What'd you say?"

"You heard me bitch." I spat. "It didn't take rocket science to figure out what happened. Edgar was a lot of things, including a drunk. But he trusted his gut. He'd admitted that he always suspected your involvement in her death. How many people just die of natural causes in their mid-thirties? It made no sense to him and at the time I thought he'd been rambling conspiracy theories...but you confirmed it for me, Trace. Thank you."

His entire body trembled below me, but I shoved the gun back into his temple. He stopped moving after that.

"You're bluffing. You don't know a damn thing, girl."

"Don't I?" I asked inquisitively. "It isn't often I'm proud to talk about my old job. But phone sex had one specific perk: men loved to air out their dirty laundry and concerns to total strangers. After some mild prompting, he easily told me about his desire to remarry and have a proper wife. To start again since his current son was such a disappointment to him that his only option was to abduct a friendly phone sex girl and pump her with the next heir to the Oak N' Son's estate. The same estate he'd been terrified to lose to you after his death."

"Shut your mouth!" He hollered.

I reared back, loving the redirection of power in the room suddenly. "Am I hitting a nerve, Tracey?"

"Oh, I'll end you once I'm up you little slut!"

I shrugged. "You're not getting it are you? Nora died the minute she was forced to live in this shitty backwater plantation!" He remained grunting on the floor, blood flowing freely from his mouth where I noticed another missing tooth. "Edgar was afraid of you. So terrified, in fact, he told me that he'd feared something would happen to him now your wife was gone. She was a cash cow, wasn't she? And once you spent all of her money, you went after him. You killed your own fa—"

My words get cut off by my own shriek as he rises with mysterious strength and blankets his body over mine.

"No!" I cry as he seizes control of the gun. "Get off of me!"

His laughter is low, dark, dangerous, and I gasp when he positions his pelvis against mine. "Don't talk about affairs you don't know about. How about that?"

I'm fighting with all my might beneath him, frantic to get out of this room and away from this man. A couple more seconds of squirming and fighting and then a sharp whelp of pain assails the left side of my face. All for me to realize after it's done that he's punched me.

"Somebody help!" I wheeze behind what I know is a busted lip. "Please..."

"Who are you?" He roars into my face. "An informant? Working for the feds?"

"No," I wheezed.

"You gotta be!" He yells, his entire face red with rage. "How else would you know about all this? About my wife's affairs and my debts? Who are you working for?"

"You're nothing." I laughed, despite the pain circulating through my face and neck from the blow. "It's just as Edgar said. You're just a little boy."

"Oh yeah? Well would a little boy come back to town after his stingy father threw him out after dishonorably discharging from the Army? Come back to take what was rightfully his? Nothing I did ever pleased that man."

"That's exactly what a little boy would do." I say, trying not to laugh some more at the man I once saw as a composed maniac. Now I see him for what he really was: a pathetic child, throwing a tantrum for not getting the less than perfect happy ending his privileged upbringing promised. It felt good to watch him sink.

Then he takes the gun and aims it at me. Just like I expected he would in this position. I couldn't explain it, but it wasn't fear I felt. Was more like a numb hyper-awareness and need to get him to spill his truth that kept me from averting my gaze from his.

"And then there was you." He grumbled. "Of course he brought you here with the intent to marry and create a new heir. That was the straw that broke my resolve to leave the old man alone. I wasn't letting no half colored baby inherit what was rightfully mine."

"You are pathetic." I say before hawking a huge spit ball at him. "Women aren't items you can possess."

"You bitch." He grumbled before wrapping hands around my neck. "That'll be the last time you disrespect southern royalty." Despite the limited air to my lungs, I wheezed a dry laugh at that statement. This seemed to piss him off even more, since he hollered, "Just what the fuck is so funny?"

I gulped. "You. To think I came here to rob you, all to hear you have nothing. You are nothing."

"I'd bestowed some pity on you and this is what it gets me." He started, his hands tightening around my throat. "Pa's Will stated I'd inherit the estate only if I had a child before my fortieth birthday. That's two years from now. Had you just cooperated, you'd have stood to make just as much cash as me. You would have been the mother to southern royalty, and I'd be a very wealthy man."

"I am...mine!" I choked out, the room going fuzzy. "Plus I know you'll cut me down as soon as I give you your heir."

"Ye of little faith," He dips low to whisper in my ear, "It's not too late you know? If you just apologize we can resume the plan. We'll both be rich."

I shook my head fiercely. "Never!"

"Gotta make shit difficult, huh?" He spat, then grinned when what looked to be realization settled over him. "Or are you so in love with my Pa that you couldn't imagine laying with me? Is that it? If that's so, then I'm sorry to report it was his time to die. Poisoning Melissa was all for nothing since she'd been cut off by her family's riches the moment she married me. But killing Ol' Eddie Oakhouse... the best decision I'd ever made in this life."

Tears rolled down my face at the reality of things: that not only was I blanketed under a confessed murderer, but my time was running out. There was so much I wanted to do. So many words left unsaid to the people who'd always mattered the most to me. To Mama, I'd say I forgive you. To Mom and Pop, I'd say you'd done your best. To my Beach, I hope you're happy wherever you are. To Sasha, keep shining bright and loving hard. To Nita, never stop fighting for what you want...

My time...I see it encased in glass...it's shattering and the shards are exploding everywhere. All around me. Same as the fog quickly engulfing me like a warm hug. This was it, I thought, as his hands strangled me tighter and the world darkens.

Except, it's not quite the end.

Sounds penetrate the haze I recognize as shouting and wrestling. Then a voice booms inside the room.

"Tracey Oakhouse you're under arrest. You have the right to remain silent. Anything you say can and will be held against you in the court of law..."

More scuffling and shouting before the weight lifts from my chest. I take a weak inhalation of breath, timidly scanning the surroundings to assess the situation.

"Nora?" The booming voice demands. "Nora! Can you hear me?"

It takes a few seconds, but my eyes flutter open again. And I nod at the man.

"Good." He says, relieved. "You did so good. You're very brave to face him the way you did."

"Okay." I squeaked out, forcing my eyes to steady enough to visualize the man beside me. "Are you an angel?"

"Far from it," he chuckles, and suddenly I'm lifted into the air.

There are sounds all around me, like crowds of men speaking in a cacophony of sound that makes my ears ache as he walks me through the house. My eyes drift closed again as I fight for breath. Then his voice comes to me again.

"Hey, Nora." He shakes me a little in his arms. "You able to look at me? I need to make sure you're feeling all right before I hand you over."

"Hand me...over?" I rasp, lifting one heavy eyelid to stare at the familiar face. "Colin?"

He nods once and I note the grim look on his face. His hazel eyes burn into me for a moment which makes me also notice the cut across his cheek.

"Are you okay?" I asked weakly.

"Asks the girl who'd nearly been choked to death." He answers, yet doesn't address the question, dryly. I'm being carried in his arms through the entire mansion: out of the bedroom, down the halls, down the stairs, before we end up at the front door. He stops to study me again. "Before I hand you over, I wanna thank you for helping us land that bastard. Trace Oakhouse has been evading police detection for years. Now we got him, thanks to you."

"Wait." I blinked a few times. "You're a cop?"

His jaw flexed a few times before he answered with a brief nod. "Something like that."

Colin, the terrifying guard of my late forced fiancé was an officer of the law?! And just how did I end up here, in his meaty arms instead of under the crazed lunatic who threatened my life? Nothing made sense, and my head swirled with a rush of new information.

"Where is Trace now?"

"In custody." He replied tersely. "No need to worry about him anymore. Nightmare's over. Had you stayed put when I told you to earlier then we wouldn't have landed you in this mess. But...we caught our guy in the end so I guess it's all good."

My mind racks from the memory of earlier. From when I woke up on the bathroom floor to Colin at the door, telling me to stay put before he made a call to somebody and I ran downstairs.

"Oh, yeah. Sorry." I whispered, rubbing my throat.

"We're all good." He repeats, staring outside for something before adding, "had you waited for me to complete the call, you'd have known that I wanted you to wear a wire. To keep you safe and coerce a confession out of him."

I shook my head. "Heck no would I have done that."

"Albert women," He laughs before walking out the door. "Had a feeling you'd say that."

I open my mouth to say something but pause when he bends down to deposit me gently inside a car. It's pitch black inside and there's another familiar collage of smells that assail my nose once I'm sat down. Colin kneels beside me and flashes a wistful smile at the open door.

"Are you feeling all right?" He asks.

"All right as one can be after nearly being strangled to death, I guess. I'll be okay."

"Good." He says again, his voice tight and eyes searching before he stands and shuts the car door. "Take care of her, you understand?"

"Who are you talking to?" I demand while looking up at him. He was glaring at something inside the car, something just behind me, and my skin crawled at the notion of turning around. "Colin, are you getting in, too?"

Silence and more glaring passes with Colin frozen at the spot. Not looking at me, but crouched at the open window and waiting for a response from...I'm not sure what he was waiting for actually.

"She'll be under excellent care from here on out." A calm, deep voice answers from beside me.

But the voice isn't calm, I realize when I swivel around to stare at the man I'd originally met in total darkness a year ago. His tone is a depthless note, consisting of zero emotion as a light fills the back of what I see is actually a black limousine.

My entire body numbs over as soon as the fear pulses my brain awake from the post-strangulation fog. It's him, the man sitting inside the car with that distinct smell is...

"Takeo Kobayashi," Colin says out loud. "Our deal is done. Take her now before I change my mind and arrest your ass."

"Pleasure doing business, Agent Isidro." Takeo, the Asian King, the bathroom attacker and killer of any shred of hope inside of me, answered Colin as the engine kicked on.

"Colin, wait!" I begged, fighting the locked door to get out of the car. "You're a cop! Please, don't do this! Help me! This man is crazy and wants to kill me."

"I'm sorry." He choked out, casting a regretful stare at me before turning around and walking back towards the mansion.

"No!" I screamed, my voice on fire but my fear heightening tenfold.

"Cleo'Nora Albert," Takeo calls when the darkness shrouds us once again and the limo begins to move. "Your deception ends with me. This will be your final chapter."

Part Three

"I will always wait for you."

27

the pieces of a girl

·❤· ·❤· ❤ ·❤· ·❤·

I wake up to the smell of burnt rubber. My head swims for a brief moment while my eyes work to understand the darkness in the room. No, it wasn't quite time for school to start, I surmised this because there was no Mom yelling at us from downstairs. She often woke right up with us to go on what she called Early Morning Jogs, where she'd walk us to Silver Spring elementary in the mornings and continue with her day from there. So, the fact that I woke up to the pungent smell of burnt rubber instead of her morning howls spoke to something really weird going on.

Curiosity at full spark, I rose and slipped on my Hello Kitty slippers. I smile as the warm tingles surge through my body at the promise of tomorrow. My Hello Kitty slippers were the first of what was sure to be tons of Christmas presents tomorrow morning. As modest Christians, my Mom and Pop never overindulge with lavish decorations or anything like that, instead spending their money on lots of gifts for me. Except, this year it wouldn't be just me, and I deflate when the memory of my new foster brother came to me.

Ashawn, my foster bro of only eight months, fit comfortably into the norm of our family. I hated his guts when I first saw him, but the hate slowly ebbed upon discovering he was a closeted doll lover. While he'd never admit to anyone out loud, playing dolls was one of the ways we bonded. Was likely the main reason we cohabitated so well together for as long as we did when our parents weren't around. And while I'm sort of peeved about sharing this Christmas with another kid, another part of me wants to do something about the permanent note of despair on his face.

I'd often catch him staring sorrowfully at me whenever my friends, Champagne and Lola, met up with us after school in the parent pickup area. He'd wear that same face during dinner most nights when he thought no one was looking, but I secretly did. My mission this year was to get my kind big bro to never make that face again.

That's right, I asserted the thought in my mind to give him the best Christmas ever. Operation Smile, I called it, and giggled giddily at the secret, special edition Ken doll I begged Mom to get for me. After pleading my case with her on how getting the doll would enrich my learning (yes, Mom made any moment a courtroom affair) she grudgingly brought me along for a covert shopping trip. She gifted Pop a new tie, Bible stand, and new shelf for his disc collection, whereas I only got Ashawn the Magic Island Ken doll and a space heater. Being anemic, Ash was always shivering cold even during the hottest days, so I figured this gift was kind of funny and practical. Their gifts were pleasantly wrapped under the tree downstairs, waiting for us to open them in the morning when Operation Smile would go into full effect.

I'm all but dancing from the excitement as I tiptoe down the hall towards the burnt rubber smell. The smell was coming from big bro's room down the hall, and I squinted at the lights shining from the slit of space under his bedroom door.

Even more confused, I knocked on his door. No answer came after three louder, more obnoxious knocks and this alarmed me. Ash was really good at being available for me whenever I needed him, and this entailed him perpetually answering the door after the first knock. Except, this time was different.

So alarmingly different I couldn't resist the urge to rattle the doorknob and hiss, "Ash! Ash! What are you doing in there, dummy head?"

The door flew open before I got the chance to finish my inquiry, and I cringed at the scary look on his face. And in his eyes.

"Quiet, Cleo!" He hissed angrily as his eyes scanned the perimeter. "Get out of here."

I frowned. "What? No!"

"I'm busy."

Arms akimbo, I just stare at the usually kind older bro we welcomed with open arms this year. I notice the huge beads of sweat on his forehead and he's sort of shaky. Or nervous, as if he'd been caught doing something he "had no business doing," Mom would have said. Even though he'd often come home after school and play dolls with me or sneakily unlock the parental controls on the TV, so that we could watch his favorite movies—now he's different. As soon as December struck, he turned more reticent and withdrawn. No more after school horror movies or doll playing with me before family dinner. Every day for the last two weeks he's come home and disappeared for hours inside his room. I almost snap a mean retort at his shady actions before Mom's words come back to me.

"Ashawn has lived a difficult life before joining our family. He didn't have all the luxuries afforded to him, like playing with toys and eating meals at a standard time each day, like you do. When he clams up, try to give him space to process. Okay?"

Of course I agreed, not really understanding the significance of what she said. Not knowing until it was too late and tragedy set our family ablaze, the likes of which we'd never recover from.

Keeping Mom's words at hand, I swallow before speaking to him again. "I miss playing dolls after school."

"Yeah," He bit his lip. "Sorry. I'll do better about that."

"Really?" I inquired, perking up at the prospect of resuming our Malibu Barbie game from several weeks ago. "So let's go play!"

I pulled on his arm, confident he'd follow me to the playroom where my dyed barbies were housed. But a flame squelches the instant he hardens under my touch, remaining rooted to the spot. I turned to him, and his eyes were casted to the floor.

"Ash, what are you doing?" I asked, a tad mortified but hiding it well.

Ash shakes his head slowly. "I ain't playing dolls no more."

"Stop being stupid!" I said, my words chased after nervous laughter. "We always play dolls after school."

"Not anymore." He says, totally serious while maintaining eye contact with the hardwood. "Not ever again."

"But why?"

"Just because."

"Because what?"

"Don't wanna talk about it. Just know I ain't playing that dumb ass doll game with you no more. We clear?"

I reared back. Horror icing me over as I sputtered a response. "I don't get it. You love dolls don't you? And so do I. Wouldn't it make sense to play together?"

He released a harsh breath and before finally meeting my gaze. I cringe again. The expression there is hard, unforgiving, and terrifying. More sweat forms on his skin as he growls, "Go back to your room, little girl. Turn around and keep walking or I'll make you."

It was as if his every word acted like a knife, stabbing into my heart with every phrase, every coldly uttered syllable meant to slice me in half and push me away. I couldn't let him do this, I thought, Operation Smile was still in full throttle and due to commence in mere hours. I could not allow his grumpy mood to ruin the early morning Christmas surprise Mom and I planned especially for him. Her logical warning flying out the window as anger reared in its place and I glared up at him.

"You ain't gonna do nothing." I said with the deepest neck-roll Mom would've disapproved of. "You're being a big jerk for no reason."

"Go. Away." He huffed with flared nostrils. "Now."

I pushed his chest with all my might, little as that may have been. "You go away!"

"How is that possible, Cleo?" He asked. "This is my room. And you're all up in my business for no reason."

"Then why won't you tell me what you're doing? Or play dolls with me?"

Frigid fury flickers in his eyes again before he gritted out, "Dolls are for babies. And girls. I ain't none of those things."

"Meany," I harrumphed.

He shrugged. "I been called worse. Now, scram."

More hurt and anger wrestled each other inside me as I glared at him. Why was he pushing me away? What did I do?

Instead of asking him these questions, I pushed him again. He didn't budge this time.

"You are the worst big brother ever." I hissed. Tears were pricking my eyes at the admission I didn't mean. But I needed my old big bro back. The one who smiled at me and laughed, instead of glared and avoided us all.

"Good thing I ain't your brother then." He said coldly, unattached and staring at me with what I could only label boredom before he added, "don't you get it? You ain't never been a sister to me. None of y'all are my *real* family. I'm betraying my real family by being here for Christmas instead of with them."

I wobbled for a second from the blow to the gut he just delivered in verbal form. Operation Smile and the merry Christmas Mom and I planned for him fading into the abyss. I realized there for the first time that we failed him. Like, totally failed him in every way possible if this was how he truly felt.

Not knowing what to say to that, I turned, preparing to launch myself back down the hall with my tail between my legs. If this was a battle, he won. Since it's pure loss that fills me instead of a giddy victory over getting him to agree to play dolls for one more time. One last time.

A hand wraps around my arm and I'm jerked backwards into his chest. He spins me around and kneels to meet my eyes. There's an emotion there I don't recognize.

"Want to see what I'm working on?" He asked.

"Uh," I sniffled. "No. You n-need space to...process?" Mom's words spill out when I have none left to give.

He draws back and laughs. "What does that mean?"

I shrug, drained from this interaction. "Whatever."

"Don't be a meany, Cleo." He goads, and I nearly shove him again, taking the bait as usual, when another voice from inside his room stops me.

"Is somebody in there?"

"Shhh!" Ash hisses, dragging me inside the room without another word of protest. The door slams behind me with a resounding bang that makes me yelp. "Get in here and be quiet. You're so irritating."

"ME?" I bellowed. "Why won't you play dolls with me?!"

He laughs in a way that isn't humorous at all. It's the opposite in fact, and I scream when the additional little boy comes into focus from across the room.

"Cleo!" Ash cups a hand around my mouth. "Shut UP!"

"Is that—" I started to ask, then faltered after casting my eyes on the sight ahead of me.

There are toys and Christmas wrapping covering the entire floor. Limited edition barbies, kitchen appliances, a tie, and so many other unwrapped gifts from under the tree line the entire floor. And I blanch at the sight of the unthinkable.

"Get off me!" I bite out after freeing myself from Ash's hold. "Are these the Christmas gifts from the tree?"

"Yep," Ash supplies proudly. "Me and Rome having ourselves a little experiment."

"No!" I whisper, my heart exploding from the sight. So many toys were unwrapped and ripped apart. And the sight that hurts the worst? The Operation Smile Official I'd been so amped to give my big brother tomorrow is savagely torn apart. The Ken doll's arms are missing as are his legs, and his head sits atop its original box, burnt to a crisp.

I sink to my knees, horrified by the sight as well as Ash's frigidity. This was a heartless act, one done with so little thought or care for the family who'd welcomed him in without condition.

"Why?" I asked, my voice hollow and tears flowing. "These are all the gifts from downstairs?" I repeated numbly, my brain hallowed out on an endless loop of horror.

His frizzy starter locs aren't hard to distinguish as he gets up from his sleeping bag and walks over to us. "Yo, bro, I forgot this fat bitch was your sister.

"Rome" is Jerome Cooper, the harshest personality to stain the halls of Silver Spring Elementary. He was two grades older than me, and I sickeningly watched Ash attach to the most criminal bully in the entire school. I sensed Ash's detachment the minute he went over to the bully's house one day after school. He hadn't been right since, and I hated to watch the sweet boy decay into a reticent clone of himself in the weeks to follow.

I don't acknowledge either of them and grimace when Ashawn bursts into a full belly laughter instead of defending me from that insult.

"How many times I gotta tell you she ain't no sister of mine?" Ash says. "Stop lumping us together or I'll throw your ass in the volcano next."

"Damn, pushy pushy bro." Jerome joked before laughing too. "Why you bring her here then?"

"I ain't." Ash answers harshly. "She just wouldn't leave. Told her to go, but hey," he pauses to allow room for a shrug, I guessed, since he's standing behind me and pausing, "is what it is."

More laughter ensues as my brain attempts to reconcile the sight before me. "What's the volcano?"

They quiet at my question before Jerome cuts in. "Oh, so fatty wanna play volcano?"

"Stop calling me that," I grumble.

"Looks like I touched another nerve." Jerome cackles before straightening and walking over to the pile of Christmas presents. "Maybe you and big brother Ash can play with some dolls? Since y'all love it so much."

"Shut the fuck up, bro. That's the last time I'mma say it." Ash sneers at Jerome, and though I can't see him I feel the intensity of his stare at the boy who was tempting fate. Then Ash comes beside me, pulling me to my feet. "That's the volcano, Cleo." He points to the space heater I chose just for him in the store the other day. It's laying on his back and the nozzle is cranked up to the high setting. "We been dropping stuff in there to see how fast it burns."

Burnt rubber. That pungent smell was the byproduct of my foster brother and his maniacal friend using the space heater to burn Christmas toys. Christmas toys purchased with care. For him. My stomach twists when he pulls me towards the backwards facing heaters, it's positioned so the grille is facing up where I see the few burnt bits of plastic inside.

"Ain't that cool?" Ash asks me, the look on his face could only be described as mesmerized. "I want to see how high the flames get."

"Why, though?"

"Why not?" He asked me back. "Look at that. It's beautiful."

"Yeah," Jerome chimed in, coming up on the opposite side of me. "We makin our own chimney fire up in here. Merry Christmas to all."

They both chuckled at his words, though I found none of this funny. No humor in watching all of my parent's hard-earned money go up in literal flames.

"Check it out." Jerome approached the space heater, picking up the remains of the Ken doll from the floor on his way. "Watch it burn."

"No!" I yelled, numbly watching him toss two rubber legs into the heater and throwing a match inside. A big gush of flames rose from the heater, but it fizzled out quick. Leaving that burnt rubber smell in its wake.

"Eew!" I coughed into my hand. "Stop ruining the toys!"

"Ruining?" Jerome parroted jokingly. "Man, look at this! This is the Christmas gift! Watch this baby burn!"

I looked at Ashawn. Hoping to find a shred of decency left in him. However, all I see is amusement. In fact, delight and excitement light up his face before he starts hooting at Jerome to add another toy to the volcano.

"Roger that," Jerome agrees before pitching another Ken leg and match into the fire. A similar flame billowed through the air and I ducked.

"I'm telling Mommy!" I screeched after watching in horror as the flames spread this time. They spread to the thick blackout curtain and quickly climbed up the one beside it. I run towards the door.

"Wait!" Ashawn grabs me, and I struggle in his arms. "Don't tell on me. I'm gonna get in a shit ton of trouble if you wake up Laurel and Ferr. Please don't!"

I just looked at him. Wondering, not for the first time, if he was inhaling paint or some other hallucinogenic shit that made him flip from Dr. Jekyll to Mr. Hyde in seconds.

"We were supposed to have Christmas tomorrow!" I whined, tears pricking my eyes and the flames kicking up behind him. "I'm scared, Ash. Let me go!"

A crazed look lit inside his eyes. "Cleo, you can't tell on me! I'll put the fire out and we'll forget all about it."

Smoke clouded the room, stealing the promise away from his previous statement to put the fire out. Smoke and flames engulfed the room in seconds, and I wondered briefly where Jerome was, but didn't linger. The room was hot and my head swam.

"Mommy!" I hollered, afraid that if he didn't release me then we'd all die. "Pop!"

A crazed expression blooms across his face as he wrestles me. I don't stop fighting, not even once, but I do get weaker. The flames get larger and Ash puts his hand over my nose and mouth.

"Mommy!" My screams were muffled by his hand.

"I never asked y'all for none of this." Ashawn bites out while suffocating me. "Y'all are gonna just leave me for dead after tomorrow anyways. That's how it always goes: we live together and get real close before the real kids get all the best toys and I'm tossed out after we take a bunch of family photos I won't be in next year. I'm just a toy to y'all. All of y'all. So, you fuck with this toy, this toy ruins your toys. I hate you so fucking much...."

His words stung, even as the smoke clouds more of the room and my thoughts float on a cloud away somewhere. He holds us both, never letting go until I hear Mom and Pop's ballistic screams when they enter the room. I black out soon after that, but the true nightmare awaited me hours later in the hospital.

Apparently, we'd all passed out from smoke inhalation. Jerome barely made it out alive since he was severely asthmatic. The flames spread so quick that it burned through the foundation of Ash's room. Parts of the ceiling collapsed onto my parents, the impact damaged my mother's spine, leaving her paralyzed from the waist down. Pop got severe burns on the left side of his body where he shielded all of us from the flames to get us out the house.

I'd never seen Ash after that, since he and Jerome got several years in Juvie from that stint authorities labeled arson. I heard Jerome Cooper's family moved to Philly shortly after and Ash would eventually be released into his biological family's care.

Christmas, just like Operation Smile, never happened. A morning filled with laughter and toys was replaced by several hours in the burn unit days later. Our house was a total loss, and the authorities discovered the reason why the fire spread as fast as it did. Apparently, Jerome stole gasoline from his dad's garage and brought it to Ash that night. Gas was found all over the floor in Ash's room, leading us all to wonder about his true intent that night. Did he want to harm us? If so, why that night? And in that way?

None of it made sense. And my family permanently packed up and moved to DC shortly after. Where we began anew. Mom navigated life as paraplegic with turbulence at first, crying through the nights from the mental and physical pain of losing her legs and son the same night. Pop held it together for us. Despite the fire, he threw himself into the church and focused on rebuilding us from the ashes.

And me? Well...

I met this beautiful guy named Luther years later. He treated me like a queen for several months before he revealed his true self to me. Luther Noonan was really Ashawn Luther, my former foster brother who vowed to make my life hell after what happened as kids. He blamed me for all of it, and I...

I did, too.

28

honor the silence

TAKEO

She does very little else but sleep.

Hard to believe three full months have passed without so much as a peep from the beautiful woman held captive in my Trenton high-rise. Three entire months she's been practically locked away in my condo and still I don't have the nerve to face her. The mere sight of her face fills me with a rage so strong I'm soon biting out more words than my name embodies.

I was The Silence, after all. Ever the calm and ruthless collector for the Kobayashi Clan, I made sure to stick to the shadows. To blacken my heart to steel to allow me the emotional freedom to execute tasks and people, alike. My Clan hailed from a long line of prestigious merchants since the Edo period and lived lucratively from those endeavors in Hokkaido's capital city. From young, my brother and I were trained to be exact. Cunning. Relentless. To remain cool under the pressure of a haggle in one of our many meat shops across New Jersey or during debt collect runs. But the mere sight of her, the girl whose name I discovered meant Honor, and I'm...unnerved. One million fucking percent unnerved.

I recall our initial interaction, and that same admiration kicked in my chest at the memory of her gallantly bowing to me. The ultimate gesture of respect in my culture.

She pleaded on behalf of the weak man who claimed to be the 590 Lieutenant, Luther Noonan. Or perhaps his legal name would be the most appropriate to use instead of the made up alias he is feared by. Ashawn Luther's file was tricky to get a hold of, but with a few strings pulled it was mine. Collected, like any other difficult to obtain debt. The guy bounced from one foster home to the next as a kid, and was finally reunited with his birth mother as a teenager just three years ago, where he was reintroduced to the drug trade. I'm almost sympathetic towards the man whose past is colored by a similar fate as my younger sister's, but the mere memory of his deeds heats my blood.

We'd strode diligently to obtain a contract with the DC based crime family turned gang. The 590's were lucrative and prosperous under Saint Millard's command, but he'd been mysteriously deposed nearly two years ago. His dead body was left alongside the equally brutalized bodies of his driver and Quincy Masters, another high profile crime family hailing from the New York area. Then Burn Man rose to the ranks to replace Saint in running the gang ops before getting arrested on possession charges. Ashawn Luther, his ill-fitted lieutenant, took over after Burn Man's imprisonment, where it was rumored he'd take on savage deals in the dark to feed a nasty drug habit. I'd been warned against granting an audience with him to negotiate a new deal towards running our ops down south.

"He's taking you for a ride, you know?" Yamada Shindo, our clan's co-collector and my late brother's best friend, said to me as we entered the Japanese Bistro minutes before our meeting with Luther. "That Luther's a real scuz. Created quite the rep for himself since his leader got pinned, too."

"Leave matters where they lie," was all I said to him for the rest of the day. I never wasted energy on speaking, since so much could be assessed from observation. From silence.

Yet, Shindo-san was right. I watched with predatory focus from the shadows as he pleaded his case regarding why he deserved our product. He'd been speaking, sure, but my mind had already been made. Taking that meeting had been an instinctive decision. One made without my full understanding until it was over. Until after I met her.

"I beg you!" She cried before bending in half before me. She didn't notice it, but the hardening of my cock demanded I readjust in my jeans. "He's had a rough time with his partner getting locked up and he doesn't know what he's saying right now."

Of course, he didn't. Ashawn Luther was a lost cause, and I didn't really need a reason to get rid of the unworthy 590 leader. Hell, disposing him would be doing our underworld a great favor, indeed, but I don't let her know that. No. Instead, I wondered for the first time just who the pretty, curvy female was with the red extensions in her hair. The Kobayashi's had a widely known affection for women and children. We protected them, always. Our centuries old decree we honored with our lives, but it isn't honor that seized my heart at the red-haired female's display. It's her actions.

She's begging for him. Pleading on this waste of oxygen's behalf to take the deal I had no intention of solidifying without Burn Man's oversight.

Financial trouble? I wondered as I studied her trembling hands on her knees.

This could be the only purpose behind her heartfelt display of pleading for this deal. She's obviously his, but rage rocketed my being at the thought of her uncared for. Unprovided for. Was this spineless wasteman making her living more difficult? As his top girl, she shouldn't have walked into an official deal wearing the cheaply made Maxi dress I could tell was from some discount retailer.

Oh yes, I noticed everything. Remembered everything. This talent served me well during debt collections and contracts I'd used to execute alongside my criminal partner called Shame. I'd readied myself to give Shindo the signal. Two finger taps of my nose would signal for him to expose his silenced gun and get rid of Ashawn Luther and his top girl. Soon they'd both be mere bodies for my crew to dispose of. A deal gone bad, one would chalk it up as, but it doesn't happen that way.

Instead, my fingers froze over my nose before I tapped it. Giving Shindo the signal to kill them both. The red haired female Ashawn Luther referred to as Nora brought fretful brown eyes on me. And this speared me.

The room blurred for moments on end as we just stared into each other's eyes. I'm not sure if she can see me from my seated position in the shadows, but I can see her. And if the steeled flesh in my boxers weren't enough, then the freezing of my heart would seal the memory into my being for eternity. Her eyes...how could I describe them? They wounded me. The intensity shining in them tugged at the dragon in my chest. Warmed the cold resolve I had a normal abundance of and shook me to the core.

Those eyes. So pure. So true. They reminded me of someone I wanted to forget. Someone I needed to forget despite my diagnosed photographic memory.

Flashes of her assailed my thoughts again. Her smile, the way she lit up when I returned home from work that had me burnt beyond repair. The way she healed the dark parts of my soul when I needed it most. Before she was gone forever.

"Maintain your bow." I bit out to the red haired female who triggered emotions inside me beyond my understanding.

As if snapping from the same trance as me, she gasped and bent again. Her eyes. I couldn't stand to have them on me, demanding me to reconcile the thunderstorm forever raging inside me since Serafina. Serafina's in the past, I remind myself. She's a part of a past I'll never be able to recreate in the present or preserve for the future even if I wanted to. Our time was, like this unexpected meeting, over.

I'd ultimately decided to allow the pair to live. Though it was difficult. Everything in my body demanded I pull my knife and carve out the waste man's throat for daring to touch the red haired female who unknowingly saved his life that day.

When Ashawn Luther failed to appear to pay his dues for distributing our product two weeks later I wasn't surprised. In fact, I expected as such. I needed a reason to get rid of him so that we could freely operate in his territory, free of interference.

Though I did not anticipate her involvement. The red haired female I discovered was called Cleo'Nora, or Nora, orchestrated the attack on my clan. The shooting of our Camden meat shop that took the lives of good men with families boiled me to the core. It took some true detective work, but I found the despicable witch who organized the attack of my clan in South Carolina where, incidentally, my sister-in-law resided in secret to remain safe from whomever murdered her husband.

Hatred, so raw and tangible, twisted my insides when I glimpsed the girl at the Obon Festival. Yume, my sister, begged to participate in the yearly festival since she'd no longer lived in Hokkaido. In our home country, she'd danced in every Bon festival, but her life had been upended for reasons I refused to dwell on since moving to the states. The woman I chased tirelessly for a year now stood a few inches from me. Her hair is in blonde plaits now, black at the root and giving her a more distinguished appeal. But something sparked when I got a look at her body. She'd lost a significant amount of weight since meeting her first. Her curves were things of yesterday, and I glowered at the fitted sundress that hugged her still-round ass perfectly.

I couldn't resist the urge to chase her back to that quiet hair salon. Couldn't resist the urge to pin her to the wall and relish the feel of her warmth against my chest at my intrusion. Fear lived in her big brown eyes as she looked upon me, sure, but also the same fire in them stoked a larger flame in me. Unleashed my beast in the most terrifying of ways that had me dying to tear her clothes away and plunge myself deep inside her heat.

A feat nearly accomplished, if not for the bullet that pierced my shoulder and headiness in the room.

She was mine now, I thought darkly. And she would pay. Though the sight of her from the CCTV in her bedroom did little to quell the beast begging to enter her, to resume our lustful meeting from months before, I ignored it. Filling my mind with the memory of her betrayal she swore against committing. It was her. Her and Ashawn Luther were responsible for the crimes against my clan, and as the clan's collector, that could not go unpunished. Ashawn went ghost. Both Shindo and I looked for him in every known place, but his trail went cold. Three months have passed. Three full months since the former red haired girl I now labeled as *Fumeiyo*, which translated to dishonor, remained prisoner in my Trenton condo until further notice. We'd negotiated her freedom if she just told us Ashawn's whereabouts, but she steeled herself. Never answering my questions or leaving her room except to use the restroom across the hall.

I grunt as I watch her toss fitfully in the bed. I expected that same fire from those eyes to awaken her. To cause her to fight back and defend her man against the allegations of his actions. But she didn't. Instead, she resigned to this room, interacting only with Yume who'd been tasked to keep her fed and hygiene intact as her permanent charge.

"Oni-sama," Yume called from the doorframe of my office. "May we speak?"

A normal man would have allowed embarrassment to dictate his actions. A normal man would have fumbled with an excuse as to why I'd been watching Fumelyo on camera asleep in her room, in the middle of what looked to be a nightmare. Not me. Instead, I slid my adopted younger sister a look that conveyed my agreeance, and watched as she spoke in fluent Japanese with a worried expression on her face.

"It's been quite a while since Nora has had any interaction with the outside world."

"Fumeiyo," I snapped, correcting her.

Yume nodded briskly, "Please excuse me, big brother. I had not meant to offend you."

I glared at her, saying nothing, but allowing the annoyance to bleed through my cold stare.

"Yes," she started as if my glare was a verbal response. "All I ask is that you consider her time outside. She speaks a lot about her mother in her sleep. And after I deliver her meals I hear her sobbing once I've closed the door. Instead of eating, she weeps for her mother. 'Mama, Mama,' she cries. And most days she cries until she loses consciousness."

I shifted in my seat. "Your point. Get to it."

Five more words than I'm used to during the day, but this time I spoke to interrupt the feelings blooming in my gut. The same ones from when I first laid eyes on her at the Obon Festival.

"Right," Yume adds, ripping me from my thoughts. "All I request is that she gets some fresh air. Or, maybe, some time to be with her mother? If I'm not mistaken from what she's said in her sleep, her mother is ill."

Again, I say nothing. However, Yume mistakes this as a pass to keep talking.

"Please consider her time to be with her mother. I am requesting this of you, big brother. If not for *Fumeiyo*, then for me? This is all I ask."

My mouth nearly falls slack as I gape at her, bowing with heartfelt fervor. Yume never asked for anything. Ever. She accepted every order ever given from me or father without a single protest. But a request? This was a rarity. A rarity that peaked my interest and caused more of those emotions I didn't like to stoke in my chest.

I nodded before telling her, "Leave."

Minutes after she departs, I'm left to stew in my thoughts at her request. I didn't flat out deny it, and perhaps that was the largest shocker of the day. The purpose of holding Fumeiyo captive here was to torture her. To punish her for keeping Ashawn Luther safe. Shindo insists I put her out of her evident misery. Asks me on a regular basis if I'd been ready to just cut off fingers to get the answers needed to find the wasteman of a gang leader and to get her talking. But I couldn't bring myself to do that.

More flashes of Serafina plague me, and I'm clutching my chest as wave after wave of guilt drowns my insides. No, I decided, this would not end the same way as it had with her. This time, things would be different.

I'm dialing the number to the phone kept inside her room before I realize my actions, and watch her jerk awake by the shrill ringing. From the looks of it via the camera, she seemed not to realize the phone bolted to the wall, prison style, right beside her bed.

"Answer it," I growl to myself, every nerve alive as I watch her cautiously tip toe towards the wall phone before raising it to her ear.

"Hello?" Her voice was rough, evidence that she hadn't used it in a while since sequestering herself inside the room. "Um, this is Nora?" She added when I didn't return her fretful greeting.

The sound of her voice leaves me tongue tied, however, and I will the wood in my jeans to calm as I sneered out the words.

"You are a traitor of the worst kind. My Clan would usually hire you dead by now, but I can't keep looking at your face like this. I'll grant you one day in your hometown to settle your affairs, but I will remain close. So don't even entertain the idea of running."

29

deus ex machina

· ♥ · ♥ · ♥ · ♥ · ♥ ·

"Lay hands on her, Jesus! Rid her of those demons that led her to the drugs and prostitution and tore her away from her motherly duties. Guide her home! For what is man without love?"

"Yes, Lord!" Amora Albert hollered in praise at the TV pastor whose voice ruptured the previous calm quiet that usually existed in our house.

I shook my head as I examined Mama on the living room couch. The quilt passed down from three generations of warrior women in the Albert line covered her minced body entirely. Her pink satin bonnet that usually teemed under the pressure from barely contained afro curls now deflated to one side from emptiness. From baldness. My heart ached to watch her perform her Sunday worship from the cheap sofa in our nearly vacant living room instead of the warm and welcoming congregation of Mt. Goliath's Chapel, our family's home church of god-knows-how-many years. I could have stayed there, stuck like glue in the door frame as I watched her proudly broadcast her love for the Lord in the empty room, but caught notice of her thin body quaking from the exertion of her hymns.

"Mama?" I asked, kneeling in front of her to assess the source of her distress.

She fanned a dismissive hand at me, her eyes trained on the TV. "Cleo, you're blocking the sermon, now. Please move out of the way!"

My hands were all over her: running their way down Mama's back, arms, and legs as if searching for the golden needle in a haystack responsible for her obvious discomfort.

"Cleo!" She protested, pushing me away from her with frail force that felt more like a nudge.

"You're so cold." I mutter, mostly to myself, but she rolls her eyes as if I threw the most ludicrous offense her way.

"I am fine. Just a little chilly, that's it. You need to turn that air conditioning down a few notches, that's all."

I gulped and forced my eyes shut, unwilling to greet the consternation in front of me. In front of both of us. While notorious for our cold winters, it was a sweltering hot day in D.C. I'm sweating like crazy from the heat beaming through the narrow windows.

The air conditioner was broken.

The weather man predicted temperatures in the near nineties all this week, and this day was no exception, but I didn't dare say anything. Couldn't breathe a word of my fear to my fearless mother. It was taking her from me, and I knew it, but I had to be strong.

I don't realize I'm crying until her bony finger wipes a fat tear from my eye.

"Mama's gonna be just fine, Cleo." Her tone was soft and her face tender as she regarded my statue of a body, frozen before her.

I shook my head. "I...I know. But the doctor said—"

"There is no fear in love, my child." She recited the bible verse flawlessly as she gathered me into her rail thin embrace. She's so cold. So, so cold..."Come on, baby." She coaxes as I sob into her chest. "Say it with me. Speak to God..."

"I'm scared, Ma." The blubbered words slip past the caged confines in my heart, and I hug her tight.

"Shhh," She croons while rocking me. "No fear, remember? Tell it to Him..."

I breathe in deep and despite the ice in her touch I'm suddenly warm as I chant the words to 1 John 4:18.

"Perfect love drives out fear; the one who fears is not made perfect in love..."

As we're completing the verse, the TV pastor's question drifts into my mind, and I'm compelled to answer it with the welled-up feelings of futility that's festered in my heart since Mama got her diagnosis. For what is man without love? Loveless.

There it was: Love. That elusive fucking virtue I'd hardened my heart against during the past few years under necessity still created yearning in me. I yearned for the days when things were simple. When my biggest worries were how long I could keep the lie about my extracurricular activities alive to my parents. When Trice and Katy and I were a unit, going out for shopping sprees and spending time together. When I worked with Nita both in DC and Greenville towards my dream. When Ty was alive and...

"Feel better?" Mama asked me with hopeful eyes. I'd almost forgotten we were speaking when I cleared my throat and stuttered back at her.

"Yeah."

"See?" She said, a satisfied smile curving her lips while she cupped my cheek. "Ain't God good?"

I sniffled, "Yeah."

A brief silence swallowed the nearly-barren room with us just sitting there. Mama, watching and rocking as she stared at the TV with the Pastor screaming now about gratitude and God's mercy. Meanwhile, I'm on complete edge at the memory I made with the devil. His cold words drift back into the forefront of my mind as I stare numbly at my mother.

"You are a traitor of the worst kind. My Clan would usually hire you dead by now, but I can't keep looking at your face like this. I'll grant you one day in your hometown to settle your affairs, but I will remain close. So don't even entertain the idea of running."

After speaking with a frantic Nita, I learned that Mama had barricaded herself inside our little blue house. Refusing to leave until her daughter came back to her. She even refused her chemo treatments and wouldn't let anyone else inside the house. Nita let me know she'd closed the shop temporarily to take care of my sick mother whose health was declining each day. She only let Nita inside because Nita somehow convinced her that she was me, and Mama's fragile mental state grasped desperately to the lie.

Mom and Pop kept Mama's bills paid since she'd been in no state to work due to her grief.

After I left home without a word, she turned into this: a skinny, sunken-in version of herself who had only one good sofa and TV where she spent most of her days. The beautiful, vibrant woman who'd once been so full of life had disappeared. And it was all because of me. Guilt piled high in my soul at the memories of what I'd done. The fact that I practically abandoned everyone I'd ever loved since being taken, not once, but both times. I could've tried harder, I thought, harder to find my way home.

But it was too late.

"Are you hungry?" The question threw me for a second, but I blinked a couple times, recentering, then answered her.

"Um, not really." I told her before standing. My one hour was almost up, and I didn't want to disobey the devil disguised as a handsome captor, called Takeo, more than before. "But you should eat, Mama."

A pained expression crossed her face as she shook her head. Declining. "If you're not hungry, then neither am I."

"Mama," I say, panicking at the thought of her missing any more meals. Nita was gracious enough to give me this alone time to spend with my birth mother, and she nearly begged me to get her to eat something while I was with her. She'd only recently begun refusing food, but I couldn't tell from how much weight she'd lost. "Please eat something. Don't wait for me."

"Cleo, I told you I am fine. Don't you worry about me, I'll fry up some party wings later on."

"Really?"

"Sure will."

Totally not believing her, I glared at her while digging in my heels. "You can't continue to starve yourself. As a daughter who loves you, I can't watch you do this to yourself."

Her eyes cut to me, harsh and sharp for a second as she studies me. Then she falters, tears collecting in her eyes and bottom lip wobbling.

"Mama?" I asked, afraid.

"I pushed you away." She breathed out, her voice tight with emotion. "My sweet baby girl. How could I do such a thing?"

"It's not your fault!" I said. "It was me. I left."

"Because I gave you no other choice, baby." She countered, her eyes more lucid now than an hour ago once I arrived. "How I'm always telling you to make good choices when every single one of mine has always been wrong?"

I opened my mouth to refute what she's saying, eager to say whatever to get her feeling better, but then I realized something: Lying and coaxing her into a false sense of reality wasn't the right thing to do. In fact, I'm sure it's the opposite of what would make her better.

Perhaps it's something I picked up on as a devil's captive, but I kneel down again and gaze into her eyes.

"You're right. You've made a lot of shitty choices. Choices I will never begin to understand. But I feel you. I know you. Even though you said I ruined your life, I know you meant the opposite. And I love you, too."

"Oh, baby..." She breathed, her voice watery and tears falling down her face. "You do get me."

"Yeah," I chuckle. "So stop punishing yourself. Eat your dinner, Mama."

Her smile cracked as she chuffed, "Suppose I will. But you need to eat, too."

"Don't wait for me, Mama," I insist, and gasp when she pulls me into her bony chest covered in silk.

"I will always wait for you." Her voice was still teary, but her words were clear, a threatening proclamation of her love that shot through me like an arrow. "Always."

A realization so raw and true settled over me as I studied my ailing mother: I forgave her. Forgiveness, as Pop preached, was a tricky thing. Something that couldn't be done for you and that hung in the air like a thin string, intent to be grabbed yet easy to slip between your fingers. In other words, it was hard to do. Normally. However, seeing the state of Mama had me reconsidering what was important. During that year on the estate, I lost so much time. I lost so much of myself I wasn't sure I could regain it. Love wasn't lost though, and I felt it tenfold as I smiled at Mama. If nothing else, love would carry us through, and my escape plan would work. The mere thought of The Devil and his cold shark eyes honed on me like a predator made me shiver. I had to get away, and even this tantamount of time with my estranged mother confirmed what needed to be done. I had to grab that string and surge on. But first...

"How about this," I start, taking her hand in mine to remove some of the tension in the air. "Let's get you beautified. I left some of my old makeup in my room, and I've been looking forward to reliving one of our post-outing makeup sessions. What do you say?"

Obviously, she agreed. After rooting through my room for the makeup I rejoined Mama in the living room. And the remainder of my allotted hour with her flew by as I filled her cheeks with the color it lost from the chemo. We laughed and laughed while reciting old tales from my childhood and the latest gossip from town.

"Forgot to mention," Mama began after I finished her eyebrows. "Your friend came by the other day asking about you. Said she missed you and asked you to call her."

"What friend?" I asked idly, not really expecting much substance in her response since I had zero friends due to being imprisoned twice in the past two years.

"Oh, come on Cleo! You remember her. The one with the little baby? Trice Newberry or Newsome, I think it was?"

My hand stilled with the brow pencil gripped tight. No way she was talking about the friend I gave up on long ago. Surely, she wasn't talking about my former Beach who literally saved me a time ago with her friendship. The friendship I fought so hard to make earnest and honest instead of the fake one we vowed to uphold for the sake of appearances and protection. We grew to be so much more than that, and if it wasn't for the sick twist of pain in my heart, I'd have the strength to ignore Mama. Could have easily relegated her name blip as a mistake and left it there.

Yet I couldn't. The Devil's statements about being honorable drift into focus, and I wondered what to do.

Instead of panicking, I breathe. In and out. In and out until I found a semblance of calm to reply. "Newbern," I breathed out. "Trice Newbern."

Mama perked up and nearly lifted out of the couch from excitement. "Yes! That's the one. Gorgeous little thing, too. She asked if you had changed your number. Did you?"

"Sort of," I nodded, and it isn't the total truth since my original phone was thrown out, courtesy of Edgar Oakhouse. But to my mother, I offer a simpering nod and add, "It's no longer in service. Did Trice say...why? Like, did she give a reason for stopping by?"

"Hmm." Mama frowned and scratched her head. "If I remember it right, she came by to tell you she was back in town for a couple of days."

"Hang on." I say coming to stand in front of her. "For a few days? So, she's permanently moved out of her parents' house?"

"I'm sorry," her shoulders sagged. "I'm not sure. She didn't go in to much detail. But she looked troubled. Give her a call, sweetheart. Looks like she needed a friend."

Anger took over and answered before reason could catch up. "Yeah, well so did I! Where the fuck was she last year when I was at my lowest?"

"Cleo, calm down—" Mama reached up to clasp my hand, but I stepped away.

"No!" I bit out, pacing now. "Do you have any idea how many times I've called her? The amount of texts and voice messages I sent until her phone stopped accepting any more? It's the audacity for me!"

"My love!" She scolded, mom-mode turning on full blast at this point. "Isn't Trice your best friend?"

"Was," I sneered.

"Was," she corrected. "Don't you think she's got her own story to tell? Her own demons? Maybe she was going through something she couldn't talk to you about."

"And why not?" I pleaded. "We were best friends! There was nothing we couldn't talk about. So tight we were practically sisters, Mama. When her stupid baby daddy was too chickenshit to change her daughter's diapers after the C-section, who do you think did that? Or when Katy developed the odd habit of putting objects in her mouth—who do you think held Trice as she cried in the ER? I mean, thank god they were able to remove the nail from her airway, but it was me. Me! Always there for her during times I shouldn't have. And where was she for me? When I needed her?"

Mama raised to her feet and flung her arms around me. Though thin and feeble, her hold was firm. Solid. And what I unknowingly needed to brace the storm of emotions roiling through me. I thought I purged my feelings for Trice. Thought that my love for her had fizzled out just like her presence in my life did, but I guessed wrong. It's a lot, but the tears pour down my face as I sob into my mother's shoulder. This wasn't just a cry. This was a release.

"I know," I mumbled as she reared back to gaze into my eyes. "Forgiveness is key to healing from it. I know."

She smiled, but the expression was tinged with sorrow. "That's right, but not what I was going to say."

"Oh." I sniffled. "Okay."

Mama exhaled a deep sigh, as though years of stress released right along with the gesture. "I want you to trust yourself. If you truly believe that your friendship with Trice is over, then let it die. People all deserve forgiveness, that much is God's law, but we need to keep it real, too. Family is who you choose, not who you're genetically saddled with. Same as friends. If you truly feel like Trice's presence in your life wouldn't be serving you, then choose what's best. That's all there is to it."

I ruminated over her words as the tears ebbed. Already I felt better by her encouragement and was reminded again why Mama was my favorite person. I'd always felt so seen when it came to her, and I appreciated the advice. Choose for me, I thought, momentarily empowered by her insight and the answer shined so clearly in front of me. Mama was right, I should let her go if I was meant to truly heal. But doubt lingered in the pit of my stomach at the thought. Was I ready to give up on Trice? Katy? Our friendship?

I opened my mouth to address Mama, to let her know what was in my heart where it pertained to my Beach, but I don't get the chance. The door flies open and we yelp at the brooding, slender man standing at the front door. Though the sun's rays shadowed most of his front side, I knew immediately who he was. And what he wanted.

"Take—" I stammered on the name he'd forbidden me to use since our bathroom scuffle. "Erm, Silence. Has it been an hour already?"

Again, his face was not visible due to the intensity of the sun, but I felt his rage all the same. "Five minutes over," He grunted. He'd not said more than three words to me at a time since he'd taken me prisoner.

That familiar tingle rose up my spine and played a sinful game down my neck. Sweat accumulated in areas it didn't exist minutes before and the urge to scream reared its way ahead. I couldn't explain the effect the fear had on my body when it came to him, but same as back in the condo, I avert my eyes the minute he gets closer.

I guess Mama didn't get the message or flat out ignored the tension rising in the room, because she smiles at him and says, "Hi! Are you one of Cleo's friends?"

My eyes are glued to the floor, like normal, but I physically jolt when his voice responds, "Yes."

This time I couldn't resist the urge to stare at him in open mouth shock. Not merely from the fact that he'd bothered to exert the extra energy on words for a change, but from what he said.

"Pleasure to meet you, uh...?" She silently asked his name and I held my breath. The last time anyone made Silence use more words than necessary ended up with a hole in their chest.

"Takeo," he groused, his tone oddly softer. "Kobayashi."

My jaw didn't just drop to the floor. It slammed clear through it as I observed the interaction. Mama beamed at him and sat back down on the sofa. "Well Takeo, it's always nice to meet any friends of Cleo's. May as well come in and get comfortable, too. I was just about to put some chicken on."

"Can't," Silence (Takeo?) said from the door. "Busy schedule."

"Sure, sure." Mama nodded with a considering look. "Are you one of Cleo's new friends or old?"

I held my breath again, afraid of what he'd say. Hell, afraid of every action from this man that didn't involve him walking away. Far away from me. Yet he paused, processed, and shot right back at her with a neutral, "New."

"Hope you like chicken, New Friend Takeo!" Mama sang and practically danced to the small kitchen. "Because I already fried it and made the collard greens, too. Lord, if I had known we'd be entertaining then I would have made sweet potato pie."

"No bother..." Silence said, but to no avail since Mama already disappeared. Now it was the two of us. Alone together in this six hundred square foot living room that felt more like a closet.

I couldn't help but fall into his dark brown eyes as the sun shifted enough to reveal his face to me. They're two dark whirlpools of snow, so cold and depthless it makes me sad to stare too long. And lost, as if I'm adrift in an ocean without a paddle.

"Don't. Stare." He bites out, his words quick and precise like an arrow to a bullseye.

"Sorry!" I gasp and cast my eyes to the floor again. Shame rolling through me at how much I forgot myself at that moment. I had to focus on the reason, the true reason behind this visit. While I longed to see my Mama, returning to the little blue house was more than a home call, but the only means to secure my escape from this psycho who still thinks I'm involved with the 590's. Who still thinks I owe him a great debt even though it's Luther to blame for everything.

The evening passes without a hitch and shockingly Silence agrees to join us for dinner. Even though this event wasn't in the plan, I secretly wondered if this was Mama's way of saving me. This bought me more time to plot, to rearrange and readjust my next moves. And after excusing myself for a bathroom break, I snuck inside Mama's room in search of the real reason I returned. My salvation. After uncovering the item from the closet, I rejoined the dinner party where Mama was regaling all kinds of vivid tales from my past to an uncomfortable looking Silence.

***

"You're planning something." Silence sneered behind the wheel of the black Mercedes to me as we drove down the highway.

A solid forty-five minutes tick by without a word since we've left my mother's house, and I freeze from the impact of his head-on collision statement. It's not a question, I note, but a statement of fact from The Devil's point of view.

"Um, no?" I say, nonplussed. Was I messy? Obvious, somehow, with that fake bathroom excuse?

"*Fumeiyo*," He growls without even glancing at me. "You're lying."

Fumeiyo. The new name he's branded me with since being taken by him. Since becoming his wrongful captive. I don't research the definition of this name that I sense is really a word that will scare me.

Instead of heading down that rabbit hole, I focused on his dinner admission when Mama asked him how a handsome young man like him was still single.

"Not single," he grumbled to her. "Cleo is mine."

I flashed angry eyes at this beautiful, yet confusing man who sought to punish me. "Why did you tell my mother we were dating?"

More silence, then he answers. "Didn't lie."

"Yeah, you did!" I howled. "Big time."

His jaw flexed a few times before he added after a full minute of quiet, "Not a lie. You do belong to me."

Fury reddens my vision and I'm suddenly back inside Luther's car. In full panic mode as I waited for him to lose it right after proclaiming that I was his property. His to do however he wants with. Not again, a voice screamed inside me. This interaction may have been the difference between me getting out of here unscathed, so I had to play my part.

"I don't belong to you! Or anyone!" I chew out through clenched teeth. "Take it back."

He doesn't answer, like I figured. So I try again. "I am not yours! I am mine!"

A smirk, but he otherwise continues to ignore my existence. To rub my nose in it, he reaches for the radio dial and turns on a jazz station.

"Figures you'd try to block me out. As if you actually respect women."

"What..." He grits out.

"Poor Yume." I pile on about his younger sister. "Her guilt leaves her stuck beside a chauvinist like you."

His face hardens for a moment, and I can practically feel the icy glare trained on the road that's meant for me. Feel it with everything inside of me, but I don't stop. We'd never shared more than a few words between us during the three months I've been captive in his Trenton condo. So this was very very new to me. To us.

"You're deflecting," I hear him say admirably past the lump of coal that's his dead baritone. I watch in seconds how the heat leaves his face and the anger subsides before he reorients and says, "good job. Enough for now."

I wasn't quite sure to be oddly flattered by The Devil's praise about my manipulation skills or afraid. A strange mix of both swirled through me as I allowed the trees to whizz by. I reflect on many things as my eyes soon drift closed. Like how my plan would come together in the end and what would be Yume's fate once I left. We'd developed a tight friendship since being taken, and I'm not sure where I'd be if it wasn't for her daily company. Similar to the estate, I had the freedom to roam the condo since his family owned the building, but it didn't get much further than that. I had no desire to leave or do anything most days, and these were the times I spoke exclusively to Yume, who'd show up and make sure I ate and showered.

I don't realize I'd fallen asleep until the car jerks violently to the right.

"Shit!" Silence hisses, his eyes trained on the rearview mirror while he makes frantic turns at the wheel. The car is speeding well past the speed limit, and I'm not certain about our location, but sure that it's somewhere almost rural. There aren't many cars on the long stretch of road, but Silence guns it like the hounds are after us.

"What's going on?!" I demand while gripping the door handle tight to steady myself. No words leave his mouth, but he keeps his eyes pinned between the rearview mirror and the road as he pushes it to near ninety. Infuriated, I shove his shoulder. "Takeo!"

"Silence!" He barks out with more emotion than I'd ever seen from him, and I'm not sure if he's demanding silence from me or demanding me to call him that, but it works all the same. I remain silent as he exits the highway and enters a town I don't know. We're parked outside a gas station soon after, where he gets out, rounds the car and opens my door. "Get out."

"What is going on? Where are we?"

"Baka." His voice is harsh and clipped as he grabs my arm and drags me across the street to a seedy motel.

The motel's sign is nearly scrubbed clean from the ages, I supposed, and the receptionist barely blinks at the odd pair we made. Just throws a set of keys without barely looking up from her magazine to tell us our room number.

"Get off me!" I shout after we get into the tiny motel room. His eyes scan me predatorially, but I don't let him speak first. "Talk to me! What is going on? Why were you speeding out of control to get here?"

He turns his back to me, his face a tight mask of emotions before he peers out the blinds. "Come see."

"See what?" I ask while walking over to stand beside him. And once I finally get a glimpse outside, my brain doesn't know how to process any of it. I also understand his decision to abandon the car at the gas station across the street and hide out.

Two men exit a black truck that looks vaguely familiar. The tall black man dressed in the suit is also familiar, but his image in my memory is blurry. He looks expensive, nothing like the threat I knew him capable of during my 590 days. I squint my eyes to make out his face, but gasp when the taller white man's face comes into view. They're both peeping through Silence's Mercedes windows, in search of us, before the white guy rears back and kicks the driver side door.

But it didn't take complex science to piece together this man's identity. I took a wobbly step back before my legs gave out completely. No, I thought, it couldn't be.

"Jack Burn." I breathed out in shock. "He's supposed to be...supposed to be—"

"In prison." Silence finishes for me. And perhaps I get the next major shock of my life when I numbly swivel around to find him, standing above me aiming a gun at my head. "This was your plan all along. Wasn't it?"

30

sunset in Morocco

·❤·❤·❤·❤·❤·

KIMMY

"Are you ready, beautiful?" Michael asks moments before kissing me.

The kiss isn't urgent or smoldering like the ones from hours before. After waking up from the strange vision I'd assumed was a dream where I met Little Helen, I couldn't kill the urge to be with the man I'd woken up to. The real man, in the flesh and blood, laid where my wife, his sister, usually did and fucked me into several sobering orgasms over the course of three hours. Hours he spent giving my body what he claimed it deserved, but I didn't feel so deserving. Pure shame ricocheted through my being at the realization that I'd been busy fucking my wife's brother instead of searching for her. She was totally disappeared, nowhere to be found, yet here I was—

"It's noisy in there," Michael breathed as he pulled back to gaze into my eyes. Then he kissed my forehead. "Everything will be okay. It's understandable to be afraid of what's to come next, but we're together. That's all that matters. That's all you should focus on."

"Can you hear my thoughts?" I asked.

His laughter rumbled in his chest and vibrated our joined bodies for a second. "No. But I guess Hollywood's to blame for how spirits are portrayed. I'm just as real as you. In the flesh and everything. No Jedi mind stuff."

"Right," I laughed then frowned up at him. "Then how could you tell it was noisy in my mind?"

All humor drains from his perfectly handsome face, making my heart race from guilt when he quietly says, "I know a thing or two about a noisy mind. Lived it for too long..."

"Oh, Mikey..." I whispered, wrapping my arms around his middle and willing some peace into him. "I'm sorry."

"It's fine." He said. "Won't be long until it's all over. And we stay diligent about getting our girl back."

I nodded. "Yes. I know. We'll be all right so long as we stay together to bring her back."

Another slow kiss and I relish the feel of his arms tightening around me. We lay naked in bed and bathed under the full moon shining into our small cabin. We bathed in it and savored it, since I wasn't sure when we'd return.

Or if we'd return.

"You don't sound too convinced, beautiful," Michael says. "Maybe it's best if I go alone."

"No!" I cried. "We do this together. She's your sister, but don't forget she's also my wife. The love of my life who's rotting away somewhere suspended in time."

Michael sits us up. "She isn't quite rotting. It's sort of a subspace. She's not suffering, but..."

"She's not fine either." I finished for him, cupping his face in my hand and bringing it to look at me. "I'm ready. Let's do this."

"You're sure?" He asks.

I bring my lips to his so eager to savor the taste of him. Before he was gone for real and for good. There would be no more Mind Mansion dwelling, no more him Taking Over whenever Vonnie couldn't deal with a problem. From now on, she'd have to face her troubles head on, but not totally alone. She'd have me, always.

His flesh hardens between us, and I grind myself into it, needing to be closer to him all of a sudden. Needing his strength so bad and with a desperation thickening the air around us.

"Shit..." He rasps between a groan when I palm his readied erection. "We're here, beautiful."

Some rational part of my brain heard him, but the insistent need from below demanded I maintain the kiss. It demanded I keep him close and slide my juices up and down his leaking steel.

"Kimmy..." He groans, a warning sound but I don't hear him. Not really, and we both cry out the second I swing my leg around and ease his dick inside me. "God damn...need to stop..."

"Michael!" I moaned.

My hips picked up speed as I sought the release my body yearned for. For hours we spent like this, waking only to scavenge the kitchen for ready-made meals Vonnie kept for when she'd pull all-nighters gaming.

That exhaustion chased me and I lost momentum as I rode his thick meat. That didn't stop him. Michael grabbed my hips and slid me up and down his dick, my juices making macaroni sounds in the hollow room. I kept my eyes closed, afraid of the monstrous wave of lust washing through my insides.

"Cum for me," he snarled, his voice laden with desire and sensual promise as he pistons into me. "Cum all over this dick."

And that did it.

"Michael!" I screamed into the universe, my eyes rolling back into their sockets and body shivering as the climax overcame me. A wave of juices flooded below, and I gasped when it didn't stop. My core clenched over his dick, milking his seed from him and pulsing as more and more and more of my wetness waterfalls between us.

"Fuck...fuck...fuck..." His words were punctuated with deep thrusts into my taut flesh. "You here with me, beautiful?"

"Mmm," I moaned. My head lolled against his shoulder as twinges of the orgasm gradually faded. "I'm here."

"Gosh, I'll miss this." He whispers with woe while wrapping me in his arms. I gasp at the feel of him lifting me in the air.

My head swirled so bad I didn't realize how thankful I'd feel that he took it upon himself to stand for both of us. I knew we had to go. Knew deep down that I couldn't prolong the inevitable since we had to get Vonnie back. Had to honor the deal he made with the spirits or all hell could literally break loose. Or worse, Mikey would be trapped in an endless loop of suffering.

"We've made it." Michael says. And I open my mouth to respond, but another voice answers him.

"That, you have. Quite the entrance you've made, grandson." A deep voice chuckles after speaking and my eyes fly open.

Realizing for the first time that this was what he meant. We were here. The subspace called The Center where my wife was kept hostage. Horrified, I scrambled out of his arms and fell to the ground.

"Oh my god!" I screeched. Covering my naked body as much as I could, I leapt behind Michael after realizing the effort was fruitless. He remained naked too, though not horrified in the slightest. In fact, he was rather neutral as he addressed the older man.

"Grandpa," He greeted, his voice gruff. "You saw that, huh?"

The older man threw his head back and guffawed some more. And even though he was muscular and taller than Mike, he seemed so much jollier and St. Nick as he spoke. "No need to feel ashamed, grandson. I'd be doing the same thing if I got one day to live amongst the living with a young body like that. Figured you'd understand the assignment soon enough, though."

"Don't get me wrong," Michael started. "I'm not sorry. Not in the slightest. What you saw was pure love between me and my woman. Nothing to be ashamed of at all. You know why we're here."

"Rightly said, son." He chuckled before turning kind eyes to me. "Nice to meet you, Kimberly."

"Kimmy," I whispered, still hiding behind Michael. "And same to you."

"You're family now since you married my granddaughter and are carrying my great grand. Congrats, by the way! Oh, and feel free to call me Grandpa. Or if you're feeling formal, Devin will do just fine."

"Wait." I paused, straightened a bit to face him, but still covered my small breasts and lower parts. "Devin, as in, Devin Carlson's grandfather?"

"Yep." A sad smile crests his mouth. "That's the one. He was a Cooper first, the same as me."

I noticed the broad similarities between the two men. Devin Carlson bore a striking resemblance to the darker complexioned male standing before us. There were subtle differences like jaw structure and ear shape, but Devin Carlson appeared more like this man than ever. It was like I was staring into a time capsule image of what Michael and Vonnie's big brother would look like in thirty years.

"So this is the grandpa you were talking about, Mike." I said to his back. His very tense backside that was getting tenser by the minute, despite our lighthearted conversation. "Sweetie, are you okay?"

"He's a bit shaken." Grandpa answered for him. "This is the last place he wants to be right now. "

I study my surroundings for the first time. Noting that we were standing outside on the curb of a craftsman style house. The house is pale blue with dead plants out front. The street itself is quiet, without a person in sight, and judging from the street sign on the corner, the house was located on Canal Street.

"Where are we?" I asked Grandpa, since Michael had metaphorically left the chat. "It's okay, babe," I cooed while stroking his back.

"It's where he grew up." Grandpa approached the house, climbing the small set of steps and stopped at the front door. He beckoned us with his hand. "Come on over!"

I gripped Michael's hand in mine. My heart dropped when I noticed the tears streaming down his face from tightly closed eyes. Raw pain written all over his face and his breathing harsh.

"Baby?" I said to him. "Talk to me. What's wrong?"

A tense minute passed without us saying anything. I allowed him a few beats to get his breathing righted, before he gulped and choked out, "This is...this is the place."

"Good job," I said to the man who brought me such pleasure just moments before, one wouldn't have known it considering the evident torture on his face. "Can you tell me why this place is so painful?"

He shook his head.

"Okay," I nodded, caressing his cheek. "Well can you show me instead? Would that be better?"

More silence before he slowly nods. Our hands entwined, I coaxed him into being calm enough to get him walking. We're now standing at the front door of the little blue house Mikey can barely stand. I don't allow my fear to stop us, because I sense we needed to do this. To move forward and enter this house to approach this entity holding us back.

Grandpa's face was just as grim as he opened the door and stepped back. "This is where we part, I'm afraid."

"Wait, you're not coming with us?"

"Can't." He shook his head. "I'm only your guide. From this point on, you both will have to decide what's next. This is Michael's journey, not mine. Trust in each other and you will be all right."

I nodded. A fierce resolve solidified in my heart as I squeezed my true love's hand. His eyes were wide open now and gaping into the open door that led to a dark hallway.

"Gramps is right," Mikey proclaimed, and I could have fainted from joy at what I saw in his eyes. There he was. My man. My Michael. The one I loved for eternity shining his light right back into me when I needed it. "We got this."

"Sure do!" I effused. "Together."

"Together." He parroted, smiling warmly down at me before placing another gentle kiss on my forehead. "Thank you, Kimmy."

"Thank you, Michael." After another moment of warmth passed between us we took the first step inside the house. Together.

***

"This is it. The place Vonnie refers to as The Mind Mansion. She's in here." Michael tells me as we walk hand-in-hand through the sinister halls.

"Wow," I breathed in awe while glimpsing at the corroded portraits on the walls and dilapidated brown paneling. Old furniture in the rooms lets me know the house has been abandoned or unattended for a long time. The floors, hardwood as they were, were rot through and an interesting smell permeated the air. In fact, it strengthened the further we walked inside the ruined Mind Mansion.

"What is that smell?" I huffed before pinching my nose and covering my mouth. "It smells like...death."

Mikey tightened his hand around mine. "That's because it is. Have you ever smelled rotten flesh before? Before this moment?"

I grimaced before turning to answer him. "No. I mean, we found Granma Stevie dead in her bed, but she'd been gone no longer than a few hours."

He grunted, but otherwise didn't respond or offer any more conversation. We're walking only a couple more minutes, but the urge to prod more on that subject rides me.

"And you know that smell? Rotting flesh?" I'm careful to keep my voice gentle, tentative, so as not to trigger any unwanted emotions in him.

The past. It's a subject we don't talk about. Like, ever. Neither he nor Vonnie ever divulge many details about their old life in DC or what exactly happened to cause Michael to end up this way. There's only one person on the farm who knows the full story, and he keeps the past just as top secret as his younger twin siblings.

"Yeah," he intones. "Come this way."

"Right," I acquiesce and allow him to pull me to his side as we approach what looks to be a really old staircase. A chill crawled up my spine. I couldn't explain it with words, but my body felt the strange charge of energy before my mouth started moving. "Somebody's up there."

"Mmhmm." Mikey agrees half grunting then he takes my hand. "I got a favor to ask."

"Anything." I told him easily because it was true. There wasn't anything I wouldn't do for him or Vonnie. Our connection was like Teflon, unbreakable through even the worst of storms. And it was through that connection where I realized a portion of that strange energy was partly emanating from upstairs and him, too. I cupped his cheek, massaging the tension stored in his taut cheek. "What's hurting you, sweetie?"

He gulped two full times before meeting my stare. "This is...fucking strange having you in this place after being here alone for so long. And it's hard to put it into words, but you don't belong here. Neither of you do. And you might encounter some...scary stuff the further we go."

All this time I thought I'd been the fearless one in this situation, considering it was his demons we'd soon be facing in the literal flesh. Okay, well the metaphorical flesh, but still. Fear never entered my heart once since entering the dark house they nicknamed Mind Mansion. Instead of fear, it was readiness I felt. Readiness to confront this thing that held them back for so long. This thing that brought both of my loves so much pain it sealed Michael in this mansion styled prison.

But now? I shiver from the dark promise in his words.

"There's nothing I'll ever see that will make me leave your side. Nothing." I said.

"Sweet Kimmy," he intones and I gasp when he brings my hand to rest across his wide chest. A ghost of a smile crests his face. And he nods before continuing. "I see what Vonnie saw in you first."

"Yeah?" I say, my heart lifting at the prospect of getting another peak into Vonnie's heart.

"Yes," he answers, kissing my fingers. "You're loyal. Always there for the people you care about one hundred percent. I wanted to tell you...thanks. For sharing some of that with me."

I fist my hand into his chest. "No thanks required, baby. It's what you do for the one you love."

"One," he said, a morose hint in his voice. "You love her that much, eh?"

"Both of you." I grit out. "One hundred percent. Together."

His light brown eyes studied me for the longest ten seconds in creation, and my heart hitches when he kisses my fingers again. But it's different now; now, he's savoring each kiss against my finger. And I shudder when his lips trail to my thumb, the final digit before casting a pensive expression my way.

"Together," he repeats, low and sultry. Then he sighs in deep, as if in preparation. "Okay. Before we head upstairs, I need you to promise me something. No matter how extreme it is, you'll have to do this to make it out of here safely."

"Go on," I encourage him gently.

"If…" he starts, then falters. His eyes are cinched shut as if he's fighting. Fighting back tears and memories and visions of something that's the likely cause for the strange energy charging the air around us. "If you see something…a person or situation that seems out off or dangerous, then you need to ignore it. We need to remember why we're here. We stay together through this the entire time. All right?"

"Ignore the dangerous person?" I ask, confused. "What dangerous person or situation will we run into?"

Now he scrunches his face in confusion. "Hold up. Vonnie never told you about our past?"

My face heats from this. From the knowledge that, even though we'd vowed our lives to each other in holy matrimony, my wife was still not willing to talk to me. At least not fully, about her past. So…

"No." I answered, retracting my hand from his chest. "IT's not something she wants to talk about. She's never comfortable enough to share, so I don't push her."

"I know you love my sis and all, but that is hella toxic."

"What?" I demanded. "It's toxic that I don't want to traumatize my wife more than she already has been?"

He shook his head. "No, sorry beautiful. That's not what I meant."

A surge of anger from depths unknown fire through my nerves and I glare at him. "No, that's exactly what you meant! You think I'm an incapable wife? That I'm just enabling her and adding to her problems? How fucking dare you?"

"It ain't like that!" He bellows, and I'd usually cower away at such an open display of hostility, but not today. Today, I stand my ground as he jabs an accusatory finger in my face. "You love her, I know. But your love can be suffocating. Stunting. You don't see it because I'm in her head, but it holds her back. Even if she doesn't want to talk about our past, about me or Mom or Dad—you make her! Make her see that staying comfortable only holds her back. Is that so hard?"

"Fuck you!" I shove his chest so hard he flies back against the dilapidated wall paneling. "I am her wife. Me! It's my job to keep her comfortable. To make her pain go away. And now you're telling me to force her into reliving that shit?"

"Damn right I am." He growls, eyes flashing and nostril flaring. "And you better watch your hands."

"Or what?" I spat before shoving him again. "What are you going to do?" Another shove. "Hit me? Shove me back?"

"Nah," he bites out, jaw flexing, but he's otherwise unmoving against my forceful prods. "Yo, stop touching me."

"Make me!" I holler from an ugly place inside. "Make me, like you want me to make Yvonne! Do it!"

Reason is out at sea. An unseen boat adrift in chaotic waters as it fights the current to get home. Just like now, the fury is so potent it's blinding me. I can barely make sense of right or wrong or up or down when I feel hands wrap around my throat. Then compress. It's hard to breathe, but the anger won't go away even as fear tries to get it to find that elusive virtue to get back calm waters.

"You are the reason," Michael snarls as his hands tighten around my throat. "You are the reason my son is dead. I will kill you where you stand for crossing me, bitch!"

It's like my throat is on fire from the rage and strange energy engulfing the room. That same energy isn't a mere reminiscent feeling as it had been when we first walked inside the house. Now, it's swallowing everything in the room. The darkness closing in on me by the second as the man who vowed to always keep me safe strangled me to death.

"Quincy, stop!" I choked out, the words regurgitated from my lips but they aren't my own. "Not in front of her. Don't do me like this in front of her!"

He casts his hateful gaze from me to the top of the steps. There, a little girl is sitting with her knees tucked into her front and a green toy in her hands. Her large puffball pony-tails alert me of her identity, and I don't need to say her name to understand who the little girl is, watching us fight like an unwilling audience in the front row.

Michael steps away. His hands falling at his sides and a tortured expression on his face as his eyes remain trained on the little girl I guessed he hadn't noticed there before.

"Vonnie!" He roars, but not in anger. There's so much pain in his voice, so much pain that it makes me gasp as a cold bucket of reason pours over me. "Vonnie, baby, I'm sorry!"

I blinked several times, looking around the room where that strange energy is still surging so strong in the air. Except, now I see it. Purplish wisps of wind swirling around us. The wisps around me have all but dissipated, but Michael continues screaming up at the little girl on the top step until his voice is raw from the strain. He doesn't run upstairs, but remains there, screaming and pleading for her to look at him and see her father's not a monster. That it was all a mistake. That he'll make everything right if she just looks at him.

But Vonnie doesn't.

Instead, her head is tucked into her chest, and from the sounds of it, she's sobbing into her plush toy I see now is a green T-rex. Something was wrong here. Gravely and sincerely fucked up.

Suddenly, Michael's warning floats back to me. Reminding me of something incredibly important about how we navigate this house.

"Mikey!" I whimper, my voice small from the force of his hands on my neck. He doesn't answer. His screams, strained, heighten and intensify so loud I have to resist the urge to cup my ears. "Baby, stop it! Look at me."

"Yvonne!" He lets out another ragged scream and this time I see streams of tears fall down his face. "Please! I will fix this! Baby girl, don't lose faith in me."

"Babe!" I choke out, a bit louder, but it isn't reaching him. The purple wisps form a tornado around his body, nearly knocking me backwards. However, I hang on. I grab onto his hand and bring it to my chest. Not knowing what else to do, I called to him over the winds that felt eerily similar to the ones from my first meeting with Little Helen.

"Michael, listen to me." I say, my words frail but projecting. "Remember what you said to me? We're here to find our girl. Our Vonnie. Try to remember. Remember me!"

He shakes his head. "No! Vonnie, please forgive me."

"Honey, I'm here!" I cried. "Remember me! Kimmy." We're naked, so it's no issue to bring his hand to cover my chest. "Feel that? That's my heart. Feel it beating. Come back to me, baby."

He's shaking all over, and I know in my experience with spirits that it isn't him. Michael has left the chat, and in his place is the father I remembered haunting me several months ago. This is a memory. Vonnie's memories, and from the looks of it, these are new to Michael, too. These are Vonnie's innermost emotions and past memories that keep her trapped here.

And we were living them.

"Mikey, please, honey!" I plead, gripping his hand tighter. "Don't leave me. Don't succumb to it. Their pull is strong, but you have to resist for me. Stay you. We're in this together, right?"

"To...gether," he mumbles in a crackling voice. "Together. Kimmy. Together. K-Kimmy. Keep safe."

I nodded, so relieved the purple whips of wind lessened as he continued to speak. As more reason came ashore. "Yes, my love! I'm here. I'm safe. This isn't you."

After another tense ten minutes of harsh purple winds, his hand tightens around mine. And everything stops. Though the ominous energy and strange winds crept inside us both insidiously, they disappear in a second. A sinister laugh sounds inside the room as more of the energy disappears—no, moves on. The energy doesn't dissipate like I figured, but slowly floats like a calm cloud up the steps, where the little girl remains.

Then Michael collapses, and I rush to his side.

"Baby!" I whimper, cradling him in my arms. "Are you all right?"

One slow, painful head gesture lets me know he's nodding. But his eyes flutter closed as he says, "Kimmy? Are you safe? Are you here?"

"Yes," I sob and fight the urge not to scream as his head lolls in my arms. "I'm here. I'm right here, unharmed."

"Kimmy!" He bellows out, jolting upright. His eyes search the room as if there's an enemy lurking in the shadows. Which it was, but I sensed its presence far from us now instead of inside of me and swallowing me whole. He swivels around, where his eyes locate me before he launches himself at me. Not to choke me, like before, but to embrace me. I'm soon swallowed into his arms where I hear his heart race. And the sobs. "I fucking hurt you! I'm sorry! I'm sorry, I'm sorry, I'm sorry, I'm—"

"Stop it," I whimper again, returning his hug and squeezing tight. "It wasn't you who did that. It wasn't us. I'm fine, my love."

He's trembling in my arms. "No! I hurt you! I d-don't deserve, I don't deserve you. Get away from me."

I shook my head and didn't let go. "No. I won't do that. We stay together through this."

This time, he's shoving me away. I'm fighting, like last time, but I'm fighting to be beside him instead of away like Helen did. The spirit of her memory felt so much anger, self-righteousness, and the most frightening of all was the emptiness. There was a depthless quality to the woman

Vonnie called Lucy, and it nearly swallowed every inch of Kimmy as it begged me to surrender to it. That amount of fury and emptiness was a powerful combination, and it lured every insecurity and doubtful thought to the surface. Causing me to hurl the ugly words at the man I loved the most.

"Go, now!" He begs me, his voice so ragged from all the screaming that he doesn't sound like himself. "Leave before it's too late. I feel it taking me over...I can't resist it."

Fed up, I took his face in my hands. His eyes remain shut as I speak directly into his face. "Look at me, Mike. This is Kimmy speaking."

"No..." he whispered.

"Do it, baby!" I bark. "You got to do this. This is the hard part we talked about. You cannot give in. You got to ignore those feelings in you. They aren't yours. It's Quincy from Vonnie's memories. These were Helen and Quincy's spirits. Her memories are so powerful we seemed to get consumed by them. The memories she tried to protect you from. Think, sweetie."

"We got possessed by her memories." He choked out, not a question, but I answered it.

"We did."

Mike's eyes open painfully slowly. His entire light brown face is red and tearstained. His eyes search mine like a lifeboat in need of an anchor. Or a reel. I willed all my love and strength into them. Praying somehow that it would be enough to bring my Michael back. To bring the second half of my soulmate back to me.

"Yes," he breathed out. "The doors she kept locked. This is...this is it. Her memories are behind them. She hid this to keep me safe. All this time it was her protecting me. Vonnie..."

"That's right!" I cried.

Anguish twists his face again through our eye-lock. "But why? Why would she hold this in? How could she shield me from all of this all by herself? This is hell..."

I nodded. "I know. She wasn't alone, though. She always had you. You say you loved my loyalty, same as Vonnie. But I never told you what I love about my wife. The reason I fell in love with her."

The anguish ebbs on his face a bit, and I take a breath before continuing. "She's tiny, but mighty. Vonnie is my lifeline and frontline defense. She'll always do her best to protect me, from anyone. Big or small. Even myself. She pushed me to be my best, and I need that. I love that."

"Yeah."

I grip his face. "Same as you. She protects the ones she loves, tooth and nail. Body and soul. This is what she didn't want you to see, but you needed to see it. And I know you said the words in anger, but you were right. We have to push past this comfort to get through to her. To save her. Thank you for showing me that."

"No." He shook his head again. "No. I'll hurt you if you stay near me."

"And I'll hurt worse if you make me go alone." I retorted. "So, make your choice. Come with me to save Vonnie, together like we promised. Or go alone."

"I'll go alone. I've got this." Mike moves to stand up, but I keep him locked in place as I drill in my point.

"I want you to understand what you're risking," I start. "If you save Vonnie by yourself, I will resent you. For the rest of my life for putting yourself in danger. This will be the same as dishonoring my dreams. It'll all be over."

"Kimmy—"

"Think about it." I say, resolute before we both stand up. "Is it worth it?"

"Your safety?" He demands. "Absolutely!"

"No," I shake my head. "My resentment. My hatred. And this baby I'm carrying will never get to know the love she was made with. Because it won't be true since it'll be hatred that follows the wake of your leaving me. Leaving us all behind."

"It's not like that." He bites out, head hanging mournfully. "I can't take it if something happens to you, Kim. I really, really can't. Everybody who tries to protect me just ends up hurting: Vonnie. Devin. Shamel. And now you..."

I shrug, arms folded as I regard him coldly. "Whether I hurt or not in the end is not your decision to make. Pain is only an indicator that we're capable of feeling. And I feel you, Mikey. Can't you feel this?" I ask quietly, bringing his hand to my chest again. "This beats for you. And this?" I move his hand to my belly. "This is our love's result. I feel her. She's fighting to live, same as Vonnie. Why can't you trust us?"

"Trust..." he breathes. Then his hand clenches around mine. "I do. I trust you, beautiful. And I'm so fucking sorry there aren't enough words in the world to describe how shitty I feel about hurting you."

I smiled at him. "How about, 'I love you, Kimmy'?"

Suddenly I'm in his arms, and his chest is lifting up and down quickly from the ferocity of his heavy breathing. And quickening heart. Where it's beating just as strongly for me as mine for him.

"I love you, Kimmy," he croons while stroking my wild red curls. "Never forget that."

"Never," I agreed, my heart lighting up from our promise reborn. "Let's make it through. Together, with trust."

"Damn right." He growls playfully, fully himself with his love shining down on me. I bask in that light for a few seconds. Then sink when darkness replaces the light in his face as he turns his gaze. He's looking at the top of the steps. I look, too, and see the little girl. She's standing now, her back to us holding the green plushy in her hands.

"Yvonne?" He calls gently, taking tentative steps with me in hand up the staircase. "Yvonne, it's me. Mikey."

Silence. But Mikey keeps going as we slowly ascend the steps as if a bomb is set to explode should we walk wrong. "Vonnie? It's me, Mikey. Do you remember me?"

"Mikey..." She whispers, but her words carry into the purple wind that reappears. "Mikey is gone."

"I know," he gulps. "But you gotta trust me. It's me. I'm here to get you. To bring you back home."

"MIKEY IS GONE!!" Little Vonnie screeches at a threateningly high octave before taking off. She runs down the hall and rounds a corner at the end of it.

More purple wind floods the air, whipping around us with such intensity I felt its anger. More of its wrath and determination to keep us out. Mikey tenses, but I squeeze his hand. "It's okay, baby. We're okay."

"You s-sure?" He stutters out in fright. His eyes are closed.

"I am," I reassure him. "Try to ignore it, remember? Just like you told me."

He nods. "Right. Right. Let's go."

For the second time that day, we began our journey to reclaim our girl. Our singular beating heart between both of us. I remain steadfast in the belief that we'll reach her, after all, I have to if it means she'll be whole again.

With ginger steps, we make our way down the hall in search of the little girl we know to be a younger Yvonne Masters. I'm doubtful if we're heading in the right direction for a second since the presence I sensed upon entering the house is gone. In its place is an eerie silence and the air is thick, choking me as I frantically inhale.

"Is she still here?" I ask no one in particular, and gasp when Michael stops abruptly in front of me.

"You hear that?" He asks, his head tilted to the side so as to get a clearer feel of the sound.

I do the same, but come up with nothing. "No," I responded. "What do you hear?"

Then, suddenly, I hear it. The discordant voices are shouting within the room we stopped outside of. There are several doors in the hallway, and all the doors are closed besides the one we're standing beside.

"Girls don't play video games, Vonnie!!" A voice snaps from the room mere steps away from us.

"Yeah they do!" Another little voice retorts. "You're just mad because I'm better at Platoon Raiders than you are!"

"Shut up, no you're not!"

"Prove it then!"

"Y'all chill out!" A deeper voice interrupts what I assumed was an argument between two other, younger kids. "Arguing like this ain't gonna change a thing. Kale said to bring one extra person since he's only got three controllers."

"Pick me then, Devin!"

"He already picked me to go!"

"I didn't pick any of y'all!" Devin sighed. "Mikey just drew the longest straw."

"He what?"

"That means he won the video game we just played over who gets to come with me to Kale's or not. So, he's going this time. Okay?"

"Because he cheated!"

"I did not!" He hollered. "I'm telling Daddy that you lied on me."

"Tell him, I don't care! He won't believe you anyways."

"Then I'm telling Mommy!"

A silence stretched between them so long there was only one word to describe it: intense. The purple wind returns, floating into the room like an ominous cloud as our eyes follow it.

I check Michael, whose standing with his back to my front, his back muscles tightening. He's tense, I sense that, mostly due to the strength of our emotional connection, but also from the tight grip on my hand in his.

"Michael?" I asked.

"I remember this day now." He whispered then squeezed my hand again. "We left her."

My brows furrowed in confusion. "Left her where?"

"Here." His voice is barely above a breath, and before I get the chance to question him further, a tall figure strides out of the room.

It's a boy, perhaps a preteen, dressed in a long white tee and blue jeans. There are deep cuts and scratches on his face that make me cup a hand to my mouth in shock. Looking up, I notice Michael watching the scene unfold with hard eyes.

"Devin." Michael says out loud, studying the young version of the man I came to know after returning to the farm. This is young Devin, I realize, one of Vonnie's core memories that are part of the pain that keeps her here. I didn't need instruction from Michael to know to be quiet and observe the scene unfold.

"Let's go, Mikey," Devin calls, but doesn't stop as he heads towards the staircase. Sniffling can be heard inside the room we dared not enter, and my eyes widened at the little boy barreling happily out of the room to catch up to Devin descending the stairs.

"Fuck..." Michael, the grown Michael gripping my hand like a vice, swears as he watched the scene. "We left her."

"Vonnie stayed behind?" I asked, going against my vow of quiet observation just this once.

He nodded. "This was the last time I left her behind. When we came back home hours later, Vonnie was different. She ended up locking herself inside our room, leaving me with no other options but to sleep in Dev's room. He was pissed, but I was just...concerned about her. It was like the light had been snuffed from her eyes. As if something happened to her." He pauses, closing his eyes and reliving an unseen trauma before continuing. "Is this...is this what she wants to show us?"

The sound of the door slamming from below lets me know they've left the house. And it's almost as if she aims to answer his rhetorical question when Little Yvonne trudges from the room. Her eyes are puffy from what I surmise are tears streaming down her face. The sniffling came from her, I realized, and looked on with mute wonder as she walked lifelessly to the staircase the boys previously descended.

"Devin!" She whimpers. And my heart explodes when we watch the little girl fall to her knees, assuming the same position at the top steps as when Quicy and Helen's spirits possessed us during that memory. "I want to play video games, too!"

"Oh, honey." I breathed, my heart wrenching at the sight. My legs move before I can stop them. "Vonnie, it's okay—"

"Kimmy," Michael's warning stops me mid sprint. As does his firm grip on my hand. "We can't interfere. It's a memory."

Tears prick my eyes at the little girl weeping at the staircase. The sobs rip through her, making her entire body jerk from the force of them. Several minutes pass by, and I'm wrestling with the idea of disobeying the rules. The idea of running over to her and embracing the troubled child hard to resist.

"She's hurting, Michael." The words fall out of me as a depthless echo.

Harsh winds blast through the hallway just then, and I shiver from the immense amount of strange energy rejoining the atmosphere. The purple air cyclones around the small child weeping at the top step, and I hate that I have to just stare in horror as she continues to cry out for her brothers.

I steel a peek at Michael, his eyes are wide open and glued on her. I can't quite read the emotion there, but I know he sees the wind same as I do, as it engulfs her.

"Don't leave me behind!" Vonnie yells through ragged sobs.

"Vonnie." Michael grits out, and this time it's me who holds him back from running over to her. "I am sorry! You will never know how bad I felt when we left you here. I begged Devin to go back and get you until Kale practically kicked us out. I'm here now, sis. I'm standing right here!"

She can't hear him, this much I know, but Vonnie's cries get louder. And stronger. And the wind returns to gale force. Michael struggles against my hold, but he's strong. A fully grown man, in fact, who easily shrugs me off of him before approaching the sobbing little girl.

"Shut that shit up, Yvonne!" A coarse feminine voice snaps from downstairs.

Everything goes deathly silent after that. Michael's eyes round in shock and I gulp at the insane amount of fear written all over his face. Then his breathing quickens as he chokes out, "No. Is that...but she's dead...M-Mommy wasn't home when we left that day. She wasn't."

"Michael," I whisper. "It's okay, honey. It's a memory. You gotta remember that. Helen isn't really here."

More silence permeates the space before Little Yvonne lets out an ear piercing scream. I cup my ears and scan the hallway for the threat. For the reason for her sudden outburst. Then I see it. The woman at the bottom of the steps glaring at her.

"You think I won't beat your ass?" She growled, branding a belt I didn't notice before in sight. "Good kids listen to their mothers when they give a command. Your dad spoils you rotten considering you got the game fucked up. Why you up there hollering like you ain't got no sense?"

A helplessness blooms in my chest as I watch the scene. Same as before, there was nothing I could do. This wasn't a peak into Vonnie's heart, I summed as the the haggard woman began a slow ascend of the steps. This was a tour in a house of horrors.

Little Yvonne stands up, casting a bitter stare I assumed at the woman down the steps since she snaps again at her.

"Of course you got nothing to say to that. You never got anything to say. But Quincy gives y'all the world like you hang the moon part time. Answer me when I'm speaking to you!"

A beat, then Little Yvonne shakes her head.

This poses to infuriate the woman more, and again, I have to restrain Michael from charging at her.

"Fucking bitch." He spits. "Threatening a little girl."

Proving Michael's accusation, Helen snarls, "Are you re-tarded? Answer me!"

Helen's getting closer and closer and the winds pick up, knocking us back. I open my mouth to call out to her but the words don't come. It's like the wind is strangling me and restraining us both in place. Neither of us can move.

But Little Yvonne revives in an instant, turning back and sprinting down the hallway in the opposite direction of us. Helen chases her until the door slams in front of her face.

She punches the door. "If you so much as look at me the wrong way, I will kill you."

Michael gasps before a tortured groan escapes him. Helen hurls several more insults at the door, and I breathe a sigh of relief when she disappears down the steps.

We're released from the temporary paralysis, and without a second thought we're running towards the room Little Yvonne barricaded herself inside. Twisting the locked knob without luck.

"Shit!" Michael swore, and I yelped when his foot came crashing into the door. "Vonnie, I didn't know that happened to you. Why didn't you tell me? Tell Devin? We would have done something if we'd have just known. My god...I am the worst brother ever."

He's on his knees now, sobbing the same as his little sister moments prior.

"Baby," I start while crouching beside him. "You couldn't have known."

He punches the door. "Fuck that! I could've done better. Could've pushed her to tell me. I could've spent more time with her. I should've killed that—"

"Stop," I say, wrapping my body around his neck as tears fall down my face. "Don't say things you don't mean in anger. Please, just don't."

Shaky hands grip my forearms and squeeze. "I shouldn't have left her."

"I know, baby." My whimper mirrors his pained one, and I'm mush when he twists to pull me into his lap, crying into my shoulder.

"Sis, I'm sorry." He bellows while rocking. "Let me in, sis. These doors were always kept locked when I searched for you in the Mind Mansion. Now I see...I see why. I fucked up."

"Baby," I start, but Michael continues talking through the door, to his sister who can't receive his message since she's only a projection. But I don't tell him that. Just hold him and listen as his heart bleeds.

"She shouldn't have said that to you." He grouses. "Dad should have been here. If only somebody was here for you when you needed us the most, then there'd be no need for rescues. No need for you to keep protecting me, in ghost or real form."

"Vonnie," I start, not able to resist the pull to soothe the storm raging behind that door. "It's me, Kimmy. Please come out and talk to us. I'm here to get you. We both want you to come back home. Can you hear us?"

I don't know what to do. I have no idea what to do to get her to open the door. Wasn't even sure if this little girl would lead us to my very real wife, but we had to try.

"Keep talking to her," I tell Michael and try in earnest not to cry when I see he's staring in a daze at the door Helen tried to punch open.

"Okay," he breathes. Nodding, then asks, "Vonnie. Do you remember that time we accidentally stole Ms. Applewood's dog?" A dry laugh escapes his chest that I sense is real, but strained. "She was so pissed at us when we told her we thought she was in danger tied up in her backyard. Even though the dog was fine, you said she'd needed rescuing. I was confused back then, but I think I know now why you did that." He pauses as if awaiting Vonnie to respond. "You always come to the rescue when someone's in need of saving. You saw that dog was all alone outside and it ate at you since that's your worst fear. So you rescued it. Like you're always doing for everyone else. For me, even."

His face falls at the end of the story. "Let it be me this once, sis. Let me rescue you. Nobody should suffer alone, with these memories, all by themselves. I couldn't save you in that basement, but let me make it up to you."

As if by magic, the doorknob wiggles. We both shoot to our feet, and I'm ecstatic that the plan worked. I resolve myself to pick the little girl up in my arms and never let her go, not giving a damn whether it broke the rules or not. I was sick of being a bystander in the middle of my wife's pain. Not anymore.

"Von—" I called, but stopped short when I got a look at the man exiting the room.

I almost ask who he is. Almost ask Michael if we'd been parked outside the wrong room, since it's a middle aged man walking out with sweat globbed over his forehead instead of Vonnie. A sinister smile twists his face as he calls behind him.

"All that pretty hair," he said before adjusting his belt. "Sure know how to make a man feel good. Until next time, sweet thing..."

Red coats my vision at the sight. So much rage and anguish needling my heart at once when I note the satisfied smug on this man's face. He's standing right in front of us, directly at eye level with Michael Masters who's seething the same as I am.

This was another memory. Another darker vision from Vonnie's past that she's either showing us or can't hide. I'm not too sure. But certain rage vibrates throughout my being at the facts: this man, whoever the hell he was, hurt her in the same unforgivable way my stepdad Gavin did me. The same way my uncle Dan perpetually hurt my mother; me and my brother's existence were the result of his abuse and products of her pain. Vonnie never went into vivid detail about the things that happened to her, as she shouldn't if she did not want to, but the thought of my favorite girl experiencing something like this? This extreme level of violation?

I'm not usually a violent person. After struggling with childhood emotional regulation issues, Mom raised us as pacifists. Yet as I stared into the eyes of the ghostly projection of this man, this disgusting piece of filth, my hand flew out before I could think twice about it.

My hand grasps at thin air since this man is only a memory in projection form. But that doesn't stop me from gritting out my next words through clenched teeth.

"You have no place here." I growl, and swipe the air from fury when his perma-smile deepens. His eyes are trained straight past me since there's no way he can acknowledge me. Or my rage. "Get the FUCK out of this house. Die!"

"Kimmy," Michael reaches for me, but I fight his arms that wound around me. "He's only a—"

"Die!" I screech. "Die! Die! Die!"

I'm all but wrestling Michael's arms as I quake with unchecked fury. Visions of the stepfather who'd touched me without permission flashing full force. Of Jeremy's face as he held our mother's abuser at gunpoint. There's nothing but mind melting anger and anguish bleeding into my vision, and I will all of it into this man.

With a final push, I spring from Miachael's arms to stand directly in this man's face, my mouth reaching his chin as I spit at him. "Pass. On."

His eyes round, as if he's seen a ghost or worse before his body shakes. The air thickens the same as before when that strange energy charged in, but this time heat scorches the room. He howls out for a solid few seconds. And then, just like that, he disappears. His entire body bursting into purple mist.

"What just happened?" Michael asked in shock.

My chest is heaving laboriously as my mind ponders the same thing. Then I come to a conclusion, my mind and heart on one accord when I say, "he won't be hurting her anymore. He's on the other side now. I can feel it."

Exhaustion rides my heels from the energy expended from that confrontation. My eyes search the open door into the room, where they soon land on the small girl huddled on a singular bed. The walls are lined with dinosaurs and posters of aliens. Action figures are scattered over the carpeted floor. It's the perfect set up for a wealthy child's room, and certainly more toys inside than what I grew up with as a poor kid in

Jersey, but there's no joy here. The little girl is shaking and one minute I'm fighting the urge to faint from exhaustion and the next I'm bolting towards the bed.

"Vonnie?" I called to her, desperate to reach the scarred little girl I resonated so much with.

"That was wild," Michael commented as he came up beside me. "You're so brave, Kim. Everybody's giving their all to bring you back, sis. Please wake up."

His words are directed at Little Yvonne huddled on the bed. She's still weeping, but it's tamer than before. Her back is to us and a wash of fear rockets through me at the thought of our mission failing. What if she stayed like this? So hampered down by these shitty memories that she can't see the light.

"Sis, it's me." He continued. "There isn't much time left now. You got to wake up."

"Oh, Mike..." I whisper, my chest constricting at the sight of the tears rolling down his handsome face.

He doesn't try to hide the tears either, opting to reach out and touch Little Yvonne's shoulder instead.

"I saw everything." He whimpered. "Saw all those memories from after I died. I watched every memory you tried to hide from me all these years. I always thought it was me doing the protecting. After all those time you got triggered or I Took Over—I was so certain it was me being the hero I should have grown up to be had my life been spared that night. You know I even convinced myself that, if I tried hard enough, that I could permanently Take Over during situations that caused you pain? I honestly thought that.

"Boy was I wrong. After all this time I'm still just a little boy. I'm that same little boy in borrowed flesh. Just like, in some ways, you're stuck, too. I've been in your head long enough to know that you're too comfortable there. Try to come out sometimes and be with the ones who care about you. Can't you see, sis?" His voice faltered on the last word and I'm weeping quietly as he strokes her afro. "They're waiting for you."

"We are, babe." I add, unable to help myself. "I'll always be here, waiting for you. I'll never stop fighting for you or your happiness. Same as you do me."

Little Yvonne's trembling ebbs, as does her crying. She's now laying eerily still with her knees pulled to her chest. I hoped with everything in me that our words reached her.

A thought comes to me, and I'm compelled to ask Michael the question that's been eating at me since his surprise inception.

"What's Vonnie's dream? It's not something she's shared with me."

"For me to come home." He said, staring down at the huddled girl before sinking to his knees. "It's me, sis. I'm back home, just like you've always wanted. Just like you dreamed." Sobs choke him up then he adds raggedly, "Let me honor your dreams for once."

I feel his words reaching her, and they're undoing something in me as I continue to listen to the man I loved bring his sister back from the shadows.

"I saw your ugly," He adds morosely. "I saw the scars, Mom, that man, and felt every bit of the helplessness you felt after we left you that day. Who do you think was with me during my final moments alive? You're afraid I'll hate you if I ever saw those bitter memories when it's the opposite. I wanna thank you for trusting me. Our woman made damn sure those ghosts will never haunt you again."

"Damn right," I confirmed, smiling. "It's just us now."

I heard Michael's grin as he spoke. "She's right. It's all on you two now to continue on. I just ask that you live the longest, happiest life possible with our girl at your side. And also, that you let me be your hero for once and honor your dreams. It's been your dream since leaving that basement for me to come home, and mine has always been to keep you safe. Since I know you'll never let me get away with doing you a favor without one in return, let's do this."

The strange energy in the room fades away. It's just the three of us in this circle of love and light as he leans down and hovers his mouth above her head.

"You can rest now. No more protecting me. And in return, do me a favor and live on." He looks over at me and adds, "We'll meet again one day. Okay?"

***

"Kimmy! Kimmy! Babe, wake up." There's an urgency in her voice as she calls out to me. My head feels like it's stuck in a jar of mud and muddle as I rise from the bed and gasp.

"Vonnie!" I scream.

My eyes search our bedroom frantically to find...nothing. In fact, our normally cluttered bedroom is spic and span. An alarming sight since my wife is the messiest human on planet earth. To my further shock, there's no alien video game powered onto the TV, nor is there the usual mess accumulated from her smoke-and-munchy sessions that ensued after visiting her older brother's house in town.

"Babe, you okay?" Vonnie asks, and I have to blink several rapid times to make out the vision hovering above me in bed. "Had a nightmare?"

My face crumples at the sight of her: fully grown, fresh haircut, yet worried as she stares down at me. I wrap my arms around her. There's so many emotions surging through me as we embrace in the sunlight: relief, happiness, panic, and...completeness. I'm not even sure if that was an emotion, but it's the truest I felt while squeezing her tightly inside my embrace.

"I should clean the house more often if this is the reaction I'll get every time." She chuckles, but I can't join her. I can't let her go either. "Baby doll, for real. You good?"

"Yes," I whimpered into her neck and taking deep breaths in. "God, you smell so good."

After a hesitant few seconds, she draws me into her arms. And they feel much more stronger from the amount of gym time she's been clocking lately at the gym in town. I nearly forgot she and Devin went to the gym every morning before her farm duties began.

"Courtesy of Irish Spring," she adds with a throaty laugh. "You know, even though it's been an hour, I miss you babe. Is that weird?"

Now to that, I do chuckle. "Not weird at all. I've missed you too." She separates us and it's my turn to cast worried eyes at the deep scowl on her face. "What's wrong babe?"

She gulps before saying lowly to me, "I, um. I don't feel him anymore. Mikey's gone. For real this time."

"Oh, honey," I cup her cheek. "It was his time."

Typical Vonnie Carlson would withdraw from a conversation like this. Typical Vonnie Carlson would merely stand up, without a word, and leave the room without even bothering to argue me down at making a statement like that.

But I sense, same as she probably does, that there's nothing typical about Vonnie Carlson at all.

She meets my eyes, and there's something resolute in hers as she says, "Everything gonna be okay. Weird. I thought if he were to ever leave me for a second time that I'd die. Right along with him this time. But...I can't explain it. It's like I've been given a new take on life. I woke up from the strangest nap two hours ago, and I felt so brand new I just started cleaning. I have this feeling that he wants me to start fresh instead of give in to the sorrow, like usual. Am I crazy?"

"No, my love." I tell her, unshed tears threatening to spill from my eyes. "That's exactly what he wanted. I know that for a fact. He wants you to live out your wildest dreams knowing he'll always be there."

"Will he?" Hope shone in her eyes at my words. "Do you mean that?"

I nodded and placed a hand over her chest. "Sure do. He's right here."

"He, uh..." She started, her tone thick with emotion. "He won't hate me for feeling this way? For doing this?"

"For doing what?"

"Living," She breathed.

And my heart ripped all over again as I watched the heaps of guilt twist her face. She's so beautiful. So beautiful that even the deepest scowl on her face makes her that much more alluring.

I bite my lip, a new need reviving my insides as I bring her lips to mine.

"Never," I answered before crushing her lips to mine. "It's what he wanted. It's what you want, deep down, too. Promise me you'll never leave me, babe."

Vonnie, stiff for a few seconds, slowly matches my pace and kisses me right back. "I can't even imagine a future without you there, baby doll. Without you, there's no home. You got me forever, baby."

Our lovemaking was slow and sensational in the hour that followed, and after arriving at my climax for the third time in her arms, I feel for the first time that everything will be all right. So long as we do this thing called life.

Together, always.

31

the truth of suffering

·♥·♥·♥·♥·♥·

JERICA

WON'T BE ABLE TO GIVE YOU A LIFT TODAY. GOT CALLED
IN TO WORK DOUBLE SHIFT. WE NEED THE HOLIDAY PAY.
FIND YOUR OWN WAY HOME.

"Saw this shit coming," I swore under my breath before
collapsing onto the bus stop bench. My mom's boldly typed
text message flashes across my phone screen before I even
got the chance to walk the block towards the bus stop. I loved
my mom, but she was deadass nobody to bet all your chips
on when it came to coming through for you.

Whatever, I thought, the old Jerica would spaz after an
unexpected turn of events like that. After another disappointment that left me so deeply pessimistic about the common good in people. The old girl with a forever chip on her
shoulder where people were concerned punched first and
asked questions...well, never. But that was the past. I learned
so much since the consequences of those actions landed me
doing an eighteen month stint behind bars. I changed my

ways since getting released, got an honest-enough job that kept the bills paid and let Mommy rest awhile from working quadruple shifts. So while the vagrant thought of chucking my phone through a parked car window and wiring it to get myself home entered my mind, I soon dismissed it. Released the violent thoughts like a free agent cancer roaming my bloodstream with a huge intake of breath. Breathing often focuses my mind and leashes my inner animal, and I smile as thoughts of my daily meditation circles from jail came to me.

"Remember that meditation is about clarity. Spending time with yourself and inhaling clean energy is most important." Damiana, my celly and best friend, instructed me during my first time at what she called Truth Circle.

I closed my eyes tight, and after trying my best to forget the cafeteria altercation involving pizza theft and the butch woman I'd rejected several times after many unsubtle advances, I sucked my teeth.

"This is fuckin stupid," I stated and turned heated eyes at my best celly, "And I'm fuckin gone."

"Whoa, Jerica, where are you going?" She asked, and I paused at the feel of her hand on my arm when I tried to stand.

"To teach that bitch not to touch what ain't hers," I tell her with a 'duh' face. "Squeeze been begging for these hands since I got here."

"You'll never win like that." She said softly, something intense shining in her eyes I didn't like. That same emotion flared in the other two inmates' eyes, too. It's a feeling I recognized and loathed to the umpteenth.

I sat back down, glaring at all three of them. "What you tryna say? Think I can't beat that bitch's ass?"

"Nothing to offend you, girl." She supplied reassuringly. "But you'll probably beat her ass. Probably beat her bad with them strong ballerina legs of yours."

"Oh," I deflate, not expecting that. "Then what's the problem?"

"That's the point of these Truth Circles. In them, we learn that there are no enemies. No winners or losers in the end. Only the Woke or Asleep. Those who see the Truth are the winners."

Interest peaked, I scrunch my brows in thought. Dami was always on about some spiritual oneness and peace within. All that talk about making love instead of war and stressing less violence was irritating to listen to during my first days inside. In fact, we got close after I blackened her eye. That was day three. And I realized she was built different than everybody else here after she smiled at me with a bloody nose and said, "I forgive you. We are really friends and you're on your path. And I can tell it will be bright."

And friends, we became.

She was the first person I'd shown all my ugly to who didn't run away or judge. Didn't fight back or slap an Angry Black Bitch label on me. Dami embraced my flaws and fury. And I didn't realize how bad I needed to be seen like that. To be accepted completely. No bars held, but all punches pulled. She'd somehow suckered me into joining one of those Truth Circles during rec time in our cell. And even though I craved fresh air and adored the sun on my skin as I danced, I grudgingly agreed to pray with her group on my last day inside. My release date was set for the following day, and oh was I fucking excited to get back home to my baby boy.

"Come on, Jeri," Dami said on a calm breath as I watched her eyes drift shut. Soon she's sitting in a meditation-style pose, index and thumb fingers pinched, same as the rest of the group, except now they're all chanting. "Rejoin the Circle."

I gulped, secretly weirded out by this cult-like display. On the inside, weakness or fear weren't luxuries afforded to girls like us. The girls in D block listened to only one top bitch, a hulking masculine presenting woman who towered over inmates and guards at a whopping six foot two. Her name was Squeeze, and since I first set foot inside this minimum security prison she'd all but declared me as hers by taking my lunch every time I rejected her invitations to chill. It was usually easy to just let her take them most days, but something snapped in me today. I was sick and tired of getting pushed around and keeping to myself as my big brother Stan told me. Keep my head down and do my time, and soon I'd be out of there with only bad memories and lessons for the future. Doing that only got me so far, and boy was I in the shittiest of moods when the butch bitch snatched my tray away on my final day inside. Everybody knew how rare pizza day was in the cafeteria. The pizza would still be considered inedible on the outs, but in here? Pizza was one of the highest in demand when commissary ran dry, which mines often did, so the couple of dollars here and there helped out. Especially during pizza day.

Anger boils my blood again at the memory of Squeeze snatching my tray away, demanding I let her give me the sendoff I deserved or starve on my last day inside.

I ran back to my bunk to grab the cell-made shiv I got off Chickadee, the country girl from down south who traded anything in our cell block for a bump. Today was this bitch's last day she'd intimidate anyone else. I swore of it, seeing nothing but red as I scoured my cell for the handmade weapon.

Only to remember the promise I made to Damiana for my final day inside, temporarily forgetting the promise I made her as recompense for punching her in the face during our initial meeting.

So there I was, pretzel style on the dirty cell floor during rec time, praying instead of stabbing like I'd wanted to.

I take the deep breath Dami instructed before closing my eyes. I hear her words over the other two women's chants whisper silkily in the air.

"No winners or losers, ladies." She intoned. "What guides us is the healing principles of Buddha. He teaches the truth to suffering. Desire and ignorance prevents us from achieving true understanding."

"What is the true understanding?" I couldn't help the question.

A beat, then she answered, "*Moksha*. The true understanding is enlightenment. Squeeze is suffering, and the old adage is real in this scenario: Misery loves company, Jeri. She wants you to partake in her suffering so as not to be alone. That is not your journey."

"My journey..." I breathed, allowing the air to fill my lungs and warmth to cascade down my body at her words. She was right, and something inside me needed to hear it. Needed, not only the comfort, but total logic her words provided.

After getting out of jail, I set myself on a path. A *moksha* of my own to achieve the understanding Dami seemed to have all figured out for herself, despite her three year sentence. Or maybe because of it.

I got my GED and continued to meditate daily. It was a practice so baked into my every day that I felt off kelter whenever I neglected a morning breathe session, or *jhāna*. I slipped into a few old habits after meeting my youngest son's father, but he's gone now. And I had to rediscover myself and set my path back to Truth, the destination which inspired my stage name. I learned the Word, studied the Four Noble Truths and used those tenets whenever I got upset or worked up over the years.

Like now, as I wrestled with the subsequent anger that tried to fester after reading Mommy's blunt text to figure my shit out. I breathed several times and reminded myself of the truth to end suffering. This wasn't the way. Wasn't my true path, and I held that notion tight to my heart as I felt the night air on my skin. The moonlight caressed my entire being as I danced at the empty bus stop, and I relished in the peace the Great Buddha guided me to.

My quiet peace dance is soon interrupted by a loud car horn, making me nearly leap out of my skin at the intrusion.

"Damn it!" I swore, squinting from the sidewalk into the rolled down window of the old school Jaguar. "You got a problem or something?"

Not that I'd looked to pick a fight, but the old Jerica revives in an instant to face off with whomever this threat was.

"Sup, Truth." The man called from the driver's side. "Saw you out here all by yourself. Need a ride?"

After a few more silent seconds of trying to piece together this strange man's identity, of wondering if I should run or find a weapon like the old days on the inside, he adds, "It's me, Coffee. You know, from the club?"

My heart beat calmed a few paces at that knowledge. Thank Buddha, it was only Coffee, the huge club bouncer who worked most nights at The Dirty Kitten Club, the Atlantic city strip club I worked at.

Rather, where I used to work before giving birth to my second baby boy, Khalil. Not only was his birth what the after school specials would call 'traumatizing,' but the emergency cesarean left stretch marks and scars that weren't received well onstage. And soon after getting the all-clear from my doc to get back on the dance floor, it was all over. Madam Calico dismissed me with a firm but loving, "you ain't getting the same clout as before, kitten. It might be time for you to find work somewhere else less...public?"

That was my last day at the club that brought me so much money. The last day working a job that felt more like therapy, since I got to dance freely and get hella paid for it. Now, my dances were reserved for my downtime and something done in the shadows whenever I wasn't working my dishwasher job at a seedy Mexican eatery or taking care of my sons.

"Coffee?" I asked incredulously as I walked over to the old car. His small brown eyes shone up at me, same as his permanent frown. "What are you doing all the way up in Pennsauken?"

He grunted. "And what you doing sitting out here by yourself on a Sunday night?"

I crossed my arms, a bit put off by the reproaching tone he took. Like I was some silly teenage girl without a clue instead of a twenty year old woman with two children. "Waiting for the bus, what of it?"

"You ain't waiting for the bus." He groused. "Now get in the car so I can take you home."

I reared back. "Say what? I ain't getting in your car."

"You ain't waiting for the bus, Truth." He gritted out my stage name.

"And you still ain't answering my question, Coffee." I shot back. "You a long way from Atlantic City."

Wordlessly, he got out of the car. And I took several steps back as he advanced towards me. Coffee had never done anything untoward in the past against me. In fact, he'd been the faithful sober presence in the club and was always there to save us dancers whenever the patrons got a little too grabby. He did his job to protect us, same as Jaimie did, who'd been the other bouncer I often caught laughing with my homegirl Shay. However, Coffee was the opposite in every regard. Never smiling. Never saying more words than necessary since his job demanded his fists stay sharper than his tongue.

"What you doing?" I whispered, willing more force into my voice but failing as I withdrew.

No answer, but I frown at him taking his leather jacket off. The leather jacket that had a patch with a name I didn't quite understand on it. A skull and bone with flames rising from the top. He was close enough for me to read the words stitched on one of the bones:

Brothers in Chaos.

I vaguely wondered if he'd been part of a gang or MC, before all the air rushes from my chest. My back officially hit the dead end of the wall to the Mexican restaurant, and in the dead night, we were all alone. Me against the six foot five bouncer who looked like he ate people larger than me for breakfast.

"Get away from me!" I snarled when I saw him raise the jacket over my head and...wrap it around me? The relieved breath that escaped me made me realize just how cold I'd been with only a dirty polo and jeans in the October weather.

"Back to my original question," he stated darkly, a storm raging in his eyes. "Do you need a ride?"

I found out minutes later as we rode in mostly silence that the bus didn't run past eight o' clock on Sundays. Still wrapped in the bouncer's leather, I stole a glance at him in the driver seat. My place in Maple Shade was only a fifteen minute drive, twenty with traffic at most, but the ride felt like an eternity with all the awkward silence filling the car. One would think we'd have more than two words to exchange, being that we worked at the same under the table establishment for over three years, but nothing but a strange quiet and heart pounding fills the space as I stare out at the streets passing by.

"My Ma stays out here," Coffee admits after parking on the street outside my apartment complex.

I stared at him in open confusion, wondering if he really was a demented psycho like all the DKC patrons pegged him as during my stint there. Then realization crashes over me as I pivoted back to my original question for him back in Pennsauken.

"Oh, okay," I nodded awkwardly. "Good to note you're a mama's boy."

Hell must have frozen over because he actually cracks a smile. Chuckled a little, even as he responded, "I ain't a mama's boy, but you'd never know it by the weekly visits I make to her gravesite."

The budding convivial vibes sparking in the car die mid air as I clutch my chest. "Shit, sorry about that."

"All good," he shrugged noncommittally as if the subject of his dead mother was a mere conversation topic fluke instead of a major social faux pas. "Not like you said anything wrong. I am a fucking mama's boy."

Now to that I do laugh. Somewhat surprised this stoically silent, brooding man was capable of...well, speaking or smiling at all. I readjusted to stare up at him. "Sorry about that."

He frowned. "Again, you had no way of knowing. Plus, it happened a fucking decade ago."

So he has a favorite word, I thought before clarifying. "No, that's not what I'm apologizing for. I'm apologizing for assuming you were an unfeeling jerk like all the regulars used to say. You know, back at the club?"

He grunted, but never actually looked at me as he answered me back. "Yeah, well, I ain't do much to convince you to think otherwise about me back then. Plus, those dudes were fuckwads, anyways. Can't put too much stock in their analysis of someone's character."

"Deadass," I said, grinning. "And thanks for the ride. I'm not too sure what I'd have done when I finally realized the bus stopped running hours before my shift ended."

More silence ate up the car that had me squirming. Was he pissed off? Did I say something to offend him in some way? The calm vibes were killed again between us, and I scrambled for an excuse to get out of the car. Then the knowledge of my kids inside with the babysitter I already couldn't afford made me remember that, hello, I was a mother! With kids inside who needed to be tucked in. By me. The responsible adult who should not be chilling with some club bouncer I suspected was affiliated with an MC and who was also literally regarded as a demented psycho at DKC.

"Uh, all right then," I mumbled while opening the car door. "Guess I'll get in the house if there's nothing else. It was good seeing you."

I almost made it. I was almost able to fumble open the door and run inside the apartment with heat surging through my body at the awkwardness of speaking with him. Of accepting his unexpected generosity. Truth, the bad girl alter ego I created to survive the club scene who was down with the violence at one point in time, is just that. A silly persona created by my need to prove myself in this world. After all that went down the past year, conversing with men like him wasn't the smartest idea if I wanted to leave that life behind. Truth was dead, and I was okay with burying her for good until…he reminded me of all that I lost.

Of all that I'd never get back.

But, to my chagrin, I never make it outside the car. Instead, I'm pulled to his wide chest and his lips come crashing against mine in a moment I'm lost in. A minute goes by, and my seriously neglected nether regions vibrate from the pleasure of his kiss before I shove him away. Then punch the living shit out of him, despite my vow in that cell against violence.

"Solid right hook you got, Truth." Coffee grunts, flexing his jaw and wiping the blood from his mouth. "Seems you're back to your old self. No more of this shy girl nonsense."

Infuriated, I shoved him again. "Why did you do that?"

"Same could be asked of you." He growled. "Why did you wait outside for a bus that would never come?"

My head throbbed now from the strange turn of his questioning and innuendos. "What are you talking about? I told you it was a mistake. I forgot the bus schedule since I'm usually dropped off and picked up by my mom. What of it?"

"Not what I'm asking." He grunts, releases an aggrieved sigh, then adds, "I mean, why did you wait for a bus that would never come to get you?"

"Okay, you're really crazy if you think—"

He tugs me back into his arms, but this time it's different. Instead of kissing me, he cradles me gently in his arms like a lost toy found. Like something to be cherished.

"Where's your guy, huh?" He asked, his voice ragged with anger. "That skinny dude you always hung around with. Seemed like you two were all simpatico and shit. He came by the club every night to see you. Y'all were always laughing about something and taking off in that flashy ride of his after your shifts. What was that little shit's name?"

I gulped, raw pain revving like an engine in my chest at the reminder of the guy I loved with every part of me during our short lived relationship.

"Shamel," I whispered the name he'd warned me against using during our last interaction. "His name was Shamel."

A gentle finger caresses my jaw when he speaks, "Shamel. Figures a pussy with a name like that would leave you high and dry like that when you need him the most. Ain't he your kid's father?"

More pain emanates, but I nod. "Yes."

I'd heard rumors in the wind that he'd been killed by some gang a while back, but I knew that not to be true. Knew that since his big sister Shay called me almost every night after my shift to talk to me about her day. Almost always we talked about her, never about the little brother she never knew fathered my youngest child, but our calls were kept short. Neither of us saying too much about our locations or the past. She'd slipped one day and mentioned how frustrated she was by her little brother's gambling habit that nearly put them in crippling debt. Only the threat of kicking him out made him stop, but even then she wasn't optimistic about his future "on the farm," whatever that meant. I'd secretly hoped he'd get his life together. Secretly wished him the best despite his leaving me with so much pain and a son he'd never meet.

"Now I'll ask you again." He rasps, still caressing my numb body while my mind reeled in the past. "Why wait for a bus that's never coming for you? All alone, vulnerable, and in the middle of the night. You still wait for that fucking dickhead even though you're probably just another notch on his belt. Why don't you get that?"

"Shut up!" I protested, hot tears stinging my eyes at all the wrong words. "That's not it at all. I'm not waiting..."

He was wrong. So, so wrong about all of it. I wasn't waiting for Shamel to come back. I knew it was impossible. I knew that, even if he wanted to, that he likely couldn't come back after what happened with Shay. He left with her, and if her situation had anything to do with his absence, then there was zero way I'd get to see him in this city alive again. Plus, I'm sure he forgot all about our time together. But still, I fought Coffee.

"You are Truth, right?" He demanded after I fought myself free of his arms. "If that's the case, then why can't you see that? Give yourself a chance to let something new in."

I almost roar the words at the demented bouncer, but remember those tenets. The truth to end suffering and my spiritual *moksha* before I hurled any harsh words at him.

"There are no enemies. No winners or losers," Dami would have said to me had she survived that prison riot. "You are on your one true path, Jeri. Don't forget peace is always with you."

There are so many things I could say to Coffee right now, but in the end, I don't. Opting for the righteous path I decided for myself after the birth of my second son, whose birth lost me my job but gained me a spot on the journey to spiritual enlightenment. For him, both of my boys, I'd choose peace. Truth and peace, always.

"Thank you for the ride, Coffee." I said, my voice mild and weary as I climbed out of the car and walked to my front door. There was nothing left to be said.

His voice stops me before I unlock the door, though.

"Jermaine," Coffee says, making me freeze in my tracks as he adds from the car, "Jeri, for short."

A light laughter bursts inside my chest at the irony of his name, his legal name, matching my own. I had half a mind to tell him how comical this was, how utterly cool it was to meet someone with a name so similar to my own and what that could potentially mean for my *moksha*, but I opt to unlock the door instead. Sliding inside the house and collapsing against the front door as the wind rushed out of me. The strength to stand was just as elusive as the cold. Memories flood my mind at the thoughts of Shamel and how cherished he made me feel. How many cold nights we spent together in my late brother's bedroom and just talked. Talked and talked and talked about what we wanted for our futures and how bad we both wanted to escape this little dangerous city where both our dreams fell apart.

This wasn't fair. How could this man make me feel so much all at once, even years later? Coffee's kiss warmed me, that much was true, but Shamel's mere smile made me burn. As did his hands that explored parts uncharted on my body, somehow touching my heart and soul in the process as he filled me with the child he'd never know. Everything was different now, and I almost laugh as the phone buzzes in my pocket. It's Shay, her unsaved number I know is a burner flashes across the screen, and I send it to voicemail for the first time. Though I'd promised to always be there for her since we reconnected, right now I don't have the strength to sit through more of her one sided drama. The drama she'd never go into exact details about, but I suspected was a hell of a story on that place she referred to as "the farm."

Remember your *moksha*, I tell myself as I snuggle into the warm leather jacket on my arms. Remember your journey, your path to liberation. I stood up to gather myself and go in search of my *Tripitaka*, the sacred pages of the Buddha I kept close to my home and heart when I needed a spiritual boost. The scriptures are roughly translated at best into English, but studying them still brought me a oneness I couldn't describe. At least, not verbally.

Three swift knocks sound at my door right when I re-member the leather jacket I'm wearing. Shit! I swore when I realized I'd still been wearing Coffee's MC jacket with the skulls on the front. It felt expensive, and of course he came back to get it. I would too, if the price tag on this thing was anywhere where I figured it to be. You can do this, Jerica. I tell myself before opening the door. Remember your *moksha*. Remember your *moksha*...

Except, my *moksha* is the farthest from my mind as I open the door to see a short woman standing before me. She's wearing only a thin black shirt without a bra, and sweatpants that look way too big for her. Her hair is a fiery red nest of curls whipping in the wintry winds, and it takes me a minute to put two-and-two together.

I don't really recognize her, though she does ring familiar in the wide set of her eyes. There are tears streaming down her face, and it's right then when I see the plump belly protruding from her. Now that, as a mother of two, I recognize. This fretful woman with wild red hair and smudged makeup, is super pregnant.

"Can I help you?" I say, perturbed by her state of dress.

"Is...is this?" She glances at a piece of paper in her trembling hands before reciting, "615 East Main Street?"

"Uh, yes." I confirm. "Do you need something, miss?"

More tears prick her eyes and she lunges forward, gripping my arms tight in her hands as she says, "Yes! Yes, I need help!"

"Okay, calm down." I tell her, still not trusting that she wasn't another drug addicted teen out to rob me. I rub her shoulders. "Just calm down, hun. Tell me your name and I'll get you to where you're going."

"No!" She groaned, clutching her belly. "Please, help me! This is the place I'm looking for. Are you Janice True?"

"That's my mother," I said. "Are you one of her coworkers or something?"

Her next words nearly made me fall on my ass from the shock. Considering her very presence was almost like a hoax or myth in our household since we'd never ever seen her before. At least, not in person.

"No, I'm not." She answers before wiping her face. "My name is Cleo'Nora Albert, Stanley True's daughter. Please help me!"

Author's Note

Loveless. To say this book has been a thorn in my side is a total understatement. Nora revealed subtle pieces of what she wanted to me during the writing process, which makes for a frustratingly complex, yet beautiful work of art.

On another note, Amora's character was modeled from my own mother, who passed away just before Christmas in 2018. While her absence leaves a hole in my heart, transforming our memories together to bring forth new life in novel form keeps me going. To my readers who've lost their own perfectly imperfect parents or guardians, my love is with you. Nonetheless I hope you've enjoyed reading about this frustratingly awesome girl who had a hard go at life. Perhaps she'll get redemption later on?

Stay tuned for that as well as the next book in The REAL Series called HONOR. Until then...

From the other side, with Love,
Laura

About the author

·♥·♥·♥·♥·♥·

Since the age of twelve, Laura could always be found writing. She writes within a wide array of genres, including paranormal, drama, slice of life, and (her favorite) romance. In her free time, if she's not writing, she's reading or listening to a steamy audio-book. Her most notable works include Something About Kyle and her ongoing, The REAL Series, which explores the narratives of various, interconnected young adults.

As an author, Laura aims to push boundaries and leave a lasting impact on her community. Her journey taught her the importance of perseverance, creativity, and staying true to one's unique vision. Support her craft by purchasing from her bookstore.

Other books in this series

GRAY
LIGHT
CAVE
EDGE (written by Laurie Ross)
HEART
SECRETS
HOME
SHAME
SAFE
LOVELESS
HONOR (coming soon)